PRAISE FOR
HISTORIC

Broken Promise is an "excellent blend of fact and fiction that will keep you involved in an unforgettable reading experience. Outstanding!"

—*Rendezvous*

In *Dark Renegade,* "the passion is primitive and lusty....Kudos to Theresa Scott for an exciting and refreshing reading adventure. Superb!"

—*Rendezvous*

"Yesterday's Dawn is an entertaining read and an enticing beginning to the *Hunters of the Ice Age* series."

—*Romantic Times*

"Ms. Scott shows that love is magical whenever it happens...[*Hunters of the Ice Age*] is a sensational series—original, exciting and romantic!"

—*Affaire de Coeur*

"Plenty of adventure and nonstop action....Readers who thrive on Indian romance should particularly enjoy *Apache Conquest.*"

—*Romantic Times*

"Forbidden Passion is a light, charming tale. Theresa Scott has penned a pleasant read for all those who love exciting stories of the days of old."

—*Romantic Times*

"Theresa Scott's historical romances are tender, exciting, enjoyable, and satisfying!"
—Romantic Times

DANGEROUS DESIRES

Yngveld freed her arms and pushed her breasts up to Thomas, mindlessly offering herself. His warm tongue laved her sensitive flesh and she curled her toes in delight, breath held, avid for his next touch. Her throat stopped working, her lips softened and she moaned as he nipped gently at her. "More," she moaned. "More!"

His head moved down her body, brushing her flesh with the caresses of his rough cheeks. His tongue flicked at her satin skin, leaving a cool trail of kisses. Yngveld sighed raggedly, eyes closed, arms limp beside her. She held her breath abruptly as she realized he was kissing his way to her lithe waist.

His tongue dipped into her navel and she moaned. Thomas gripped her rounded buttocks tighter and pressed his face into her. She could feel the strength of him, the hardness of his manhood. He wanted her and she moaned again. He pressed further until her legs parted of their own will.

Other *Leisure* and *Love Spell* books by Theresa Scott:
SAVAGE REVENGE
LOVE'S AMBUSH
CAPTIVE LEGACY
APACHE CONQUEST
BRIDE OF DESIRE
SAVAGE BETRAYAL

Hunters of the Ice Age:
BROKEN PROMISE
DARK RENEGADE
YESTERDAY'S DAWN

Forbidden Passion

Theresa Scott

LEISURE BOOKS NEW YORK CITY

A LEISURE BOOK®

January 1998

Published by

Dorchester Publishing Co., Inc.
276 Fifth Avenue
New York, NY 10001

ISBN 0-8439-4344-0

Printed in the United States of America.

Chapter One

Swords, a village north of Dubh Linn, Ireland
988 A.D.

Thomas Lachlann wiped wet, dark curls away from his sweating forehead as he slowly straightened up from the water barrel in front of his mother's small hut near the edge of the forest. Drops of water glistened on Thomas's broad, naked chest and dripped down the waistband of his rough-spun black breeches. He dried his sun-browned, flat torso with lazy circular motions that belied the intensity in his narrowed green eyes as he watched an oncoming rider. The rider cut ruthlessly across the front field, churning up the neat, newly mounded rows that

Thomas himself had planted but yester eve. He watched as the man flailed the beast mercilessly until the snorting, trembling gelding finally slid to a halt in the dust before Thomas.

"Flee, Master Thomas, flee!"

"Whoa!" Thomas reached for the bridle, his strong arm muscles flexing as the skittish roan gelding tried to dance away from him. "You rode this beast too hard, mon!" His eyes glittered in anger as the sinewy man slid off the horse's back.

"Couldna be helped," retorted the other as he drew himself up in front of Thomas. He wiped his furrowed brow hurriedly, his breath coming in quick pants.

Thomas saw the fear in the man's eyes and went still. "What has happened, Caedmon?" he asked in a low voice, stroking the gelding's nose to calm him. " 'Tis not like you to treat a beast so, nor to ride carelessly across a newly planted field." He added wryly, "That is more my brother Aelfred's manner."

"Master Thomas, 'tis your father! Lord Harald is dead with this morn's sunrise. And your brother rides this way with armed men! He seeks to kill you!"

Thomas compressed his lips and his green eyes glittered. So, it had come to this. His father had finally died, God rest his perfidious soul, and now Aelfred was seeking to destroy the one person who stood between him and the Viking overlordship of Swords—his bastard Irish half-brother, Thomas.

"He seeks to steal your birthright! You are the eldest son. The land should be yours." Caedmon's wiry body tensed with his words. "He steals from you!"

Thomas fastened his gaze on the panting Caedmon.

"Steals?" He laughed, a falsely light-hearted sound in the little clearing. The sound brought a woman to the door of the hut, and she stood watching the men whilst she dried her hands on an old rag. "Steals from me?" Thomas repeated. "Why, Aelfred cannot steal my birthright, Caedmon. He was *given* it. By my *father*." Thomas upper lip curled as he sneered the last word.

Caedmon glanced from the young man's bitter face to that of the woman leaning against the hut's doorframe. And, as was the custom for so many of the local people, he turned to her. She wore a gray, shapeless dress with a gray woolen shawl over her shoulders to keep off the chill spring breeze. Her hair stood in a great black and gray knotted mass around her head, and her green eyes, the same green eyes that she had passed on to her son, held Caedmon as spellbound now as they ever had before her accident.

"Caedra," Caedmon breathed and touched his forelock in a gesture of respect.

Thomas glanced sharply at him, hearing the loss, the sadness, and knowing that Caedmon longed for the past, for the time when Caedra's vast family, the Lachlanns, were the powerful ruling family at Swords.

Caedra nodded regally, the gesture some half-forgotten vestige of what her parents had taught her in the long-ago days before the coming of the Vikings.

"Lord Harald's dead," said Caedmon and waited.

Caedra stepped into the yard, her first steps uncertain. A shadow crossed her face as she tilted her head curiously. "Dead?" she asked, a quaver in her voice. "It is certain?"

"Aye," Caedmon assured her gently. "He is dead, Caedra. He is dead." The two old ones stood there looking at each other, so many unspoken words between them.

Caedra's shaky steps brought her to stand at last next to her green-eyed son. She looked at him. "Thomas," she murmured, and 'twas as though she spoke in a dream. "Thomas, you are the new lord, the new lord of Swords!"

He looked at her, his eyes softening. "Aye, Mother, by right of being the eldest son, I should be the new lord." His eyes took in her faded face, the still generous mouth, the green eyes now framed by lines. As he looked at her, he felt the pain knot deep in him that he would have to leave her and she knew it not. "But," and his voice lowered, "it is not to be, Mother."

"Not to be?"

She looked startled, unbelieving, and he cursed the fall she had taken—the one that had given her the vague, staring look that told him she could no longer understand his words as well as before.

"But you are his son!" She clenched her fist and reached for him. "I bought you that birthright! I paid for it with my own blood! My own pain!"

"Mother." Thomas winced at hearing her speak of what had happened—even in front of Caedmon, trustworthy though he was and knowing every word of the story, Thomas's story. "Mama, 'twas long ago." He stroked her forehead and patted the mass of her hair, and she calmed, as the gelding had calmed under his same sure touch only minutes before. "Mama, I must go."

"Go?" She reached for him and clutched his hand, her face again wearing that vague, startled look.

In irritation, for Caedmon's eyes warned him there was little time, Thomas said, "I must go. Aelfred seeks me."

At the mention of his half-brother's name, a cunning look crossed her face. "Aelfred? Oh, aye, Aelfred." She turned to him, her eyes clear once more. "Go my son, flee!"

In relief, Thomas hugged her. He turned to Caedmon and placed his hand on the old man's. "My thanks, Caedmon, for your loyalty in bringing me word."

"Hurry, master, *hurry*! You may yet save your life!"

"Aye, I intend to do just that," muttered Thomas grimly. He would waste not a moment in taking possessions with him. He had known that when this time came he would leave and take nought with him but his weapon.

He ran to the small hut and emerged only heartbeats later, looking paler and grimmer than before. His naked torso was now covered in a handwoven, oft-mended black cloak, and he clutched a small bundle of food. At his side swung the silver filigree-handled Viking sword, *Thor's Bite*, the sole legacy of his Viking father.

Caedra gave a small shriek when she saw the sword and then quickly stuffed her fist in her mouth to let not another sound escape.

Thomas neither glanced at her nor halted in his rapid strides to the roan, but he had heard her cry and it pierced him to the heart. He wanted to assure her that 'twas a necessity that he take this sword, the one that he had secretly oiled and sharpened when he thought she was not looking. He would need it now, both as a weapon and as a desperately wanted sign of his father's acceptance, when all other acceptance had been denied him in his life.

This sword was all that he had of his father, and he still remembered the day Lord Harald had come to the hut, suddenly standing there in the doorway, blocking the sun. 'Twas on Thomas's twelfth birthday and his father had at first merely stood there, awkwardly it had seemed then to the young Thomas. At last, Lord Harald had entered, though Caedra had not bidden him do so. Thomas remembered her leaving her place by the fire, running to a corner of the hut, and throwing her apron over her head when she realized 'twas Lord Harald come to call. 'Twas after her fall, when she had hit her head so severely that her behavior had become strange.

His father had looked at him and then asked him to come out into the light. Thomas had done so, heart pounding in fear, but he had followed the one man who had so marked his life, the man whom he had seen but a handful of times previously. While they stood outside the hut, Lord Harald staring at Thomas, Thomas's attention had been drawn to the beautiful black stallion that stood pawing the dust, impatiently waiting for his master to mount so that they could be off and running through the fields once more.

Lord Harald, seeing the boy's interest, had invited him to sit atop the horse. He had laughed as he lifted Thomas onto the black horse, showing him where to place his foot, where to grasp with his knees. Then Lord Harald had stepped back.

Thomas, eyes shining, breath held, had urged the stallion forward. The beast took several steps, then suddenly reared up, nostrils wide, eyes rolling. Thomas had landed butt-first in the dirt. Lord Harald had stood there laughing heartily at the boy sprawled in the dust.

Humiliation ran high in Thomas at that. In a fury, Thomas had lunged to his feet and run at his father, slamming into Harald's stomach with his head.

The attack on his father, far from enraging Lord Harald, seemed but to delight him. With great whoops, his father had then proceeded to beat Thomas to a pulp. Thomas, his nose bloody, his arms bruised, his stomach scraped, had only ceased fighting when Lord Harald stood over him with a sword at his throat. With one final laugh, the big, bearded blond man had grinned and thrown the sword into the dust. "*Thor's Bite* is yours," he had said then, gesturing at the magnificent weapon. "And so are my lands, *if* you can take them." And with this parting remark, tossed casually over his shoulder, Lord Harald had strolled over to his horse, though Thomas now saw he had to limp to do so.

Lord Harald had swung up onto the stallion and surveyed Thomas once more, from bleeding head to dusty toe. Thomas stood with sword in hand, glaring at Lord Harald who, laughing, pulled tightly on the reins. The horse reared, spun on its heels, and galloped back across the fields to the manor where Lord Harald dwelled.

Thomas had watched him go, and in that moment he hated his father to the depths of his heart for the violation of his mother, for the humiliation of himself sprawled in the dirt, for the years of indifference. But mostly he hated him for that tiny spark of yearning, for that desperate desire for his father's love and acceptance—while he received neither. The love and acceptance had gone to Aelfred, the son who lived behind the manor walls with Lord Harald—Aelfred, the legitimate issue of Lord Harald's marriage to Lady Ingrid.

As Thomas watched Lord Harald disappear that day, he swore that he would find a way to take his father's land from him. Or from Aelfred.

Thomas' brooding thoughts brought him back to the present. One look at Caedmon's concerned face and Caedra's worried one convinced Thomas that he must lose no more time.

Caedmon handed him the reins of the sweating, sorry-looking nag that he had managed to steal from Harald's—now Aelfred's—stables. " 'Twas the only horse I could fetch," he mumbled apologetically to Thomas.

" 'Twill do, Caedmon," Thomas assured him, swinging himself up onto the beast. Thomas's black hair shone in the sun and his large frame dwarfed the thin horse he perched atop of, its ribs showing through the dull red coat. Yet Thomas looked every inch the lord that his father had denied he was by rights these many years.

Horses ridden at a pounding gallop raced over the rise in front of the hut.

"Too late!" cried Caedmon.

Aelfred Haraldson and three of his henchmen yanked their lathered horses to a stop. Thomas watched, green eyes narrowed, as Aelfred swayed precariously atop his horse. 'Twas his father's black stallion. Aelfred tightly held the reins on the beast, pulling at the sensitive mouth, and the horse tossed his head several times, eyes rolling.

"So. You have heard," grunted Aelfred, walking the skittish black over. The stallion stood taller than Thomas's nag and Aelfred obviously enjoyed the advantage the height gave him. He sneered down at his older brother and waved a hand deprecatingly at Caedmon, who had joined Caedra in the doorway of the hut.

Thomas sat his nag stonily and looked up at his brother with an impassive face.

"Our father died. This morn." Aelfred's cold blue eyes watched Thomas.

"And you have wasted no time in taking his horse," observed Thomas.

" 'Tis *my* horse." Aelfred frowned. "My horse. *My* lands. *My* village." The black took a step closer. "And what are you still doing here? Why did you not run like he"—Aelfred pointed to Caedmon—"told you to do?" Aelfred's lips twisted in a grin. "Or were you just on your way?"

Thomas eyed his half-brother coldly. "I know you do not want me here."

"I want you dead!" spat Aelfred.

"Then why do you not try and kill me?" Thomas was surprised. 'Twas not like Aelfred to warn a man before he killed him.

"Because," spoke up a cynical voice behind them.

Thomas turned to look at Helmut, a Dane swordsman who had recently attached himself to Lord Harald's manor. Obviously the man thought well of himself, well enough to interrupt his new patron, Aelfred.

Aelfred gaped at Helmut, then relaxed and

grinned. He turned back to Thomas. "I do not kill you because Lady Ingrid specifically forbade me to kill you. *This* time."

Thomas raised an eyebrow. "How unlike your mother to be so kind."

"Oh, 'twas not kindness at all," chortled Aelfred artlessly. "She thought that if I killed you, the men and women on our lands would rise up and attack the manor house in revenge. Lady Ingrid did not want that."

"Mmmmmm. 'Twould prove inconvenient," observed Thomas cynically.

Helmut, a hardened man whose scars indicated he had survived several battles, walked his horse over and sneered, "Get out, Lachlann. Get out and do not return."

"Or what?" Thomas's face flushed at the man's impudence.

"Or else we will kill your mother and"—Helmut nodded negligently in Caedmon's direction—"and anyone else we care to. Anyone who is of your kin. Anyone who names you friend."

Thomas turned to Aelfred. "You let this—this outsider—speak for you?" Rage swelled in his voice.

Aelfred grinned happily and nodded. "Aye. He is a good fighter. A good planner."

And Helmut planned to take over Swords and the manor, Thomas saw in an instant. He glared at Aelfred. "You are a fool, Aelfred. Do not let this man guide you. He will take everything he can—"

"I said get out!" Helmut's sword was in his hand and he slashed the air within inches of Thomas's face. Thomas read his deadly intent in the man's pale gaze.

Thomas glared at Aelfred, cursing his half-brother's stupidity, his ambition, his ignorance. Thomas knew that if he said but another word, Helmut would slice him through.

"Thomas!" 'Twas his mother's voice. Thomas slumped in the saddle. For himself, he could fight, but what of his mother, his cousins, his friends? He could not protect them all against Aelfred, Helmut, and their deadly ilk.

"Go, Thomas," cried Caedra. "Your brother will be here any moment!" There was an urgency in her voice.

Aelfred smirked. "Still as crazy as ever, I see."

Thomas felt humiliation wash over him at the amused look in his half-brother's eyes and at the smug looks of Helmut and the other man. His mother could not help it that her mind was not quite right since her fall.

Thomas drew himself up straight in the saddle. He could not, would not, discuss his mother or her affliction with Aelfred. "See that she is not hurt," he said tersely. "And if word ever reaches me that you have harmed her, I will return and kill you. All of you."

Aelfred's mount took a step back, responding to the icy coldness in Thomas's voice. Aelfred himself looked taken aback at Thomas's words. The half-brothers glared at each other.

Caedmon slapped the thin flanks of the nag

in a desperate effort to get the roan moving and to get Thomas away and out of danger. "Ride!" he entreated.

Thomas reined in the nag and looked down at the trembling man. His green eyes steadied with purpose. "My thanks, Caedmon!" he said. "I willna forget your help!"

"Master, ride!" The desperate pleading in Caedmon's voice reached the youth on horseback.

"Aye. Get!" sneered Aelfred. The men with him laughed coarsely.

With one final nod, Thomas kicked the spindly flanks of the sorry roan and moved slowly off toward the forest.

He looked backward once.

"And do not return!" cried Aelfred.

His voice reminded Thomas of a petulant child's.

"If you do, I will kill you!" Aelfred's words, however, did not belong to a child.

Insolently, to goad his half-brother and Helmut as much as to communicate with his loved ones, Thomas waved at his mother and Caedmon, a last farewell. His mother waved back and finally Caedmon, too, lifted his hand in a sad, disheartened gesture of farewell.

Thomas swung around and kicked the horse harder. The gelding, though sorry, was not without heart, and he broke into a rolling canter, every stride taking Thomas farther away from the raucous laughter of his half-brother and his companions.

Shuddering, red-faced in anger and humiliation at the coarse taunts, Thomas's fists clenched the reins. He guided the horse into the forest and onto one of the many trails that crisscrossed the woods in a fine network like so many veins on a leaf. Within heartbeats, Thomas was swallowed up by the dense forest.

Chapter Two

Dubh Linn, Ireland
Ten Years Later

"You asked to see me, Ivar?" It was dusk as Thomas Lachlann stepped into a large military tent, ducking his head to avoid the ornately carved dragon's head that adorned the top of the tent frame.

Ivar Wolfson swung around on the stool he was sitting upon. A large, slow-moving man, he dwarfed the stool. His eyes were set in a web of lines from squinting for years in the sun of hotter climes. His short blond hair betrayed his Norwegian heritage, and his skin was ruddy from those same years in the sun.

Two of Ivar's lieutenants were with him.

Thomas saw the wide parchment with the black outlines in Ivar's hands and knew the three had been discussing the strategy for yet another battle. Ivar nodded, then jerked his head silently toward the tent's opening. Without a word, the lieutenants left the tent, Ingolf with a smirk and Dirk the Dane with a wink.

"You too, Jasmine," said Ivar. "Out."

Thomas watched as a sinuous, dark-haired young woman slowly unwound herself from the thick pile of pink, blue, and turquoise pillows in one corner of the tent. A dark bundle of rags in the other corner moved, got to its feet, and revealed itself to be an old woman who hobbled after the younger woman, who ignored her. Jasmine pouted and glanced angrily at Ivar through the thick lashes of her almond-shaped black eyes; then she busied herself in wrapping a voluminous black robe around her shapely contours until naught was visible but her lovely eyes. With one last unreadable glance at the commander, the young woman left the tent. The old woman shuffled after her.

Ivar waited until they had gone. "Sit," he ordered.

Puzzled, Thomas sank down onto the richly patterned Moorish rug that covered the ground in Ivar's tent. Ivar had gained the beautiful carpet, the pillows, the small, elaborately carved table, the flickering lamps, a taste for luxuries and his lovely concubine, Jasmine, during profitable military campaigns against the Moors in southern Spain.

Thomas waited for his commander to speak. Yet still Ivar said nothing, his blue eyes watching Thomas almost dispassionately. Nevertheless, Thomas perceived an intensity to the look that almost took his breath away. He swallowed once, and waited.

At last Ivar said gruffly, "You have been with me for ten long years."

Thomas waited.

"During that time you have fought for me. Risked your life for me. Pulled me out of battle when I thought I was half way to Valhalla with a Valkyrie on each arm."

Thomas said nothing, but the memories flooded over him and he nodded. The battle that Ivar spoke of had been the first time Thomas had ever met the man, though he had soldiered for him nigh on half a year. Ivar's life was being threatened by three rock-hard fighting Irishmen who had attacked him as one, and Thomas, not liking the odds, had chosen to even them. Half-naked and howling like a berserker of old, he had descended upon the three, *Thor's Bite* swinging. He had killed the Irishmen in several hacking blows. Ivar looked up from where he had been pinned to the earth and said, "I want you in my personal guard."

And so Thomas had been with Ivar as one of his bodyguards ever since that day. Thomas liked the prestige that went with the position. And he knew he had gained a reputation as a ferocious fighter, not only from that fight but from countless others against both Norse and

Irish. His growing reputation served Thomas well; the other soldiers of Ivar's command, always a rough lot, gave him a respectful distance when he had need of it.

"Never asked from whence you came . . ."

Thomas was about to speak but Ivar held up a strong hand. "And I will not ask now."

Thomas subsided, silent. Mayhap 'twas best if even Ivar knew nothing of Thomas's past.

Ivar paused, as if assessing his man. At last he said, "I have contracted a bride."

Thomas started. This *was* news. Ivar, to be married?

Ivar was quick to spot the incredulous look on his bodyguard's face before Thomas could wipe it off.

"Do not look so. Even *I* have need of a wife. Of a son."

Thomas nodded slowly. Ivar was carving out a large territory around Dubh Linn, ostensibly to help King Sitric Silkenbeard. In return for Ivar's loyalty, Silkenbeard left him much power. And some land. Ivar had fought hard for Silkenbeard. But there were ferocious contenders, Norse and Irish, for Dubh Linn and were Ivar to die, his efforts would come to naught. It seemed natural to Thomas that Ivar would want to pass his command on to a son or sons. And though Ivar's concubine, Jasmine, was lovely, she had so far proved infertile. She had been with Ivar for as long as Thomas had known him and had not produced a child, boy *or* girl.

"Another concubine?" suggested Thomas delicately. Verily, he thought, his brow sweating, he had no experience in advising military commanders about such things, but surely a woman was all that was needed. No need to marry her, he thought dismissively. "A wife might find the field living difficult . . . too rough. . . ."

Ivar frowned. "I have thought about it. A wife is what I need. No contest for legitimacy that way."

"Ah," said Thomas, suddenly bitter. Indeed, Ivar would not want his illegitimate son fighting with the legitimate one for power and land. The irony was not lost upon Thomas. Why, 'twas the very situation that had driven him from Swords village. Lord Harald had sired Thomas upon an Irish woman and Aelfred upon his legal wife. Thomas clenched his teeth. 'Twas ten years later, and he was no closer to fulfilling his vow to claim his father's land today than he had been on the day he fled from Aelfred. "Aye," agreed Thomas shortly. "You have the right of it." How well he knew that!

Ivar nodded. A little silence grew between them; Thomas was lost in his thoughts.

Ivar continued, "I have arranged a ship for you. I want you to sail to Greenland and bring back my bride."

"Greenland!" Thomas' interest quickened. He had heard of such a place. As a boy he had once met a man who claimed he had sailed there. Why, 'twas at the ends of the earth! "Greenland!"

"Her name is Yngveld Sveinsdatter."

Thomas stared at his commander, pulling his thoughts forcibly back from the sea.

"Her father," continued Ivar, "is Svein Skull-crusher, an old comrade-in-arms of mine. We fought together many years ago." A shadow crossed Ivar's face and for a moment he looked cruel. Then the look was gone. "The betrothal agreement is there." He nodded at a yellowed, rolled-up parchment wrapped in a red ribbon that sat on the delicately carved Moorish table. "Take it. 'Twill convince Svein that you are my emissary."

Thomas took the scroll gingerly and barely glanced at it.

"Svein should be expecting you," said Ivar. "I sent a message two years past, by ship, to remind him of the betrothal and to tell him that I, or my representative, would come to Greenland." He eyed Thomas. "Unfortunately, I cannot get away at this time. Too much fighting—'tis a critical time." He sighed. "The Irish are in rebellion again. Brian Boru is gathering more men."

Thomas nodded. Brian Boru was a powerful Irish warrior and had enjoyed much success in raids against the Norse.

"I have chosen you," Ivar went on in a gruff voice, "because of all my men, I trust you the most."

Thomas started.

" 'Tis true," said Ivar. "I trust you as my bravest and most loyal man. I want a man who can bring my bride to Dubh Linn safely."

Thomas swallowed, cognizant suddenly of the immense responsibility of his mission. "I will do my best," he assured Ivar.

"See that you do." Ivar watched him carefully. "You may have your pick of forty men to take with you, except for Ingolf and Dirk the Dane. Choose any man you think will fight hard and sail straight. Choose loyal men. You will have need of them."

Thomas nodded, his mind racing. Whom to choose? There was Caedmon's son, Neill, who had searched until he had found Thomas in Dubh Linn, stayed, and was now a presentable soldier. Thomas would take him. And Torgils—he fought well and he, too, was a half-Norse, half-Irish bastard like Thomas, and also from Swords village. And what of Connall, another trusted friend? No, Connall he would leave at Dubh Linn. Mayhap Connall could make one more visit to Swords and give Caedra the few gold coins that Thomas had saved. Connall had done this regularly for Thomas over these past years. 'Twas too dangerous for Thomas to go in person. Aelfred had not stopped searching for him. And each time Connall returned, he had brought truly disturbing reports about Aelfred's treatment of the Swords peasants. 'Twas most unsettling.

Ivar was looking at him.

Thomas shook his head, coming out of his thoughts. He said, "Very well, I will choose."

Ivar answered, "Good," and nodded several times.

Thomas would need a cargo to sell so the voyage would bring a profit. And he must get a huge supply of food, though doubtless he and his men would catch fresh fish to supplement their diet.

Ivar interrupted, "There's talk of finding nine men hanging in Odinn's grove of trees."

The change of subject caught Thomas unawares. "Men? Hanging? Oh, aye, aye, so I have heard."

"Know you about it?"

Thomas shook his head, slowly coming round to the topic. "I do not have confidence in Odinn—or any of the Viking gods. I do not sacrifice to him."

For the first time Ivar's face split in a grin and he slapped Thomas on the back. "Aye, I know that well enough, my friend. Who do you sacrifice to?"

Thomas shook his head. "No one," he answered sullenly. 'Twas a sore point between him and his commander. Ivar favored the old gods, but Thomas could find little use for them *or* for his mother's Irish Christian god. He knew many of the Dubh Linn Norse sought and found the favor of Thor, Odinn, Frey, or whoever could be of help to them, but he himself did not choose that route. "No one," he said again.

"Well," said Ivar, getting to his feet. " 'Tis of little importance. I but wondered who had done it, 'tis all."

At Thomas's inquiring glance, he added, "Seems we did very well, very well indeed, the next day in our fight against some ratty Irish rebels." He grinned. "Mayhap the sacrifice worked."

"Mayhap," said Thomas noncommittally. The joke did not set well with him. He moved to rise.

"Get some rest," advised Ivar. "You leave a sennight hence."

Seven nights! Little enough time to prepare a ship, and men.

Something of Thomas's thoughts must have shown once more upon his face, for Ivar said, "The ship is ready. And has supplies enough. I have made a deal with an honest merchant of the town." He snorted. "Somewhat of a rarity! He assures me the ship is seaworthy."

Then with a wave of his hand, Thomas too was dismissed from Ivar's tent.

Thomas had just lifted the tent flap when Ivar's voice halted him. "Thomas Lachlann!"

Thomas turned.

"I want Yngveld Sveinsdatter brought to me virgin!"

Thomas smiled, a slash across his rugged, good-looking face that did not quite reach his hard green eyes. "You shall have your bride," he answered shortly. "Untouched."

Ivar nodded.

Thomas turned once more to leave.

"Tell Jasmine to get in here," said Ivar to Thomas's back before the tent flap closed. "I want her. Now."

Chapter Three

Godthab District, Greenland
998 A.D.
Springtime

Yngveld Sveinsdatter crouched in what she was certain was the only clump of scrub willow trees on the entire barren coast of Greenland. She waited in the waning light, brushing at the tendrils of long blond hair that had escaped her single thick braid, scratching at mosquito bites, and staring at her sweating palms as if willing herself to see her future therein.

At her belt hung a small bundle containing her most valuable possessions: one set of embroidered undergarments; two leather sacks, one filled with gold coins, the other with silver;

three precious hair ribbons, one yellow, one red, and one purple; her dead mother's breast pin of amber set in delicate silver filigree in the shape of a flower; Yngveld's own favorite breast pin of heavy worked silver; two silver armlets in the shape of entwined snakes; a tiny vial of floral scent; and five carefully wrapped slices of dried seal meat for her desperate journey. Yngveld fondled her precious treasures for as long as she could still see, then she listened to the heavy flap of duck wings overhead, scratched some more and waited for even deeper darkness to descend.

Presently she peeked out stealthily from behind the willows. No one. Good! She had not been followed. Bjarni had been so certain of himself that he had seen no need to post a guard at the farmhouse. She had slipped away undetected. Good, she repeated to herself. She might yet get out of this terrible situation.

At last the purple dusk became the velvet dark of night. With trepidation, Yngveld watched the rise of the huge silver moon from her hiding place. While beautiful, the full moon posed a danger to her: she might be seen. Yet it would also help her pick her path down the hillside to safety.

At last Yngveld felt free to leave her shelter. Rising, she snagged her laboriously embroidered dress on a thorn. She gave it a yank and it came free with a little tearing sound. No matter, she thought ruefully. Why, only a sennight past such a thing would have sent her into a flurry of activity matching the right color of thread and repairing the rent. But the little tear to her best dress mattered little—now.

Her blue eyes widened, darted everywhere, scanned the bleak hillside for enemies—human, bear, or wolf. Nothing moved in the moonlight. Carefully she took a step, then another. She paused, her ears straining for a sound, any sound. But naught was to be heard, not even the evening cry of a bird.

Then, heedless to traitor moon, stealthy adversaries, all, she dashed down the mountain trail to the farmhouse nestled far below. She knew the trail by heart, having traversed it many times with her father, now dead, God rest his soul. She brushed a tear from her eyes as she flew along the trail. *Father would understand*, she thought. *He would want me to do this*.

Yellow light spilled from the open door of the small farmhouse, giving the place the look of the true haven that she knew it to be. She heard the sound of low voices talking, but gave no pause as she hurtled across the threshold. She was home, or as near to home as there was left for her in the world.

Her race run, she collapsed in a heap upon the hard-packed dirt floor. The two inhabitants looked up in alarm from their evening meal at the specter of the young woman suddenly in their midst.

"What?"

"Who?"

"Why, 'tis Yngveld!" Karl Ketilson, a middle-aged man with graying hair at the temples, jumped to his feet and ran to the woman.

He was followed more slowly by Patrick, his blond male thrall, who hung back but could not take his eyes off the woman. "Is she hurt?" asked the slave, appearing not to breathe. "Yngveld?" He knelt beside his master, who was gently patting her cheeks, trying to bring her round.

"She is so gently bred," Karl was muttering. "I fear she is . . ."

But he did not finish, for the object of his concern was slowly waking up. "Karl? Karl? Patrick?" asked Yngveld, dazed. "Ah, then I truly made it." And she would have sunk back into a swoon had not Patrick taken her hand and squeezed, hard.

"Stop that!" Yngveld sat up suddenly, irritated at the pain in her hand.

Patrick's narrow face fell and he looked sheepish. "I was only—"

She smiled tremulously and forgave him at once. " 'Tis only that I thought 'twas Bjarni," she said, and her smile disappeared.

"Bjarni? Do you mean Bjarni Bearhunter?" asked Karl.

"*Ja*, the same."

A closed look came over Yngveld's face, and Karl decided not to question her further. She would tell him when she was ready and not a moment before. Gently bred she was. And she had been through enough these past days, what with her father's death.

Then the incongruity suddenly struck Karl.

Here was Yngveld Sveinsdatter in his home on the very night she was supposed to sit with the body of her father for the last time.

"Your father," he began. "He is alone?"

She sighed. "He is. Alone like me."

Karl nodded. "*Ja*. 'Tis hard to lose a father," he said. "Especially one so fine as Svein Skullcrusher."

"*Ja*," said Yngveld sadly. "And I am angry that I cannot keep my vigil at his deathbed even now."

Thinking that she had fainted from grief or mayhap hunger, Karl helped her to her feet and said, "There, my child, we shall feed you and then we shall walk you home, Patrick and I."

She waved away his suggestion of food. Her stomach had not felt hunger since her father's death. "Alas, my father's friend," she said, her big blue eyes fastened on Karl's dearly loved, familiar face, " 'tis to you that I have run for safety. I cannot return to my father's home. Not now."

"Safety? Not return? What is this?"

Yngveld walked over to the table. The remains of a simple meal were there—cheese, buttermilk, seal meat. She sank down on the bench, head averted, unable to abide the sight or smell of the food. Weariness invaded the very bones of her body. " 'Tis as I said," she answered. "I cannot go home. Bjarni waits for me there."

"Ah, *ja*. Bjarni." Karl waited.

Yngveld watched him out of haunted blue

eyes. "Bjarni wants to marry me," she announced at last.

"*Ja*, has for some time, I believe," said Karl. He frowned in perplexity. He feared the young man would not make a good husband—for Yngveld or any woman. But he kept his own counsel, not wanting to discourage her if she wanted the young man.

"*I* will not marry Bjarni."

Relief crossed Karl's blunt, plain face. "*Ja*, I understand that. Bjarni is, well, mayhap not the best prospect for a husband that a young woman like yourself might find," he ventured.

"Oh, Karl! He is worse than that. He is a lying, dishonest, dangerous fool."

Karl thought about that. "*Ja*, he is." After a moment, Karl asked, "What has he done?"

Yngveld threw up her hands. "He has taken over my farmhouse and my lands with a band of his friends. Both my servants have run off in fear of him." Her voice trembled. "And he would force me to marry him."

Karl flinched and paled. "He would not dare!"

"He does. In the full light of day. He came to me this morn and told me so as I was sitting in vigil beside my dead father's body. 'Yngveld,' says he, 'marry me. I will fair waste away for want of love of you.'

"'Love of me?' says I. 'Love of my property, you mean!'

"'That too,' says he with barely a flicker of an eyelash. Aaaargh, but he does take me for a fool!" she cried.

Karl nodded judiciously. "He does." After a pause, he added, "Bjarni does not know you well, 'tis plain."

"He knows well enough that I have no one to call upon now, whilst I wait upon a message to reach my father's cousin in Norway."

Karl considered this. "Think you that your kinsman will answer your call for help?" he asked. There was doubt in his voice. "Your father fled Norway, was driven away, called outlaw. Mayhap this cousin will not come to your aid."

"What choice have I?" cried Yngveld. Indeed, Karl had given voice to her own fears. There had been little word from Norway over the long years. But where else had she to turn? "To stay in Greenland is to give Bjarni all he wants—my land, myself." Her blue eyes flashed. "And that I will *never* do! *Nej*, to appeal to my kinsman is my only hope now."

Karl nodded, but he was doubtful, she could see that.

"You have me," said Karl at last.

"*Ja*," agreed Yngveld gently. "And I need your help." She looked around the simply furnished room, at the scarred furniture, and beyond the open door to the small dirt plots where Karl and his only slave scratched out a meager living. "But you do not have the servants," she said sadly, "or the men that I need to reclaim my farm, to protect my person."

Karl nodded. " 'Tis true," he conceded. "But I would help you nonetheless." He met her eyes steadily. "I was your father's friend. I will help you. Stay here. Patrick and I will protect you."

She held his gaze and warmth flitted through her veins at his loyalty. She touched his hand then, a thankful gesture. "*Nej*, Karl, I must flee—flee Bjarni, flee Greenland. I shall never marry him! He is a murderer!"

"You speak of the thrall woman?" Karl asked.

"*Ja*. Bjarni Bearhunter was the last to be seen with her, walking over the hills. He returned. She did not."

"Her body was never found. It cannot be proved 'twas Bjarni," reminded Karl.

"'Tis enough for me," retorted Yngveld heatedly. "He could have pushed her into the sea, or thrown rocks on top of the corpse." She threw up her hands. "*I* do not want such a man for my husband."

"*Nej*, I would not want such a man for you," answered Karl honestly.

Patrick coughed gently.

Karl turned to him. "*Ja*?"

"Master," began Patrick, "are there no other farmers in this area, men who were friends of Master Svein Skullcrusher, men who will say *nej* to Bjarni? Mayhap you could tell them of Yngveld's circumstance and they would come to her aid."

Karl looked at Yngveld. "'Tis a good idea," he said.

Hope rose momentarily in Yngveld's breast, but then subsided swiftly. She shook her head sadly. "Alas, *nej*, there is not. In the old days, mayhap, when your sword hand was strong and my father's was too—but not now. Now these younger sons do as they like, lawlessly taking land. I know not how to stop them." She added slowly, painfully, "And most of our neighbors—" She broke off, and her face crimsoned.

Karl writhed inwardly for her.

"Most of our neighbors no longer wanted my father around at the end. His rages—"

Karl reached out and placed a hand on her shoulder. "They did not know him like I did," he said kindly. Her huge blue eyes were riveted on his face and Karl flushed at the desperation he saw there. "To me, your father was generous, kind, honest. . . ."

Yngveld squeezed the hand on her shoulder and the tears in her eyes fell and wetted the back of his hand. "Thank you, Karl Ketilson, my father's friend," she whispered. "Thank you for those kind words."

Karl nodded wordlessly, embarrassed for her, for himself. Svein Skullcrusher had not been an easy man to deal with in his later years. Many of the local farmers had turned against him with his unpredictable ways, but Karl—though insulted at times, fearful of the man at others—had refused to turn his back on his old friend. And seeing Svein's daughter now, pleading, with no one to turn to, Karl was glad that he had not broken faith with his old, mad friend.

Yngveld's round eyes were fastened on him

now. "You understand why I cannot ask the others—"

Karl nodded. Patrick too.

With a rush of expelled breath, Yngveld relaxed. Her voice steadier now, she named the young men who had been with Bjarni when he had made his shameful offer.

Karl started in surprise. "But those men are from some of the best families in Greenland!"

Yngveld nodded.

"Younger sons," Karl mused. "Looking for land."

Patrick sat down on the bench, his blue eyes filled with silent sorrow as he watched Yngveld.

"What about Einar?" asked Karl. "Your father looked to him as a trading partner on occasion."

"*Ja*," said Yngveld. "I had thought to ask you to come with me, Karl. And you, too, Patrick. We must go to Einar. I must depart for Norway. And I must find a ship. Einar will know."

"When will you leave?"

"This night," said Yngveld.

"So soon?"

"Bjarni will not wait," she said ruefully. "I was barely able to get him to promise me a single night of freedom afore we wed. He thinks we are to be married in the morn. And," she added with a determined gleam in her blue eyes, "I do not intend to be here!"

Patrick coughed delicately.

"Einar will help us," said Karl at last.

"For a price," added Patrick wryly. He smiled.

Yngveld did not. She took out a jingling sack

of coins from the bundle at her waist. "I brought this. There is another sack inside." She patted the little bundle. " 'Twas all I could take with me."

Karl nodded. He looked inside the leather bag and whistled. " 'Twill be enough," he assured her, "for ship to Norway."

Yngveld nodded, relieved. She had hoped so. No one could have been more surprised than she was when her father had called her over to his side as he lay near death. Seeing him point to the firepit several times, she had thought he was cold and had built up the fire. When he shook his head, she understood he wanted something else. Little could she believe when he told her what lay buried under the pit. But when the fire had died down, she dug and found the gold, more gold than she had ever seen—or thought her father to possess. They had lived a difficult life in Greenland, careful to husband what crops they grew, and Yngveld had never expected that her father had so much money. To her questioning look, he had but said, "Take it, my daughter. 'Tis yours." Later, he had fallen asleep, then lost consciousness and mumbled nonsense for days before his final, merciful end.

Sadness haunted her blue eyes as she thought of her father. Then, carefully tucking away the sack of gold, she rose to her feet. "Well?" she asked, her voice scarcely quavering. "What are we waiting for?"

Chapter Four

As it turned out, Einar had the solution to Yngveld's problem.

"So you must ship for Norway by dawn," he yawned. With hair askew and his nightshirt falling off one pale, hairy shoulder, Einar sat at the wide table in the main room of his heavily furnished house and looked like nothing so much as a great, plump walrus. The wooden bench he sat on groaned from his weight. A lamp flickered on the table and Einar yawned once more, his jowls stretching with the effort. Yngveld and Karl sat across from him and Patrick waited quietly near the door.

Yngveld took a secret ruthless pleasure in the knowledge that she had awakened the merchant from his sleep.

And she was relieved to sit across from Einar, out of his reach. She too easily remembered the one time when, as a girl, she had been left alone with him in this dark, stifling house whilst her father was out in the yard examining a supply of Markland lumber that he and Einar had jointly purchased. Einar had oozed his way across the room to her, talking softly. He had touched her shoulder, then had slid his hand lower until it was curving her newly budded breast. Frightened, Yngveld had shrugged out of his oily touch and run out of the house and across the yard to her father, her heart pounding the while.

Svein had glanced up absently from counting the lumber when she had thrown herself at him, hugging herself to him as she had done when but a tiny girl. Her father had patted her absently, then gone back to his counting. Yngveld had hovered near her father for the remainder of the visit, refusing to leave him for a single moment. She never did tell him what Einar had done, but every time she saw the oily man she wanted to run from his presence. Her skin rose in great goose bumps whenever she felt his sly, beady eyes studying her. As they were now.

Yngveld bravely locked gazes with the fat merchant and felt a wave of revulsion wash over her. But she would not let him drive her away. Not this night. 'Twas too important—her life hung in the balance.

'Twas also the reason she had wanted Karl to come with her when she sought Einar's help.

Had there been anyone else in the whole of the Godthab district to ask, she would have, but Einar was the most influential farmer and merchant in this part of Greenland. He knew everything, from what crop a certain farmer was planting to when the next shipment of precious lumber would arrive from Markland to what price a man could get for a polar bear skin were he to sell it in Iceland.

"Slaves, my girl," Einar was saying, smiling across the table at Yngveld and Karl in a falsely hearty manner. "Slaves."

Yngveld's senses recoiled as he wet his lips. "Slaves?" She could not imagine how slaves would help her get away from Greenland. Mayhaps Einar's greed had at last warped his mind.

"Slaves will give you no trouble. They will sail your ship for you, row themselves to death for you. *Ja*, slaves are the answer."

"Ship? What ship? I have no ship, though a place on a ship is what I need." She did not trust Einar. He had some scheme on his mind—she knew the look of him when he was up to something. She had seen that look before—the smug little smile, the darting eyes—when he had told her father to count out his own share of the lumber when Einar's ship had returned from Markland that time. Einar had claimed that his ship had needed vast repairs after the voyage, hence she was drawn up on the beach of another fjord. Einar, incidentally, was generously willing to pay for the repairs out of his own pocket and not demand a share from

Svein. Svein had pointed out that 'twas not so generous since Einar owned the ship. Why should Svein pay for Einar's repairs? Einar had huffed about that, and gone on to say that he had already taken the liberty of ordering the ship's crew to unload Svein's share of the lumber at Einarsfjord.

Svein had counted the logs and found the amount short, much lower than the partners' previous lumber ventures between Markland and Greenland had produced. But Einar had explained in his oily voice that the ship had been injured, that she could not carry as much wood that voyage, and on and on until Svein had accepted the count as his fair share. Later, Svein had discovered that there were only the usual repairs made to the ship after such a voyage, and that whilst he had been counting his lumber, Einar's crew, far from making repairs, had instead been unloading half again as much timber in the quiet little fjord just over the hill from Einar's home. Einar had then proceeded to sell the extra timber to a buyer, all for Einar's own profit. And this at a time when the price for straight, strong Markland timber was at the highest.

Ja, Einar bore watching indeed, thought Yngveld.

"I have a ship," announced Einar.

Yngveld's wariness heightened. "You do?" she said. Karl echoed her.

"*Ja*." Einar waited and Yngveld thought he enjoyed the power he held over them.

"I have a ship that can leave at next dawn. On the high tide. And with it a fine captain," Einar simpered, then coughed once, the words choking him a little. He decided he need not mention that the man he had available to captain the ship was an old grizzled outlaw who even now was hiding in one of Einar's outbuildings with five of his vicious friends. Or that Einar owed the outlaw a favor. Or that this outlaw, Ole Olafson, had recently killed a man on Greenland and had bullied Einar into hiding him. Or that Einar himself did not like Olafson, indeed feared him. *Nej*, such things were best not mentioned at this delicate stage of the negotiations.

A ship! This was news! "How much?" asked Yngveld cautiously. She was under no illusion as to Einar's motivation. "How much for my passage?"

"My lady," Einar looked pained. "You wound me."

"How much?"

Einar rubbed his hands together as though he were washing them. "We can speak of that later." He smiled.

"Why do you insist upon slaves?" asked Karl.

Einar turned to him. His little eyes flitted over Karl twice before he spoke. "The ship I have cannot leave without a full complement of sailors. At present it has only a handful of men to row it—the captain that I mentioned and five of his crew. Thirty more men are needed to complete the crew." He smiled smugly, but his beady eyes watched first Karl, then Yngveld.

"And . . . it so happens that I have a crew of thirty experienced sailors."

"The slaves," sighed Yngveld.

"Of a certain, my lady." Einar continued to watch her, and Yngveld wanted to veil herself. The man's eyes made her feel soiled.

"Ja," Einar smiled a little more expansively. "Irish slaves. Strong, sturdy. Took them off a ship myself not long ago."

Einar's activities would bear closer examination, thought Yngveld. And sailing on a ship where most of the crew were slaves sounded dangerous to her.

"But," said Einar, and his face took on a tragic cast, "I do not have a load of trade goods aboard the ship, and as you want to leave at dawn, I do not have time enough to fill the ship's hold." He shrugged, and his nightshirt slipped a little farther off one round, hairy shoulder. "I am a merchant, please understand. I must make the trip to Norway profitable for me, else why do it?" He spread his hands. "So, we have a problem." He sighed.

"*Nej*, we do not," said Yngveld. She shook her head, not liking the danger despite her desperation to leave Greenland. "For I am not interested."

Einar glanced at her sharply. "Then you will stay in Greenland until next spring. There is not another ship or another crew available in the whole Godthab district. And if you do not leave now, soon it will be too late—the seas will ice up."

Yngveld sat pondering. Could she afford to have scruples when they might very well cost her her one chance at leaving Greenland and Bjarni's long reach? Should she let her fear of difficult conditions on shipboard rule her when Bjarni was waiting to marry her? What a choice, she thought—to risk her life on a ship with desperate men or to marry murderous Bjarni. Her mouth turned down at the thought and her empty stomach churned.

"More ale?" Einar asked, giving her time to make her decision. Yngveld shook her head, as did Karl. Patrick was not offered any.

Presently, when Yngveld had still not said anything, Einar ventured, "But for you, Yngveld Sveinsdatter, I am prepared to be generous."

All Yngveld's senses went on alert.

"For you I will do something that is not my habit. I will *sell* you the ship, the slaves, *and* the captain's services for a *very* reasonable sum." He watched her closely. "To help you, you understand."

Seeing the suspicious look on her face, he added, "Of course, if you do not want to buy the ship, I understand. But please understand that I cannot just outfit a ship, feed the crew, pay the captain, send the ship across the seas to Norway and then back to Greenland, all for the price of one woman's passage." He spread his hands again. " 'Twould not do. Why, I would go out of business." His smile did not reach his beady eyes.

Karl caught Einar watching Yngveld. He did

not like the calculating look in the wealthy farmer's eyes. 'Twas as though, with Svein Skullcrusher dead, Einar thought he could turn against his old trading partner's only daughter. And Yngveld probably knew it. Mayhap 'twas why she sought out Karl to come with her to bargain with Einar. She knew he would not give her a fair deal. Karl sighed.

Yngveld tossed her long blond braid back from her neck as she considered Einar's words.

Karl noticed the action. So did Einar. And Yngveld had wide blue eyes which Einar must find most alluring, Karl thought. Her slim body and manner of dress were very attractive, and 'twas most obvious that Einar, given little encouragement, would soon be making designs on the young woman.

Karl sighed again. Yngveld was not even out of Greenland and already she was in danger. Karl looked at Patrick, then back at Yngveld again. 'Twould not do, he thought. He must go with her. She would need his protection and Svein, his old friend, would have wanted it.

But Einar's rising from the table signaled that a decision must be made. "Would you like to see the slaves?" he asked Yngveld.

Yngveld looked at him. "Very well," she answered. "I will look. I am not saying that I will buy, mind you," she added sharply, "but I *will* look."

Einar smiled broadly. He had her! The sale was as good as done. "You will like what you see," he promised in a smooth voice as he reached for his heavy cloak hanging on the wall.

Karl cleared his throat. "As I am going with her to Norway, 'tis best if I examine the slaves too."

Yngveld looked at him in surprise and, though she said nothing, the grateful glance she shot him spoke volubly. Patrick dropped the piece of wood he was carving and retrieved it, also without saying a word.

Yngveld, Karl, and Patrick tramped with Einar through the newly sown fields. The full moon overhead cast its broad beams of silver to light their way.

Einar lived on a large farm with much arable land, and a cluster of outbuildings lay at some distance from his house. Farther down the hillside was the fjord, Einarsfjord.

Yngveld squinted through the darkness to the fjord but 'twas too dark to see the ship that Einar had spoken of. She wondered if he had spoken truly or if 'twas but a ploy to get her gold.

Einar led them to one of the long, low outbuildings. Several sheep scattered at their approach. All three men had to duck as they entered. Yngveld followed and Einar held high the lamp he had brought with him. The pool of light fell upon half-clothed, sleeping bodies.

The smell of human sweat hit Yngveld full in the face. The interior of the building was a long, low, dark room lit only by the lamp Einar held. Men—large, muscular men—sat up blinking, and Yngveld caught the clanking of chains.

Einar said, "They are strong and hearty."

"And you fear they will flee," added Yngveld.

Einar shot her a discouraging look which she ignored. Instead she surveyed the slaves. She thought that the men had been taken into captivity but recently, for they looked healthy. Also, she did not know Einar to trade in slaves all that often; he would probably want to sell them as quickly as possible. She wondered how great was the demand for slaves in the Godthab district. Selling them would probably be a major concern of Einar's.

Einar walked past the half-naked men, who glared at him and Karl and Patrick. Yngveld they devoured with their eyes. She shivered as she walked along behind Einar, carefully keeping to herself, not letting even the hem of her dress brush a slave.

Einar continued on, oblivious to the slaves' pulsing hatred, holding his lamp up and peering at the foreign faces. Obviously he looked for one man in particular.

At last he halted in front of a man casually lounging on the dirt floor, his back against a wooden stall. The man's green eyes glittered in the lamplight, but he stayed where he was. He looked supremely indifferent to Einar's presence, and indifferent to the others, too, including Yngveld.

She felt creeping irritation at his lack of reaction to her, realizing suddenly that the other slaves' devouring stares had excited and flattered her.

"Get up!" barked Einar.

The man slowly got to his feet, just barely obeying the order, Yngveld thought, shivering. She watched as he stood, strong, muscular legs planted apart, arms folded across his naked chest, only a small, ragged loincloth keeping him decent. He towered over the portly Einar, as well as over Karl and herself. And Einar expected her to take to sea with such as him? Why, were she to go anywhere with this slave, she could expect at best reluctance or even defiance to every order she ever gave him. And what did she know about ordering slaves? True, she had had the two house servants at home, the ones who had fled into the fields the moment that Bjarni Bearhunter had curled his lip at them. But *these* slaves? Big, muscular brutes they were. Especially this one. How would she order *him* about?

Yngveld chewed her lip as she pondered this. Not a good beginning, she decided. All she had wanted to do was to flee Greenland and get to Norway, where she knew her kinfolk were. They would return to help her take back her land from Bjarni and his minions. That was all she wanted. Yngveld sighed and looked closely at the standing slave.

In the light of the lamp, she was unable to look away. He was magnificent—muscular, with curling black hair covering his head and brushing his shoulders. His face was strong-boned, his nose as straight as a knife, and his square jaw looked as though he were gritting his teeth. Glittering, ruthless eyes impaled Yngveld's when the slave turned his fierce gaze upon her.

Yngveld stared back. The shock of looking into those fascinating eyes held her mesmerized. Green they were, a beautiful sea green with thick black lashes, incongruous in that masculine face. The sneer he gave her added a brutal contempt to his handsome face and sent shivers down her spine. Yngveld stood the straighter then and turned away as though unaffected by the slave's rudeness, or his beauty.

But she was affected, very affected. Her pulse was pounding, her heart smacked against her ribs, and she wanted nothing so much as to turn back and stare at him, mayhap even touch that wide, hair-sprinkled chest of his. But she did not. Instead she asked Einar, "How did you get these men?" Anything, anything to forget that the hostile, fascinating slave was glaring at her.

Einar shrugged nonchalantly. "My men took them off a shipwreck."

Yngveld's jaw dropped. "You mean you rescued these men?"

"*Ja*, but I could not do it for free. After all, it took time and gold to save them. I wanted something for my efforts. Their cargo was gone, destroyed by the seas, and so I had no choice but to take them. As booty, if you will." Einar laughed.

Thomas clenched his jaw. This piece of human dung, Einar, had schemed with another treacherous Greenlander—a man who had given his name as Bjarni Bearhunter, a man who had pretended to befriend Thomas. A storm had landed Thomas's ship, *Raven's Daughter*, on the rocks of a small island off the Greenland coast. For two days he and his crew had tried feverishly to repair the ship, but they could not find the wood they needed. Then the treacherous pretender, Bjarni, had sailed out of the fog in his longship, offering to tow the stricken vessel to a safe fjord where Thomas and his crew could get the necessary wood to make repairs.

Thomas had eagerly agreed to Bjarni's help and had trusted him, telling him of his mission to find and take the woman, Yngveld Sveinsdatter, back to Dubh Linn with him as Ivar's bride. From that point onward, Bjarni, Thomas's new 'friend,' had acted suspiciously. Still, Thomas had not suspected any betrayal until Bjarni had knocked Thomas unconscious, seizing his crew and ship. When Thomas awoke, he and his men were in chains.

Even now the humiliation of it infuriated Thomas. That he, a veteran soldier, should be taken in so easily by a lying pup and his band of young thugs! And Bjarni's men would have killed Thomas and all his crew were not Bjarni so greedy for Einar's gold. Instead, Bjarni had held out against his men and sold Thomas and his crew and ship to this piece of human offal, Einar.

Thomas sneered in contempt at Einar. 'Twas obvious he was trying to impress the pale woman at his side. Then Thomas turned his glance on her. His eyes boldly raked her body and he sneered at her too. So, he and his crew were to be sold once more, were they? And to a woman this time! Well, from the look of her, the woman was another treacherous Greenlander. Blond hair—if you liked it. Thomas perferred black hair. Wide blue eyes. Thomas preferred any other color. Pale skin. Thomas preferred brown. A steady gaze. Insolence, obviously. By the look of her expensive clothes, she was some rich farmer's spoiled brat who had never done a day's work in her life.

Thomas felt his fury mount. Mayhap 'twas because she was beautiful to behold and he was in chains, a slave. He wanted to spit at her feet. He glared at her, daring her to say something, anything. Then he would attack her and this piece of offal, Einar.

Karl Ketilson watched the Irish slave. It was clear that the slave understood Einar's words, for his glittering eyes bespoke rage, and his whole body was held taut. Karl thought privately that the man was barely refraining from launching himself at Einar. Or Yngveld. Once more, Karl sighed and was glad that he had decided to accompany Yngveld to Norway. She would need his help, he knew that now, especially if *this* slave were to be aboard ship.

In a way, Karl almost felt sympathy for the slave. He himself would not care to be "rescued" by one such as Einar—ever.

"This one is the captain," smirked Einar, spitting on the dirt floor. "He is the one I deal with. The others do what he says."

She was forced to look at him now that they were discussing him. His proud, chiseled face was cold, his body poised in coiling tension. There was an aura of danger about him. Yngveld took a step back. "What kind of deals?" Einar was revealing new depths in deceit.

"He agreed to go quietly if I did not kill his men." Actually, 'twas Bjarni who had stumbled across this way of subduing the captain—keeping the fierce fellow quiet by promising not to harm his men once they were captured. But Yngveld did not know that. Let her think it was him, Einar. Let her think what a *man* he was.

Yngveld swung back to stare at Einar. "You would have killed them?" she gritted out between her teeth. Einar was, by every indication, a monster.

"Nothing so obvious as that." He laughed, amused. "I would have left them where they were."

Yngveld watched in fascination as the slave's big hands clenched into tight fists. "And where was that?"

"Oh, on an island, a rocky little piece of land that would support a goat or two, in good weather." Einar seemed to find the whole topic a good joke. "When Bjar—uh, when I found them, they had been shipwrecked for two days and had managed to catch a few fish. I guess they would have survived for a while. No water, though. They would have been reduced to drinking sea water in no time."

"And their ship?"

"We were able to repair it. 'Tis the ship I spoke of. The one I have offered to sell to you."

Yngveld's jaw dropped at Einar's duplicity. Never, never had she suspected such depravity in her neighbor. To rescue a man, throw him and his crew into chains, seize their ship, then sell them all—why, 'twas beyond crediting!

Einar, oblivious to his own depravity, continued, "I am told that this one"—he indicated the green-eyed slave captain casually—"actually risked his life in the storm to save four of his men. No telling what fool thing some men will do."

The chain between the slave's clenched fists was drawn so tight that Yngveld expected it to snap. And then two pairs of glittering eyes centered on Einar—the green-eyed slave's and Yngveld's. Einar did not appear to notice.

"I will take them," ordered Yngveld sharply.

"What?" asked Einar in surprise.

But the surprise on his face could not match the surprise on her own, she was certain.

"You have not yet seen all of them," protested Einar.

"No matter. I will take them. Every one of them."

Suddenly Einar looked crafty. Yngveld realized then that she might as well have told the man to name his highest price for the slaves.

Einar did some rapid calculations in his head and stated a price that caused Yngveld's strong sense of justice to blossom anew. She had heard of greed, but Einar was ridiculous.

"*Nej,*" she said. "I will not pay you that outrageous sum."

"But it includes the ship."

"No matter."

Einar contrived to look sorrowful. "I understand. 'Tis a lot of gold. Still"—he sighed—"if you want the full crew . . ." He let her think about it, certain that the fool woman would pay his price.

Yngveld calculated rapidly. Then she named a figure half as much. She reached into the bundle at her waist, Einar's greedy eyes following her every move. She brought out the leather sack of gold coins. She hefted it up and jingled it. The coins inside clanked dully.

'Twould have to be enough, she thought. Her offer took every last gold coin in the sack. Now she had only the silver left, but she would not tell Einar *that*.

Einar swallowed.

"For the full lot," said Yngveld, swinging the leather sack back and forth under his nose. "No inspection, no questions asked. Tonight! Tomorrow, I will not give you a single coin. 'Tis tonight or not at all." She started to tuck the sack back into her bundle.

She would marry Bjarni if it came to that, she thought. How could she let this greedy merchant wield such power over her? And she refused to pay him the outrageous sum he demanded. "I will take them off your hands, the ship off your hands, and you will have a sack of gold. Think on't, Einar. Gold! What say you?" Yngveld's voice was crisp. 'Twas robbery and Einar knew it.

The sack was slowly disappearing, being lowered carefully into the bundle.

Einar toed the dirt. Hemmed and hawed. One or two of the men were injured and might be useless at the oars. He would get little for them.

" 'Tis my final offer." Yngveld could barely bring herself to speak civilly to the merchant. The sack had disappeared now, contained safely in the bundle.

Einar swallowed, eyes on the bundle, mind racing.

Yngveld slanted a glance at the green-eyed slave to see the effect of the transaction upon him. Her heartbeat quickened and she stifled a gasp when she saw his eyes, hot and predatory, slide over her. He was watching her as a falcon does its prey. The men with him moved restively, like caged beasts.

Yngveld knew now that she would have trouble with the slaves, and she felt a prickle of fear. But Einar had wronged them terribly and she *did* need to get away from Greenland. Tonight! 'Twas her only chance, and she knew it. Already, through the open doorway, she could see the sky lighten. Desperation seized her. She knew that when Bjarni found her missing, he would search the whole of Greenland for her.

Einar's little eyes darted from Yngveld to Karl to the slave captain. Einar sensed that Yngveld was indeed making her final offer. He knew that Yngveld was angry, though why he knew not, and made her offer in haste, yet 'twas still a most excellent offer for all that. And he did not want her to come to her senses and retract it, which she just might do if he prolonged the haggling.

With a great show of reluctance amidst haste, Einar nodded at last. "*Ja,*" he agreed. "I will accept your offer, low as it is, out of friendship for your dear, departed father."

'Twas the final blow. With a snort, Yngveld whipped out the leather sack and slapped it into Einar's upturned palm. Turning on her heel, she strode out the door. "Karl, see to it that they follow!" Blast that Einar! The man would sell his own mother were he given the chance!

Einar called out behind her, "A good bargain, my girl. You will not regret it!"

Yngveld, remembering the glittering bold eyes of her newest possession, the slave captain, wondered if Einar's words were as false as the man himself.

Chapter Five

"Wait!" 'Twas Einar. "Wait for me!"

With a gusty sigh, Yngveld slackened her pace and looked back over her shoulder. She swung around, waiting for him to catch up. As she waited, arms akimbo, tapping her toe rapidly on the hard ground, she watched the slaves shuffle slowly along, ropes linked through their manacles, their loosely chained feet hampered at each step. Karl and Patrick straggled to the rear.

Before Einar could reach her, the green-eyed slave captain at the head of the line shuffled close to her. *He* had been the reason she had hurried ahead. Yngveld held her ground, though her toe stopped tapping and she felt suddenly short of breath. Her heart pounded. Still he came on. She dared another breath. He came so close that she could see the black curling hairs on his chest, hear his breathing, smell his pungent sweat. Another step and she would run.

He halted. "Three of my men are injured," he said, his voice low and deep.

She shivered at the intimacy his voice and nearness evoked. She looked up into his eyes warily, expecting she knew not what, but caught off guard by the simplicity of his words.

"Y-your men?" she stammered, floundering for meaning. He was so close she could not think. His face swam before her. Only those green burning eyes held her upright.

Einar came up from behind and slammed the slave leader in the shoulder. The slave spun to the side, off balance, his weight jerking the three slaves closest to him in line. They braced themselves and he recovered his balance, watching Einar with eyes cold and ruthless, lips grimacing, manacled fists half-raised.

"Damn cocky Irish bastard," cried Einar. "Stay away from her!"

Karl ducked his head nervously as though expecting further trouble. Patrick's head swiveled, alert. The pudgy Einar glared at the slave leader. Yngveld realized then that only the iron chains on the slaves' wrists and legs stood between her and a knife in the ribs, for the four of them could not hold off thirty determined slaves. Indeed, she wondered briefly why the slave leader allowed Einar to bully him, then swiftly drove that frightening thread of thought from her mind.

Slowly, the formidable man shook himself, the chains tightened, and Yngveld saw his muscles gather to spring at Einar. She shivered. In an effort to take command of the situation, for she thought Karl too timid and Einar too uncaring, she cried out, "I will see to it that they have medicine and food! 'Tis all I can promise." She held his hot, tortured glance with a piercing gaze of her own.

Thomas eyed her suspiciously, his shoulder throbbing. He was a mere handsbreadth from launching himself at the fool Einar, yet to do so would give the game away too soon. This pale slip of a woman had bought him and his crew—and his ship as well. He must do nothing—nothing!—to tip her off as to the danger he was to her.

She needed them to row her somewhere. Good. That would fit in well with his plans. As he watched her, he saw the quiver of her lip, the furrow of her brow, the way she held her hand to her breast to still her rapidly beating heart. The ruthless, predatory sense that served him so well in battle was fully alert now. She feared him. He could smell it. She sensed the danger that he was to her and to the other three.

The thought gave Thomas strength. With a shuddering breath, he forced himself to take a tiny step back, but 'twas enough for her to see it. He read the relief in her blue, darkened eyes. She thought herself safe now. Good. He would use that against her. Ruthlessly. Once he and his men were back on his ship 'twould be time to take the ship back. What wondrous good fortune! Odinn, Thor, the Christ—whoever—was with him at last! But he must leash his temper. And he would yet make good use of this woman—very good use.

He took another step backward and reluctantly lowered his fists, the action slow and riveting to Yngveld's eyes. When she saw the tension leave his body, she started breathing once more.

"'Tis enough," he said, his voice gravelly.

Yngveld's body jerked at the snap of his voice. Again she was caught off guard by him. She could sense the coiled tension in him. She continued to watch him warily, but when he made no further move and only stood there, she nodded cautiously.

The march continued in tense silence on the trail back to Einar's farmhouse. Now and then the silence was broken by the clink of chains or a rough Irish curse as someone stumbled.

Rotund Einar ran at Yngveld's side, panting as he tried to keep pace. She snorted under her breath at his efforts but refused to slacken a single step. Karl and Patrick followed at the rear.

As she walked briskly, Yngveld marveled at the desperation that now forced her to cross deserted fields with a crew of thirty big, hungry, ferocious Irish slaves at her back. Was Bjarni Bearhunter really that bad?

Ja, she answered fiercely, he was. Marriage to him would be hell! Not only was he land-hungry, he was cruel. And she could never forget the murdered female slave. That deed she laid at Bjarni's door, though others, like Karl, were inclined to say that mayhap the woman had wandered away and not been murdered. *Nej*, Yngveld cared naught for Bjarni's company and refused, utterly refused, to marry him.

Her thoughts returned to the present. Now the only thing standing between her and a knife in the ribs, she mused as she hurried along, was likely her promise that the Irish wounded would be physicked and fed. Little enough to stand between a woman and eternity, she thought, shivering again.

It seemed a cunning stroke to her now as she thought of it, that promise of care. The little that she knew of the Irish slave captain indicated a strong loyalty to his men. He had certainly backed off once she had promised aid.

Well, she would use his loyalty. Carefully. She would give medicine and food to the three injured members of the crew, and in return she would demand strict obedience from them all and especially from their dangerous, green-eyed leader. Otherwise she would leave them with Einar and be done with them.

And marry Bjarni? Not likely. She increased her pace. She reached Einar's yard only to find that the heavily embroidered back of her dress was soaked from sweat, pasting it to her skin. As the night was cool, she knew that wetness came from fear.

Einar halted the slaves and roughly lined them up. Yngveld surveyed the Irishmen. Most of the thirty men were in good health, but the three wounded were badly off—so badly that Yngveld wondered if they would ever actually man an oar. Nevertheless, she had given her word to the Irish slave captain and she would do what she could to aid the wounded men.

She cornered Einar and insisted that he give her some medicine for the men. After all, she had paid for them and she had a right to expect that medicine was a part of the bargain. Einar frowned but gave it to her, reluctantly, as she knew he would, but she was past caring what Einar wanted. She, Yngveld, wanted only to get aboard the ship—her ship!—and leave this place. Already the thin pale fingers of dawn crept across the sky to warn her of Bjarni Bearhunter's threat.

Seen in the pure light of dawn, the pale woman's beauty suddenly struck Thomas like a blow to his stomach. Her blond hair had come loose from her braid and the wisps blew gently around her face. Her features were clear and perfect. Her graceful form and gestures made him long for something feminine to hold to himself. He shook his head, trying to dispel the yearning, and sought refuge in anger. Whatever was she doing, putting herself in with a bunch of rough, desperate slaves? He turned to glare at the older, graying man with her, the one she frequently consulted with. He must be mad to let her do this, Thomas thought with a sneer of contempt.

Karl noticed that the Irish slave captain had locked his glittering green gaze upon Yngveld, and Karl's heart stopped. The hunger he read in the man's gaze appalled Karl. He resolved then that he must never, *ever*, leave Yngveld alone with these slaves and certainly never with the Irish slave captain.

Roughly, Karl pushed past the slave, knocking him in the gut with an elbow to let him know that he was subordinate. "Fetch your wounded," Karl growled. His elbow throbbed from contact with the slave's iron-hard stomach.

Thomas grinned to himself to see a spark of courage in the older man. He had thought him weak before. Thomas grunted an order and the three injured men shuffled forward.

One man had a deep gash in his leg, the second a broken arm that he held at an odd angle, and the third suffered from a festering chest wound.

Yngveld cleaned each wound as best she could, set the arm, and searched through the paltry selection of herbs that Einar had provided.

While Yngveld was physicking the wounded men and trying to determine the extent of their injuries, Einar disappeared into a large outbuilding near his house. He returned leading a barrel-chested, grizzled man of middle age and his five equally unsavory companions.

"Who do we have here?" asked Karl, not liking the look of the men. He thought he recognized one of them, a troublemaker who had worked odd jobs on some of the local farms.

In a hearty voice, Einar announced, "Meet your new captain—Captain Ole Olafson!"

Yngveld stopped in mid-conversation with one of the injured men. "What?" she cried. When Einar only grinned, she hurried over.

Thomas turned a cold gaze to watch.

The new "captain" kept looking around as if he expected to take flight at any moment. When whatever he was expecting did not appear, he shifted his gaze to Yngveld. "You need a captain," he said in a hollow voice. "I need a ship."

"I do not need a captain this badly," hissed Yngveld to Einar. "This man looks, looks—" Words failed her as she stared, horrorstruck, at the rough-looking man in front of her. "Take him away!"

"*Nej, nej,*" soothed Einar, hands out to push her back into place. He wanted Olafson gone. The man was dangerous, and Einar did not care to hide him or his rough friends a day longer. And there was no one else in Greenland available to captain a ship at such short notice.

Einar's little eyes watched Yngveld, willing her to silence. Were the silly wench to refuse Olafson as captain, she might refuse to buy the ship and slaves, too! And Einar would never get a better price. He cleared his throat and lifted his hands, palms open, at his most persuasive. "Why, Captain Olafson is a man of the sea. He is from our very own Greenland! And he knows ships, knows them well. He and his men can control a ship full of slaves for you. You could do no better than Captain Olafson."

Yngveld transferred her horrified gaze from the Greenlander to Einar, then to the watching, silent slaves. She felt suddenly as though she was in the midst of a nightmare. *I must wake up*, she thought desperately, shaking her head. *I must wake up*.

For a moment, Thomas almost pitied the woman. He did not like the look of this "captain" either. The man had a hard, cruel look about him that Thomas had seen before. Such a man would not hesitate to use slaves, and use them harshly, tossing their bodies overboard when they died at the oars. Thomas, too, shook his head, not liking the idea of such a man commanding the ship. *His* ship.

Yngveld blinked several times, trying desperately to come out of the nightmare. 'Twas not working.

"Captain Olafson is ready to leave whenever you are," Einar was saying briskly. "The dawn," he added, pointing at the lightening sky. "I believe you said you must leave at dawn?"

Yngveld turned a dazed glance upon Einar. Bjarni! She must get away from Bjarni Bearhunter. If only her brain were thinking clearly.

The long night, the fatigue, the grief at her father's death, the fear of spending a life as Bjarni's wife, the slave . . . 'twas all too much for her suddenly. She swayed on her feet and Karl barely caught her.

"Very well," Karl muttered, propping up his beautiful burden. Yngveld shook her head, trying desperately to rally. She glimpsed the curious faces of the slaves, Patrick's worried one, and Einar's smug one. A surge of anger rallied her. She was damned if she would succumb to weakness in front of that toady Einar. She shook off Karl's hand.

Karl stepped back, relieved to see that Yngveld was herself once more. He turned to Einar. "We will accept Captain Olafson's help. Now let us proceed to the ship." Yngveld let him lead her along the trail after Einar, accepting Karl's help whenever she felt shaky.

And as she walked, she worried about her predicament. She had a terrible feeling of dread that it was too late, far too late to change the course she had embarked upon. She was leaving Greenland, true—but oh, what unknown fate awaited her?

The slaves followed, several of them burdened with bundles of dried seal meat, reindeer meat, round cheeses, and barrels filled with water or ale—food and drink that Karl had tremulously demanded of Einar. Einar had only parted with the food and other possessions after Karl had flashed three of his own carefully hoarded gold coins. Yngveld wondered if the quantities of food she saw would be enough to feed all the men on the ship. She did not trust Einar not to sell them short.

Other slaves carried blankets, furs, and large rolls of coarse material to be used for tents. The green-eyed slave, she saw, carried a big barrel on his shoulder. She dragged her eyes away from the smoothly rippling muscles of his powerful arms.

They reached the fjord and Yngveld saw, for the first time, the ship that she had purchased. The vessel floated silently upon the still green waters of the fjord. She was long and clinker-built, with overlapping one-inch planks to ride out the storms. Her prow curved majestically. The mast was up, but there was no wind and the sails hung limply. My ship, Yngveld thought exultantly—my ship! She perked up, suddenly feeling more hopeful.

The sight of the dragon ship lifted Thomas Lachlann's spirits. Ah, but he had feared never to see her wild beauty again. But there she was, *Raven's Daughter*, with the huge black raven painted on her red sail. He narrowed his gaze. The barnacles had been scraped off her proud hull and the terrible gash in her side repaired. He smiled grimly to himself, heartened.

Captain Ole Olafson produced a large whip and strode forward amongst the slaves. Suddenly he lashed out with it, flailing freely to left and right.

Yngveld watched uneasily. "What does he do that for?" she asked.

Einar remained silent, a smug smile tugging at his lips. Karl shrugged and ducked his head. Patrick watched as though his bloodless face were carved in stone.

"Got to," panted Captain Olafson, "let them"—more pants—"know who is boss!" And again he flailed about with the heavy leather.

The green-eyed slave leader spoke several words, rapid-fire, in a language Yngveld did not understand. Not a single slave cried out. 'Twas an eerie sight—the grizzled, heavy-set man laying about viciously with the whip while his victims scowled in deadly silence.

Thomas winced inwardly as he watched the snaking whip fall upon Neill's bare shoulders—faithful Neill, Caedmon's son. After Thomas's long ago escape from Aelfred's wrath, 'twas Neill who had searched the countryside of Ireland until he had at last found Thomas at Ivar's military encampment. Later, they had been joined at Dubh Linn by Torgils. Brave Torgils, whose naked flesh now jerked under the same heavy lash. Both men had always shown unwavering loyalty to Thomas.

And this is how they are repaid, thought Thomas bitterly. He gritted his teeth and turned away, unable to bear the pain and anger upon his faithful friends' faces. When this is over, he vowed, his brown hands clenched, they would be avenged. He would see to that.

Yngveld closed her eyes, flinching each time she heard the whip lash at bare flesh. Then of their own volition, Yngveld's traitorous eyes flew open and sought out the slave leader. She shuddered as the whip struck him on the cheek, raising a mean red welt. Her hands flew to her mouth to keep from crying out and she felt her face flame in humiliation for him.

He turned at that moment and green eyes locked with blue. Yngveld looked into the furies of hell. *What have I done?* she screamed inwardly. *What have I done? What is happening to these people?*

And yet, she could not go back, for Bjarni awaited. She could go only forward, into the unknown. Her blue eyes wide in horror, she faltered and jerked her glance away from that harsh, unyielding gaze.

"Get on board," ordered Captain Olafson. He glared at Yngveld and Karl as he said it. Karl started forward to the small skiff on the beach. Yngveld stumbled helplessly after him, holding her flaming cheeks. Two of Olafson's uncouth companions stepped into the skiff with them and Yngveld shuddered anew at their shifty glances.

As Yngveld was being rowed out to the ship, a breeze cooled her heated skin and she calmed a little. Then she noticed Patrick waiting on the beach, standing apart from the others. She suddenly remembered that he, too, was an Irish slave.

"What of Patrick?" she whispered to Karl. "Think you that Olafson will lash him?"

"He had better not," gritted Karl, a worried frown upon his kindly face as he watched the heavy-set man cruelly belaboring the slaves. Yngveld could hear Olafson yelling at them, but she was too far away to understand the words.

Yngveld and Karl arrived at the ship and clambered aboard. Yngveld clutched her precious bundle, determined not to drop it into the clear, icy-green waters of the fjord. Then she stood on deck, hands clenched on the railing, and watched as the Irish slaves were rowed out in groups of three or four with a surly overseer, one of Olafson's companions, on each trip. At last the laborious transport of men, food, water barrels and other possessions to the ship was completed and Yngveld let herself relax. They would leave soon and Bjarni would be naught but a bad memory.

"You," Captain Olafson snapped at Yngveld, "set up your tent there!" He pointed to a place on the stern deck.

Yngveld did not like his tone. "This is *my* ship," she said evenly. "I will put my tent wherever I wish."

"*Nej*, you will not. *I* am the captain. What I tell you to do, you will do." His beady little eyes watched her and he fingered his whip surreptitiously.

"And if I do not?" Yngveld's stuck her jaw out. She refused to be bullied by this man. "Will you whip me too?"

Olafson grinned, as if the very thought appealed to him. "You will not like what will happen," he warned, and his little eyes continued to watch her like a snake's.

"How dare you speak to me like this," exclaimed Yngveld. "I *own* this ship!"

"*Ja*, but you cannot sail it to Norway without me. 'Tis a ten-day voyage, eight days if the weather is good. You cannot leave Greenland on this very morn without me." His grin widened and he thrust his face closer to hers.

The odor of his breath hit her and Yngveld clutched the rail, suddenly nauseated. She was trapped. Einar had already paid this man, so she had no hold over him that way. And if she wanted to leave Greenland before Bjarni Bearhunter discovered where she was, then she had to leave now. There was no time to find another captain. Damn that Einar! Wherever had he come upon such an unsavory specimen?

"So," Captain Olafson was saying in measured tones, his little eyes squinting at her, "you will do as I tell you. There is only one captain aboard this ship and that is *me*!" He tapped at his chest with a thick thumb.

"Karl?" she asked, looking to her father's friend for help.

"Best do as he says, Yngveld, for the nonce," was Karl's advice. Patrick stood beside him, bent over and nodding. Watching Olafson's cruelty to the other slaves had seemed to greatly unsettle the older thrall. He looked very pale and leaned on Karl momentarily for support. Yngveld, seeing the two comfort each other, wondered suddenly what this voyage was going to bring to each of them—herself, Karl, and

Patrick. Would they all survive?

"Get!" 'Twas the captain.

With a most unladylike snort, Yngveld flounced to the stern of the ship and set her bundle down. "I do not like that man," she muttered as she set up her tent. "I do not like him one bit!"

While Yngveld fussed with her tent, unaware of the many pairs of masculine eyes that followed her every move, the ship's anchor was pulled aboard and the sail was raised. Below each oarhole, along both sides of the vessel were placed rowing benches. Each bench was occupied by a slave.

Raven's Daughter swung out toward the open sea. The wide sail caught the wind and the vessel glided smoothly across the water.

Evening was approaching when Captain Olafson again prowled amongst the slaves, finally untying them from each other but leaving their manacles and ankle chains on.

Thomas had thought Olafson meant to keep them roped for the entire voyage. His cramped muscles ached and 'twas a relief to stand while waiting for Olafson to untie him. Just then Thomas's sharp eyes spied the filigreed hilt of a sword tucked into Olafson's wide belt. Thomas smiled grimly. The last time he had seen his sword was when Bjarni, his "good friend," had stolen it from him. Thomas wondered how Olafson had come to receive the beautiful weapon. Then he dismissed the thought. 'Twas enough that *Thor's Bite* was here when Thomas had expected never to see it again.

Thomas shifted from one foot to the other as he stood next to his assigned seat, the first bench closest to the bow, and waited for the Greenlander captain to work his way down the slave line.

As Thomas waited, his eyes roved the ship. They riveted upon the blonde woman who was once more fussing with her tent at the stern. Cheeks red from her efforts, hair loose and blowing gently in the breeze, she kneeled in front of her small dwelling, arms busy.

Once, she bent over to put something in the tent and Thomas had to swallow. He wanted that woman, he realized suddenly. Wanted her badly. Wanted her so that he could prove to himself that he was a man, not a slave. That he was bigger, stronger than she. That she did not own him, no one owned him—nor this ship! Thomas's large fists clenched as he held the looped rope in his hands.

"What are you looking at?" demanded the burly Olafson as he drew abreast of Thomas at last. Olafson followed the Irishman's icy gaze to where Yngveld was unconcernedly straightening her tent.

The Greenlander swung back to Thomas and backhanded him across the face. "Keep your eyes to yourself, big fellow," he snarled. "She is not for you." With a vicious jerk, he cut the walrus hide rope and his knife grazed one of Thomas' fists. "Oops, a little accident."

With an evil grin he watched Thomas's fury rise to his eyes and then Olafson laughed at the chained man's helplessness. He leaned forward. "Listen to this, you piece of Irish dung, and listen good. While you are out here rowing your ass off, I am going to be in that tent humping mine! You just think about *that* while you row us all to Norway!"

Thomas lunged at Olafson then and had his hands around the man's throat before even one of Olafson's Greenlander companions could move.

Olafson struggled uselessly, his face turning purple, his eyes bulging. Finally one of his men, Sweynson, noticed and gave a shout. All five Greenlanders came running and leaped at Thomas, dragging his manacled fists from Olafson's throat.

Olafson, gasping and coughing, held his thick red throat, his bulging eyes never leaving Thomas's face. When he finally stopped choking, his face lost the dark purple color. Thomas struggled against the beefy men holding him, but they held on tenaciously, dragging him down to the deck like wolves upon a stag.

"I got a special little present for slaves like you," Olafson snarled, and his eyes were malevolent.

Thomas looked up and saw the hate in the man and knew that whatever Olafson planned 'twould not be pleasant—might in fact, be deadly. He clenched his jaw and said nothing. Sweynson kicked him in the back.

"Come, come," sneered Olafson, still rubbing his throat. The Greenlanders with him grinned expectantly. Evidently they had shipped with Olafson before. "Are you not curious?"

Thomas's icy gaze watched Olafson. Not a word escaped Thomas or the Irish slaves on their benches. Sweynson, furious at the slave's silence, kicked him again.

"Well, now, I will just have to show you, I suppose." Captain Olafson slowly, ominously, reached with a beefy hand for Thomas's arm. His grip was iron as he led Thomas to the stern of the ship. Two of the Greenlanders, their eyes showing their fear, still gripped Thomas's arms.

Yngveld sat outside her tent carefully arranging her bone needles in their little skin packet. She glanced up to see the muscular, green-eyed slave in the grip of a red-faced captain and two of his men. She got to her feet, frowning. "What goes on?"

"A little fun, my lady," leered Captain Olafson. "You will enjoy it."

Yngveld glanced from Olafson's snarling face to the darkly fierce Irish slave's and back again. Her voice faltered. "Somehow," she sighed "I do not think I will enjoy it at all."

Karl and Patrick joined her and moved behind her like silent shadows, waiting.

"Wh-what are you going to do, Captain Olafson?" Yngveld watched him unlock the chains around the Irish slave's ankles. Next, Olafson tied a thick rope of tough walrus hide around the slave's narrow waist. Still the two burly Greenlanders held on to the big slave's arms, obviously afraid to let him go.

"Aww, 'tis nothing, my lady," Olafson assured her in a falsely hearty voice. "Just a little swim for the slave here."

"A swim?" she asked, bewildered. "Why, that water is cold! Men die in water like that if they are left for even a short time!"

Her lips tightened as Olafson pushed the big slave up against the stern rail.

"Jump," ordered the captain.

"Wait!" cried Yngveld, running to him. "You cannot force this man into the water! 'Twill kill him! Stop!"

Olafson swung his stout arm and halted Yngveld in her tracks. Two of his henchman moved to either side of her. "*I* am the captain on this ship," he proclaimed. "Stay back!" At his nod, the two grabbed Yngveld's arms.

She struggled furiously. "Unhand me!"

"Not until this slave has had his little swim," snarled Olafson. Then to Thomas, "Jump, I said!"

"His hands are chained! How can the man possibly swim in chains? Stop!"

Yngveld's desperate cry had no effect on the vengeance-seeking captain. "He will think of a way. Har! har!"

And with a hard push, Thomas was in the water. The freezing liquid closed over his head and he struggled to the surface. Dragged along by the rope at his waist, he floundered and, lungs bursting, tried desperately to get his head above water. The ship was sailing swiftly and he was being pulled through the waves faster than he could swim. His chained hands allowed for little movement and he kept going under. He kicked strongly—at least his legs were free.

He was dragged past a huge, floating chunk of ice. Thomas knew he would be fortunate to last for five minutes in the freezing depths.

He managed ten before Olafson had him hauled out.

"Now," snarled Olafson, once a dripping Thomas stood on deck in front of him. "Some of the fight gone out of you, boy?"

Furious green eyes met Olafson's. Thomas's lips compressed tightly.

"Next time I let you drown! You understand?"

Thomas refused to acknowledge the man. He had no sensation in any of his limbs. He clamped his jaw tightly to keep it from chattering. As he looked into the Greenlander's flat blue eyes, Thomas knew with a certainty that only one of them would survive this hellish voyage to Norway.

Chapter Six

Thomas lay slumped on his rowing seat, his nearly naked body shaking with chills. He had been wearing little enough ever since his "friend" Bjarni had sold him into slavery. At that time Bjarni had apparently taken a sudden liking to Irish fashion and had gleefully stripped Thomas and his men of military cloaks, warm breeches, short woolen tunics and leather boots, leaving them with only loin cloths. And now it appeared that the theft of Thomas' clothes would cost him his life.

Several of his men had stealthily passed a few pieces of salvaged, ragged clothing to him since Captain Olafson had retired for the night watch, but Thomas' chills had shaken the rags off. And now he appeared insensible to doing anything to keep the ill-fitting garments on.

And then there was Captain Olafson's vicious comrade, Sweynson, the overseer taking the night watch. Sweynson, like his captain, openly enjoyed laying the whip vigorously upon any slave he perceived to be resting at the oars. Thomas had already been slashed with the leather snake twice this eve. And felt nothing.

He nodded at the oars, his body wanting nothing so much as to sleep. He had stopped shivering, his body temperature had dropped dangerously low, but he was beyond caring about such things. Sleep, sleep, 'twas all he wanted. Sleep.

Across the deck sat Patrick, half-awake, half-dozing. He had been unable to sleep this night, for the sight of the Irish slave leader dragged through the frothing, icy waves had been the stuff of his own worst nightmares. Restless, Patrick had left the small tent that he and Karl shared so as not to awaken his master with his uneasy tossings.

The faint sound of the Irish slaves whispering teased Patrick into wakefulness. He peered into the night gloom and frowned. One of them pointed at the slave leader slumped at his oars.

Just then Sweynson swaggered out of his tent. His head swiveled left and right as he watched the slaves row. Patrick knew he was looking for a shirker. Sweynson lashed out at a captive, the man with the broken arm.

A slash of the whip fell upon the slave leader for a third time this bitter night. Patrick saw the slave's body jerk convulsively, saw Sweynson laugh and then swagger back to his tent to pass some more time gambling with his cronies.

Patrick knew they were gambling because earlier in the evening Sweynson had invited Karl Ketilson to join him and two of his Greenlander thugs for gaming and ale. Sweynson had covetously eyed Karl's leather sack of gold as he made the invitation. Karl had politely refused, but Patrick's relief had been short-lived. Sweynson had then eyed Patrick with the same mercenary glare he had given the sack of gold and made a joke that if Karl did not want to play for gold, they could play for his slave instead. Patrick's heart had thumped against his ribs at that, but Karl had merely turned away with a mild answer. Later, in the privacy of their tent, he had assured Patrick he would never gamble him away. Patrick merely nodded, his face impassive. He had decided, however, that Sweynson bore careful watching.

Patrick could see but little in the gloom now, but his curiosity was whetted by the whispers of the other slaves. He admired the slave leader, wished that he could fight back against the bonds of slavery as did that one. Seeing little movement from the slave, Patrick left his place on deck and crept closer.

When Patrick saw the large, mostly naked slave leader nodding at the oars, warning bells went off in his head and he gasped. The man was in danger, severe danger!

Hurriedly glancing about until he was certain

that no one had seen him—except for the wide-awake slaves and who would they tell?—Patrick scuttled back to his tent and shook Karl awake.

"Master! Master, wake up!"

Karl blinked and woke. He sat up wearily, the warm blankets falling away. "Eh? What is it, Patrick?"

" 'Tis the big slave, the leader. He is in a bad way!"

"How mean you?"

"He nods at his bench, does not row, tries to fall asleep."

"Well, let him. He probably needs a good night's sleep after that icy swim." Karl reached for the covers to pull them back up.

"*Nej*, master. He must not sleep. Remember when you fell into the fjord on that long ago winter day?"

Karl frowned thoughtfully. "*Ja*, I remember."

"Remember how cold you were? How, when I pulled you out of the water, you shivered, then the chills came upon you and you wanted only to sleep?"

"*Ja*, I remember."

"And how the old witch woman said to keep you awake and warm and not to let you fall asleep else 'twould be your death? And how I and young Johannes got into the bed with you and lay one on each side, skin to skin, stark naked, our body heat feeding yours until you finally revived?"

Karl needed no further reminders. He was on his feet now and pulling on his cloak. "You are right. If he sleeps, he will die!" Karl snatched up the flickering seal oil lamp he liked to keep burning during the night.

Gratified, Patrick smiled slightly and said, "We must warn the slave."

Karl halted suddenly, his head only part way out of the tent. "Wait! What is it to us if he dies?"

Patrick looked pained. "He is a man, like us. Why should we not try to save him?"

"Why *should* we try to save him? Captain Olafson will not like it."

" 'Tis obvious Olafson is trying to kill the slave, true." Patrick shrugged. "Very well, we will let Olafson go ahead and do it." He watched the struggle on Karl's face.

"But Yngveld?" muttered Karl, almost to himself. "What would she say?"

"*Ja*," said Patrick slyly. "He is her property. Mayhap she should make the decision to save him or not."

"Very good," said Karl, nodding his gray head. "We will go to her."

And so it was that Yngveld found herself being implored in whispers outside her little tent: "Yngveld, wake up!"

She poked her head out. "Karl! Patrick! What do you want?" she whispered back.

" 'Tis the slave leader—" began Patrick.

Karl held up a hand. "Patrick thinks he is in danger of dying."

"Dying? How can this be? What has Olafson done to him now?"

"Shhh, *nej*, 'tis not Olafson. 'Tis the cold!

Patrick—uh, that is *we* think the slave leader is too cold and will die soon. Already he seeks to sleep, a bad sign."

Yngveld's heart pounded and she felt the blood pulsing in her ears. The green-eyed slave in danger! While she pondered how this information was affecting her whole body, Karl added, "We thought you should know. He is, after all, your property."

Yngveld said nothing to that, but a curious warmth ran through her at the thought.

Patrick added, "Methinks he is a valuable slave. Mayhap you do not want to lose him." He shrugged, trying to appear casual. Letting a brave man die as a sop to Olafson's petty rage disgusted Patrick.

Yngveld made her decision. "Very well," she said, drawing her mantle about her, "I will go and see about this."

She was out of the tent and had taken two steps toward the slave leader when Patrick put a hand on her arm. "Mistress," he cautioned in a low voice, "do not let Sweynson see you." He nodded in the direction of the overseer's tent. "He comes out with the whip and lashes the slaves every few minutes. I fear he would not take kindly to you interfering with them."

"That is correct," added Karl. "Sweynson is a troublemaker. Stay away from him."

"How can I?" pointed out Yngveld reasonably. "If he comes upon me while I am examining the slave, I will just have to tell him to go back to his tent."

Patrick dropped his hand and nodded dubiously at Yngveld's determined sounding voice. He doubted that the bullying overseer would do a single thing that Yngveld told him to do, but he and Karl followed her upon silent feet to where the slave leader nodded at the oar.

Yngveld stood at the bow watching him. She could see the naked backs of the other slaves as they pulled in unison. She, Karl, and Patrick stared at the slave for some minutes, Yngveld wondering what to do, when one of the Irish slaves twisted his head around and spoke over his shoulder. "Thomas has been nodding like this for a long while. I fear for his life."

Yngveld murmured, "Thomas? So that is his name."

"Aye, my lady. Thomas Lachlann. My name is Neill."

Yngveld turned to study the man by the light of Karl's little lamp. Neill's back was to her once more. The moon was out, and she could discern a head of shoulder-length brown hair. Taking several steps forward on the middle plank, she stopped to peer at him. She could see the flashing whites of his eyes, a prominent nose, and a scar across his left cheek. The soft regular clink of metal as he rowed reminded her that his hands were manacled and linked by a short length of chain.

Neill glanced in the direction of the overseer's tent. "The lash has been laid upon Thomas several times already this eve," he informed them bitterly.

Yngveld followed his gaze to the overseer's tent. She could see the shadows of Sweynson and his two comrades against the walls, lit by a lamp inside. Great guffaws came from the tent, and she watched as one of the men—she guessed it to be Sweynson—raised his drinking horn, his silhouette clearly observed by all. A great belch followed and Yngveld winced.

"I see," she said, turning back to Neill. "What can we do to help this slave?" She felt at a loss, knowing little about how to treat a man who went from shivers to dull nodding. She shrugged, holding up her open palms. "I have little experience with this sort of thing. . . ."

Patrick and Karl shifted a little upon the deck. Neill, too, was suddenly silent. "Well," asked Yngveld impatiently at last, "does anybody have any ideas? We cannot just let him die!"

"*Nej*, my lady, 'tis not that," answered Neill. "We do not want him to die. He is our captain—and our fellow soldier." She saw several of the slaves nod their heads and heard their mutters. It was evident to Yngveld that the slave leader enjoyed the considerable esteem of his own men.

"What is the problem then?" asked Yngveld.

Patrick looked at her, struck by her curious innocence and turned his head away. When no one else spoke up, he cleared his throat. " 'Tis—ahem, 'tis only one way that I know to save him. . . ."

"*Ja*," joined in Neill eagerly. Two other slaves echoed him.

An awkward silence followed.

"Well?" demanded Yngveld. "What is to be done?"

More silence.

"Blankets," said Patrick heartily then, as if by sudden inspiration. "*Ja*, that is it! He needs blankets!"

"Blankets," echoed the slaves. "Aye, he needs blankets!"

"Why did you not say so?" Yngveld whirled and ran to her tent. She returned with her arms laden. Karl met her with blankets of his own. They both dropped the blankets on the deck and Yngveld chose a large warm one to wrap around the broad back of the slave.

Thomas continued to nod and ignore them entirely. The blanket slipped, and Yngveld found herself reaching around him once more, this time to tie the blanket on.

Yngveld watched Thomas's nodding head keeping rhythm with the pull of the other slaves' oars. Her forehead wrinkled in thought. "What now?"

Patrick cleared his throat. "More blankets?" he suggested hopefully.

Yngveld dutifully picked up another coverlet and spread it over Thomas's back. She regarded him doubtfully. "He is still nodding," she observed. "The blankets seem to make little difference. . . ." Her voice trailed away as she pondered what to do.

At last Karl broke the tense silence. "We could gamble," he suggested.

Patrick stiffened in dread. "Aye, master, we could. We could gamble. Sweynson would be kept busy. . . ."

"Gamble?" asked Yngveld. "Whatever do you mean? I thought we were trying to save this slave's life and now you speak of gambling?" She broke off as she saw Karl and Patrick exchange silent looks with each other and the listening slaves. Her mouth tightened. "Will someone please tell me what is going on?" she demanded.

Patrick looked at Karl. Karl looked at Patrick. They both looked at Neill, who continued his rowing, his jaw set, eyes focused determinedly straight ahead.

At last Karl's shoulders slumped. "You see, Yngveld, my dear," he began.

When several heartbeats went by and he did not continue, Yngveld stamped her foot impatiently. "Tell me what is going on!" she hissed. "Now!"

Reluctantly, Karl dragged his eyes from Patrick's face and locked them on Yngveld's wide blue ones. "The slave needs someone to be with him under the blanket. Naked."

"Well, what is the problem in that?" cried Yngveld. "Surely one of his men—"

"We cannot stop the rhythm of the ship, my lady!" chimed in Neill. "Were even one man to stop rowing, Sweynson would notice the change in the speed of the ship and be out here with haste to see what is going on." Neill glanced at the overseer's tent and added, "He would lay about with the lash, 'tis certain. Not that we would not bear it for the captain. We would. But Sweynson would probably kill the captain or whoever was with him under the blanket. He and Olafson want Thomas dead. Torgils overheard them talking."

"Torgils?" Yngveld asked.

Neill nodded at the broad, strong back of the slave in front of him. This one had a thatch of pale blond hair.

"Ahh, *ja*, Torgils," acknowledged Yngveld politely. Then she shivered as the import of Neill's words sank in. "They want him dead?"

"Aye, my lady."

She turned to Karl. "Well, what of you and Patrick? Surely the two of you could strip and . . ."

"We would, Yngveld," said Karl softly, "but someone must needs keep Sweynson occupied." At the look of incomprehension on her face, Karl explained, "So that he does not come out of his tent for a long while."

"We will gamble with him," continued Patrick. "Earlier in the evening he suggested a game to Karl." Patrick's face was white in the flicker of the little lamp, and Yngveld wondered at it.

"Do you not like to gamble, Patrick?" she inquired gently.

"*Nej*, I do not," he said shortly.

Karl added, "There is more, Yngveld. Sweynson wants to gamble with me for gold, *ja*—but also for Patrick."

"Patrick?" she gasped.

"*Ja,*" said Karl grimly. "Sweynson thinks to win my slave from me."

Patrick stared impassively straight ahead and Yngveld's heart went out to him. She clutched Karl's arm. "Karl! Do you think you should risk it?"

Karl shrugged. "I have spent some time gambling in my life. Why not now?"

"But Patrick?"

"I will not wager him unless I have lost every coin and you still need more time with the slave," said Karl stubbornly.

So, it had come to this. The words had been spoken. "Is there no one?" pleaded Yngveld. "Is there no one who will get under the blanket with him?"

Karl, Patrick, and Neill watched her. "No one," said Karl finally.

Yngveld looked at Neill. His powerful wrists in chains, his feet too, he did not look as if he could move far off his bench, certainly not close enough to aid his friend. And his rowing was sorely needed.

She turned to Karl. He was willing to risk his own small hoard of gold to Sweynson's gambling skill to help her.

She glanced at Patrick. He was risking an even greater sacrifice—the possible transfer of ownership from kind Karl Ketilson whom he had waited upon for fourteen years to the brutal man Sweynson.

Lastly, she turned to stare at Thomas Lachlann, who nodded on, oblivious to the men and the lone woman who were about to decide his fate.

Yngveld's thoughts raced. Did one slave matter so much? Surely she would get to Norway without this one man's rowing ability. There were thirty-four others, enough to row the ship. Why then need she risk herself and her honor to warm the likes of this slave?

Because, came back the answer, 'twould be a terrible thing to let such a magnificent man die. She remembered the first time she had seen him, in Einar's outbuilding, the presence of him, the glittering green eyes—eyes that were now closed, unknowing. She remembered the slave leader's proud, straight back, his defiant glares at Einar, his willingness to challenge brutal Olafson. And had not Einar mentioned something about Lachlann rescuing four of his men at the risk of his own life in the storm that had shipwrecked him on Greenland? *Ja*, she rather thought that he had.

Yngveld bit her lower lip nervously as she turned over in her mind all the things she had observed about Lachlann and all the things she had heard.

With a sigh, she looked away. And caught Neill watching her.

" 'Tis up to you, my lady," whispered the Irishman in his thick brogue as he pulled on his oar. She caught a flash of the white of his eyes. "*You* decide if he is to live or to die."

Chapter Seven

Yngveld drew herself up the straighter. Her heart pounded, and her hands were sweat-coated. She could scarcely think for the blood pounding at her temples. What should she do?

Should she let her fear, her feelings, or her head triumph?

Her fear was of touching a stranger with her naked body, of actually embracing a man that she did not know.

Her feelings were that she found him tempting, dangerous and more than a little exciting. She knew that she would do well to stay away from him.

Her head told her simply that a man would die if she did not act.

And what if the situation were reversed?

Would she want him to save *her* that way—skin to naked skin? Her face grew hot at the thought and she was glad of the night that hid the sudden flush on her cheeks.

She breathed in the cool evening air, she who was alive, who knew she could go to her little tent, sleep and awake the next morning still alive, the blood coursing through her veins. Oh, why did she feel she had to rescue this man whom she did not know but felt vaguely responsible for? Was it because she owned him as slave? Or was it something else, something more—personal? Her soul writhed in a torment of indecision.

She turned and caught Karl and Patrick watching her. Neill and Torgils were staring over their shoulders. Waiting. She glanced out to sea, her eyes passing over Lachlann's broad back as she did so. She took a shaky breath, wondering what words would come out of her mouth. "Very well," she heard herself whisper, "I will do it."

Yngveld watched relief cross Torgils' grim features. Neill let out his breath in a whoosh. Karl slowly nodded his acceptance. Patrick looked drawn and worried.

"Come then, Patrick, let us away," murmured Karl, taking his slave's arm and pulling him along. "We will challenge Sweynson to a little wager." With a nod to Yngveld, Karl slipped away, Patrick reluctantly in tow.

Soon there were five silhouettes on the tent wall. Bursts of rough laughter drifted across the deck to where Yngveld continued to stand as though anchored to the wood.

She turned once more to gaze at Lachlann. There was enough moonlight that she could see the outline of him. Indecision gripped her as she stared at his broad back, the striped fabric of the coverlet rising and falling with his every breath. His head had slumped forward, and he leaned against the rail of the ship with his arms dropped in his lap, his big hands shackled together. The oar he had been manning now dangled uselessly in its oar hole. His long legs were stretched out before him. Olafson had forgotten to fetter his ankles, she noted.

Neill kept silent and rowed, Torgils too, their eyes focused on the stern of the ship. Yngveld understood this as a gesture for privacy in a place where there was none.

Realizing at last that if she was going to do something to help Lachlann, she had best do it *now*, Yngveld crept over to where he was slumped on the seat. She peered around him as best she could. He did not look to be tied or chained to the seat. Nor were the other slaves. Was this a presumption on Captain Olafson's part—that the slaves would stay in their seats? Mayhap. He relied on the whip to keep them in their place, she supposed.

She sat down gingerly on the bench next to Lachlann. There was very little room. A sudden swell of the waves rocked the ship slightly and sent Yngveld careening into his side. He groaned, but that was all.

Yngveld righted herself, rubbing her arm that had been crushed momentarily between his large body and hers. She glanced at Neill, seated directly in front of Thomas, and surprised his eyes upon her. Swiftly he turned away. Yngveld flushed anew and gritted her teeth. Would that she was with Bjarni Bearhunter in her farmhouse kitchen, she thought with grim humor, instead of trying to cozy up to this naked barbarian.

With gritted teeth she sat there, making no move to lift the blanket or coverlet off Lachlann's broad back. The sea had no further surprise swells, however. All was calm, and Yngveld gathered her courage once more.

Gently, almost tenderly, she lifted the coverlet edge. Thomas did not move, but continued to lie half-slumped against the side of the ship. With a little more courage, she lifted the blanket higher.

She took a gulp of air and eased her lithe body up against him. Now there was a coverlet over them both and a blanket between them. She looked down at her garments, loathe to shed them. They, too, remained as a barrier between her and Lachlann. A protection.

But she could feel the cold of his body seeping through the thin blanket next to his skin. She chewed her bottom lip. With one trembling finger she touched his heavily muscled upper arm. She traced the line of a blue vein there. His skin looked pale, and felt cool—too cool.

She listened to the slow sound of his breathing and watched him. He was nodding less now. *Already he sleeps*, she thought. Panic raced through her then. Mayhap she had waited too long, mayhap he could not be revived! In a sudden frenzy of concern, she lifted the blanket and pressed her clothed body against the length of him.

How very cold he felt! She stayed like that, pressed to him for several long moments, wondering frantically what to do, her panic gradually receding. If left like this, he would warm on one side and no doubt freeze on the other. She reached her arms around him, her hands barely meeting and clasping each other at one muscular shoulder. Oh *nej*, she moaned, he is too big. She herself was not small, but of a tall height for a woman, yet there was still so much of him that she could not reach to warm.

Her heart pounded as she held the slave, but nothing more happened. She found she could no longer think of him as 'Lachlann.' With their new physical closeness, 'twas foolish not to call him 'Thomas,' she decided.

The ship continued to ply its way through the sea, the moon shone down on her, and she could hear the oars of the other slaves dipping in the water. *What now?* she thought.

Pressed stiffly against Thomas, she could not tell if he was getting any warmer where her clothing touched him, but she thought not. With growing dread, she realized that what Karl had said was true—only her nakedness would truly warm him.

Glancing surreptitiously about and feeling foolish for doing so, she noted with relief that all the slaves were facing the stern, their backs to her, as they pulled on the oars.

Using the wide coverlet as a shield against any curious eyes, she wedged one corner of it between Thomas and the ship's side, firmly anchoring the blanket. Then she grasped the other corner with one hand and pulled it tightly over Thomas's back and hers. That left her one hand free with which to undress. She bent, trembling fingers pausing at her hem.

Slowly, trying not to think, knowing she would cease all movement were she to give in to her fear, she cautiously lifted the hem of her shift. She got it as far as her waist, then struggled fruitlessly to lift it further.

'Twas impossible. She needed two hands to get the garment off her body. Taking a deep breath, she looked at the moon, hoping for a cloud to scud across it and give her the privacy that she so desperately wanted. She said a tiny prayer—to the Christian god, she decided. The Irish slave was no doubt of that sect, though she herself was of indifferent religion, reflecting her father's bias. He had not pressed the old Norse gods upon her, nor the more recent Christian one.

Alas, her prayer was not heard. The moon shone brightly, traitorously down upon the deck of the ship and upon her. The night was clear, stars sparkled, and nary a cloud was to be seen.

Yngveld stood up then, her legs trembling, her

breath coming in quick pants, her ears straining for a sound, a word, anything, from the rowing slaves ahead of her. But she heard nothing—only the usual ship sounds of creaking wooden oars against wooden ship and the soft bubbling sighs as the ship slid through the swells.

With deft movements, she whipped her garment over her head. Her undershift hit the deck. Then she was back under the coverlet and pressing herself close to Thomas's naked frame. She moved swiftly as though for protection from unknown watching eyes. And she refused, utterly refused to remove her skimpy pantalets, her one remaining undergarment.

At last her frantic breathing slackened, her thrumming heart calmed.

Her eyes roved over Thomas's face. His green eyes were closed, his square-jawed face rough with beard, and she thought she could see a slow pulsing at the side of his neck. The breeze fluttered a black curl on the nape of his neck. It caught her attention and she stared, fascinated. "Thomas?" she whispered, a warm sweat forming on her trembling body. "Thomas? Are you awake?" she pleaded. Oh, if only he were awake, she would not have to do any of this.

But, half-conscious, he merely leaned against the wood and gave an occasional nod to the side of the ship. She listened desperately to his breathing. Her hand touched her wildly beating heart when she heard his ragged breaths, fewer with each passing minute.

She clutched the coverlet tighter and moved

the blanket away from his pale skin. The blanket was rough beneath her touch; Thomas's flesh felt dry and cold as her fingers brushed it. Her heartbeat quickened and she touched him lightly on a shoulder. He flinched.

There was nothing between them now. No blanket, no coverlet, for those two barriers now covered their backs, keeping out the cool night breeze.

Taking up her courage once again, Yngveld feverishly pressed her warm self against him. He felt cold and firm where she pressed her warm, soft flesh against his ribs.

"Thomas?" she whispered imploringly. The breeze carried the sound away. "Thomas, please wake up!"

" 'Tis no good, my lady," came Neill's grunting response. "Our captain sleeps the sleep before death."

Neill's words were stark and sent a thrill of terror through her. Already she had wasted too much time on concern only for herself, *her* modesty and *her* clothing. Thomas was not going to wake up, not unless she could warm him. Yngveld knew that now.

Grimly, with gritted teeth, she reached across his broad chest, pressing her arm to it. 'Twould do little good, she realized. He would get little warmth from one limb.

"You must get on top of him, my lady," whispered Neill over his shoulder. Yngveld was glad he could not see the blush that rose to her cheeks.

"Very well," she said. Something of her new determination must have carried in her voice because she saw both of Neill's white fists pull harder on the oar.

Thomas was still slumped against the side of the ship. She must get him laid out on the deck. Then she could climb on top of him.

She swung round to face him, wrapped against him like a lover, his back to the bench. His arms dangled between them, the manacles clinking with every sway of the vessel. Carefully, not daring to let him fall too fast, she eased him down, aiming his back for the bench so that he would land upon it. He sank slowly against the bench, and his head fell back over the end of the short seat. She had done it! He was on his back! She stood there panting, trembling, amazed at the weight of him.

The position he now lay in would be most uncomfortable, she reflected. So, she clambered over to one side of him. On the other side, the bow side, was the flat deck of the ship; the heavy oak planks would make a hard bed.

She picked up three of Karl's blankets piled on the deck where he had dropped them. She spread one out and folded the other for a pillow. With great care she pushed at Thomas to roll him onto the deck. With a sickening thud, he fell the short distance.

She looked around, mortified. Suppose his friends thought she was trying to kill him? But they kept to their rowing task, eyes straight ahead.

With a sigh, she turned back to the unconscious man. She arranged his naked limbs carefully, shackled hands centered on his torso, legs straight out, and covered him with another blanket.

Then, with flushed face and one last glance around, she climbed under the blanket with him. A cloud mercifully drifted across the moon at that moment and she sent a little prayer of thanks winging its way skyward to the Christian god.

Lying atop Thomas, her own limbs felt heavy as they touched his. And she touched him at every part, from mid-shin to head. Her thighs felt the cold, hard, muscled length of his legs. Her intimate region pressed against his hands and she unknowingly clutched at the tough muscles of his arm in reflex. She swallowed once and wondered if the Irish slaves had heard it over the creaking of the oars.

Her stomach lay flat against his, navel to navel, and she could feel his hipbones. His arms buttressed her on either side, but his joined hands were uncomfortably close to the center of her pantalets. Her naked breasts were crushed against his wide chest, the tips tickled by his chest hair. Her entire body covered his. She could feel the cold of him, feel it drawing the warmth from her. Snuggling against him, she rested her head in the crook of his neck and drew the blankets tightly about them.

And waited. And waited some more. At last, feeling the cold as though *she* were the one who had been thrown into the sea, Yngveld gently moved atop his nearly lifeless flesh. Time to warm the back of him, she decided.

Crawling off him, she leaned against him and then pushed until she got him on his side. With another heave, she rolled him over, face down. He let out a moan.

She stopped for a moment, peering at him. She touched his hair, one black curl of it encircling her finger. Holding her breath, thinking that he would surely waken now, she waited, the pounding beat of her heart the only movement in her body.

Disappointment welled in her. He was obviously not about to wake up soon. She clambered onto his back and lay there panting. This was a little different. She ran her arms under him and grasped him at the shoulders, pulling herself into him. His back was strong, muscled and hard. She tried to press her stomach into him, but her intimate parts were hung up on his buttocks, leaving a gap between her torso and his. What do I do now? she wondered. Will he recover if I do not warm his back?

She lay there for a time. Then, uncomfortable, she got off. With a grunt, she rolled him onto his back once more. 'Twas much more comfortable, she thought, as she climbed atop his large frame once again.

Suddenly the rueful humor of the situation struck her, and she began to giggle. Here she was on her mad, desperate flight from murderous Bjarni Bearhunter and Greenland, lying naked atop a handsome, insensible Irish slave. Truly, 'twas not something she would have ever predicted! Furthermore, the two boon companions who shared her plight were busily gambling away the only gold they owned in a tent with Greenland ruffians. She hoped Karl and Patrick did not lose.

Yngveld chuckled. 'Twas all too odd!

Chapter Eight

She slept. When she awoke, she chuckled softly once more at her strange plight atop a naked stranger. She was still chuckling when he rolled her over. He slipped his manacled wrists over her head and down her back, catching her neatly.

Eyes wide in shock, heart pounding, Yngveld stared past the curling dark hair, the closed green eyes, the dark winged brows, to the now brightly shining moon. She pushed at Thomas's shoulders, and his smooth skin felt very warm to her feebly moving hands. She tried to move her legs, but they were anchored by the heavy weight of his. She moaned once, weakly, in protest.

The delicate flutter of her limbs against his

teased Thomas. He dipped his head to the gently parted lips.

Yngveld gasped when she realized that she could not budge him. His shackled hands were flattened behind her and supported her spine against the ship's hard oaken planks.

Her gasp was swallowed by Thomas as he pressed devouring kisses upon her soft lips. Heart pounding, Yngveld struggled against the muscular arms that so easily encased and pinned her to the deck. Both her wrists were caught to her sides, held in his powerful embrace. She could not move an inch, no matter how great the strength she put into the struggle.

Thomas held the woman securely. His senses reeled, spinning dizzily as he kissed her leisurely and to his fill. How good she tasted! Mmmmm . . . must be Katelyn, one of his favorite lovers. Nobody could kiss like Katelyn. Though, strangely, she did not smell like Katelyn, unless Kate had recently taken to wearing the salty scent of the sea. No matter, 'twas Kate and they had managed to slip away from the watchful eye of her father and out to the byre where the sweet-smelling straw made a soft bed. Ah, but 'twould kill Kate to know he planned to leave her, that he would not return for a long while. He was reluctant to tell her now. There would be tears, frantic pleas, even begging, for she loved him much, he knew.

He touched her lips firmly and met only resistance. He felt her squirm beneath him. Why was she fighting him? Why was he reeling? His eyelids fluttered as a wave of dizziness hit him.

"Let me in," He ordered. He took a breath, struggling against his wandering senses. "Ahh, Katelyn," he murmured. "'Tis our last chance to make sweet, passionate love before I return with Ivar's bride. I will make it good for you. Only let me in." He nudged at the top of her thighs with his knee, but met further resistance there. "Katelyn, my sweetling," he pleaded, the Irish words muffled in her long dark hair, "'tis our last chance. . . . Do not behave so, I implore you."

Yngveld thrashed frantically, pushing at his huge body. She tried to cry out, but his lips covered hers and now his tongue was plunging into her very mouth! Eyes wide, she pushed desperately at those strong shoulders that budged not an inch. Her tongue sought to push the invader out, but he would have none of it. And now he was pressing his knee into the very vortex of her being and she had on only her skimpy little pantalets. Oh *nej*!

He was muttering soft words in her ear, his breath sending sweet shivers down her spine, the words running together and making no sense that she could tell. But 'twas obvious he was a most determined lover, she *could* tell that. He had worked his manacled hands down to her buttocks and now held them, squeezing rhythmically. Oh *nej*! Oh, help!

But she did not cry out. She could not. For the sweet sensations of her body wherever he touched her soon drove everything else from her mind.

And her body was warm now too, the blanket creating a delicious coziness. Thomas' head glided over her neck as he searched blindly for her breasts. With his mouth he teased one nipple, and she moaned. His breath on her naked skin warmed her and she tingled wherever his roughened beard touched her flesh. He caressed her breast gently with his cheek while his arms held her securely. Her breathing quickened and she gasped. Her other nipple ached to be touched. With deliberate thoroughness, he tongued that one too, causing the little nub to spring erect.

Yngveld freed her arms and pushed her breasts up to him, mindlessly offering herself. His warm tongue laved her sensitive flesh and she curled her toes in delight, breath held, avid for his next touch. Her throat stopped working, her lips softened, and she moaned as he nipped gently at her. "More," she moaned. "More!"

His head moved down her body, brushing her flesh with the caresses of his rough cheek. His tongue flicked at her satin skin, leaving a cool trail of kisses. Yngveld sighed raggedly, eyes closed, arms limp beside her. She held her breath abruptly as she realized he was kissing his way to her lithe waist.

His tongue dipped into her navel and she moaned. Thomas gripped her rounded buttocks tighter and pressed his face into her. She could feel the strength of him, the hardness of his manhood. He wanted her, and she moaned again. He pressed further until her legs parted of their own will.

Thomas moved up and rubbed his knee into the center of her being. His hands skimmed the pantalets down over her buttocks and partway down her smooth legs. He arched his back and began kissing his way slowly, tauntingly, to the very core of her.

Yngveld went wild, moaning, head tossing from side to side. Thomas's manhood was poised at the very entrance of her now. He braced himself, both hands under her hips. As he lifted her to meet him, he shook his head groggily and opened his eyes. "Katelyn?"

The word may have been said in the Irish tongue, but 'twas enough for Yngveld to understand. She froze, and slowly, heart beating frantically now not from arousal but from a terrible dread, she opened her eyes. He had lowered her and was now looking down at her. Horrified blue eyes met glittering green ones.

With a frantic push, Yngveld scrambled back from him, and somehow, wriggling and kicking, she slid out of his grasp. She snatched up a blanket. "*Nej!*" she whispered. "Oh, *nej*!" She clutched the blanket in front of her as if that wretched piece of cloth could protect her from this staring, aroused male with the flaring nostrils.

Thomas, panting, watched as she backed away from him. He shook his head, trying to make sense of this. He eased back onto the deck. 'Twas not Katelyn. His body and his mind reeled with frantic passion and confusion. He was on the deck of a ship. A ship? But who then? Where? He shook his head again, trying desperately to clear it. Trying desperately to quell the trembling within his body. And his soul . . .

Yngveld, cheeks flaming, snatched up her clothes from the deck and, still clutching the blanket around her nakedness, stumbled blindly toward her tent, oblivious to the eyes that followed her. Her blond hair flapped behind her in the night breeze.

Hiding in her tent, she could still feel the press of Thomas's skin against hers, his firm mouth on hers. She could smell his scent upon her. Her nipples were still wet from his tongue's caresses. The flesh of her back bore the marks of his manacles. She felt branded.

Yngveld dropped her clothing and held her flushed cheeks and moaned. Oh, what had she done? The way he had moved, the slow, arousing kisses he had given her—why, her whole body still tingled wherever his lips had touched!

She sank to her knees on the blankets and put a trembling hand to her wildly beating heart. Her body throbbed with new awareness. Her eyes darted about the small space, her ears straining to hear if *he* had followed. A frisson of fear darted down her back at the thought that he would come for her. But she heard nothing—only the creaking of wooden oars, the splash of waves against the sides of the ship. Gradually, she relaxed; her breathing became less frantic and the pounding of her heart less deafening.

She glanced around the little tent where she crouched. She felt safe in it, she realized. Safe from Thomas Lachlann.

"But *ja*," she muttered in silent anger, fighting the lingering memory of his sensuous, marauding lips. She pounded her fists into the crumpled blankets. Then she paused suddenly, one fist raised in mid-air. A tiny smile flashed across her face and then was gone like lightning in a thunderstorm. "*Ja, ja* . . . at least I warmed him. . . ."

Chapter Nine

"She what?!" roared Thomas.

"Quiet, mon!" hissed Neill. "Do you want to wake up Olafson? Or mayhap you prefer Sweynson and his heavy whip?" Neill's eyes shot toward the Greenlanders' tent where drunken Sweynson's booted feet poked out of the entrance.

"I do not give a damn which one I wake!" Thomas growled. His eyes fastened upon the little tent at the stern, the woman's tent. He glanced back at Neill. Thomas lay on his back on the deck boards and rubbed at his eyes with trembling hands. Lord, he felt weak. He pushed off the rough wool blanket that covered his chest. "What is this?" he demanded. "How did this get here?"

Neill sighed. "'Tis a wonder you are alive, mon," he answered. "And of such sweet temper, too!"

"Enough," snapped Thomas, forcibly throwing off his thoughts of the woman as he did the blankets on his chest. "Tell me what I am doing here? The last thing I remember—" He frowned, rubbing his forehead in concentration. "Was—was being dragged through the freezing sea!" He sat up and looked around. His fellow slaves continued to row only because no one had told them to stop. "Where is Olafson?"

"Asleep."

"At this late time of the morn?" Thomas snorted. "The man is a pig, not a sailor."

"True enough," agreed Neill. "Shall we take over the ship now?"

Thomas smiled for the first time. "You know me well, my friend," he said getting to his feet. He looked around the deck. No one moved except for the constantly rowing slaves. And even some of them were slumped, asleep, at the oars. Thomas shook his head. "Piss poor way to run a ship," he commented.

Neill grinned. "What better time to take it away from them? Let us do so. Now!"

"Easy, my enthusiastic friend," cautioned Thomas. "We wait."

Neill frowned, obviously not liking this answer. "Wait? Why?"

With a rueful look, Thomas sat down at his place on the short rowing bench. He shivered and picked up a blanket off the deck. He dropped it on the seat beside him and then wordlessly held up his manacled hands for Neill to see. The crude irons glinted dully in dawn's weak light. "These," he said grimly. "I must get the key first. The men will not row back to Ireland in these."

"Aye. True." Neill rowed, his back tense with expectation. Thomas's deep voice growled at him and he relaxed. Grinning to himself, he twisted around to hear his captain's words.

"Tell me again what she did." Thomas kept his voice neutral. He shook his head, scarcely able to believe what Neill had told him minutes ago.

Neill gave an exaggerated sigh. " 'Twas nothing. You would be bored."

Thomas cast him an impatient glance. "Tell me, Neill," he said evenly.

Neill knew his fellow Irishman well enough to recognize the tone of voice. He shrugged. "Very well," he said over his shoulder. " 'Tis as I told you. The woman lay upon you and warmed you with her bodily heat. That is all."

"Naked?" asked Thomas, dragging out the word lovingly. The picture he conjured in his mind of the blond woman, nude and embracing him, was a delight. But then he frowned, confused. He seemed to remember Katelyn . . . long dark hair. . . . He shook his head, trying to make sense of his muddied thoughts. When Neill did not answer, Thomas demanded, "I said, was she naked?"

"Aye," came the surly reply.

A satisfied smile crept across Thomas Lachlann's face. "I thought so." Vague memories of a warm, soft body with fragrant skin came to him as though from a dream. Had Neill not mentioned it, Thomas would have dismissed the strange memories as mere wisps of dream, or fantasy.

"You were close to death," said Neill. His voice interrupted Thomas's pleasant reverie.

Thomas shrugged. "'Twas not the first time."

"I know that," said Neill. "But I am rather fond of your old carcass. We did not want to lose you."

Something of his concern came through the casual words. "My thanks," Thomas said soberly.

"Do not thank me." Thomas could hear Neill's grin. "Thank the wench."

Thomas smiled. It was a predatory smile, the kind that warned a woman of his delightfully wicked intentions for her. "Aye. I will." A few moments later he added, "Tell me again what she did. You say she got up and ran for her tent just as I was waking up?"

And Neill told him once again, in detail, all that had taken place between Thomas and the beautiful Greenlander woman when Thomas had finally emerged from his close meeting with death.

In her tent, Yngveld wanted to hide and never, *ever* come out. Mortified, she held her hot cheeks and wondered over and over how she could have ever been persuaded to lie atop a naked slave—herself naked! Madness. It had to be!

And to think that *he* had seen her. And—and touched her! And, oh *nej*, kissed her! 'Twas too much! None of Karl's and Patrick's protests, of which there were many, could convince her that Thomas had awakened and not realized that it was she, Yngveld, his erstwhile owner, who had been lying with naked breasts pressed into his naked chest! Even now she writhed at the thought.

And here she was, hours later, resisting the pleadings of her friends. "*Nej!*" she cried, still holding her cheeks. "I will not step out of this tent for the duration of the voyage!"

"But Yngveld," said Karl in the same reasonable voice he had used all morning, "you cannot stay in here forever!"

"There you are wrong!" she cried. "I can! I can and I will!"

Karl shrugged, and his eyes met Patrick's helplessly. "Your turn. I hope you have more success," he murmured as he walked away from the tent.

Patrick sat down, his long hands hanging between his knees, his blond head drooping. After a while, he pushed aside the door flap. He looked at the flushed woman and wondered where to begin as he toyed with the small leather sack he held in one hand. At last he brightened and said softly, holding the sack aloft, "Look, Yngveld. We won!"

Yngveld spared barely a glance at the leathern sack. "Oh, how could I?" she moaned. "Naked . . . Kissing him . . ."

Patrick let her run on at some length. Finally he said quietly, "You saved his life, Yngveld Sveinsdatter. Mayhap he shall be merciful and spare yours." And with that, Patrick, too, got up and left the tent.

It was some minutes later that the full import of Patrick's words trickled into Yngveld's awareness. "Spare me?" she asked, glancing up at the tent's opening. "Spare me? Whatever did he mean?" A puzzled frown wrinkled her pale brow. "Patrick? Patrick! Come *back* here!" She got to her feet and ran after him.

Chapter Ten

She raced out of the tent only to skitter to a halt under the watchful green gaze of Thomas Lachlann. He had braced his feet on the seat ahead of him and was pulling with all his might on an oar. He nailed her with his hot glare.

He was bigger than she remembered and very much alive, in full health, his color restored. Unbidden memories raced through Yngveld's mind of how she had lain naked atop him, of how he had kissed her, kissed his way down . . . Her face burning, Yngveld glanced away, groping at the wisps of hair about her face as though they truly irritated her. In truth, she was shielding her flaming face from those unyielding green eyes. "Patrick?" she squeaked.

Patrick waited in front of his tent as Yngveld

staggered over in time with the gentle swell of the sea. She peeked from behind her fingers to the bow. Oh *nej, he* was still watching her. She wanted to sink through the floorboards. In fact, to sink through to the depths of the sea sounded very enticing at this terrible moment of her life. Anything, *anything*, so long as she would not have to meet that knowing green gaze again.

Yngveld focused upon Patrick, willing herself to think of nothing else, especially not *him*. "Patrick?" she asked, her voice atremble. "What did you mean? You said that mayhap the slave will be merciful and spare my life? It does not make sense, Patrick." She blushed anew under Patrick's thoughtful gaze. "I am the ship's owner. My life is not at risk."

Patrick's blue eyes moved consideringly down one row of almost-naked, rowing slaves, then slowly back up the other row. He swung back to Yngveld. Should he tell her of the dream he had had? He had dreamed that the slave captain had freed his men and taken the ship. Patrick sighed heavily. Already the dream fragments were becoming mere wisps in his mind. Mayhap 'twas better not to say anything. " 'Twas nothing," he said at last. "Merely a poor slave's fancy."

She waited for him to say more, but he was silent. " 'Tis not right for you to scare me so," she frowned. "I—I—" She broke off because Patrick was not listening. He was watching something, or someone, behind her. Yngveld did not dare turn around, for she knew who that someone was.

Patrick locked gazes with the slave captain and shifted his feet uneasily when the big slave continued to stare at him. Something in that cold green gaze flared, and Patrick felt a momentary dread. He had underestimated the Irish slave captain. They had all underestimated him; that knowledge came to Patrick in a flash. And he was in danger—indeed Yngveld, Karl, all of them were. Then the feeling passed and Patrick was himself again, watching just another sullen Irish slave row.

Unable to resist, Yngveld peeked round once more. 'Twas worse! Thomas glared at her with hot bright eyes. Neill and Torgils watched her too. She turned back to Patrick, but he was no help.

Yngveld flounced back to her tent, careful to keep her gaze averted from the bow—and *him*.

Thomas Lachlann watched her go and his green eyes narrowed. He switched his brooding gaze to the thin blond older man she had been speaking with mere moments ago. A slave he was, if Thomas was any judge.

Thomas continued to row and to think, and later in the day he caught sight of the older slave once more. With a subtle nod of his head, Thomas ordered the slave to approach.

Patrick glanced about nervously. Sweynson was nowhere to be seen, and Captain Olafson was drinking ale in his tent. The Greenlander at the tiller looked half-asleep. Patrick hesitated. He was certain that none of the Greenlanders would want him talking to the big slave captain. He glanced at Thomas. Again, that same little sidelong movement of his head.

Sweat stood out on Patrick's brow. What did the slave want? Patrick took a step toward him, then stopped. Karl was asleep in the tent. What would he say? Would he want Patrick to speak to the slave? Mayhap not. Would Yngveld? Definitely not. But something in the big Irishman's manner was enticing.

Patrick glanced quickly up and down the deck, then sauntered as casually as he could on shaking legs over to the big man. "What do you want?" The words came out in a hiss. Patrick took a nervous step back and waited, glancing hastily up and down the deck once more.

Thomas laughed low in his throat. "What is there to fear from me, little man? Are we not both slaves—mayhap from the same land?"

Patrick nodded uncertainly. So Thomas's guess had been correct. This slave was Irish too.

"I was born free," stated Patrick after some moments.

"As was I," came back Thomas.

Patrick was beginning to wonder what he was doing speaking to the big Irishman. 'Twas one thing to watch the slave captain when he was nodding off, close to death. 'Twas another to face him when he was very much alive. Patrick's eyes ran over the big muscles of those powerful rowing arms. He jerked his eyes away and swallowed. "What do you want of me?" he asked. He heard the quaver in his own voice. Strange how fourteen years of slavery had changed him. Now he was cautious, subservient. Before his capture, he had been blustery and, aye, mayhap careless.

"What is yon woman's name?" asked Thomas, pointing to the little tent where he knew she was hiding. He asked the question in a deceptively gentle tone of voice.

Patrick's eyes widened. Somehow, to tell this imposing slave Yngveld's name would be traitorous. "Oh, *nej*, I will not tell you," he answered stoutly.

Thomas smiled, a flash of white teeth. "No matter," he said lazily. "I will learn it."

And Patrick heard the supreme confidence in that deep voice. He backed away, slowly, a shiver of dread coursing through him. The slave captain would indeed learn Yngveld's name, of that there was no doubt. But it would not be from Patrick!

Thomas, however, was not finished with him. His eyes narrowed as Patrick stepped back and said in a gravelly voice, "How would you like to be a free man, slave?"

Patrick froze and his eyes widened once more. "F-Free? How?" he croaked.

Thomas grinned, his white teeth catching Patrick's fascinated eyes. "Think on it," he said only. "Are you willing to risk your life to be free?" One black eyebrow lifted in challenge. "If you are, come to me. Then we will talk."

Patrick knew he was dismissed. With quick steps, he hurried to his tent, tripping in his haste. He was brought up short suddenly, realizing that Karl was in there. Karl, the man who owned him. *Owned* him. Suddenly the words left a raw, bitter taste in his mouth. Feelings of anger, long buried, and fear and disloyalty all warred in his heart and he stumbled blindly to the side of the ship, ostensibly to stare out at the vast ocean. Tortured thoughts went round in his brain. *Freedom, freedom,* taunted his mind. You could be a free man. *Nej, I could not. The slave captain can do nothing to free me,* he argued back. *He is but a slave himself.* Oh? He is strong. He is wily. How can you be so certain he will stay slave? Why do you not seize freedom with both hands? There was a time when you would have, chided the little voice, before you grew to accept your lot as slave.

Thomas watched the Greenlander thrall stumble away. He pulled at his oar thoughtfully. 'Twas a gamble. He knew that. But there was no one else on the ship he could get to help them. The slave, a son of Ireland, seemed intelligent. Now Thomas would find out if he was also brave.

Thomas stared thoughtfully out to sea, chains clanking as his arms kept easily to the rowing rhythm despite Sweynson's quaint habit of lashing the floorboards with the leather whip to set the pace he wanted. Intimidation, Greenland style, did not sit well with Thomas, but there was little he could do for the nonce. He gritted his teeth as Sweynson's whip snapped in the air just behind his ear. Thomas refused to give the irritating man a second glance.

Sweynson came sauntering over, hitching his belt aggressively over his rotund stomach as he dragged the whip after him. He stood, legs spread, glaring at Thomas from his low height. "What do you think this is?" he demanded. "A picnic? Or mayhap you think this is an old lady's burial ship?" He cracked the whip once more and Thomas could feel the leather tip whistle past his cheek. Sweynson was good, very good with the whip. He could place it exactly where he wanted. Still, Thomas rowed and stared out to sea as though Sweynson was a mere harmless gnat.

"Answer me, you son of a bitch!" snarled the overseer. Another crack of the whip and this time the tip of the whip bit into Thomas' cheek. He jerked once and kept rowing, gripping the oar in a two-fisted hold that threatened to snap the strong oak.

Sweynson's confrontation with Thomas caught Olafson's attention. He, too, swaggered over, staggering once as if from the gentle swell of the sea. But Thomas had noted that Olafson enjoyed his ale—morning, noon and night. In fact, since they had been aboard ship, Thomas could not recall seeing the man without a drinking horn in his hand.

"He giving you trouble?" bit out the crusty captain. Thomas moved his eyes from a point off the stern to glance at the Greenlander captain. The interesting thing about Olafson, to Thomas's way of thinking, was that the man rarely showed the effects of his liquor consumption. He merely stayed all day in an alcoholic haze that passed for his usual manner.

Sweynson blinked and gripped the whip tighter. Clearly, he feared that his superior would whisk the weapon away from him.

Thomas smiled grimly as he rowed. The whip would not protect Sweynson for long. Or Olafson either. Thomas's glance slid to Olafson's bulging waist. Thomas's filigreed sword still swung at Olafson's side. Thomas blinked. And there, dangling, swaying back and forth with each step in the place of honor in front of Olafson's crotch, was the key, a simple iron key—the key to Thomas' chains, and the key to his men's chains.

Thomas shut his eyes as hope washed over him. When he opened them, his eyes jerked back to the key. How to get that beautiful, tantalizing, beckoning key away from the Greenlander captain? Suddenly, the key took a step closer, jangled musically, now stood in front of Thomas as he rowed. Thomas raised his eyes slowly from where the key played peek-a-boo with Olafson's crotch, past the tight belt that bit into the bulging stomach, past the colorless, food-stained blouse, past the shrivelled chest with the white hairs sprouting out the top of the blouse, up the red, wattled neck to Olafson's stormy countenance. Flat blue eyes regarded him suspiciously. Olafson took a swig from the horn he held in one hand. "I said, this boy bothering you?" He glared at Lachlann, then at Sweynson, evidently expecting an answer.

Sweynson fingered the neck of his own faded blue tunic. "*Nej, nej*," he answered. "Nothing that I cannot handle."

Olafson studied Thomas while he rocked back and forth on the heels and toes of his feet. Then he pointed his drinking horn at Thomas. "He is a dead man," he said conversationally to Sweynson and nudged the smaller, rotund man. Sweynson chuckled gently, still fingering his collar, looking distinctly uncomfortable. Thomas wondered why.

"*Ja*," continued Olafson expansively. "A dead man." He leaned toward Sweynson. "Why, we might as well toss his rotten Irish carcass into the sea right now. That's how dead he is!"

"Oh, let us not do that, Captain." Sweynson's voice sounded distinctly subservient.

Olafson hesitated as he lifted his drinking horn to his lips. He peered at Sweynson. "Why not?"

Sweynson hesitated. Olafson glowered.

"Because I or one of our men would have to take his place at the oars."

The captain let out a belch and slapped his knee with his free hand. "Har, har! So that is it! You do not want to take a place at the oars, is that it, Sweynson? You like holding the whip, eh?"

Sweynson fingered his collar. Thomas turned away to hide his fury. "*Ja*, captain. I do not do slave's work." Thomas could hear Sweynson spit over the side. Olafson took a great swallow from his drinking horn.

Olafson patted his comrade's shoulder in a paternal gesture. "There, there, my friend. You will not have to. We will keep this stinking Irish slave around a little longer. You will not have to row." He walked away, guffawing loudly.

Sweynson wiped a brow and then turned to find Thomas watching him. "Get to work, you lazy son of a bitch," he snarled. "I just saved your worthless hide, and by Odinn, I will get the work out of you for that!" Snap! The lash fell across Thomas' back twice before Sweynson strode away to whip some other unfortunate rower at the stern end of the ship.

"When?" demanded Neill. "How long do we put up with these fools?"

Thomas kept rowing. He had to get the key off Olafson; he wanted to do it when at least two or three of the six Greenlanders were either asleep or passed out. Of the six Greenlanders, Thomas knew that Sweynson and Olafson were the most vicious, taking any opportunity for reprisals against the men. Those two were fairly cautious, however. Each carried a knife and sword or whip upon his person and always one or the other was awake and standing at the tiller, amidships, even at night. Because they were so far north and because it was summer, there was only a short twilight instead of full dark.

Therefore Thomas could not hope for cover of darkness to hide his men's movements. And he still did not know if the little Irish slave, the one puking his guts over the side of the ship at this very moment, would do what Thomas required of him.

Thomas pulled on the oars. His men would not take Olafson and Sweynson's brutality much longer. The tension aboard ship was palpable and fighting could erupt at any time. Thomas knew he could not afford to wait much longer or open, unorganized rebellion would swamp the ship. No. He must not let that happen. Better that he take command.

Thomas's low voice filtered back to Neill. "Tell the men to expect my signal as twilight falls tomorrow night. Pass the word to the men. We mutiny tomorrow night!"

[illegible]

[illegible]

[illegible]

[illegible]

[illegible]

Chapter Eleven

One thing about rowing, mused Thomas, was that it gave a man plenty of time to think. And thinking was all he had been doing this day, for when twilight came, he and his men would take the ship.

Thomas turned and squinted into the thick fog, peering over the bow to see where in hell they were going. He swung back and watched Olafson at the tiller. The Greenlander captain was wiping his mouth with the back of one hand as he leaned against the steering mechanism. All day, Captain Olafson had been taking swigs from his ever-present drinking horn, yet his stout frame showed no ill effects. It was difficult to tell, of course, from this distance, but by Thomas's calculations, the captain should have been falling down drunk on the deck and passing out. Instead he was swaying on braced feet, shouting guttural orders now and then at Sweynson, who leaned out over the bow searching intently for Thor knew what. Landmarks or icebergs, Thomas supposed.

Thomas sat up a little straighter to watch Olafson rummage through a sack at his feet and pull out a small rock. The captain held it up at arm's length, one eye screwed shut, the other squinted almost closed as he stared at the stone.

Sunstone, thought Thomas. It looked like an ordinary dull rock until it was held up lengthwise to the sun and then it glowed warmly. Viking captains had discovered they could use the stone to determine the sun's place in the sky on foggy days such as this one. Thomas smiled to himself. He would be certain to take that stone from Olafson after the mutiny. Thomas would need it if he and his men were ever to return to Ireland. His own stone lay somewhere on the bottom of a Greenland cove, lost when he was captured.

Olafson glanced at the sky, obviously certain as to where the sun was now. He swayed a little at the tiller and Thomas hoped he would at least pass out by twilight, a few hours hence. 'Twould make him quieter when the key was stolen from his waist.

The stomp of Sweynson's leather boots behind Thomas warned him of the overseer's approach. Thomas sighed, expecting a crude word or a blow upon his back, but the man hurried past him, intent on speaking with Olafson. The two conferred at the tiller. Olafson swayed slightly as Sweynson gestured with tight, short movements. The captain made a careless gesture with his drinking horn and Sweynson turned away, shrugging, a worried look upon his face.

Thomas lifted a brow. Was Sweynson uneasy because of the fog? Bah, these Greenlanders knew nothing of the sea if such a little fog could make them uneasy. And Sweynson had much more to fear than a little fog, if he but knew it.

With a leisurely sweep of his glittering green eyes, Thomas surveyed the backs of his men. He could see the two rows of Irishmen only as far as the tiller. The remainder of the two rows were blurred in the dense mist. He wondered idly why Olafson and Sweynson had elected to take to sea with a crewful of slaves. Normally, 'twas not done. Too risky. They must be desperate men indeed. Either that, or the woman was paying them a pile of gold.

Aye, the woman. Thomas's handsome face looked carved from stone. His lip curled. Her ownership of him rankled greatly. He had been watching her the three days since she had saved his life. At first he had found it difficult to believe Neill's words, but the woman's behavior gave her away. Whenever he caught her eye, or even looked in her direction, high color would rise to her pale cheeks. She would turn away quickly, as though something at sea had suddenly caught her attention, but Thomas knew it was he that was the cause of her obvious discomfort. Neill spoke true then—she *had* lain naked atop him to revive him.

Thomas wondered why she had saved him. Did she do it because she owned him? He thought so, thought that she was one of those women who counted her every spindle whorl, every needle, every armband and breast pin as dear, knew its value and held it close to her. His lip curled once more. Aye, he had seen greedy, controlling women like her before. That he owed his life to her mattered naught if she had saved him merely to keep her wealth. He owed her nothing. What did matter was that he retake this ship and turn the broad sail and noble prow for Ireland. After *Raven's Daughter* was his once more, he would decide what to do with the woman—*if* he let her live.

He felt warm suddenly, and his heart pounded in his breast. His narrowed eyes sought the stern, where her little tent was. He could not see her through the white fog, but she was no doubt there, safely ensconced in her tent. Stay there, woman, he laughed to himself. Stay there so that I will know where to find you when the fighting is over and I can come for you.

"The men are ready," came Neill's hoarse whisper.

Thomas shook his head to clear it of images of the blond woman. "Good. Olafson should be drunk by then." He frowned. "And Sweynson should be passed out soon after that. When I get the key, I will go along the rows and unlock the manacles on all the men. Then we attack the remaining Greenlanders. Any questions?"

"Several," answered Neill. "How will you get the key? How do you know Sweynson will be drunk? It does not take a seer to know that Olafson will be drunk—but Sweynson? Or are you just hoping?"

Thomas laughed a bitter, low laugh. "I have my ways," he answered. When he was not more forthcoming, Neill risked a glance over his shoulder. But Thomas merely shook his head at him, an enigmatic smile upon his face. Neill shrugged. "Tonight, at twilight fall," he concurred.

Yngveld huddled in her tent, a warm down blanket wrapped around her to keep out the chill of the evening fog. Of late she had found that it was best to stay in her tent. To go walking on deck was to risk her every move being followed by those bold green eyes.

Or mayhap 'twas that she was so aware of him. She could easily see him from the doorway of her tent. He sat in the last seat at the bow and her tent was placed in the middle of the ship at the stern. Although the length of the ship separated them, she found that the distance provided little protection. Always those burning eyes followed her. Except in fog like this, of course. Then she was safe. She had walked on deck earlier in the evening, but she found the dense fog little to her liking, so she had decided to spend her evening sewing in her tent instead.

She was sewing the tear in her favorite embroidered dress, and though there was little light to see by, she thought she had done a fine job of it. She held it up near the light from the door, eyeing the stitches.

She was about to take up her needle once more when she heard a slight noise just outside. Peeking out, she saw that the fog was lifting and she could see past the first several banks of rowing men. She could also see enough to notice Patrick approaching Olafson's tent, set not too far from her own.

"That is odd," she muttered to herself. "I wonder what Patrick wants with Captain Olafson?" She frowned. "It is not like him to seek the captain out." Heretofore, Patrick had been most scrupulous about keeping a distance between the Greenlanders and himself. Then she chided herself. " 'Tis nothing, you nosy girl. He is but on an errand for Karl."

She took several stitches before the thought struck—what could Karl possibly want with the Greenland captain? He too, had only talked to the man when necessary. Besides, everyone aboard ship knew that Olafson had retired for the evening over an hour ago.

Curious, she poked her head out of the tent once more. *Ja*, she could even see Olafson's skin boots protruding from the entrance of his tent. Patrick was inside the dwelling. Nothing but guttural snores came from inside the tent.

Suddenly Patrick came dashing out of the tent and darted down the plankway toward the bow of the ship. Then Yngveld could see no more for the fog still curtained the last few banks of rowers.

Yngveld clasped nervous hands together. Something had happened. Dare she go and see? Her heart pounded and she felt dread at taking a single step outside the safety of her tent.

Something had happened to Olafson. She knew it. Patrick had done something to him. But what? Olafson's boots still lay there, unmoving, as they had before. Mayhap the captain had merely gone back to sleep, she told herself.

And Patrick? What of him? She thought she had heard a clanking, jangling sound as he ran but she could not be certain. Whatever was going on?

She peeked outside the tent, and her disbelieving eyes registered a large figure walking out of the fog. 'Twas the slave captain! He was no longer confined to his seat! He crouched beside a prisoner—it looked to be Torgils. She heard a faint clanking and then the slave captain moved on to the next prisoner. He was working his way swiftly down one side of the ship, stopping at each seat and undoing the manacles of each prisoner!

Then loud yells assailed her ears. Oh, *nej*, she moaned. Whatever could be happening? The vessel suddenly jerked as though whoever was steering her had suddenly abandoned his station at the tiller. Yngveld's eyes swept the deck. There, amidships, where Sweynson had been—now there was only a slumped body. Her horrified eyes saw a dagger protruding from his back. Oh, *nej*!

Yngveld was on her feet now, ready to dart out of the tent. She whirled in time to see Lachlann enter Olafson's tent. Only her shaking hand clapped to her mouth prevented her outcry. She must get away! But where? Her confused mind raced, trying to make sense of what she was seeing, trying to figure out where to run. Suddenly Patrick came dashing down the center planks heading directly for her tent. He reached her, panting. "Get inside! Quickly!"

Yngveld obeyed, tripping over her own feet in her haste. He joined her on the blankets, his chest heaving. When he had caught his breath, he turned his large blue eyes upon her.

"Patrick? Whatever—?"

"Sssh, quiet! You must be very quiet," he insisted, placing a hand over her mouth.

Her eyes were huge in her face and he saw that she would do as he asked. He took his hand away.

Several minutes went by, and Yngveld heard a scream, then more cries. Unable to bear the cries a moment longer, she leaned toward the tent flap, intending to open it, only to have Patrick push her back.

"Really, Patrick," she whispered. "This is too much! I know we are friends, but—"

He shook his head, gesturing for her silence, and the hard look in his eyes froze her tongue. She stared. 'Twas so unlike him. She scooted back a little from him. Whatever had happened to Patrick?

He saw her put distance between them and grunted. "You have naught to fear from me, Yngveld. I am not your enemy."

"Who is?" she asked, eyes huge.

He jerked a thumb at the door of the tent in answer.

The grunts and thuds were growing quieter. Yngveld took courage to ask, "What were you doing in Captain Olafson's tent, Patrick?"

"I stole the key," he said tersely. "For my freedom."

"Key? What key?"

"The key to the slaves' irons."

She frowned and opened her mouth, about to say something, when he cut her off with a sneer. "Freedom, Yngveld. But what would you know about freedom? You, who have been free all your life! You, who have never known what it is like to be at the call of another, your life forfeit at a whim! What would you know?"

Yngveld stared at him, unbelieving. Never, in the whole of her life, had Patrick ever been anything but polite and gentle with her. Now he was sneering and speaking cruelly to her. She gasped and turned tear-filled eyes away.

No more was said until the cries had died down. Then the front flap of her tent was suddenly pushed aside by a bloody sword tip.

One of Yngveld's hands sought her throat for reassurance, and with the other she reached for Patrick. But when she saw who was standing in front of her tent, feet planted firmly on deck, her hand fell away. It was Thomas Lachlann—unchained, unfettered, a vicious sword in his grasp.

Yngveld gazed up at him, her heart pounding. His broad, naked chest rose and fell with each heavy breath and gleamed with moisture. His craggy face looked ruthless and dark in the dim light, and she could see the bunched muscles of his clenched jaw. But it was his eyes, those eyes the color of a stormy sea, that frightened her the most. They were arrogant and demanding, hot as they ran over her. He licked his lips once, then sliced through the thin tent flap with a single hacking stroke.

Yngveld shuddered and clutched her middle as if by hugging herself she could somehow protect herself from his terrible threat.

With the bloody tip of his sword, Thomas Lachlann coldly beckoned her out of the tent.

Chapter Twelve

"*Nej*," Yngveld whispered. "Oh, *nej*!" Blindly, she fumbled for Patrick's hand, seeking support and comfort. She closed her fingers over his warm ones. He squeezed her hand momentarily, then let it drop. His message was clear. She was on her own. "Steady," he murmured once.

But her eyes were on the massive man standing outside her tent, still beckoning her. She tried once, twice, to get to a crouch from where she sat, but her limbs refused to move.

But the man outside her tent was through waiting. He tucked his bloody weapon into the ragged waist of his loincloth and bent low. With ruthless intent, his brawny arms reached for her and Yngveld froze in disbelief as he dragged her out of the tent. Her legs were like water when he tried to force her to stand, and she swayed toward the deck. He caught her with a grunt and scooped her up, his strong arms imprisoning her.

His gaze warred with hers. Her heart stopped beating. His square jaw clenched and he strode with her over to the tiller. There he let her slide down his hard, lean length onto the deck. She gave a little cry before she hit the hard planks.

For once her legs obeyed her and she started off on a shaky run for her tent. There was nowhere to seek safety on this accursed ship, she thought, but there *was* her tent. She raced for it instinctively.

"Come back here," roared a voice. He did not even have to take a step toward her, for one of his men—a great, burly blond man—reached for her and caught her effortlessly. Though she struggled, she was no match for him and she was soon deposited, trembling and defiant, in front of Thomas Lachlann once more.

He smiled grimly, his bold gaze riveted to hers. "Welcome to my ship."

"It is not your ship," cried Yngveld and she stamped her foot. "It is mine!"

He threw his head back and roared with laughter. Then he faced her once more, a smile curling his sensuous lips, lips that had touched hers, that had touched her breasts, that had fluttered down her stomach. . . . Face burning, Yngveld strove to let her sudden fury at him for taking her ship give her the courage to cover her very real fear of him.

All around her were Irishmen—big, strong men, some taking down the sail, some taking their place anew at the oars but without chains, some just watching the confrontation between their captain and the woman. She gazed wildly around the deck. "Where are they?" she cried.

Thomas smiled lazily. The wench was an amusing diversion after the bloodletting. "I presume you mean your Greenlander captain," he drawled.

"*Ja,*" she snapped.

His eyes met hers ruthlessly, deliberately, all hint of amusement gone from his cold green eyes. "Overboard."

"You—you killed him?"

"Aye, Sweynson too."

Yngveld looked away for a moment. They had been cruel to him and his men, and she knew she should have expected no less a fate for them.

"Where are the others?" she demanded.

Thomas jerked a thumb over his shoulder toward the stern. With a shriek, Yngveld whirled around, expecting to find the ship's white, foaming wake littered with bobbing bodies. Instead, lined up along the stern were the four remaining Greenlanders. She relaxed in relief before she swung back to Thomas. It was better than she had expected. Four were still alive. "I am surprised you did not throw them into the sea too," she said caustically.

Thomas bowed mockingly. "Thank you for the fine idea. We are just about to do so."

"*Nej,*" she cried before she could stop herself. "Do not do such a terrible thing!"

He raised a brow. "Who are you to beg for their lives?" demanded Thomas arrogantly. "You are but a prisoner yourself."

Yngveld bit her lip. What could she say to that? She swayed a little, her hand going to her throat. "What of—what of Karl?" she managed to choke out.

"I suppose you mean the gray-haired man. Is he your father?"

She shook her head. "My father's friend," she said before she stopped. She did not have to explain anything to this—this ruffian, this mutineer!

Thomas looked over Yngveld's shoulder with one brow raised. She turned when she heard soft footfalls come up behind her. It was Patrick.

"She wants to know about Karl," explained Thomas to Patrick.

Yngveld glanced from one to the other. " 'Tis obvious you are in league," she said.

Thomas's eyes stroked her face. "That we are. Why, 'tis to Patrick here that I and my men owe our freedom from your good captain and his henchmen."

"He was not 'my good captain,'" snarled Yngveld.

Thomas turned away to hide a little smile. His own eyes had told him that she had not liked or trusted Olafson. When Thomas turned back to her once more, his face was stern. "As for what happens to Karl," he answered lazily, "that is for Patrick to decide."

Yngveld started. "Patrick? I—I do not understand."

Thomas looked at her coldly. "Patrick will decide how we dispose of Karl. After all, he was the man's slave for thirteen years."

"Fourteen," corrected Patrick.

"Where is Karl?" demanded Yngveld in a voice that shook. "He is a good man! He was my father's friend. If anything should happen to him—"

Thomas held up a hand. "That is for Patrick to decide," he said. "Not you."

"And does Patrick decide if *I* am to live or die?" spat out Yngveld. Fury shook her voice.

One corner of Thomas's lips tilted up. "*Nej,*" he said. "That is for *me* to decide."

"Oh!" gasped Yngveld. "Oh!" She whirled away only to be pulled back by a sharp grasp on her arm.

"I have not dismissed you, wench," said Thomas in a silky voice. "Do not be in such a hurry to offend me again."

Yngveld clamped her mouth shut. She tried to shrug out of his tight grasp and, not succeeding, contented herself with crossing her arms in front of her breasts and tapping her toe upon the deck, looking the very picture of impatience.

"Aah," whispered Thomas in her ear, "are you so eager to find out how I will dispose of you then? Which is it to be, my little Valkyrie, the sharks or the sword?"

She blanched until she realized that he was laughing at her. "You, sir, have a very sick humor," she replied haughtily and then refused to say anything further. The lengthy silence that grew while Thomas hungrily eyed her lovely form was interrupted when Karl was dragged over and made to stand in front of the new captain.

Yngveld winced when she saw the purple bruise over one of Karl's eyes and the scrapes across his cheek. "Gave us a fight," puffed one of the newly freed slaves, still holding Karl's arm.

Thomas looked at Karl, then shrugged and turned to Patrick. "Well, Patrick?" he asked. He pointed to the stern where the Greenlanders stood waiting for their watery fate. "Which is it to be for Karl? The sharks, the sword, or your custody?"

Yngveld gasped. Thomas Lachlann had not been joking, after all. Her hand sought her throat as she wondered which terrible choice would befall her. Then she glanced at Karl. He was pale and trembling. She held her breath, her eyes watering. He was her father's old friend. Loyal Karl. He had only sought to help her escape to Norway and now here he was, facing death because of her. Misery invaded her soul and she wanted to weep.

Karl's blue eyes met hers for a fraction of a second. She read sorrow in his eyes, but no blame. In that short glance she understood that he did not hate her for what had happened.

Karl turned to face Patrick. For several heartbeats the two stared at each other, and Yngveld wondered what passed between them. How do men weigh fourteen years of slavery in the twinkling of an eye?

Finally Patrick said in a hoarse voice, "Release him into my custody."

Thomas nodded. "He is your slave, then," he said. He waved to the two Irishmen. "Leave him with his new owner."

They stepped back from Karl and left him staring at Patrick. Both looked pale; Karl looked shocked at the swift change of events. "Patrick?" he asked hesitantly, reaching a hand toward his former chattel.

Patrick stepped back and Karl's hand fell short of touching him. "Patrick, *master*," he corrected sharply.

Yngveld hardly dared glance at Patrick, he looked so furious. She wondered if he had carried such anger in his breast through the fourteen years of slavery, and only now let it show. Strange how such thoughts had never occurred to her before. . . .

Karl reddened, then swallowed. Several moments went by. "Patrick . . . master," he repeated in a dull whisper.

But those words gave Patrick little triumph that Yngveld could tell. She watched in a daze as Patrick whirled and led the way to their old tent—once Karl's, now Patrick's—and stepped inside, motioning Karl to follow with a sharp gesture. Head bowed, Karl took slow steps. Then the tent flap swung closed and Yngveld was left staring, wondering at the sudden change in the relationship between the two.

Subdued now, and thoughtful, Yngveld glanced worriedly toward the stern. The Greenlanders looked grim; one was praying, two others looked as though 'twas but an ordinary day and they were not facing Death. The fourth was sobbing and crying. She turned away, sick. How soon would she be forced to join them?

Thomas watched her out of narrowed eyes. He had seen her glance at the stern and swallow. So she was mulling over what fate lay in store for her, was she? Good. He would find out what she was like before he decided what to do with her, though truth to tell he no longer entertained seriously the idea of killing such a beautiful woman, however selfish or greedy she might be. "Before we discuss what is to happen to you," he began conversationally, "I want to know something. I have wanted to know it ever since you bought me."

She looked up at the sneer in his voice.

"Why," he asked, "did you leave Greenland?" When she opened her mouth to answer, he shook his head. "No lies," he warned. "Only the truth between us."

She tossed her head. "Why should I lie?"

He smiled grimly. "Some people say and do strange things when they face a—shall we say difficult situation?"

Yngveld hesitated, then swallowed once. "I—I left Greenland to flee a man," she said at last, her voice a mere whisper.

He had to lean forward to hear. He frowned. "A husband?" Strange, he could have sworn she was not married. She had an air of innocence about her.

She shook her head. "*Nej*, another. Not a husband. Though he wanted to be. He fancied he was my betrothed."

Thomas Lachlann's chiseled face cleared. He could understand such a lovely woman as this one attracting a number of men, and not all of them would be desirable mates, he supposed. Still, all that was in the past. She was his, now. For as long as he wanted her.

"Who was he?" Thomas asked lazily, while his burning eyes lazily perused her graceful form. Her high, full breasts were made for a man's hands, he decided. His. His eyes shifted lower. Her stomach was flat. He could see the roundedness of her slim thighs. Aye, he thought. He could have a most pleasant time with this woman. Most pleasant.

Yngveld saw his appraisal and turned away to look at the sea for a moment. She did not want to accept that her life hung on what he read of her in that one blazing glance. She swatted gently at a wisp of blond hair that blew across her eyes, then turned back to him, holding her breath, wondering if she could read life or death in his eyes. She read lust, amusement, and something more—but was it life? She could not read her fate in his green eyes. She sighed, and a giddy, powerless feeling overwhelmed her.

Thomas Lachlann reached out a hand to brush a wisp of her hair back from her forehead.

Startled, Yngveld took a step back.

"Let me," said Thomas in a low voice. She stood stock still, forcing herself to show no fear, when all she wanted to do was to turn and flee the second his fingers touched her flushed skin.

"You must get used to me, to my touch, to my body," he said hoarsely. The blood pounded in his veins. Lord, he wanted to take her right here on deck. In front of his men. He took a deep breath and released it in a long shudder. He must get control over his desires. "After all," he added softly, " 'tis not as though we do not know each other."

She drew back and her blue eyes darkened. "What do you mean?"

"You, naked, atop me," he whispered.

Yngveld gave a little cry and jammed her fist in her mouth. Oh, the barbarian! How dare he remind her! "Much to my regret!" she burst out.

His gaze riveted to her face, he asked, "Do you regret our interlude, fair Valkyrie?" He fingered her hair, not waiting for an answer. "I do not. I find the memory quite . . . sweet." He leaned toward her and kissed her forehead.

Yngveld's knees buckled and she almost swooned.

His arm went around her, holding her upright. Good, he thought. I have the same effect on her that she does on me. He inhaled the fresh scent of her hair before reluctantly letting her go. "What was his name?"

"His name?" repeated Yngveld. "Who?" She opened her eyes to find him watching her in arrogant amusement.

She was beautiful, Thomas decided. Aye, he would keep her.

"His name?" She tried desperately to reel her thoughts back to the question he had asked.

Thomas nodded. Lord, she had beautiful eyes.

"Bjarni Bearhunter," she said at last.

Thomas froze, staring at her intently trying to determine if she had played him false. How could the wench know? "Bjarni Bearhunter," he repeated for good measure.

She nodded.

Thomas began to laugh. He was still laughing when Neill approached him. Neill bowed to Yngveld, and she smiled shyly. Surely they were not going to kill her when they were busy bowing to her, she thought hopefully. She turned her blue eyes back to the great boob in front of her, laughing his head off.

Neill waited until Thomas was down to gasps. "What ails you, lad?" he asked.

Thomas, bent over, pointed at Yngveld. "Her betrothed," he sputtered. "Her betrothed is . . . Bjarni Bearhunter!" And he started laughing all over again.

Neill joined him.

Yngveld stood, hands on hips, toe tapping the deck impatiently, now watching two great boobs laughing their heads off. Her face wrinkled in disgust. This must be the merriest mutiny that ever was pulled off, she thought. "And what is so funny?" she demanded. "If you knew Bjarni, you would not think 'twas a laughing matter!"

"Oh, we know Bjarni Bearhunter," Thomas assured her between fitful gasps. Neill nodded, too overcome with hilarity to speak. "We know him very well. 'Twas he that captured us!"

"Then what is so funny?"

" 'Tis that we—you, you are—we have his betrothed!" And both held their stomachs and doubled over again, almost falling to the deck in their hilarity.

Yngveld stamped her foot.

Finally Thomas was able to regain some semblance of order. He wiped his eyes and was now down to mere chuckles. "Ah, 'tis a fine revenge," he said at last. Neill fell against him, still laughing. "Aye, fine indeed. You see, he took our ship, which we have just taken back. And we—why, now we have his lovely betrothed! We won! Oh, 'tis too fine a revenge!" He looked as if he wanted to start laughing again.

Yngveld frowned. "What," she asked cautiously, "are you planning to do with me? Return me?" She could hear the hope creep into her voice and it surprised her. Surely she did not want to return to Bjarni. Did she?

"Return you?" asked Thomas incredulously. "Not now. Not now that I know Bearhunter wanted you!"

Yngveld turned away. "I see," she whispered. Yngveld could find no humor in the situation. None at all.

"Why, now *I* keep you!"

Chapter Thirteen

"Keep me?" whispered Yngveld, her voice listless. So now she was to be a slave. Her proud spirit felt battered at the realization of her thralldom, yet it was what she had begun to suspect would happen to her. She wondered briefly if the sword or the sharks would have been kinder to her proud Norse blood, but then she glanced at Thomas and her blue eyes hardened. Whatever way she could, she would escape this man and the servitude he planned for her, she vowed. She would not stay a slave—that she would stake her life upon! She came from proud Norse ancestors. Her father was Svein Skullcrusher, raider, berserker, once the proud bodyguard of an illustrious Norse chieftain!

Nej, this fool did not trifle with some peasant farm girl. There was Viking blood in her veins, by Thor, and he would learn of it. Firsthand!

She turned to him, her blue eyes glinting. "So you think to make me your slave."

Thomas nodded, watching the proud tilt of her head. She was a fine-looking woman. He would be most pleased to have her as his concubine. Lazily, he reached for her and his strong arms surrounded her.

She tried to push him away, but could have easier moved a mountain.

"You *are* my slave," he said hoarsely. "And a warning, fair Valkyrie—what I take, I keep."

She shivered at his words. He sounded so arrogant, so confident that he could hold what he took. That he could hold *her*. She tried to pull away once more, but he entangled one large fist in her thick hair and laughed softly as he held her head immobile. He bent to kiss her. A little cry sprang to her lips and he muffled it with his own.

Lord, she tasted sweet. Thomas lifted his head to gaze at her and met outraged blue eyes. He dropped his head once more, slanting his lips across her and pulling her body up against him. He molded her frame to his so that she could feel how much he wanted her. He groaned as her struggles served to rouse him further.

"Let me go! Let me go!" Somehow Yngveld managed to free her arms. Her fists beat ineffectually on his shoulders. "Let me go, you barbarian!"

He looked down into those furious blue eyes. "*Nej*," he answered. "I told you that what I take, I keep." He could not take his eyes off her quivering lips.

"You will not keep me!"

His nostrils flared. "You will stay with me for the rest of the voyage. And warm my bed!"

"Never!"

Her cry of outrage could be heard from one end of the ship to the other. Several heads turned, but Thomas cared not a whit. Let his men see her in his arms, know that he had claimed her. He hugged her to him then, freeing her hair, and she erupted into a kicking, pummeling bundle. He laughed at her struggles. "Methinks you will make a most amusing slave—in bed," he whispered in her ear.

Humiliated, writhing in pain, fury, and fear, she turned away and he released her. Stumbling, dazed, she tried to steady her faltering steps. That she, the proud daughter of a once valiant Viking fighter, should come to this, this demeaning state of slavery smote her heart deeply. She clenched her fists until the knuckles were white. Oh, how would she ever get free? And oh, how her poor, mad father's heart would have broken if he could see her now. 'Twas as well that Svein Skullcrusher was dead. Dazed, in searing pain, she took a step toward her tent.

Thomas would have dragged her back to him, but he saw the despair written large upon her fair face before she turned away. Something about her touched him; mayhap it was her thin, shaking shoulders, or the pitifully clenched fists, or her tense, straight body, the head proudly turned away. He did not know what it was, but something of her despair touched him.

He discovered that he did not want her to leave, not yet. He reached out a hand to stop her, but her back was to him and she never saw his outstretched hand. He dropped it. "I do not know your name," he said softly.

She did not answer, only stood there frozen.

"What is your name?" he asked again.

She turned at that, blue eyes full of reproach, lips tightened. She shook her head once, denying him answer. Then, with a little cry, she fled to her tent.

"Let her go," he muttered to Neill, who would have gone after the wench. "She needs time to get used to her new status."

"Aye," said Neill. He swung a curious gaze back to Thomas. "But she did save your life," he reminded his captain. " 'Tis a poor way to repay the good deed she did you."

Thomas's steely glare pinned his friend. "I spared her life. 'Tis payment enough. And make no mistake," he warned. "She saved me to protect her own wealth. She did not do it for *me*." At Neill's disbelieving wince, he added, "And when I need a prodding of my conscience from you, I will ask for it."

Neill nodded shortly. "The prisoners?" he asked.

"Put them to work bailing."

Neill looked at him askance. "You are not going to drown them?"

Thomas did not meet his eyes. "She—she pleaded for their lives." Then he cleared his throat and straightened, all compassion gone from his eyes. "I do not find it convenient to rid ourselves of them just yet. We can work them. Hard."

Neill snorted. "Aye, aye." He strode to the end of the ship shaking his head and muttering something about ungrateful, illegitimate, half-Irish soldiers who did not know their own minds.

Thomas watched him go, and some of his tension lessened. What was the woman doing to him? He answered himself—making him soft, that was what.

He turned to watch as the four surviving Greenlanders knelt on the deck planking and used wooden scoops to haul up the excess water below deck.

In satisfaction, Thomas surveyed the ship—*his* ship—once more. His men were at the oars, but as free men now. His beautiful *Raven's Daughter* was flying her broad red and white sail with the black raven painted in the center. The fog had dissipated, twilight was approaching. All was well with his world.

He cast an eye to the stern where sat the little tent with the savagely slashed flap fluttering in the breeze. *Almost* all was well with his world.

Chapter Fourteen

"Why are we turning the ship around?" demanded Neill. "I have set the course for Ireland."

Thomas looked up and saw his lieutenant's frown. The puckered scar across Neill's left cheek was red, a sure sign that he was angry. Towheaded Torgils silently joined them, also frowning.

With a sigh, Thomas slowly straightened from where he had been resting at the ship's bow, keeping one eye out for changes in the weather pattern and in the color of the sea water. "I ordered it," he answered.

When he volunteered nothing more, Torgils growled, "What is going on? Why do we not return to Ireland?"

"Because," said Thomas patiently, "we have

not completed our mission."

"Mission be damned," swore Neill. "We got out of Greenland with barely our lives. Why go back?"

"Ah, so you have guessed," said Thomas.

"Aye, I have," answered Neill shortly. "I know the way that you think, Lachlann. You think to return us to Greenland."

The use of his surname was a sign that Neill was truly angry. Thomas dropped his foot from the side of the ship and swung to fully face his two comrades.

"We are some distance from Ireland," he said slowly. "I do not know for certain the exact distance."

"So?" shrugged Neill. "Sail for the nearest coast. We can find our way from there."

Thomas flexed his hands. Patience, he warned himself. They are landsmen and do not understand the ways of the sea. "I do not know the exact place," he explained carefully. "That means I cannot be certain how far off the coast we are. Or even which coast. The nearest coast could be days away, or"—he squinted at the sun—"it could be mere hours."

"When we were boys, you were the one always sneaking off to your father's dragonship. I always supposed you to be the sailor," Neill accused him. "You should know these things!"

"Aye, and I do," answered Thomas, unperturbed. His eyes twinkled. "And you could have come with me, except you always pleaded seasickness." Neill grimaced at the barb, but said nothing. Thomas continued, "I know enough to tell you that the safest route is to return whence we came. We are only three days out of Greenland. We can touch shore there, get our bearings. And, as we are short of food and water, we can get those—"

"And what will we pay for food and water with?" broke in Torgils. "Our good looks?"

"'Tis true we have no gold," agreed Thomas amiably. "But we are strong, we can work."

"Or steal!"

"If we have to," answered Thomas equably.

Neill flushed with impatience. He looked frustrated. Thomas patted his lieutenant upon the shoulder. "I understand your frustration," he said. "'Tis mine, too. But we have a job to do."

"Aye, find some Greenland wench for Ivar Wolfson." Neill sounded bitter. "I would as soon get home. Methinks this sea life is a poor one." He spat over the gunwale.

Unfortunately, thought Thomas, many of the men probably agreed with Neill. The euphoria of retaking the ship was now over. It had been brief. His men wanted to set foot on Ireland, and soon. Thomas could understand that, but he still had a commitment to Ivar to fulfill. He must do that first; his men would have to bear with him.

"I cannot risk the men's lives," said Thomas. "We have risked enough. Why, we do not even have clothes, should a storm arise."

"Clothes?" Neill snorted and waved a hand.

"What matter? The men are tough, 'tis summer. 'Tis not a group of infants we have aboard."

Thomas smiled. "You are tough, Neill. So are you, Torgils. But some of the men are sick and injured. They have been whipped and have not had decent food." He shook his head. "*Nej*, I do not care to risk them further."

"What of the wench, Lachlann?" remarked Neill slyly. "Should you return to Greenland, mayhap she will seek to escape. After all, 'tis her homeland. She will know people there who would help her."

Thomas sobered. "Leave her to me. I am well able to take care of one small blond wench."

"I thought your taste ran more to brunettes," added Torgils. "With large breasts." They both knew he spoke of Katelyn.

Thomas frowned. "Enough." Thoughts of the generous farmer's daughter who lived near Dubh Linn were not so welcome to him now. Her image seemed weaker to him; 'twas the blond wench he found himself thinking on.

"I have decided the matter," stated Thomas. "We return to Greenland, make inquiries for Yngveld Sveinsdatter, find her and take her back to Ireland with us. That was our mission and by Thor, we are going to carry it out."

"Who are you trying to convince?" answered Neill. "Us or yourself?"

"Aye, you have the right of it, Neill," answered Thomas. "If I could, I would set our course for that emerald jewel, Ireland, this very day. But, alas, I would have to explain to Ivar why I arrived in Dubh Linn shirtless and without his precious bride."

Neill and Torgils looked thoughtful. " 'Twould not be a pleasant conversation," acknowledged Neill at last.

Torgils snorted. "He would run you through with his blade once he realized you did not bring his betrothed. Out of disappointment, of course."

Thomas sighed. "I do it out of loyalty to the man, not out of fear. Wolfson has been a good commander."

Torgils raised one light eyebrow. "As Vikings go, he is not bad."

"Not bad, man! What do you want?" Thomas glared at his friend and lowered his voice. "We half-Irish bastards are treated decently at his military camp. No man makes snide jests or thinks to attack us because of our heritage."

"Aye, and 'tis because of your own prowess with your blade, not because of Wolfson," growled Torgils. "He could care less whether you are Irish or Viking, so long as you fight where he tells you and protect his precious back."

"That is the way I like it," scowled Thomas. "No questions to answer to anyone. I let my blade speak for me." He fingered the sharp blade of the sword his father had given him. 'Twas the first thing he had retrieved upon becoming captain once more.

"As for me," said Torgils, "I would prefer someone who fought more often for the Irish."

"As would I," snapped Thomas. "But the old days are gone. Then, you could choose your side, Irish or Viking. And fight like hell to win. These days Ireland is split up into little pockets of Viking and Irish. Look at Dubh Linn. For the past few years, Ivar has held the town for the Vikings. But the Irish will try and retake it, mark my words. If not this year, then the next. Brian Boru is stubborn and he gathers men even as we speak. Ivar has a tough job to do.

"And alliances are constantly shifting nowadays. Why, in one battle we will have Irish and Viking allies fighting against invading Vikings. In the next battle, it's back to Irish against Viking. And do not forget the half-Irish, half-Viking men like ourselves, the folk who get caught in the middle." Thomas's bitterness showed in his hard eyes. "We are neither one nor the other. The best thing we can hope to do is hire out to the best paying commander and loyalties be damned."

"They can *try* to take Dubh Linn," said Neill. "But they willna succeed."

"Your loyalty to the Vikings is commendable," said Thomas, "considering you are fully Irish."

Neill looked at him in surprise. "Do you not have the same loyalty? After all, you joined them first. I know you hated your Viking father, but I thought, these past years, fighting for the Vikings, that you had come to terms with—"

"With nothing," snapped Thomas. "My loyalty is to Ivar, not to the Vikings."

"Aye, Ivar is good enough," said Neill. "I have taken the measure of the man. He is fair, and he is honest. And he keeps his word. 'Tis all I know about the man." He spat again. " 'Tis all I need to know."

Thomas looked at Neill and Torgils. " 'Tis a far cry from when we were growing up as boys, is it not, my friends? Here we three are, two bastards begotten on Irish mothers and one full-blooded Irishman fighting for the Vikings. Back then, I hated anything to do with Vikings."

"Hated your father, Lord Harald, you mean," said Torgils.

" 'Twas different for you, Torgils," responded Thomas. "You did not know your father. Oh, you knew he was Viking and that he had raped your mother, as happened to mine. But you did not have to see him every day, know that he rejected you and chose his other, legitimate son." Now it was Thomas who spat over the side of the ship in disgust.

Torgils' blue eyes, no doubt inherited from his absent Viking father, snapped. "If I could find the son of a bitch, I would kill him."

"Him or all Vikings?" asked Neill.

"Him," answered Torgils curtly. "And then I would cut off his head and present it to my mother on a platter." He smiled ferociously. "Aye, she would like that."

Thomas laughed. So did Neill. "That is why Ivar Wolfson likes you fighting for him, Torgils. You are so bloodthirsty!" He slapped his friend on the back.

Torgils looked at his friend and smiled grimly. "Aye," he agreed.

All three were solemn and quiet for a moment. At last, Torgils sighed and glanced at the little tent at the stern. "Be gentle with her," he said, his pale eyes unreadable as they fastened on Thomas's green ones.

Thomas was the first to look away. The thought suddenly struck him that he would be loathe to force the blond wench to carry his son, a son that would carry the load of hate and guilt that he and Torgils carried against their sires. Thomas vowed to himself at that moment that he would do things differently from the way of his father, and of Torgils' father. Strange, how he had never thought about such things before. He glanced at the little tent with the ragged flap and sighed.

Torgils heard his sigh and shook his head. He stretched, yawned, and said, "I take my turn upon the oars now."

Thomas and Neill watched him stride away. When Thomas's glance caught Neill's, Thomas suddenly found that he had nothing to say. But much to think on.

Chapter Fifteen

Yngveld crawled out of her tent and went to stand at the rail near the stern. From where she stood, did she care to turn, she would be able to see the full length of the ship, the Irishmen rowing—unchained—and the Greenlanders bailing or winding the thick walrus-skin ropes into neat coils. Thomas would be at the tiller, and mayhap Neill or Torgils or some other Irishman would be with him.

But Yngveld did not care to turn to survey the ship. She preferred to stare at the sea, watching for the animals that lived upon the ice or swam in the cold green depths. She knew she was avoiding Thomas, but she could not face him, not just yet. So she gazed instead at a huge brown walrus clumsily trying to climb up onto a flat piece of ice. Five times the beast clambered halfway up out of the water, perched on the ice, then slid back into the sea with a big plop! Yngveld chuckled to herself at his antics. The sixth time he made it and lay, panting, king of his little ice floe. She clapped her hands together in glee at his triumph.

"Fascinating animal, is he not?" came a deep voice behind her.

Yngveld whirled, her hands up to protect her rapidly beating heart. "What—what do you want?" she cried in alarm.

"I did not mean to frighten you," murmured Thomas. Lord, she looked lovely on this day. Her blond hair was tied in some kind of a knot at the base of her neck, but all the fine hair that framed her face had come undone in a gently blowing halo. Her wide blue eyes, startled, dominated her beautiful, pale face and two spots of color blossomed in her cheeks, like roses. He would go gently with her, he decided, the conversation with Torgils still fresh in his mind.

She had on the richly embroidered tunic he had seen on her before. He was disappointed to see that it hid her curves. Up close he could see that 'twas a costly garment. The sight of it reminded him of all the qualities about her that he did not like—her previous ownership of himself and his ship, her wealth, and her saving of his life.

"Why did you do it?" he asked abruptly.

"Do what?"

Her blue eyes, framed in golden lashes, were all he could see. The ship and its sounds were blotted out. The sky, the sea—nothing existed, only her.

"Why did you save my life?" He reached for her wrist and pulled her to him. "And I will have no lies about it."

"Lies?" she cried, trying vainly to release her wrist. She looked down at her hand and his dark fist against her pale skin scared her. He was so strong. "Let me go," she hissed, "or I will tell you nothing!"

He released her then and she fell back against the railing. She touched her sore wrist to her lips, brushed her mouth across it as if trying to heal it unconsciously.

He watched her through narrowed eyes. "A rich woman like you," he snarled. "What difference does one slave more or less make?"

She heard the contempt in his voice and it bewildered her. As hard as she could, she had fought to forget the part she had played in saving his life. Even in the privacy of her tent, whenever she thought of how she had lain naked against him, she could feel the heat rush to her face and neck. And here he was, snarling at her, as though she were throwing the whole thing in his face.

She shrugged as casually as she could, as though the matter were of no great import—indeed, as though it were an everyday occurrence for her to lie naked atop a giant. "No need to thank me," she said quietly. Let him think on that!

"Thank you?" he roared. He swung her around to face him. "I did not come here to thank you, wench! I came here to find out why you did it!"

His green eyes were furious. His lean, hard, half-naked body loomed close to hers, and she wanted to shrink away from him. Instead, she held her ground. "I did it," she hissed, "because if I did not, you would have died."

He stared at her, unwilling to believe any good of her. "And you would be the poorer . . ." he encouraged in a soft voice, determined to wrench the truth from her.

She turned away and shrugged her slim shoulders. "In truth," she said, "the thought of your value had not entered my mind." Patrick had mentioned it once, she remembered, but she had quickly moved past that consideration to the one about life or death. And—she flushed to remember it now—she had thought about how attractive he was and what a sad thing it would be for a beautiful man like him to die. She clenched her fists. *More fool I*, she castigated herself.

Thomas did not believe her. The rich women he knew—Lord Harald's wife, Lady Ingrid, and her friends—thought of little else than the cost of this, the value of that. He stared at her with flinty eyes. *Nej*, my fair Valkyrie, he thought. I do not believe a single word.

He stepped back, increasing the distance between them in the hope that she would feel safer and forget the threat that he was to her. "And would you have saved Olafson?"

She shivered. Lie naked atop Olafson? The very thought of his hairy, rotund body made her feel sick and she paled.

"Or Neill? Or Torgils? You would have done the same for them, would you not?" *You greedy wench*, he finished silently.

She thought about it. If Neill or Torgils were dying, she supposed she would have tried to save them. She nodded. But Olafson? She stopped nodding.

He saw her indecision and it intrigued him. Lord, he wished he knew what she was thinking. "Not Olafson," he guessed softly.

She shook her head. "Not Olafson."

So his guess was confirmed. She would not seek to "save" the captain, a free man—only the slaves. So he was correct, thought Thomas triumphantly. She had done it to keep her wealth. Just as he had thought. But the triumph soon dwindled away to be replaced by a hollow feeling.

Yngveld looked at him then, wanting to explain. "It was different with you," she began.

"How so?" he purred. *Because you owned me*? But he did not say the condemning words. Something in him held him back. He did not want to fully know the callousness of her. She was too beautiful, he supposed. Or he was too weak. Mayhap he would cling to his illusions about her a little longer.

She glanced at him, and he saw her blush as she turned away to watch an iceberg float past. "I—I had seen you stand up to Einar. I had heard that you saved four of your men. You were brave. I wanted . . ." What had she wanted? She tried to remember, but his close presence was driving every thought from her mind. She could smell his scent—sweat and salt and sea—and out of the corner of her eye, she could watch the rise and fall of his wide, tanned chest. Her pulse was beating in her ears and she could not think straight. "I wanted . . ."

He frowned. This was not what he had expected. "Brave?" he echoed. What was the wench thinking?

Yngveld grasped the railing for support. "I thought you were too beautiful to die," she gasped out.

Thomas opened his mouth and stared at her through narrowed eyes. Too beautiful? For a moment something soft in him longed to believe her. Then anger took over. So she thought to get to him that way, did she? Thought to flatter him into thinking that she—that she what? Her nearness was pushing every thought from his head. Her white neck, bowed before him, was all he could center his thoughts on. How vulnerable she looked, with her pale blushing cheek, her gracefully bent head, her hands twisting on the rail. Then his eye caught her rich robe fluttering in the wind and calm descended upon him once more. She was rich, and she sought to keep her wealth. That was how it was. He should not forget it. She was like any other rich woman.

He smiled grimly. "I see," he said softly. Let her think she had fooled him, that he believed she was overcome by him. He knew better. He reached for the sleeve of her garment with its heavy red and yellow and purple embroidery. "This is a lovely dress," he said.

She glanced at him, obviously surprised at the change of subject. She smiled tremulously. He was not going to mock her for saying that he was beautiful. Some part of her wanted to weep in relief. "Th-thank you," she murmured. "I sewed it myself."

He was surprised. He thought she would have one of her women do it for her. He rubbed the rich work between thumb and forefinger as he watched her. "Do you—do you make most of your own clothes?"

Now it was her turn to be surprised. She bobbed her head. "All of them." At his frown, she added hastily, "I had only to sew for myself and my father. The servants took care of their own clothes, of course."

"Of course," he muttered. Servants. He dropped the sleeve as though it had bitten him. His face was hard as he looked out to sea. "What did you pay for the ship?" he asked casually.

She gaped at him. This man jumped from topic to topic faster than a polar bear on ice floes. "The ship?" she asked, bewildered.

"Aye, the cost." He turned a grin on her, a wicked half-grin that utterly charmed her.

She blurted out the price and saw him wince.

"You were taken," he said.

"Pardon?"

He sighed and said slowly, "You were cheated. The ship is not worth that. Even with the men."

"I had to get away," she said. " 'Twas worth it to me." Actually she felt humiliated that Einar had cheated her. And that this handsome man should be the one to tell her so. Her face was red, she could feel it. She stuck her chin in the air, trying to salvage her pride.

He saw the gesture and was amused. He placed a hand on her cheek, bringing her proud face around to him.

Yngveld wanted to snuggle up to that warm hand. She did her best not to lean into him, but she thought he could tell how he affected her.

"Why did you have to get away?" he whispered.

She blinked as she stared into that green gaze. His eyes had little flecks of black and gold in the green part. She opened her lips, but no words came. She swallowed once. "I—I told you," she breathed. " 'Twas to get away from Bjarni."

"Ah, Bjarni. Bjarni Bearhunter. Aye, so you did." He paused, licking his lips as he saw her pink tongue dart out to wet her own dry lips. "Bjarni wanted you?" he asked softly.

She nodded her head, trying to break his spell. "He—he claimed he did. But I think he wanted my land. And house."

"Land and house," he mused. "Just how much land and how many houses?"

She named a figure of acreage that by Irish standards would have been a large farm. By Greenland standards, because of the lack of arable land, it was barely enough to make a living when farmed by an old man, his daughter, and two servants.

Thomas straightened hastily. Any more of this kind of questioning and he would have the girl in the tent and under him.

"We return to Greenland," he said curtly.

"Greenland? Why? Do you—"

Thomas saw the hope light up her face. She thought he was taking her back to her home. He would promptly disabuse her of that notion. He shook his head.

"*Nej,*" he said gently, but she heard the rock-hard firmness in his voice. "I am not returning you to your home. We but go there for fresh supplies."

Yngveld turned away, biting her lip to keep from crying out. For a moment, she had thought . . . She had hoped . . . But *nej*, he had dashed that little ray of light. And what would she do in Greenland, even if she were to escape Thomas? She had no money, and she still had to get to Norway to plead with a kinsman to help her take back her land.

She squinted in the direction of the sun. In the days that had passed since her flight, of course Bjarni Bearhunter would have taken her farm. Her thin frame shook with silent sobs.

Thomas watched her, feeling suddenly guilty for his role in her plight. He swung round to look at his men, and every single one of them had amazingly found something else to stare at—which convinced him that they all had been watching him and the woman. He turned back to her. "Woman?" he asked.

Yngveld turned to him, her lips trembling, great blue eyes filled with tears.

Thomas flinched inwardly, sternly crushing down all soft feelings that arose at the sight of her. He forced himself to remember the terrible lesson he had learned about the deceit of women. 'Twas the first time when, as a lad of ten years, he had sneaked aboard his father's dragonship moored at the sheltered harbor of Swords Village. One of his father's men had discovered him and, recognizing him as the bastard son of the Lord, had dragged him by the ear all the way to Lord Harald's mansion. The sailor had thought that the lord would be halfway pleased at his offspring's desire to learn about ships.

Unfortunately, Lord Harald was not at home, but Lady Ingrid was. Upon hearing that her husband's bastard was waiting in the front yard, the Lady Ingrid and several of her friends had come to stare at him. Thomas had stared back. He had never seen such pretty ladies, dressed in such gay colors. His mother and the peasant women he knew wore roughly woven clothing and went barefoot. These ladies were lavishly dressed and decorated and wore soft gray boots upon their feet. Thomas stared open-mouthed at them.

Apparently, the frowning Lady Ingrid did not like what she saw, for she gave orders that Thomas should be whipped for trespassing aboard her husband's ship. When the indignant sailor refused to wield the whip, the irate lady snatched up the lash and did the job herself, whipping Thomas soundly in front of her tittering friends.

Thomas refused to cry out, though the lash cut into his back. When the Lady Ingrid was done, she threw the bloody instrument into the dirt and warned the watchers to say not a word to her husband. She warned that she would lie to him and that he would believe her over anyone else. With that hissed warning ringing in his ears, Thomas waited as the Lady Ingrid then calmly invited her friends back into the mansion for refreshments and left her husband's bastard sprawled face down in the dirt.

The sailor, with a look of disgust, had helped Thomas to his feet, his aching back streaming with blood. To Thomas's knowledge, no one ever did tell Lord Harald about the incident, though in truth, Thomas did not think his father would have done anything even if he had learned of it.

But from that day onward, the sailor, Gudleif, had proven himself to be a friend to Thomas.

When next the young boy disobeyed his mother's orders and went to stare at his father's dragonship, Gudleif invited him aboard for a sail. And the other sailors treated him well too. Soon the dragonship was the one place where Thomas could go and be accepted and where he learned about his Viking heritage. *Ja*, he had learned a powerful lesson that time. Women were not to be trusted, men were.

Thomas's green eyes focused on the teary face in front of him, his heart hardened by the old memories. *Ja*, women were deceitful and cruel when they had power. This one was rich and beautiful, like Lady Ingrid and her friends. No doubt she would be just as cruel. Well, he would not let her work her wiles upon him. "Get to your tent," he said curtly.

Yngveld started, not understanding the coldness in the deep voice that had been so warm and gentle mere minutes before. With a startled glance from her large blue eyes, she hurried to her tent. With a last look at Thomas, she dipped and entered.

But he was not done with her. Thomas strode over to the little dwelling with the slashed flap fluttering in the wind like a black ribbon. He squatted down in front of the doorway and peered into the depths.

Yngveld sat, crouched, her head resting on her drawn-up knees. She wiped at her eyes and looked up hastily when she heard him halt in front of the tent.

Thomas caught the pitiful gesture and Torgils' words returned to him. "Be gentle with her," Torgils had warned. And Thomas's own inclination had been to be gentle.

"Woman," he said. "I will take my evening meal with you. Make it for me." There, that should not be too difficult, he thought. She could cook for him and he would get to speak with her again, let her get to know him. She would not find him a cruel man. If she did what he wanted, which was bed him, then they would go along very well. Very well, indeed. He strode away whistling, picturing her soft, naked body in passionate surrender to him. *Aye*, he would have her and then this unease he felt with her, these soft feelings—they would be gone like that, like the snap of his fingers.

Yngveld watched him walk away and her hands shook as she pressed them to her open lips. He demanded that she cook for him, did he? Very well, she would cook for him. And 'twould be a meal he would not soon forget!

Chapter Sixteen

To Yngveld's dismay, Thomas had also invited Karl and his new owner, Patrick, to partake of the dinner she was preparing for him. "Is he going to invite the whole crew?" she muttered irritably as she knelt beside a contained box of sand where the fire would be built. She blew upon the tiny curls of wood, trying desperately to get the fire started. If only she knew more about cooking aboard ship. She supposed, after some thought, that it would be similar to cooking at home.

Yngveld had not often cooked for her father or herself. Dimples, the woman thrall, had done that chore. But Yngveld had watched Dimples. Cooking did not look difficult. She knew she could do it, but first she must get this fire to burn.

And she wanted the fire to burn, by Thor! She wanted it to burn down to tiny embers so that she could go ahead and burn the lordly Thomas's meal. See if he would demand that she cook his dinner ever again! The problem was, 'twas difficult to fan the flames when one was snickering to oneself.

She finally managed to get the little orange tongues of flame to lick the wood and was heartily congratulating herself on that small triumph when a red slab of bloody meat landed on the deck beside her with a loud, wet splat.

Torgils stood beside her. "Fresh seal," he growled. "Neill harpooned it this afternoon." Then he walked away, his bare feet soundless upon the oak planks.

Yngveld eyed the large chunk of meat. Already she could imagine it a scorched, charred mess. Humming happily, she built the flames a little higher and then sat back and waited calmly for them to die down. Ah, *ja*, 'twould be a fine meal. 'Twould also be the last that Thomas would demand she cook for him!

Busy with her preparations, she did not hear him come upon her until he was right behind her. When he spoke, she jumped at the deep voice. "Ah, seal meat. My favorite," he said in a voice filled with male satisfaction.

She glanced at him from where she crouched, her face suddenly wreathed in a smile. "Your favorite, is it?"

Lord, she looked a lovely sight. Her hair had come loose and hung down her back in a great blond web. He fancied that he could see white streaks in it, so fair was it. Her eyes, bluer than the sky overhead, were sparkling. And her lips—ah, those full lips were beginning to be the stuff of his every waking thought. He shook his head, trying to dispel the temptress's image, but 'twas difficult when she was there in front of him.

With a sweet smile at him, Yngveld carefully laid slices of meat on the embers. The fragrant smell of roasting meat soon filled the air, and Thomas's mouth watered. He watched the woman's delicate white hands as she cut through a chunk of yellow cheese, carefully laying it out on a wooden platter.

With his eyes fixed on the gentle swells in the front of her sack-like tunic, Thomas said, "I invited Karl and Patrick so that you would feel more at ease."

Ah, that explained it. She smiled at him brightly. "And why did you want me to feel at ease?"

She was standing, waiting for his answer, but Thomas's tongue could not seem to move. At last, he dragged his eyes away from her breasts. He swallowed once and then raised his eyes to hers. "I, uh, I—"

Damnation, what was wrong with him? His tongue felt tied in knots whenever he was around this woman.

His eyes fell upon her white, flower-embroidered tunic, and he followed the path of one yellow-and-orange burst of color with a long green stem that wound its way up one sleeve. With a great effort, he tried once again, "Uh, your tent—we must—"

Yngveld watched him, her eyes narrowing.

"Get in the tent," he croaked, placing one hand on her arm and dragging her toward the dwelling.

She tried to shrug his large hand off, outrage visible in those clear blue eyes. "What do you want of me?" she cried. But her efforts did not hamper his yanking her into the tent.

"To talk," he said at last and sank down upon the soft blankets, pulling her down beside him.

"Talk? Why could we not talk outside?"

"Because," he said, reaching for her and dragging her across the small space that separated them, "what I have to say is not meant for any other ears but yours."

"And what might that be?"

His hands were everywhere at once and 'twas all she could do to get hers there a split second after his. "You," she panted, "are like one of the giant squid—"

"Giant squid?" he frowned, his hands halting their restless quest while he stared at her with furrowed brow.

"The giant squid that latch onto its prey," she explained, smartly pushing both his hands from her and getting to her knees ready to flee the tent.

But she was too slow, and he reached an arm around her waist and dragged her back to him.

"Thomas Lachlann, stop!" she cried then. "This must stop!"

"Why?" he whispered, nuzzling her ear. "I do not want it to stop."

"Well, I do!"

"You do not mean that." His nuzzling mouth was now working its warm way across one cheek. One hand was firmly clasped to the swell of her breast and she felt as caught as though she truly were in a giant squid's grip. "Let me go!"

"*Nej*. I want you," he replied and she could hear the amusement in his voice.

"That does it!" she cried. " 'Tis one thing to be seduced, 'tis another to be laughed at!"

He turned her around to face him, and she stared up at those green, green eyes. He lowered his lips to hers, cutting off any further protests.

"Seduced?" he repeated lazily. "Could I seduce you?"

Without half trying, she thought. Aloud, she barked, "*Nej!* Do not even try!"

He bent his lips to hers once more and all protests were stilled until, minutes later, the kiss ended. By then, Yngveld noticed in a daze, the top of her tunic was peeled back and his hands were busily stripping the garment off her. She lay there, gasping, looking at him out of staring blue eyes, heart pounding, wondering how she had come to be in this half-naked state.

Thomas, however, was wondering no such thing and, having dispensed with his modest loincloth, again reached for her and pressed his heated length against her.

"Wait!" she held up a hand, drawing a slow breath. "We must not—I cannot—"

"*Ja*, you can," he whispered. He kissed her again, his kisses drugging her senses until she was limp. She pressed a hand to his broad chest, intent on summoning the remainder of her resistance to him, but instead of pushing him away, her traitorous hand gently closed upon the crisp male hair and pulled him closer.

Thomas smiled into his kiss at the little pain of her pulling him toward her and he went with her, avidly. His tongue had claimed the virgin territory of her mouth, and he was just about to press forward to other virginal parts when the woman suddenly heaved him off her.

"What?" he cried in bewilderment, panting. "Why did you do that?"

"I cannot!" she cried, snatching up her tunic and holding it in front of her heaving, naked breasts as though it were a shield. "I will not let you bed me as though—as though I were a conquered plaything! I am a woman! A woman with thoughts and feelings, and I will not be bedded at a barbarian's will!"

Thomas leaned back, trying not to grimace at the ache in his loins. He toyed with a lock of her blond hair, twisting it around his finger as he fought to regain control of his body and his breathing. "I do not take you for a plaything," he said at last, though his conscience gave a slight twinge.

Something of his guilt must have shown upon

his face, for she narrowed her eyes at him. "Ahhh," she whispered, "but you do."

He was about to say more when a loud cough outside the tent caught their attention. Yngveld's lovely face swung to the opening, and she prayed that no one would look inside. " 'Tis Karl and Patrick," she whispered.

Thomas cursed one frustrated, completely graphic curse, then he rearranged his loin cloth. The woman kept her back to him and he looked at that long naked spine until it was completely covered by the embroidered tunic once more.

With a great sigh, he got to his knees to move out of the tent. As he lifted the flap, he turned back to watch her frantically combing her hair, trying desperately to untangle the snarls resulting from his lovemaking. He reached for a lock of hair that lay upon her breast, lifted it to his lips and kissed it gently. "I do not even know your name," he murmured.

She heard the quiet supplication in his voice and she thought to herself that it was the first time he had *asked* anything of her. She had just opened her mouth to tell him, when suddenly Patrick called out in a merry voice, "Yngveld Sveinsdatter, are you in there?"

Yngveld shrugged in amusement and met Thomas's green eyes to see if he appreciated Patrick's uncanny timing. In disbelief, she recoiled at the fierce look she saw thereon.

"Yngveld Sveinsdatter?" Thomas's bronze tan did not hide the sudden bloodlessness of his shocked face. "It cannot be!"

Chapter Seventeen

Yngveld frowned as she served up a second helping of seal meat to Thomas. She placed an incinerated square of blackened meat in the center of his wooden platter, where it lay like an unappetizing, scorched lump—which was exactly what it was. Carefully, as though placing a prized gem in front of him, she lowered the platter to his slack hands.

And watched the charred piece of meat slide off the platter onto the deck. Resolutely, she picked it up and dropped it back on his plate. Thomas still sat there, staring into space.

Whatever was the matter with the man? She watched him chew, that square jaw methodically working the meat which she had personally tasted and knew to be as tough as walrus hide. She shot a glance at Patrick and Karl, who sat quietly on deck with untouched little black squares on their platters. Their faces revealed nothing of their thoughts, but Yngveld knew that she herself could only pretend to chew one bite of the blistered black stuff before surreptitiously spitting it into her hand. Once, she had tossed the mess overboard and Thomas had merely smiled vacantly at her as though she had made a comment about the weather.

Nej, something was definitely wrong, had been ever since he had left her tent like a man in a trance and had plunked himself down, unseeing, on the deck near the fire. Yngveld herself had served him the well-burned meat decorated with bits of cheese. He had eaten it all—all!—and had placed his platter on the deck. As though his action was a request for another helping, she had filled up the platter, only to watch him work his way through another charred slice.

She frowned again. When she had first conceived the idea to burn the meat, it had been for sport. Now, with Thomas completely unaware of what he was eating, there was no amusement in it at all for her. With a sigh, she pushed the miserable meal away. Glancing over at Karl's plate, she saw that he had taken one bite. Patrick, she saw, had taken none.

Patrick looked at her with chastising blue eyes. She smirked, hoping he would say something about her fine cooking, but he did not. Disgruntled, she returned her stare to Thomas.

And met angry green eyes.

Thomas spat out the mouthful of scorched meat. "What the hell is this that you have been feeding me?" he demanded.

At last! she thought exultantly. With a tiny smile, she looked down at her plate, as though with maidenly modesty, then back up to him. Her laughing eyes met his furious ones. "I am a good cook, *ja*?" she simpered.

"*Nej!*" roared Thomas. "I have never eaten such charred, foul fare in all my days!" He looked at her with furious eyes as he wiped at his mouth.

Yngveld hugged herself in delight.

Thomas glared at her. Ever since he had discovered that the "wench" he had tried to bed was actually Yngveld Sveinsdatter, Ivar Wolfson's betrothed, Thomas had been in shock. He had come very close indeed to bedding Ivar's bride and, despite his new knowledge, he still found himself greatly attracted to her.

Thomas wanted to beat his fists on the deck in frustration. What the hell was he supposed to do now? Take her back to Ireland, hand her over to Wolfson, and say, "Here is your bride, Ivar, good luck"? He snorted in derision—at himself and at the ill-fortune that had landed him in this particular dilemma. He knew what he would like to do. He would like to bed the wench and keep her. That was what he would like to do.

But he had sworn to bring Ivar his bride

"untouched." Thomas had no wish to cross Wolfson, but more than that, he respected Wolfson, and as his bodyguard, Thomas felt a very strong loyalty to his military commander.

Thomas was not Wolfson's only bodyguard. Dirk the Dane and Ingolf, both berserkers, and one other, Helmer Halfdan, were also responsible for protecting Ivar with their lives. But Thomas had been with Ivar the longest. Thomas was aware that Ivar preferred Dirk the Dane and Ingolf to himself and Halfdan, but Thomas still felt an allegiance to Wolfson.

But more importantly, Thomas considered himself to be a man of honor. He had given his word to bring Wolfson's bride back untouched and he felt honor bound to do so. Were he to break that word and violate the woman, by seduction or force, then he would no longer be a man of integrity. He would be less a man, both in his own eyes and those of his fellows.

With a snort, Thomas fastened glittering green eyes on Yngveld Sveinsdatter's lovely form. There she sat, smiling so sweetly at him, as though she had planned a wonderful feast. And instead had offered him charred seal. He chuckled to himself. She was becoming most amusing, this bride-to-be of Ivar's. His amusement fizzled. She was Ivar's. Not his. But a little voice challenged him. She would be Ivar's upon their return to Ireland, but she was not Ivar's yet.

Thomas sighed and glanced to where Neill stood steering the ship at the tiller. Neill would not find it amusing. He would expect Thomas to do the honorable thing and deliver the woman to Wolfson. As would Torgils, or any other man whose opinion Thomas respected. Thomas himself would expect it of another, if anyone else were involved. Anyone but the blond, blue-eyed Valkyrie laughing at him from across the platter piled high with the incinerated remains of dinner.

With a slight grin he asked, "I suppose I kept you too long in the tent and the meat burned?"

Yngveld gave a yelp. "I will have you know I planned it," she snapped. "I burned it apurpose!"

Thomas bent his head so she would not see his smile.

"I will not take orders from you, Thomas Lachlann," she said evenly. "So do not demand that I cook for you again."

Thomas eyed her. If only it was as small a matter as her cooking that truly occupied him. With a sigh, he got to his feet and felt a tiny flash of pleasure at the look of dismay that crossed her face. He bowed. "Thank you, Yngveld Sveinsdatter, for a most . . . uh, memorable meal." He turned and walked away.

Yngveld's narrowed blue eyes followed him and then, in a fit of pique, she reached for the last blackened square on his platter, picked it up, and flung the hard, crusty piece of ash out to sea. "There!" she cried to the wind. "That is what I would do with him!"

Patrick got to his feet, Karl too. Karl bowed politely. "It has been a pleasure." Patrick bowed.

"Come, Karl." And away they went, back to their tent.

A frowning Yngveld sat beside the embers of the fire, surrounded by platters of burned meat and wondering what had gone wrong.

Chapter Eighteen

Thomas stood at the bow of the ship, directly behind the magnificently carved dragon head. He could easily discern each burnished scale on the back of the sinuous wooden neck, work so fine that it must have been wrought by a master carver of Dubh Linn. He patted the rail of the ship affectionately and stared out to sea. Aye, *Raven's Daughter* was a beautiful ship, one he thought of as his own, though it actually belonged to the merchant friend of Ivar's who had outfitted the vessel as a special favor to the military commander of Dubh Linn.

Ah, yes, Ivar. Ivar Wolfson occupied Thomas's thoughts overly much these days.

With a sigh, Thomas straightened, arms across his broad chest. He had made his decision. There had never been any doubt in his mind as to what was the correct, the honorable thing to do. He would abide by his word and bring the woman to Wolfson.

That it had taken him a day and a half to reach this decision testified to the strength of the blond wench's attraction, he thought ruefully. Then he corrected himself. She was Yngveld Sveinsdatter, Ivar Wolfson's betrothed, and must be treated with all the dignity and respect that her position as betrothed to the powerful military commander of the town of Dubh Linn entitled her to. He winced as he remembered holding her in his arms, of caressing her naked breasts. . . . Stop! That way lay madness, he chided himself. She was a pretty wench but claimed by another. He would do well never to forget that.

He stretched lazily, then turned and sauntered to the tiller where Torgils and Neill were conferring. Neill, his hand on the tiller, nodded at Thomas's approach.

"Another day," said Thomas, "and we will reach Greenland."

"The same spot where we first landed?"

"Aye, Neill. The same."

"Hmmmph," growled Torgils. "Let us not sojourn on the little isle we first came to."

Thomas flashed a wide grin. "There are no storms in sight, so it is not likely we will repeat *that* disaster." He paused thoughtfully. "We will, however, see our good friend Bjarni Bearhunter once more."

"It cannot be too soon," said Torgils in his low, gravelly voice.

Thomas laughed. "Ah, Torgils, so you too, want revenge. As do I."

"I, myself, am not averse to a fight now and then," added Neill cheerfully. "Especially with Bjarni. I must thank him for the chains."

All three laughed.

"What about Einar?" joked Thomas. "Anyone want to stop and pay their respects to old Einar?"

"I do," said Torgils.

Thomas slapped him on the back. "We will." He frowned. "What I cannot decide is whether to give him gold for the food he will give us or merely take it."

"A difficult decision," agreed Torgils sarcastically. "For myself, I say, take the food. We have already paid for anything from that man with our blood."

Neill and Thomas nodded solemnly.

"Do tell me," began Neill casually, "why we are going to visit Bjarni again. Did you not get enough of his treachery the first time?"

Torgils snorted at that.

Thomas hesitated, then bit out, "To take back a farm." At Neill's uncomprehending look he added, "It seems that our fair passenger is none other than Yngveld Sveinsdatter, Ivar Wolfson's betrothed."

"What?" yelped Neill.

"*Nej!*" exclaimed Torgils at the same time.

Thomas eyed them both. "I see that you are as

surprised as I when first I learned her name."

"So," observed Neill slyly, "that is why I have not seen you near the fair maiden this past day!"

Thomas locked eyes with him. "I respect Ivar. I will not toy with his betrothed."

Torgils whistled—a long, low sound. Neill nodded, a hooded look to his eyes. "I would expect no less of you," he said soberly.

Thomas did not tell his companions of the difficulty he'd had in making his decision. Doubtless they would have had no trouble at all putting their loyalty to their military commander over the errant call of their loins. Thomas did not need their needling remarks on *that* score.

He sighed, gathering his courage for the coming encounter with the daughter of Svein Skullcrusher, betrothed of Ivar Wolfson, and fair Valkyrie of the North. With an absent wave to his friends, he headed for her tent.

"What?" hissed the fair Valkyrie of the North. "I will do no such thing!"

She was not taking his news well, Thomas decided. Not well at all. He repeated his words patiently. "I have come to tell you that I am the emissary from Ivar Wolfson, of Dubh Linn. I have come to take you back to him to be married."

Yngveld pointed to the tattered remnant of her tent flap. "Out! she order. "And do not come back!"

Thomas bowed and stepped out of the tent,

his teeth biting the soft inside of his cheek to keep from laughing.

Seeing that he had quietly obeyed her command reassured Yngveld somewhat that the man was not completely mad. She poked her head out of the tent and demanded, "Are you a berserker?"

Thomas looked at her with bewilderment, then slowly shook his head.

"Strange," she said, "I would have thought you were. Sometimes they are a little odd," and she tapped her temple significantly.

Thomas frowned. Dirk the Dane and Ingolf were berserkers, and outside of battle they were decent enough fellows. In battle, 'twas a different story. Then they acted like invincible crazy men, naked, twisting, leaping and writhing with sword in hand and hacking at the enemy. He himself had never had the strange mood come upon him—'twas said to be a gift from Odinn and Odinn's protection came with it. Thomas was not certain that he would ever want such a gift, but he saw no reason to disparage it, as the wench was doing.

Seeing his frown, Yngveld added, "My father was a berserker, and in his later years he acted and said things most strange." She saw Thomas's bewildered look. "As you are doing now!"

Thomas scratched his head. "I see nothing strange about explaining to you who I am. Surely you received Ivar's missive two years ago telling you that I would arrive."

"I know nothing of any emissary, any missive, any Ivar! You are clearly, without a doubt, mad!"

The man obviously was mad. Most unfortunate because he was so devastatingly handsome—but mad nonetheless. She swung around and presented her back to him, just in case he should stay at the tent entrance.

"Yngveld?"

She tapped her foot impatiently as though she could not wait for him to leave. Thomas smiled to himself, feet planted apart, arms across his chest as he waited for her to turn around and face him.

"Yngveld?"

Tap, tap, tap.

"Yngveld, I am not going to disppear just because you want me to."

Reluctantly, she swung around. "Will you please leave?" She tried to speak gently; she must keep him calm. "I do not know any Ivar Wolfson, I do not know of any missives. Please, *go*."

But Thomas stood there, an obdurate stump on her doorstep.

When she saw that he would not leave, Yngveld decided to take a different approach. After all, the man was bigger than she, stronger, too, and the rest of his men seemed to think he was in his right mind—that is, no one had yet run up to him and dragged him away. So, trying to keep a calm demeanor, though her heart was pounding and her palms sweating, she said cautiously, "When did you first get this idea?"

At his blank look, she explained, "The idea that I am to marry this—this Ivar Wolfson." She tried to keep an impassive look on her face; 'twould not do to rile the man.

Thomas watched her out of amused eyes. She thought he was daft. He could see it in her manner, in her gentle, new, slow way of speaking to him. As one would speak to an idiot.

"Yngveld," he said, just as slowly. "Let me start at the beginning." And he did.

When he had finished telling her about Ivar Wolfson, about sailing to Greenland, about the betrayal of Bjarni, Yngveld found herself tongue-tied. She sat down on deck in front of her tent because she knew her legs would no longer support her.

"So you see," Thomas was saying, "now that I have discovered that you are Yngveld Sveinsdatter, the woman I was sent to fetch for Ivar—well, there is nothing for me to do but release you from our former—uh, agreement."

"You mean my slavery, do you not?" she inquired archly. Thomas coughed, and Yngveld watched in surprise as he flushed under that glorious bronze. So the man had a conscience after all. Then quickly, before he could change his mind, she snapped, "Done. I will accept release from our—uh, agreement."

Thomas nodded, wanting to get past that delicate subject. Were Ivar to discover that Thomas had enslaved his betrothed—well, Thomas did not care to imagine his commander's rage.

But Yngveld was not done. "I do not know Ivar Wolfson. I have not heard of him."

"Think," pleaded Thomas. "Did your father never mention him? Ivar said that your father and he were comrades-in-arms many years ago."

Yngveld frowned thoughtfully, casting her mind back over the years. Her father's old fighting comrade . . . She tapped her chin with one forefinger. "*Nej*," she admitted at last. "I remember nothing."

At Thomas's disappointed look she added, "Mayhap later 'twill come to me."

"Mayhap," agreed Thomas, but there was no hope in his voice.

"Thomas," Yngveld said gently, "whether I remember the man or no, the question remains, why should I want to go and marry a perfect stranger?"

"Oh, you would like Ivar," assured Thomas. He looked at Yngveld thoughtfully, his eyes roving over her slightly turned-up nose and the graceful arch of her brows as he wondered what she would want in a husband.

"Ivar is rich." Thomas was doing an admirable job of keeping his face impassive. "He wants for nothing. Ivar has brought back many valuable articles from his travels in the east and he has wealth aplenty."

There, that should impress her. But to his chagrin, Yngveld yawned.

"Ivar is strong and healthy," Thomas volunteered.

Yngveld nodded, but her face showed only polite interest.

"Some women consider him handsome," he added.

Yngveld perked up a little at that, he thought. "And he is a brave fighter, commander of the full garrison at Dubh Linn. He has hundreds of men under him, good tough fighters, all. Why, he even has four bodyguards, so precious does King Sitric Silkenbeard consider him to be to Dubh Linn's security."

"Four bodyguards. And you are one of them, you said."

"Aye." Thomas fell silent for a moment, suddenly feeling like a fool in pressing another man's suit with a beautiful woman. Damnation! If only Ivar were here to do the job himself. He could be the one to say the sweet, honeyed words needed to convince this woman to marry him. Thomas merely felt like an awkward fool.

He watched Yngveld's lovely face in an unguarded moment and saw the fear there. "There is nothing to be afraid of," he tried to reassure her. "Ivar is a good man. He would not hurt you."

"Does he . . . like women?"

"I will say he does! Why, he has had Jasmine and any number of—" Too late the words were out and Thomas tried to stop, tried to turn her from the anger he saw gathering suddenly in that sky-blue gaze.

"Jasmine?" she said softly. "And . . . and others?"

"Aye," said Thomas shortly. He felt thoroughly miserable, as though he had somehow betrayed Ivar and yet all he had done was tell the truth. Many men had wives and concubines and worried not about what they thought. But mayhap 'twas the wounded look in those lovely eyes staring at him that caused that guilty feeling. "Well," Thomas said lamely, trying to repair the damage he had done, "at least Ivar is kind to women."

"Kind?"

Thomas nodded. "Generous. He—he gives gifts—"

"To Jasmine?"

Thomas nodded bleakly.

"And others?"

Another nod.

"I see."

That was what Thomas feared. That she saw only too well. " 'Tis not as it sounds," he tried, but she held up a hand to stop his flow of words.

"I must think on it," she said and retreated to her tent.

"Mayhap he will want only one wife," said Thomas encouragingly to her graceful back and bowed head. The minute the words were out, he wanted to call them back. Ivar was a lusty man. One woman had never satisfied him.

"Mayhap." But her voice did not hold an abundance of hope, he noticed. He sighed, feeling like a bumbling fool in presenting Ivar's suit. He turned to walk away, only to be brought up short by her voice.

"Thomas, tell me. Do I have a choice in whether to marry this Ivar?"

Thomas green gaze met Yngveld's, and for a moment he hesitated. She thought she saw a softness, a gentleness. Then his eyes hardened and he shook his head. "*Nej*," he said.

She looked at him with eyes deep and knowing. " 'Tis as I thought, then," she said softly. "I have but traded one slavery for another."

Thomas swore and swung around and marched down the planks, away from the little tent and the sad woman in it. "Damn you, Ivar, why could you not pursue your own woman?" he demanded, shaking a fist at the sea. "And why could *she* not be mine?" he whispered.

Chapter Nineteen

Godthab District, Greenland

Yngveld stared at the steep hillside that towered above the waters of the fjord. She took a step backward on the deck of *Raven's Daughter* and let two of the brawny Irishmen pass by. They were obviously eager to set foot on land once more but she herself could summon little enthusiasm for the visit. 'Twas too disheartening to see Greenland again. She thought she had escaped it, and Bjarni Bearhunter, once and for all. But now she was back.

Yngveld glanced stealthily toward Thomas Lachlann. Though he appeared to be deep in conversation with Neill and Torgils, at first she had thought he was staring at her. Then she saw him shift slightly and deduced that he was intently engaged in the conversation, his full attention upon what Neill was telling him. Disappointment surged through her and she turned away to stare unseeing at the steep shore.

Ever since he had told her that he planned to take her to Ireland to marry Ivar Wolfson, Thomas had ignored her. Not once had she caught those fierce green eyes upon her as she had done so many times earlier in the voyage. He was keeping his distance from her now.

Listlessly, for want of anything else to do, Yngveld stabbed one big toe at an oaken plank, her face downcast, her little sack of belongings over one shoulder. The Irishmen were stopping to get fresh supplies; she had overheard the men talking amongst themselves. She would just as soon stay on the ship, but Torgils had informed her earlier that Thomas expected her to leave the ship with them. Six Irishmen were to be left to guard *Raven's Daughter* and the four Greenlanders who were tied up and sitting sullenly on deck in the hot sun.

"Yngveld!"

She swung round at the sound of her name.

"Karl." She nodded. Karl had become a recluse on the voyage, ever since he had become Patrick's slave. Whenever she had seen him these past days he had looked sad and mournful. Now he looked more alert, but wary. " 'Tis good to see the old country once more, is it not?"

Yngveld shook her head. "Where is Patrick?"

A shadow crossed Karl's face. "He is in the tent." Karl glanced uneasily in that direction and lowered his voice. "Have you noticed how Patrick has changed?"

Curious, Yngveld waited.

Karl stepped closer. "I cannot take it, Yngveld. I am going to escape him."

Yngveld looked at him in shock. "Whatever do you mean?"

"He—" Karl paused and shook his head. "He is not the man he used to be. I cannot tell you. . . ."

"Try," she whispered urgently. Karl's face looked tired, his eyes sunken. Her heart squeezed painfully at seeing this old friend of her father's so agitated. Why, he was positively wringing his hands.

"When I was his owner," said Karl, "I was kind. When I had a little food, we both shared it. When work needed to be done, we both did it." He frowned seriously in the direction of the tent. "But Patrick is not like that to me now."

Yngveld felt bewildered. "Does he beat you?" she asked. "Hurt you?"

Hastily Karl shook his head. "*Nej, nej,* 'tis not that. 'Tis that I cannot . . . stand his contempt."

"Why would he be contemptuous of you?"

"I know not. But he is. And when he looks at me, 'tis often a look of hate." Karl glanced over to where crew members where climbing steps cut in the steep rocky slope of the fjord. "Methinks he has hated me all these years, years when I thought him calm and unruffled and accepting of his lot, years when we shared board and bed. . . ." He glanced hastily at Yngveld to see how she took his words.

"I have long known how it is with you and Patrick," she said gently. Then she frowned, "Mayhap you angered him somehow when he was your thrall."

"I have asked him. He cannot name a time or place or event where I hurt him. 'Tis all of it, he says. The thralldom. Says he is glad that now I know what 'tis like being a slave. Oh, I can tell you, he is very bitter."

Yngveld reflected silently. "I know not what to say, Karl," she said at last. "If you think that 'tis best to escape, then go. I will not tell the Irishmen." She glanced at Thomas in time to see his eyes slant away from her. "I will certainly never tell *that* one."

Karl nodded. "I wanted you to know," he said. "I trust you will not tell Patrick?"

Yngveld shook her head, her lips tight.

Karl nodded hastily. "Very good, then. Well, I must be off."

"Here?" Yngveld was astounded that he would bolt in the full light of day. "Now?"

Karl smiled with trembling lips. "I must go." And he was off, stepping onto the long plank that slanted between the ship and the slope of the land.

"Come back here!" came a cry just as Karl reached the end of the plank. He turned once to see who had called out, then started running.

"Seize him! Seize him!" cried Patrick, running to the side of the ship and pointing at the fleeing Karl. "Escaped slave!"

Several of the Irishmen halted to see what all the shouting was about. One of them chased Karl and grabbed him by the scruff of the neck. Patrick went running up the slope until he reached the two. Yngveld could not hear what he said to them both, but she watched as the Irishman dragged Karl back to the ship. Patrick disappeared only to reappear moments later holding a thick walrus-hide rope. She watched in horror as Patrick knotted it about Karl's neck and then took up the end in his hand. Why, Karl looked like an animal on a leash!

For a moment, Yngveld thought she detected a fleeting, tortured look on Patrick's face. Then it was gone, to be replaced by a cruel smile. She watched, numb, as they crossed the gangplank and scrambled up the steep side of the fjord. Several times Karl slipped on the slick shale. Whenever he faltered, Patrick yanked on the leash, dragging Karl after him. They headed in the direction of Karl's old homestead.

Yngveld turned away, sickened. How humiliating for poor Karl. And how she pitied Patrick. She shook her head. It would have been better if they had never left Greenland with her, she thought. That it should come to this between them!

Her morose thoughts were interrupted by a deep voice. "Are you ready, my lady?" Thomas held out an arm, but Yngveld turned away, refusing to take it. Thomas dropped his arm and leaned instead on one hip. "Very well, we go." He led the way down the gangplank and she followed, taking dainty steps along the narrow plank. She felt a sudden desire to sneak up behind him and push him into the deep, cold water, but she squelched the impulse.

Thomas waited for her on the rocky slope. Lord, but she looked beautiful this day. There was a clearness to her skin that he had never noticed ere this. And those eyes! He had seen their luster when she had sent him a flashing blue look just before she had refused his help. He could feel his manhood stirring as he watched her graceful form cross the gangplank. How he wanted her!

He reached for her hand to aid her that one last step onto the moss-coated rock. She let him hold her hand for only a second, but 'twas enough for him to give a little squeeze. She flushed, and turned away.

He gazed down at her blond head and thought to himself, *I must remember that she belongs to another*. But by Thor, 'twas difficult. Something about her cried out to him, and he wanted nothing so much as to pick her up in his arms and march back across the gangplank, lay her down in her tent, and have his way with her. But of course, he could not. She was Ivar's.

In anger, he started up the steep hill and his voice came out harshly. "See that you do not lag."

Yngveld fell into step behind him, wondering at his sudden surly tone.

They reached Einar's only to find that he was not in. Several of his slaves were there, and one of them eagerly told Thomas that if he wanted to do business with the master, he would find him at Bjarni Bearhunter's. The slave mistakenly read Thomas's wide grin to mean he was another of Einar's customers and he happily pointed Thomas to the east.

Yngveld opened her mouth to correct the slave. Bjarni's farm lay to the north. The slave had pointed to where her own farmstead lay. Then she snapped her mouth shut. So! Her farm was Bjarni Bearhunter's now, was it? Well, *she* would have something to say about that!

Yngveld followed the men, muttering to herself as she trod the narrow path to her old home.

They stopped at the top of the path. Below them stretched the fields and land that Yngveld and her father and servants had so rigorously farmed. She could see the farmhouse and her two goats eating the rich green grass on the roof. Anger washed over her at the thought that Bjarni had taken her home and the goats from her. 'Twas not right!

Thomas issued terse commands to his men, and they started forward. He jerked a thumb at Yngveld. The rude boor was telling her to stay with him. She wanted to snap at him, tell him that she was not one of his men to command, but then she glanced at her father's farmhouse and her shoulders slumped a little. Bjarni owned it now. Bjarni had taken it from her, and she could do nothing to get it back. She shot a black look at Thomas's back. What did he care about Yngveld and her land? Nothing. All he wanted was to marry her off to his military commander. She trudged along, fuming in tense silence.

They reached the yard and Thomas signaled her to stand next to the outbuilding that housed the goats. The look on his ruthless features indicated that he would brook no disobedience to his order. With a sigh, Yngveld crossed her arms and took up a position where she could watch the front door of the house. She tapped her foot impatiently, her only way of letting Thomas know of her displeasure at being forced to miss whatever was about to take place. She wondered why he did not just march into the house, speak with Einar and Bjarni, and be done with it. Surely getting supplies could not be this complicated!

Thomas and his men entered the house and Yngveld heard one sharp yelp, a scream, several gasps—then nothing more. Glancing cautiously about the yard, she determined that she was alone. She tightened her lips and took a breath. She tiptoed across the yard and pressed herself up against the side of the dirt house next to an opening that served as a window. She could hear Thomas's voice and Einar's and Bjärni's but she was too far away to hear what was being said. Carefully, she peeked into the window and gasped.

Three men lay dead on the floor of the main room. A panting, sweating Bjarni Bearhunter was on his knees with Thomas's sword at his throat, and Einar, gasping, lay flat on his back staring up the blade of Torgils' weapon. Without pausing to think, Yngveld ran to the door and darted into the crowded dwelling. Bjarni, slumped sullenly on his knees, grasped his right forearm; his sword lay on the floor beside him. 'Twas obvious that someone, no doubt Thomas Lachlann, had hacked it out of his hand.

Yngveld ran up to Thomas. "What is the meaning of this?" she gasped, her eyes darting from him to the dead men and the two on the floor.

"Yngveld? Yngveld, is that you?" cried Einar.

He looked dirty, she saw, as though his great walrus body had been wrestled to the dirt floor. She could see the clean streaks where tears had run down his puffy face.

When he saw that it was indeed Yngveld, he heaved himself in her direction. "For the love of God, Yngveld, do something!" he wailed piteously. "He's going to kill me!"

Torgils placed a foot in his face and kicked. "Get back, oaf!"

Yngveld recoiled a step, then turned a flashing look upon Thomas. "What is the meaning of this, sir!"

Thomas grinned at her. "Unfinished business."

"Yngveld! For the love of your father!" implored Einar. "He was my friend. Do not let them kill me!" He struggled to his knees, then shuffled toward her, hands out in supplication.

Yngveld felt a wave of distaste run through her at Einar's groveling. That he should call upon her father's memory disgusted her. Einar had been only too happy to cheat her father whilst he was alive. As he had cheated *her* on the high price of the ship.

But despite her disgust, she could not let him be murdered right before her very eyes. She cast a quick glance at Bjarni, who stared right back at her, a crafty look on his blunt face.

Touching Thomas's sleeve, Yngveld asked, "What—what do you plan to do with them?"

"What do you suggest?" answered Thomas playfully. Then, before she could answer, he said, "Bjarni here, is treacherous, too treacherous to live, methinks. And Einar—why, Einar, enjoyed putting the chains on us, did you not, Einar?"

Einar shook his head quickly, the fat on his neck shaking.

"And he sold us like meat." Thomas's grin had disappeared. "So he dies, too." He fixed the two culprits with a steely glare, and Yngveld had no doubt that she was witnessing Einar's and Bjarni's last moments upon this earth.

"Wait!" she cried, her thoughts racing. Oh, what could she say that would make him spare them? True, they were dishonest and cruel, but to cut them down like this—'twas too horrible!

Thomas turned to her. "Why do you beg for them?" he asked in anger. "Bjarni has stolen your farm, Einar cheated you for gold. Why in

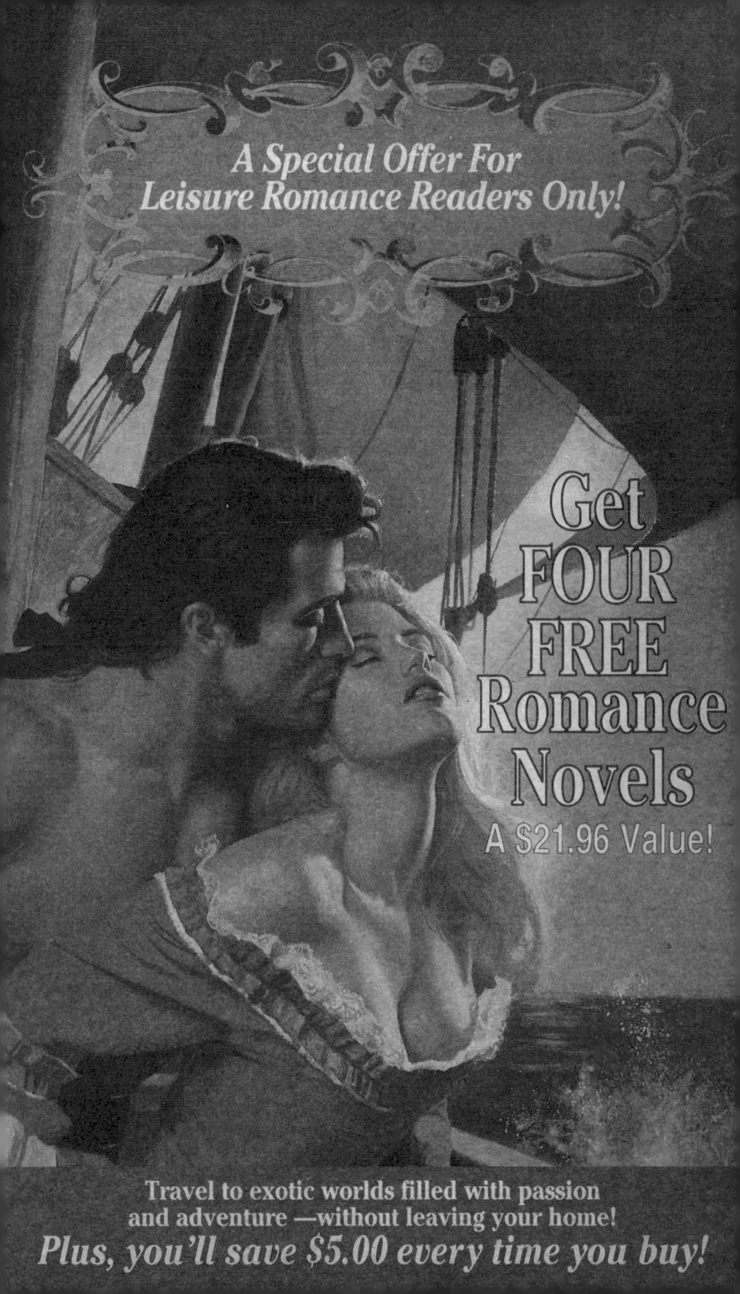
A Special Offer For
Leisure Romance Readers Only!
Get
FOUR
FREE
Romance
Novels
A $21.96 Value!
Travel to exotic worlds filled with passion
and adventure —without leaving your home!
Plus, you'll save $5.00 every time you buy!

Thor's name do you plead for them?"

But he saw those blue eyes widen and knew he could refuse her nothing—nay, not even the lives of this miserable, treacherous pair.

Yngveld choked, the words not able to come. Oh, what could she say? Suddenly she gasped, "What about the supplies, the food? Take what you need of Einar's. Only let him live!" She had known him since childhood. *Ja*, he was deceitful, but pitiful, too.

Einar was clutching at Thomas' knees. "*Ja, ja*, take the food. Take supplies. Take whatever you want. Only spare me!"

Thomas jaw clenched and he poked at Einar with the blade of his sword as though Einar was a slimy sea creature to be kept at bay. Einar fell back, a tiny drop of blood oozing from his shoulder where the blade had punctured the plump white skin.

Bjarni snorted in disgust at the frantic ravings of his fellow conspirator.

"You are silent, Bjarni Bearhunter," observed Thomas, turning to him. "Are you not moved to beg and plead for your life?"

"Will it do any good?"

"*Nej*." Thomas' voice was deadly.

Yngveld looked at Bjarni's impassive face, secretly impressed that he did not cower in fear like Einar. "What about Bjarni?" she asked hoarsely. "Will you spare him?"

Thomas turned from Bjarni's narrowed eyes to Yngveld's wide ones. "Is there anything you want of Bjarni?" he asked softly. "Ask, and if it is in my power to make him give it to you, 'twill be done."

Yngveld's blue stare met Bjarni's malevolent one. He hated her, she thought. Waves of hate emanated from him, she could feel it. But there was something else too—fear. She could almost smell it.

"She was to be my wife," snarled Bjarni.

"You did not want me," cried Yngveld. "You wanted my land!"

Bjarni spat. "I do not want you now—Now that you have been used by an Irish slave!" Disgust rippled across his florid countenance.

But his disgust was no match for Thomas's. "Get up," he snarled. "You do not speak to Yngveld Sveinsdatter that way and live!"

Bjarni got shakily to his feet. He looked wider than Thomas, but mayhap 'twas the thick hide coat he wore. Thomas towered over him.

Thomas kicked Bjarni's sword. It skittered across the floor to him. "We fight to the death for the insult to Lady Yngveld. Prepare to die."

"*Nej!*" shrieked Yngveld, throwing herself at Thomas. Her hands splayed across his naked chest as she clutched at him.

His eyes never leaving Bjarni's sneering face, Thomas shoved her aside. "Be silent, woman. 'Tis my choice now, not yours!"

Torgils caught her and held her. His tight grip on her wrist told her 'twould be foolish to try to stop Thomas again.

Bjarni swayed a little. Thomas saw the blood running down his opponent's sword arm and cast his own sword aside. "I will match you," he said. "Your wound and sword against my bare hands."

Bjarni smiled then, a wicked, cruel smile. "Fool," he growled.

Torgils laughed. "We will see who is the fool," he snorted. But Yngveld winced as his hand on her wrist tightened.

Bjarni lunged for Thomas. Thomas leaped to one side, then swung to face Bjarni, arms up, legs in a crouching stance. Bjarni lifted his heavy sword and brought it down to bash Thomas across the head. But Thomas was not there. He was a whirling blur and now behind Bjarni. With a leap, he kicked Bjarni in the back. Bjarni collapsed on the floor, and Thomas swooped up his sword. "Child's play," he panted, blowing on the blade of the weapon. Heavier and clumsier than his own sword, it could still cleave a man's head from his neck. He flung it to one side and leaped for Bjarni's throat.

He had a grip on his struggling foe's neck, and Bjarni was turning purple when Yngveld shrieked, "*Nej!* Stop!"

Thomas glanced at her in time to see the look of horror on her lovely countenance. With one last savage squeeze, he got to his feet, throwing Bjarni away from him.

Bjarni's head bounced on the dirt floor, and then he lay still except for clutching his throat and sputtering. Gradually the purple faded until he was his normal florid color once more. "I could have killed you," he croaked at Thomas.

Thomas grinned. "You had your chance, my *friend*." His voice cut like the blade of his sword. "But how many more poor wretches will you deceive as you did me?" His eyes narrowed. "None, I will warrant."

Bjarni wiped his mouth with the back of one hand and blood from his wounded arm streaked across his cheek. He attempted to rise, but his leg had been injured in the fight and he collapsed. He cursed lividly.

Thomas turned to Yngveld. "Tell me, fair lady," he began conversationally. "What would you have me do with him?" Thomas lifted one inquiring black brow. "Or have you no plans for him? From your outcry, I assumed—"

"Assume nothing," she cut in. "I did not want you to kill him! That is all."

Thomas's face darkened. "He was to marry you, I understand. Have you a tender passion for him then?" He waited while she stared at him, open-mouthed. "If so, let me warn you that you are now betrothed to Ivar Wolfson and I will not allow—"

"You will allow nothing!" she screeched, outrage evident in every muscle of her body.

Torgils groaned and stepped away from her, a glint of amusement in his eyes that only Thomas caught.

"I am not yours to command! Did I want to marry the man, I would!"

Thomas' eyes glinted and narrowed. He walked over to her. "Am I to understand that you wish to marry this—this treacherous wretch?" Disbelief echoed through his voice.

Yngveld, tired of being told where she was to stand, where she was to go, and whom she was to marry, thought suddenly to push him. "And if I do, 'tis none of your business." In truth, the thought of marrying Bjarni Bearhunter fair turned her stomach, but she would not let the odious man in front of her know that. 'Twas enough that she was taking some power into her own hands. "I do not even know this Ivar Wolfson that you speak of! At least I know Bjarni!"

Bjarni, partly lying, partly kneeling on the floor, listened intently. Now, with Einar's faltering help, he crawled to his feet. "I might be persuaded to marry the wench," he conceded, a look of mingled triumph and greed upon his face.

Yngveld turned a withering stare upon him. "I do not want you," she said. "I never have."

Bjarni contrived to look wounded. "But Yngveld—"

"You, sir, are a murderer," she began.

Bjarni held up one hand to stop her words. "*Nej*, I did not—"

"You did. You were the last person seen with the thrall woman."

"The thrall woman?" Bjarni's blank look would have been comical were the topic not so serious. He hesitated, then waved a hand. "Oh, her."

Yngveld looked at him aghast. "You killed her, did you not?" she persisted.

"And what if I did? She was a nothing. No one missed her. Why, she was not even good in bed." He turned to Einar and they both laughed, as though sharing a good joke.

Yngveld was outraged. "I would never marry you," she said in a choking voice. She looked wildly around the room. Thomas was watching her, a calm look on his face, as though waiting to see what she would do next. Neill and Torgils and the men, were watching to. Suddenly an icy calm settled over Yngveld. She knew now how to make the situation work in her favor. "I demand my farm back!"

Bjarni, who had been having a little chuckle with Einar, stopped. With a scowl, he answered, "It is not yours." He glanced nervously at Thomas and his men to see if they believed his words.

Thomas stood with arms crossed and jaw clenched, waiting, his green eyes glittering. "Tell us more, Bjarni," he said softly, menacingly.

Bjarni swallowed. "'Tis mine. Svein Skull-crusher gave it to me."

"He did," piped up Einar.

Yngveld swung on them both. "Lies!" she cried.

"'Tis not," said Bjarni stoutly. Einar bobbed his head several times in agreement, and his jowls swayed with each movement.

Yngveld stood with hands on hips, eyes flashing fire. "I will not argue with you about this," she said with as much dignity as she could muster. "This is my farm, given to me by my deceased father. You took it from me." She held out a hand, palm up. "I demand that you pay me for it."

Bjarni began to laugh. Einar soon joined in with little chuckles.

"You are exceedingly confident for men so recently facing death," observed Thomas.

Einar's chuckles ceased, and Bjarni halted in mid-laugh. "Keep out of this," he said insolently.

Thomas took a step closer until he was face to face with Bjarni. "Does nothing frighten you, Bjarni Bearhunter?"

"*Nej*," answered Bjarni. "Nothing. And certainly not you." The tiny step he took back belied his words.

Thomas smiled and Yngveld shivered to see the ferocity in his face. "You would be wise to be afraid."

Bjarni glanced at the bloody body of one of his men where it lay off to one side. He shrugged. "Were you going to kill me, you would have done it ere now. As I am still standing, I assume you are only good for threats." Though his voice shook, he shot a smirk at Yngveld. "Methinks you will not kill me because *she* has asked you not to." His voice sounded more confident.

There was a small silence in the room.

Yngveld broke it. "Do not be too certain," she said coolly.

Bjarni looked at her, the smirk gone. "Yngveld?"

"I said, do not be too certain that I will protect you."

Bjarni glanced at Thomas, who was fingering his sword.

Torgils and Neill were smiling. " 'Twould not take much," growled Torgils. "I have not forgotten the lovely welcome party you arranged for us."

Thomas laughed. "Torgils loves revenge," he explained to Bjarni.

Bjarni swallowed. "Yngveld! You have known me a long time—"

"Too long."

"—and if you want me to marry you—"

"I do not."

"—then you must call off your dogs."

Thomas yawned. "I grow bored." He turned to Yngveld. "Shall we kill him?"

Yngveld faced Bjarni, liking the sudden surge of power that she felt. She felt grateful to Thomas for backing her like this. Holding out her hand once more, she said softly, "The gold, Bjarni. The gold to pay for this farm—"

"He does not have any," spoke up Einar from the floor.

"—or I will let Thomas and his men run you through."

Bjarni looked at her searchingly, obviously wondering if she meant what she said. At last, with a deep sigh, he slumped and reached into his tunic. He pulled out a heavy sack and Einar's eyes narrowed.

"*Nej!*" he cried. "Do not—"

Thomas' sword touched the thick folds of Einar's throat. "Silence," he said.

Bjarni pulled out five gold coins and threw them onto the hard-packed floor. They rolled in several directions. "That's for this pitiful farm," he snarled. " 'Tis nothing but rocks and gravel, no dirt—"

" 'Tis a good farm," said Yngveld firmly. "Else why steal it?"

Her logic was impeccable and Bjarni snapped his mouth shut.

Yngveld picked up the coins, her face flooding red. She clutched them to her chest.

"Is it a fair price, Yngveld?" asked Thomas softly.

She looked at him and wet her dry lips with her tongue. "I—I know not. I think 'tis."

Thomas nodded, and Bjarni started to tuck the sack back into his tunic, a small smile on his face. Einar, too, looked pleased.

"One moment," said Thomas. With the tip of his sword he plucked the sack by its drawstring from Bjarni's hand.

Bjarni stepped back as though burned, and fury leapt to his eyes. Einar howled.

Thomas smiled, his eyes icy. He tossed the sack carefully to Yngveld. "Methinks this would be a better price."

She caught the sack and the weight of it alarmed her. " 'Tis very heavy," she exclaimed, peeking into the contents. "Oh," she breathed. "Oh, my."

Bjarni looked livid. Einar's face was mottled in fury. "Give me back my money!" cried Bjarni.

"And mine!" echoed Einar.

"Consider it Danegild," growled Thomas. "You bought your lives with it. For the nonce."

They left then, Yngveld walking close to Thomas. She turned in the doorway to see the black looks upon Bjarni and Einar's faces.

"Come," said Thomas, dragging her away. "They got a good bargain. They retained their lives."

Yngveld looked up at him and smiled, the pouch of coins heavy in her hand. "My thanks," she said shyly. The triumph of besting Bjarni coursed through her. No longer was she penniless. No longer was she powerless. She had been paid for her land and there was a justice to it that suited her well. Very well indeed.

Thomas looked at her, his green eyes twinkling. Her face was flushed and she glowed; Lord, she was beautiful. Suddenly he longed to take her in his arms and hold her to him. To tell her that he wanted always to be there to protect her. *And love her*.

He pushed the treacherous thought away. She was Ivar's. He must not forget that. " 'Twould not do to bring you to Ivar without a dowry," he joked, trying to make light of his feelings, of his need for her.

The smile disappeared from Yngveld's face. He had not done it for her. He had been thinking of Ivar the whole time. And Ivar's rights.

"*Ja*," she said dully. "Ivar."

Chapter Twenty

Einar's house, thought Thomas in grim satisfaction, looked as if it had been ransacked by a band of thieves. Which of course it had. The rooms were empty of the great heaps of furniture that Einar had crowded them with. Clothes and cloth and pots and useless trinkets were scattered on the floor, all picked through and then discarded by the discerning eyes of the Irishmen who took only what they could sell in the teeming markets of Dubh Linn.

Thomas's men made several trips from the house to the ship, and now *Raven's Daughter* was a floating warehouse of Greenland artifacts. There was a huge polar bear skin, white in the middle, fading to yellow at the legs, that Thomas had torn off Einar's wall. Now it lay draped over six elaborately carved wooden chairs tied on deck.

There were two score tusks of walrus ivory, precious items that Thomas would get an excellent price for in the ivory-starved markets of Dubh Linn. And there was more furniture—carved wooden tables and polished wooden bed frames. Thomas surmised that, despite the expense and scarcity of wood in Greenland, Einar had commissioned the beautiful pieces and had hired master craftsmen to carve them—and now all to Thomas's profit!

There was a huge pile of seal skins that took seven men to load. Einar had obviously been saving up a great store of them for a trading voyage to Iceland or Norway. But now, thought Thomas with a grim smile, *he* would be the one to gain from Einar's diligence. He shrugged his broad shoulders. Einar was merely paying the price for throwing Thomas and his men in chains, and Thomas would waste no sympathy on the merchant.

They raided the outbuildings of Einar's farm too, bringing with them several sheep, great quantities of dried and smoked fish and caribou meat, bales of edible seaweed, baskets of corn, grain for porridge, dried fruit, and great pieces of cheese and butter. Yngveld's eyes rounded in amazement at the huge quantities of food carried past her onto the ship. She knew that thirty hungry men would soon eat their way through it, but still, the quantity was astounding.

Thomas watched in satisfaction as Torgils

staggered by carrying a bale of whalebone. Behind him came Neill, loaded down with soapstone bowls, another item much in demand in the Dubh Linn market. Along one side of the deck there were neat coils of walrus-hide ropes and lastly, near the bow, a bundle of that most elusive luxury of all—four twisted tusks of the narwhal which, upon reaching the Irish market, magically metamorphosed into unicorn horns.

Aye, he would be arriving in Dubh Linn in a ship laden with treasures, enough to make him and every member of his crew wealthy men. Thomas smiled. And all thanks to Einar—and Bjarni, of course.

He slanted a glance at Yngveld. She, too, had done well. The gold in that sack she carried at her waist would make her a wealthy woman by Irish standards. Ivar would have to treat her well when she came to him with a dowry so rich.

The smile faded from Thomas's face. He did not like to picture Yngveld with another man, even if 'twas Ivar. While Thomas did not regret helping Yngveld get the money owed to her for her farm, and he did know that the wisest use for the gold was as a dowry, still he did not like to think of Ivar claiming the money, for to claim the money was to claim the woman.

Thomas sighed. Loyalty was a strange thing, he mused. He had never known it to pain so. He had always given his loyalty, unquestioningly, with his sword arm—'twas expected that a man fighting for the Vikings would keep his word to his fellows. Not to the enemy, of course. To get inside a castle, or to board a ship, why, any promise made could be easily broken. 'Twas only your word to the enemy. But amongst one's fellows, especially the Vikings—that was different. A man was expected to keep his word, and honor was a highly prized quality in a man.

And Thomas had always been loyal. And honorable.

He stared at the blond woman who was watching the passing parade of goods. Strange how one small woman could make a man think of throwing over the very virtues that he had lived his whole adult life by.

When Thomas had first arrived in Dubh Linn, he was leading a spavined horse and clutching the single silver coin he had to his name. His father's filigree-handled sword was stuck in his waistband, and the warm cloak upon his back was his best garment. He had been a hunted man, on the run thanks to his half-brother Aelfred's murderous attempt on his life.

Then Ivar Wolfson had accepted Thomas as a soldier, and later gave him the position of bodyguard. With that post went respect, a decent living wage and a life not dependent on Aelfred's deadly whims. In short, Ivar had helped Thomas when he had needed help the most. And Thomas had repaid that help with steadfast loyalty, with honesty, and with the risk of his own life in battle. And now, for the first time, unbidden thoughts crept through Thomas's mind. Disloyal thoughts. Thoughts about what it would be like to take the fair Valkyrie and sail to another part of the world. And not to return with her to Dubh Linn.

Thomas tore his gaze from the subject of his thoughts. He must be going mad, he thought, to question his mission like this. What kind of a hold did she have on him? Had she bought his soul when she purchased his body? She must have, to make him question his loyalty to Ivar.

Teeth clenched, Thomas stared out to sea. Suddenly, he longed to be away from this place. Away from Greenland. Away from the cruel test to his loyalty. And away from *her*.

But alas, 'twas not possible. He would be seeing her every day on the ship. Watching her graceful form as she walked about the deck. Gazing at her as she cremated seal meat at her little fire. With a groan, he ran a hand through his tangled jet curls. Would that he had never accepted this mission. *Nej*, would that this voyage was over, his mission completed, the wench delivered to Ivar.

For 'twas with a sinking heart that he realized he faced a formidable battle with himself about what to do with Yngveld Sveinsdatter.

Yngveld stood at the rail by her little tent and watched the activity far into the twilight. The men had been loading the ship for hours and 'twas late, but she was too excited to sleep. The bleating of the nervous sheep would have kept her awake even if she had wished to sleep.

She wished now that she had thought to take

some of her dresses from her father's farmstead before she had left. Her hand absently sought the heavy leather sack at her waist, and she heard the dull clink of the gold. No matter, she decided. She would order many dresses to be made upon reaching Dubh Linn—beautiful new dresses, of every hue imaginable, and with jewelry to match.

She may not have a choice as to *who* she was going to marry—now her eyes flashed dangerously in the direction of Thomas—but she *did* have a choice as to what she would wear, by Thor! And she would not go to Ivar as a humble bride from the colonies, oh *nej*. She would go with dignity and pride, and wearing a beautiful dress. And he would know that he could not trifle with her. And he would love her. And he would rid himself of Jasmine and prefer her, Yngveld, to all others. . . .

Then, realizing the direction of her thoughts, that she was halfway to accepting the marriage being forced upon her, she blushed in the dusk. Had it come to this? Just because she had no home, nowhere to go, no kin but strangers in far-off Norway, was she now reduced to thinking that she must marry whatever man Thomas told her to?

Her blue eyes narrowed as she watched Thomas and several of his men lifting the heavy mainmast with sail attached, putting it in place for sailing. Thomas's corded arm muscles bulged with the heavy weight of the wood. His long muscular legs were planted firmly apart so he could better bear the weight. Sweat dripped from his brow, and wet dark curls framed his stern jaw. He concentrated completely on what he was doing, and she held her breath until the mast was plunked into place. She let out her breath then, not even realizing that she had been holding it.

Thomas wiped at his forehead with his hand. He turned then, swiftly, and his bright gaze impaled hers for the space of a heartbeat. Too late, she glanced away. She tightened her grip on the railing as her blush rose once again.

Yngveld's lips tightened in chagrin at being caught staring at him. Then she shrugged her shoulders, telling herself it mattered not. What was he to her? Why, nothing.

And *nej*, she was not yet reduced to such pitiful circumstances that she would marry the man *he* said she had to marry, some man she had never met, some man she had never even heard of! Why, Thomas Lachlann must think her a blithering idiot, a sheep easily led to the slaughter.

Her long fingers gently brushed the rough leather sack dangling at her waist, and a small smile played upon her lips. Now that she had the gold, she had a choice. Several choices, in fact. Once she arrived in Ireland, she could flee Thomas and go into hiding. Or, she could take ship for Norway. She could—what else could she do? Truly, she must think about this. Why, there were so many possibilities, her brain was befuddled as to which ones to consider. She would give it some time, she decided. *Ja*, that was it. She only needed some time to work out a plan of what she wanted to do next. She smiled to herself. She was young, she was rich, she was traveling to new lands. Something would occur to her, she knew it.

Her blue eyes scanned the deck, stopping at Patrick and Karl. She gazed at them curiously, wondering what they were up to now. The leash around Karl's neck kept getting in his way as he piled clothes and goods haphazardly into the tent. Evidently the two had returned from Karl's home laden with their possessions, possessions they had not had time to take with them the first time they had left Greenland. Patrick stood nearby, pointing out what he wanted done next. Karl looked redfaced and sullen and he muttered to himself. Patrick looked frustrated. Yngveld turned away, shaking her head.

And caught Thomas' glimmering eyes upon her. He strode over to her. His nostrils flared as he approached, and she swallowed.

"I trust that you are settled in well, Yngveld Sveinsdatter?"

The solicitous words were at odds with the hot look in his eyes. Yngveld clutched her gold, and stuck her chin out. "I am most settled," she stated confidently. There, let him see that she did not need his help, that she was not some bleating sheep. . . . She turned away, but he grasped her arm and spun her round to face him.

"Let go of me!"

He let go of her, gingerly, as though he thought she might bite. "I merely wanted to warn you."

Her gaze met his and she frowned. "Warn me?"

"Aye. The men are going to be celebrating tonight." He glanced around the deck and she followed his gaze.

"I am ordering you to stay in your tent. I do not want—"

"I do not care what you want!" she hissed. "I can think for myself. I do not need you to tell me what to do, or whom to marry!"

Thomas rocked back on his heels. "Ah, so that is it."

She faced him squarely. "*Ja*. That is it." *Careful,* she warned herself. *Do not let him know your plans too soon*. But she could not keep her anger down and the words tumbled out. "Who is this Ivar Wolfson? How do I know he even exists? How do I know this is not some plot of yours to take me to Ireland and then sell me as a thrall? I have only your word—"

"And it is not enough?" Thomas's voice was deepening in his anger. "You dare question me?"

"I do not know you! I only know that I bought you—"

"Ah, yes. You did. We must not forget that!" His jaw tightened as he remembered the humiliation. His grasp on her arm made her wince. "I am not likely to forget it, either, with you reminding me."

She was glad she had angered him, glad her words had hurt. "I owned you," she taunted, the words out before she could stop herself.

"Aye," he said coldly and the icy look in his eyes matched his voice. "And then I owned you." He took a step closer and lifted her chin with one strong brown finger. The hand grasping her arm loosened for a moment, then he was holding her waist, pulling her closer to him. "And aye, who is to say that you are not still my slave, that I have not lied to you to keep you quiet?"

His lips moved closer and for a moment she stopped breathing.

His warm breath on her lips made her heart jump frantically in her chest.

"Let me go," she whispered.

"No, I will not," he murmured back. He lowered his head until their lips touched. It was a searching, gentle kiss, at odds with the heaviness of his breathing and hers. Then he pressed forward, pulling her tightly up against him until she could feel his full arousal. She raised her hands to his broad chest to push him away, but he moved not a bit. His lips were harder on hers now, and his tongue was demanding entrance to her mouth.

Eyes wide, head pressed back on her neck, she pushed frantically at him. "Stop," she cried, but it came out as a muffled groan.

Which only served to entice him further. An answering groan from him caused her to close her eyes in despair. She felt him press against the length of her body and she shuddered.

Thomas felt her tremors and his tongue eagerly continued plundering her soft, open mouth. Plunging in and out of her in imitation of what he really wanted to do with her, Thomas held her until he felt her gradually go limp in his arms. Her surrender would be sweet, he knew. His hand came up the sides of her, searching for the fullness of her breasts. He pressed into her, his awareness centered on where their groins met. Ah, but she fit so well! He buried his face in her neck then, inhaling the warm scent of her. She smelled wonderful.

"Please . . ." she whispered weakly. "Please . . ."

But Yngveld could say nothing further and leaned into him, trying desperately to slow her breathing.

Then Thomas froze. He lifted his head and dropped his arms. He took a small step back from her. What in Thor's name had he been thinking of? She was Ivar's! Had always been Ivar's.

With trembling fingers, Thomas gently touched a strand of her hair and brought it slowly to his lips. "You had better go," he murmured, regret in his voice and in his green, green eyes as he gazed at her.

Yngveld lifted one hand to her swollen lips, her blue eyes heavy lidded and dark from passion. She looked at him, fear and desire warring in her gaze. Then, without a word, she whirled and fled to her tent.

Thomas watched her go with bleak eyes.

Chapter Twenty-one

They had left land some time ago. Left behind also were the four Greenlanders, set free with a gruff warning from Thomas. Yngveld breathed a sigh of relief at leaving behind Einar and Bjarni Bearhunter; she hoped never to see them again.

She stood on the deck of *Raven's Daughter* next to her tent, and relished the jerky bucking of the ship as it sailed over the choppy, gray-green sea. To her surprise, she realized that she was happy to be sailing away from Greenland once more. Whoever would have thought that Yngveld Sveinsdatter, a woman who had spent her girlhood and young womanhood on a landlocked farm, would grow to love the life aboard a sea-going vessel? Yet she already did.

The gentle rolling of the ship, the immensity of the blue sky, the endless gray expanse of sea, the fresh sea air that streamed past her nostrils—all of it held excitement for her, all of it heralded a wonderful new adventure. She was excited to be a part of this voyage. Not even the thought of marriage to Ivar at the end of her adventure bothered her at this moment.

She sniffed the tangy sea air. That was what she liked about the smell of the sea—'twas the smell of freedom!

But something was disturbing her wide sense of freedom. 'Twas the loud singing and roistering coming from various sections of the ship. Warily, she took a few cautious steps closer to her tent. Mayhap she should move into it as Thomas Lachlann had warned her. She glanced around the ship. Everywhere she looked, she could see men. Only ten were at the oars, five on each side of the ship. The rest were scattered in groups all over the ship. There were men singing drinking songs, men shouting insults at each other in the Viking tradition of insult contests, men with drinking horns raised to their lips, men staggering and falling about the deck, laughing and getting up and staggering some more.

Yngveld regarded the opening of her tent, glad suddenly that she had earlier repaired the rents in her doorflap. She wondered uneasily if one of the drunken fools would accidentally blunder into her tent. It was set back at the stern far enough that she should be in no danger, she tried to assure herself.

Still, she shot a questioning glance at Karl and Patrick's tent, wondering if she should seek shelter with them for the nonce. When she saw Patrick stagger out of his tent and scoop up a drink of ale from the barrel, she decided to stay where she was.

Then Karl, too, came out of the tent, staggering as he crossed the deck to join his new master at the ale barrel. Karl's neck leash dangled and swayed down the front of his tunic like a giant broken necklace.

Yngveld watched uneasily as Karl lifted his drinking horn in a silent, obsequious salute to Patrick. Karl's lips drew back in a feeble attempt to smile. Yngveld cringed inwardly when she saw Patrick return the smile, but coldly. Then Karl gave a massive hiccup, leaned forward, and threw the entire contents of his drinking horn directly into Patrick's shocked face.

Yngveld hurried back into her tent and let the flap fall closed behind her. It did not matter now that Thomas Lachlann had ordered her to keep to her tent—oh *nej*, now she saw for herself that 'twas the wisest thing to do after all. And she did not want to see what Karl and Patrick would do to each other next. She did not want to look at drunken, boisterous men a minute longer.

Unfortunately, her hearing was very keen, and her sharp ears soon detected small cries and harsh expletives coming from the direction of the ale barrel. With a sigh, she lifted her doorflap to see Patrick straining to push Karl over the side of the ship. With a small moan, she jumped to her feet and ran out of the tent.

"Patrick! Patrick! Stop!" She pulled frantically at Patrick's arms. He had Karl bent backward over the rail and had yanked one of Karl's legs off the deck. Karl had grasped the rail with both hands and his knuckles were white from his grip. He kicked at his master with his free leg.

"Stop! You must not do this!"

Yngveld's grasp on Patrick's arm was tight, but he shook Yngveld off like a harmless gnat as he let out a frustrated roar at Karl. Patrick's face was contorted in fury and red with exertion; Karl's was pale with fear.

"What is going on here?" Thomas Lachlann's deep voice invaded Yngveld's awareness.

Thomas strode up to her and she shuddered in relief that he was there. "Help me! We must stop them. He is going to drown Karl!"

Thomas shrugged. Yngveld reached out her hand to him. Then, when her gaze caught those blazing green eyes, her hand fell awkwardly. He was not going to help. She could see it in those bold, bright eyes.

Throwing herself into the midst of a drunken fight, thought Thomas in disgust. He had ordered her to stay in the tent! What was the matter with her? Did she never think of her own safety?

The two combatants, master and thrall, appeared to be doing little harm to each other.

In any event, Thomas was not concerned about them. They could kill each other for all he cared. 'Twas the woman he must watch, must protect.

He stepped between Yngveld and the struggling men. His big body blocked them from Yngveld's view. Thomas seared her with a scorching look. "I told you to stay in your tent." His hands clenched into fists at his side. Had he not seen her in time—why, she could have been dragged off by some of his men, violated, her broken body left in some dark corner of the ship, and he would have been none the wiser.

Yngveld darted her head to one side to see what Patrick was doing to Karl now. But in the intervening seconds, Karl had managed to get Patrick bent over in a headlock and was now drumming enthusiastically on his ribs with a fist. Yngveld bit her lip. The two looked evenly matched.

Thomas stepped in front of her once more, his green eyes raking her. "Get back to your tent."

Why was he so angry? "But Karl, Patrick—"

"Leave them. Let them fight. Do you not know any better than to throw yourself into the middle of brawling men? You could get hurt!"

Yngveld was still biting her lip in agitation. "You do not understand! Karl was my father's friend. It is all my fault that he has come to this. If he had not come away from Greenland and tried to help me . . ." She turned away, guilt strong upon her.

Thomas swung her back to face him. "The problems between those two were born long afore they left Greenland with you. 'Tis between them, not you. Let it go."

His green gaze was hot and mesmerizing. She swallowed, her eyes holding his until she desperately tore them away from his ruthless features. "I—I know not what to think" . . . *when you look at me like that.*

In truth, she had forgotten about the brawling men and was aware only of Thomas—his scent, his broad, naked chest, his blatant aura of *maleness*. She could not think with the man so close to her. She should hate him, or at the least be furious with him. He was taking her to a man she did not know, and marrying her off against her will.

He was pompous, arrogant—and oh, so handsome. She peeked at him just once. A nerve jerked in his cheek as those glittering green eyes stared boldly right back at her.

She could feel her cheeks flush. Her eyes fell upon Patrick and Karl once more and she gave a start of surprise. She had forgotten all about them. Patrick was bent against the rail, and Karl swayed beside him. Neither appeared much damaged. She slumped in relief, whether 'twas because of the end of the fight or because she had something else to look at besides those bold, glittering eyes, she did not know. "They—they have stopped," she murmured.

Thomas caught the direction of her gaze and turned. "Aye. And now, get you back to your tent. The celebrating has only begun."

She took a step away.

"Yngveld."

She paused in mid-step, keeping her back to him, not wanting to turn around, not wanting to see that bright, bold gaze sweeping her body.

His voice came to her, harsh and deep. "I cannot be with you, to protect you the whole night. I have a ship to sail. But know this, do you stay in your tent. I will not have you beaten or raped."

"Beaten? Raped?" she cried. "Surely they would not—"

"They are men," he said simply. "Fighting men. Hardened, desperate men at times. They work hard and play hard. You are the only woman on this ship. These are men used to taking any woman that catches their eye, if they can get away with it. And the ale just makes it worse. I cannot run the ship and guard you too. Stay in your tent."

She knew he was watching her. But still she kept her back to him. She would not give him the satisfaction of seeing her fear. Without another word, she flounced to her tent.

Thomas stared after her for a long moment, his burning eyes following the sway of her hips. Then, with a wicked oath, he swung away, punching one rock-hard fist into the open palm of his other hand. If only she were not so beautiful. If only she were not so desirable. If only she were not destined for Ivar!

He stalked away, ignoring the swaying, staggering pair in his path. Arms around each other, their singing sounding like the caterwauling of sick wolves, Patrick and Karl wove their way across the deck, stopping now and then to lift their drinking horns high.

With a growl, Thomas pushed past them and seized the tiller from Neill's grip. Neill shot him a look of surprise, but seeing the dark look upon his friend's face, forbore from questioning him. Besides, he had seen Thomas at Yngveld's tent and guessed the reason for his captain's ill-humor.

Neill rubbed the scar across his cheek thoughtfully as he ambled over to the ale barrel. If what he suspected was happening to his battle-hardened confederate was in fact happening, then Thomas was in for a very difficult time. Neill knew Ivar Wolfson, and he knew Thomas Lachlann, and he also knew that neither one of them would ever back down on what he wanted. And Neill strongly suspected that now they both wanted the same woman.

Chapter Twenty-two

Yngveld was plastered up against the side of a madly plunging ship. A furious storm lashed the vessel as she clutched the railing, fearing at any moment that she would be thrown into the swirling depths. She could see the huge black shapes of sea monsters roiling under the surface of the water from where she cringed on deck. She looked to where her father stood at the tiller, his long white shock of hair blowing wildly about his face. She barely recognized him. And now, out of the darkness of the storm, came a second ship, its proudly curved prow on a collision course with the ship that she and her father stood upon. "*Nej,*" she screamed. "*Nej!*"

But still the second ship came on. 'Twas closer now, close enough that she could discern the ruthless, laughing figure of Thomas Lachlann leaning over the bow. He beckoned her. She wanted to go to him, but something froze her.

She raised stricken eyes to the huge figure that suddenly loomed behind Thomas. 'Twas Odinn, she recognized instantly, the one-eyed Norse god of war. Odinn's great red mouth opened in a cruel, soundless, slathering laugh. Between his great clenched fists strained a strong rope, knotted for hanging. And then, while Yngveld's horrified eyes were riveted upon Odinn, her father suddenly seized her from behind, lifted her high over his head and hurled her into the waves between the two ships.

Yngveld plunged down, down, down through the sea's cold green depths. A twisting black sea monster grazed her leg and she recoiled from the cold, rough feeling of its scaly hide. Her heart pounded; her lungs were about to burst. Then, just as her life's breath was escaping bubble by bubble, she awoke.

Yngveld shuddered as she lay in her damp bedclothes. The powerful, frightening dream had seemed so real—as real as the fingers she now fluttered in front of her eyes to determine that she was, in fact, awake. Blankets were entangled around her long legs; her forehead and torso were drenched with sweat. The dream. Was it an omen? What did it mean?

Trembling, she hastily donned her long tunic, then put on her armlets, bracelets, and heavy brooch pin. While she coiled her hair into a tidy knot at the base of her skull, her mind raced frantically, trying to make sense of the dream. Her father, though dead, had been very much alive aboard the dream ship. And Thomas, when he had reached for her, had wanted her, and oh, she had wanted him, too. Then, Odinn looming up behind Thomas, laughing with a hangman's rope. Her father had thrown her overboard as though she were but a sacrifice to appease the storm—or Odinn? And the sea monsters that she had feared had not hurt her, merely brushed by her. Oh, what did it mean?

Her bewildered brain could make little sense of the wispy images. Yet, try as she might all morning long to banish them, the images stayed with her, strong for all their apparent frailty. And when she glanced at Thomas Lachlann, standing at the tiller, it was with new, thoughtful eyes. In the dream, he had symbolized protection and desire. Her eyelashes fluttered closed as she pondered that thought. Desire. Did she desire Thomas? And what of her father? In her dream, her father was wicked, sacrificing her to the elements. Her real father would not have done that, would he? *Nej*, never, she assured herself. 'Twas almost, she thought, as if the dream were telling her that danger came from another direction, not one she had anticipated—not the sea monsters, not Thomas' desire for her, but something beyond him. Her father in fear of Odinn? She shook her head, her brain growing weary from trying to interpret the puzzle and at last, with a sigh, she set it aside.

She sat in the warm sun, eyes closed, her mood contemplative. The problem, she realized, was that she, Yngveld, had no plans for her life. Had never had any. She had not thought to question her father's plans for her, whatever they were. She had always assumed that he had wanted her to stay on the land and farm it. He had never really suggested she get married, now that she thought about it. He had always brushed the topic aside whenever she had brought it up—which was with waning frequency in the past few years. She had understood that he was not receptive to her marrying, but he had never said so in words. Now she wondered if it was because, as Thomas avowed, her father had already promised her to Ivar Wolfson. And if so, why had Svein Skullcrusher never told her? Had his occasional bouts of madness and rage also sapped his memory?

Her father's death had brought into sharp relief her lack of planning for her own life. To flee Bjarni Bearhunter for unknown relatives in Norway did not seem like such a sound plan now. At the time, 'twas the best she could come up with. *Nej*, she must think, she mused, upon what she, Yngveld, wanted for her life. Did she want to drift through her life, tossed here and there like a ship by the storms of chance? Or did she want to plan what she wanted to do? And would it do any good? If she had wanted something, if she had had plans of her own upon her father's death, would they not have all been for naught, anyway?

Gravely she reflected, oblivious to the groans and moans of men at the oars who suffered from having consumed vast amounts of ale the night before. As her head nodded in gentle time with the soft waves rocking the ship, and as the pleasant heat of the sun warmed her closed eyelids, Yngveld fell fast asleep.

She awoke to hear loud exclamations on deck. Sitting up, she looked about with dazed eyes. She blinked several times, and then stretched. Getting slowly to her feet, she stood staring at the men who crowded around something on deck. Most of the men had left the oars, and even Thomas Lachlann had deserted the tiller. She could see his tall form among the other men. She blushed and looked away. Then, her curiosity getting the better of her, she strolled over to halt behind Patrick and Karl. She peeked surreptitiously from behind their heads, finally standing on tiptoe as she strained to see what everyone was staring at. Yngveld could see nothing, but the men's excited comments drew her closer.

"Ever see anything like it?"

"Wot the hell is it?"

"Looks to be . . . Why, 'tis longer than a man is tall. . . ."

"Hell, 'tis longer than two men!"

"Look at those teeth! They could take a chunk out of a man!"

"Must be some kind of—"

"Fish! That's wot it is. Some kind of weird fishie."

"Nah, not a fish. 'Tis a sea monster. Look how long it is."

" 'Tis no sea monster. I have seen one of these before." Patrick stepped forward, careful to remain at some distance from whatever it was they were discussing. He had the full attention of the gaping Irishmen, and Yngveld too. One man used his sword to prod the long fleshy lump with fins that lay upon the deck.

"What is it, mon?"

"A Greenland shark, we call it." Patrick stared at the fish that lay where it had been flopped by the man who caught it. The shark looked as dazed as Yngveld felt. Or mayhaps it was asleep.

She brushed past some of the men, and they parted ranks to let her pass. Squatting down to get a better look at the fish, she crouched eyeball to eyeball with the strange creature. She saw that one of the shark's eyes was open and looking directly at her. The mouth was closed and she reached out to touch the creature.

Just then, the fish gave a half-hearted flop. Before she could move, Yngveld was grasped from behind and hauled up against Thomas Lachlann's hard frame. "Have you no sense, Yngveld Sveinsdatter?" he growled. "That creature looks as if it could swallow you whole and then ask for dessert!" Several of the men chuckled.

"These sharks have been known to attack whales," said Patrick softly.

Yngveld shuddered suddenly in Thomas's arms. The creature looked so sleepy. Surely 'twas not so dangerous?

"This fellow," continued Patrick, "is far from his hunting grounds. Usually these beasts are found under the ice in winter. Greenlanders do not catch many in the summer months."

The men looked at the fascinating fish and murmured amongst themselves.

"Are they good eating?" asked one of the men. There were several guffaws and comments.

"*Ja,*" spoke up Karl slyly. "Very good eating. Especially raw."

Patrick whirled on him. "You would like to see these men get sick, would you not? Think then that you would go free?"

Bewildered looks appeared among the crowd at this interchange.

"What mean you?" asked Torgils.

"I mean that should you eat the raw flesh of this creature, you would get very sick—shark sick!"

"Shark sick?" murmured several voices.

"Aye," said Patrick. " 'Tis like being drunk. The meat of this shark must always be boiled to cook the poison out of it. Otherwise, one can get sick to one's stomach." He glowered at Karl. "Not very funny. I will deal with you later."

Karl bowed his head, looking appropriately subdued at the threat. But Yngveld, watching the two, had a suspicion that things would not go any better for them even if they did discuss the matter later in privacy. Karl and Patrick had a way of thwarting each other that was inimitable, she decided.

"Give me a knife," cried a wag. "I want to get drunk again, just like last night!" There were several answering guffaws, but Yngveld noted that no one actually hacked off a piece of the now dead animal to eat.

She was relieved when the muscular arms holding her slackened. She stepped away from Thomas and would have run for her tent, but he gripped her arm. She turned angry blue eyes upon him. "Let me go, sir!"

Thomas watched her with hard eyes. When he had seen her crouching so close to the big shark, he had thought of nothing but her safety. Now it irritated him to see that she wanted nothing to do with him. "A fine thanks for saving your life," he needled, unable to help himself. He wanted to goad her, just a little. See the fire leap in her eyes, see the proud tilt of her head.

"Consider us even," she snarled. "I warmed you from your swim in the sea. And now you have saved me from the snapping jaws of death." She turned away.

Thomas still gripped her arm. She looked up at him, the flare of anger darkening her blue eyes. "Unhand me."

"That's not what I would like to do to you," he whispered low. The words were out before he could stop himself. He watched the color rise in her cheeks.

Yngveld stared into those ruthless green eyes watching her, waiting. As she watched, they suddenly warmed, and his gaze went hot. Her eyes widened to see the lust in his.

"You forget yourself," she answered carefully, slowly. "I am to marry Ivar Wolfson. Or have you forgotten so soon?" And with that, she yanked her arm from his suddenly loosened grip and stormed away.

He watched her go, cursing himself for forgetting. And for being so vulnerable to her blond beauty.

Chapter Twenty-three

Yngveld watched Thomas. She watched him through her lashes; she watched him through sidelong glances. She watched him when she thought he was not watching her. She was even watching his straight back one time when he stood at the ship's rail, legs splayed and answering nature's call. When she realized what he was doing, she blushed and turned away. She could not help it, she told herself guiltily; her eyes followed his every movement of their own accord.

She was watching him now as she stood near the rail of the ship. But then Thomas turned and nailed her with his ruthless gaze. His burning eyes lanced through her; he was a healthy male animal that suddenly scented the female's blatant interest.

Only her interest in him was not sexual, Yngveld assured herself. 'Twas merely that she was curious. Ever since she had dreamed about him, she had pondered his role in her life. The dream had distinctly told her that he was beckoning her to come with him. Yet, that image did not square with the facts. He wanted her to come with him, but it was so that he could present her to his military commander as a bride.

Mayhap the dream was a warning. Mayhap Thomas Lachlann had some insidious plan for her, something involving Odinn. She wondered idly if he were an Odinn worshipper. He did not look as she thought an Odinn worshipper should look, she thought critically. Her blue eyes roving his frame, talking in his finely chiselled lips, his flaring nostrils, those green ruthless eyes, the lock of dark curls that dangled over his forehead. Odinn worshippers were . . . well, they were fanatical men and women, relentless in their attempts to appease the harsh god of violent death. Odinn was capricious, in Yngveld's view. He would protect his worshippers in battle, send them into a frenzy, and freeze their enemies on the battlefield with a paralysis called 'battle-fetter,' but sooner or later inconstant Odinn would withdraw his protection, and the betrayed worshipper would be slain to join him and his Valkyries in Valhalla.

Yngveld did not find such a god trustworthy, for herself, but she was aware that others, especially berserkers and fighters, found Odinn's protection to their liking. And those who favored the dark arts—the seers, the sorcerers—they too worshipped Odinn.

How she wished now that her father had been more forthcoming about teaching her of the Norse gods, but he had mentioned the Norse deities only when pressed to do so. She remembered that Svein Skullcrusher had preferred Odinn in his youth, but she also remembered that he had spoken more often of Thor in the years just before his death.

Hammer-wielding Thor could send good or bad weather to farmers and seafarers. He was the guardian of justice and law. He fought off giant wolves, serpents, and dragons with his hammer blows and could be counted upon to fight evil in any shape. *Ja*, her father had definitely preferred Thor in his old age, now that she thought on it.

Yngveld sighed. 'Twas all too complicated. Like her life. When she was a girl, there had been naught for her but her father, taciturn at times, gruff and hearty at others. It had been a good life. She had never doubted his love for her, though in recent years, his madness and rages had come upon him more frequently. She had learned that when he was in the grip of one of his rages 'twas best for her to disappear.

At first, she had thought to hold him down, to help him with the strangeness, but he would kick and yell and see men who were not there—men she did not know, men whom he would fight with over and over in silent, sickening pantomime. And later, when she realized that his mind and body were fighting something beyond what she could see or help him with, she had crept away.

And so she would take one of the goats, usually Flowerface—Bent Horn, the male goat, was too cantankerous—and head up into the meadows, away from her father's frightful fits.

And with the goat she would wander the hillsides, feeling alone and with no home, even if 'twas for a short time. When they reached the high hillsides, she would sit upon a jagged rocky outcropping. Then Flowerface would come to her, and Yngveld would bury her face in the little goat's wiry, crisp coat and sob. Out of her would well up all the sadness, the hurt, the abandonment, the fear.

And 'twas there that the gift of her voice had come upon her.

She had lifted her voice to give vent to all the pain and grief and sorrow and fear, and what had come out of her throat was not an ugly, hideous noise as she had expected, but a high, sweet voice that had drifted over the hills and back to her and brought her solace. She could sing.

And then Flowerface would bury her head in Yngveld's lap and she would pat the faithful beast, and her voice would sound all the sweeter.

She would sing to Flowerface and to the bent scrub saplings that passed for trees in Greenland. She would sing to the sky and if necessary to the moon, if her father were in a long fit. And her voice would float over the meadow and the hills and the fjords and would come back to her and sound so sweet and mournful to her ears that she would cry at the sweetness of it. And when she had cried until she had no more tears left, she would sing again.

And so it went. 'Twas a way she had found that she could cope with the bewilderment and frustration she felt when her father would take such strange turns. She had done the only thing she could do at such times. She sang.

There was no one she could talk to about her father. The little farm that she and her father lived on was not that distant from others, and Karl Ketilson and Patrick lived fairly close by. Yet Yngveld found she could not confide in them her confusion and fear and shame about her father's strange moodiness, kindly though Karl and Patrick were.

And girls she had known since childhood had now grown up, married, and moved to farms at some distance, and were busy with their own families.

Her father's servants, both elderly now, were quiet and humble—aye, even respectful in their own way—but she did not count them as friends and could not bring herself to speak of her father's strangeness with them.

So there was no one in whom she could confide her troubles, no one to whom she could reveal her fears and shame about her father's strange behavior when the madness was upon him.

The servants, too, would hide from her

father's madness. And when they all returned to the little farmhouse, 'twould be as if naught had happened. They would not speak of it, and Svein himself never spoke of the strange moods that came upon him. Indeed, Yngveld wondered if he even remembered them or his actions during such times. And so Yngveld would shrug the incident off, though she thought that somewhere deep inside her mayhap she did not shrug it off so lightly.

And she knew too, that a dread lodged in her breast about what she would do the next time he acted thusly.

Now he was dead. She felt sorrow, regret, and something more. Guilty relief?

Musing on her memories, Yngveld began to sing. Softly at first, then, as she was caught up in the song, and her feelings, she sang with more volume, the rich notes floating up over the sea, curling around the sky and sweeping back down to the deck of the ship.

Around her, men stopped rowing, heads turning this way and that to locate the sound.

Thomas Lachlann, standing at the tiller, master of all he surveyed, suddenly froze. Chills ran up and down his spine at the sweetness, the purity, that he heard in that beautiful voice. Like one in a trance, he left the tiller and walked slowly over to where Yngveld was standing at the railing, singing.

Yngveld, eyes closed, voice soaring, finished the exquisite song on a long, triumphant note. When she opened her eyes, Thomas Lachlann was standing next to her.

"You truly are a Valkyrie," he said in hushed awe.

Yngveld smiled, able for the moment to look her fill at him. His words warmed her. Men went back to their rowing, and a thoughtful look appeared in Thomas's long-lashed eyes. "You sang of sadness," he said softly, "and yet 'twas the most beautiful sadness that I have ever heard. I did not know there could be beauty in sadness."

Yngveld shrugged. " 'Tis not so much the sadness that lends the beauty," she observed. " 'Tis the acceptance of the sadness. The knowing that 'twill not go away. The willingness to say, very well, you are here, Sorrow. What can I do with you? And for me"—she turned to watch the gray swells—"for me the answer is to sing."

"And then your sadness goes away?"

She shook her head. "*Nej*. It does not go away, but becomes, somehow, more bearable." She looked at him brightly, amused at his efforts to know why she sang. "Is it not like that for you?"

Now he shook his head. "*Nej*. 'Tis different." He looked out to sea for a while, then turned to look at her, a new look, a curiosity, in his eyes that she had not seen before. "And from what comes your sadness, sweet Valkyrie?"

Yngveld watched a seabird wheel away from the ship. "We must be near land," she observed. "Such birds do not fly far from land."

He nodded, silently accepting that she did not

want to speak of her sorrow.

Yngveld, perversely, feeling his acceptance, offered in a low voice, "My father died recently. On the night before I boarded this ship. 'Twas of him that I was thinking."

Thomas nodded. "The thought of my father, too, gives me pain." But his voice was cynical and cold.

"And you hate him?"

"You make much of what you hear in a man's voice," he said, neither confirming nor denying her guess.

"Voices do not lie. Words do, but voices do not."

Thomas looked at her, at the wisps of hair blowing gently from her cheeks. At the cerulean blue of her eyes. At her face, open and frank, one of the first times that he had seen her gentle like this. He cleared his throat. "I would have you sing for me, this eve. Would you do it?"

Supplication was in his voice. She nodded. "I will."

He smiled then. "Notice, I do not ask you to cook my meal for me, Yngveld Sveinsdatter," he admonished. "I ask only that you sing." He grinned, showing his even white teeth against the tan of his skin. "And no croaking."

They both laughed then. Yngveld watched him, his head thrown back, the tanned column of his throat strangely vulnerable to her. She heard his deep voice blend with her own higher one and she thought that they sounded lovely together.

Chapter Twenty-four

'Twas time for the evening meal. Yngveld leaned over the little square of deep sand where the cookfire burned. With fingers that shook she added a few more curls of firewood to the flames, then carefully placed cooking stones in the flames to heat. That done, she reached to take up the heavy iron pot used to boil water. Her hand slipped on the wet handle and the pot dropped to the deck, splashing cold water on the hem of her dress and narrowly missing her toes. She jumped back; her hands flew to her red cheeks in mortification at her clumsiness. A few of the rowers glanced her way, but she would not look at them. She bent and picked up the pot, walked to the water barrel and half-filled the pot once more, then returned to her cooking station at the stern, never once looking at the men, and especially not looking toward the tiller where she knew Thomas Lachlann stood.

There was no reason to be so nervous, she assured herself. 'Twas a common enough thing for her to be asked to sing. And 'twas not as if she was about to sing for the King of Norway, after all! Why, back home in the Godthab District, she had sometimes been asked to sing at gatherings during the harvest and in the winter. 'Twould be no different now. 'Twas a slightly different audience than she was used to, of course, one that she had not yet sung before, but still, 'twas not so different as all that. It certainly was not so different that her hands should be shaking as she sliced through the white slab of shark meat. Or that she should accidentally nick her finger with the blade.

She plunked the round hot stones that would bring the water to a boil into the pot. Then she carefully placed the shark meat in the hot water. When the shark meat was done, she used two long sticks to pull the boiled meat out of the water. She set it aside neatly on a platter.

Glancing up, she saw that her dinner companions, Karl and Patrick, had arrived. With a hesitant smile, she wondered if it had been a mistake to invite them. But in truth, she had thought she could not get through the evening otherwise. Even their companionship, bickering as they had been with each other of late, was welcome.

She glanced quickly toward the tiller and

then away as disappointment surged through her. 'Twas Neill at the tiller, not Thomas Lachlann.

She set her lips in what she hoped was a smile and indicated to her two guests to sit down. Patrick smiled and sat, yanking hard on Karl's leash to pull him down beside him on the deck. Karl half-fell, and landed in an undignified sprawl.

Patrick frowned.

Karl glowered.

Yngveld sighed. 'Twas going to be a long evening. Her mind flitted through numerous topics to find one of sufficient neutrality for discussion with the two men, but she need not have bothered. Patrick, it seemed, had something he wanted to speak about. "What are you going to do upon reaching Dubh Linn, Yngveld?"

Karl shot Patrick a nasty glare. " 'Tis no business of yours," he sneered.

For a moment, Yngveld was taken aback. What had happened to the slow-moving, slow-speaking Karl she had always known? Who was this angry stranger? " 'Tis not amiss," she defended Patrick hastily. "I do not mind telling him."

"Hmmph," grunted Karl, obviously in disgust, but whether at herself or Patrick, Yngveld could not tell. She settled herself down and placed the platter of cooked shark meat directly in front of her guests. She was careful to place the platter exactly between them, favoring neither the one nor the other.

Patrick helped himself first; his fingers were barely out of the way before Karl snatched a piece of fish. Karl began wolfing the hot meat down, and Yngveld watched him with something akin to amusement and worry. She chose her piece of shark meat with care, with as much care as she selected the words she was about to say. "I think you know that Thomas claims I am to be wed to a man called Ivar Wolfson."

Patrick and Karl nodded together, and Yngveld smiled secretly to see them agreeing on at least this one little thing. "I, however," she continued, "do not know this man. Nor have I ever heard of him."

She chewed her fish thoughtfully before asking, "Karl, didst ever you hear my father speak of him?"

Karl frowned and nodded. Yngveld stared at him. "You did?" 'Twas news to her and she wondered now why she had not thought to ask Karl sooner.

"*Ja.*" He shot an unreadable glance at Patrick and again Yngveld had the strange feeling that the two agreed suddenly about something, though they spoke no words.

"Tell me."

Karl watched her, and she felt suddenly that the old Karl was back and all was as it had been. " 'Twas after your father first arrived in Greenland. You were a tiny girl at the time."

Patrick said nothing, evidently content to let Karl speak, and Yngveld wondered uneasily what was to come.

"One of the local farmers was joking with your father. Saying things like mayhap your father was on the run, mayhap someone pursued him." He eyed Yngveld kindly. "Many outlaws have come to our shores to hide from enemies in Iceland and Norway, you see."

Yngveld nodded, scarcely daring to breathe. Her meal lay forgotten.

"At the time, your father laughed along with everyone else. He answered that he was merely looking for farmland. He said he had spent his time in raids and fighting, and now he wanted nothing more than to settle down and make a home for his six-year-old motherless daughter and himself."

Patrick nodded.

"Were you there, Patrick?" she asked.

"Aye," he answered shortly. " 'Twas soon after I, too, arrived in Greenland." He shot an angry glare at Karl, who appeared quite unmoved by the unspoken threat. Patrick subsided into sullen silence.

Yngveld waited for Karl to continue, but when he merely reached for another piece of the boiled shark, she cleared her throat. "And was it true?" she asked.

"Why, Yngveld, of course 'twas true."

But Yngveld wondered.

"Or at least parts of it were true," acknowledged Karl.

Aha, she thought.

"Your father later confided to me that he was in fact on the run. That he had been outlawed first from Norway, and then from Dubh Linn in Ireland."

Yngveld's mouth dropped open.

"But by then, Svein Skullcrusher and I knew each other better and he knew that I would not betray him." Here Karl shot a quick glance at Patrick. Patrick glowered back at him.

Yngveld's heart was pounding. "That explains why—"

Karl nodded. "Why you had so few family members to call upon after your father's death. For most Norse, family is everything. Yet your father had no one—except you."

"I always thought 'twas because my father was an only son."

Karl raised a dubious eyebrow. "Mayhap."

"Outlawed?" Yngveld was having a difficult time taking in everything Karl was telling her. "Why should my father be outlawed?"

Karl shrugged. "I do not know why he fled Norway."

Yngveld watched Karl, her mouth dry.

"But in Ireland, your father murdered a man. A man with powerful relatives. Those relatives, especially the dead man's brother, swore to avenge their kinsman's death. Svein told me the brother meant to kill him, and so he fled, taking you with him." He paused.

Yngveld was silent, bewildered by the information Karl was telling her. It all seemed so unbelievable, and yet some of her earlier memories . . . She asked, "And Ivar Wolfson? Did my father speak of him?"

Karl nodded slowly, almost reluctantly.

"What did he say?"

"He did not like the man."

"Then why would he pledge me in marriage to him?" Her eyes narrowed.

"I do not know." Karl shrugged. "I remember Svein speaking of a pledge. You were so little, that at first I thought I must have misunderstood him. But Svein said *ja,* he had pledged you to Ivar Wolfson." Karl said slowly, "I thought at the time that mayhap your father had no choice."

"No choice?" muttered Yngveld. "It makes no sense."

Karl shrugged. "Nevertheless, 'twas what I thought at the time."

" 'Tis very little to go on," reproached Yngveld.

"Mayhap," suggested Karl, "Svein thought to keep you from ever fulfilling the pledge by hiding out in Greenland with you."

Yngveld looked doubtful. "Mayhap. But 'tis more than passing strange."

"Aye," agreed Karl. "I like it not, Yngveld." His forehead wrinkled in a worried frown. Patrick, too, looked suddenly concerned.

Yngveld's stomach tightened. She, too, felt something was not right. She was sailing into danger, that much *was* becoming clear. She glanced around the deck, seeking the tall, dark form she knew so well. But Thomas Lachlann was nowhere to be seen.

And what did he know? she wondered. Did he know why Wolfson wanted her, why he really wanted her? Or was Thomas merely a messenger? She shivered. Thomas would do whatever he thought his duty to be. Thomas Lachlann might very well pose more than a threat to her heart. He might pose a threat to her very life.

Chapter Twenty-five

"Why the frown, fair Valkyrie?"

Yngveld looked up to see Thomas grinning down at her. He looked relaxed, younger than his years. She wondered suddenly if his command and responsibilities weighed heavily upon him. At times, she decided, they must.

She returned his smile as best she could, though her lips quivered. To be thinking of him, of his possible threat to her, of his ruthlessness—and then to see him smiling at her, an open look upon his face, why, 'twas confusing. She wondered what he knew about her betrothal, what Wolfson had told him. Then with a shrug, she put the question aside. She would learn of it eventually. Dubh Linn would hold the answer to many secrets.

She rose slowly to her feet. "We were just eating," she explained. She gestured to the shark meat on the platter. "Would you like some?"

Thomas shook his head and peered at the meat. 'Twas pale and boiled, not overdone or underdone as he had expected. "*Nej*, thank you," he said politely. "I have already supped." His eyes twinkled. He had not been about to foist himself upon her as an unwanted guest. He had decided to eat his own cooking because his imagination had balked at what she would do to the shark meat if he had demanded that she cook it for him. Would she leave it raw and lightly cooked in an attempt to poison him? Or merely burn every morsel like the last time? Rather than give her the opportunity to wreak havoc with his digestive system, he had made his own meal. Inhaling the fragrant scent of the meat before him, he wondered now if he had made a poor choice. But nothing of his thoughts showed upon his face.

"If you wish me to come back later to hear you sing . . ."

"*Nej, nej,*" Yngveld answered hastily. "This time is fine. Please, sit and we will talk. Then I shall sing for you."

He bowed and sat down cross-legged on the deck where she had indicated. He nodded to Karl and Patrick, and they politely murmured a greeting. The three men talked quietly while Yngveld washed the platter and the eating knife. She carefully sprinkled sand over the flames to put out the fire and then sat watching the men;

she was in no hurry to interrupt them. She merely wanted to look at Thomas.

She leaned back against the rail and let her eyes rove over his strong jaw and straight nose. The sea breeze blew gently at the curls of his forehead. She followed the tan column of his throat to where the neck of his collar brushed his skin. She felt a tiny twinge of disappointment that he was no longer wearing the loincloth. She had grown used to seeing that strong, broad chest of his and those firm, muscular legs. Now she must rely on memory to remind her of what he looked like.

Thomas could feel Yngveld watching him, but he promised himself he would not look at her. Let her think that he was indifferent to her. That was much better than for her to know the truth—that he had watched her many times on this voyage and that he was fighting a battle with himself about her. Once he glanced at her, while Patrick was speaking. Yngveld flushed and jerked her eyes away as though she had been caught stealing. He smiled to himself and turned back to what Patrick was saying. He nodded and pretended to be listening as Patrick described the Irish town where he had grown up, but all of Thomas's attention was actually focused on Yngveld, fair Valkyrie of the North. What, by Thor, was he going to do about her?

He knew that Ivar expected that she would be delivered to him. Hell, even Yngveld expected it. She had not fought against it much that he could tell, except for those few times when she had compared his taking her to Ivar with slavery. It appeared to him now that she had accepted her forthcoming marriage to Ivar, and he was glad of it. Or so he told himself.

While Patrick was talking, he noticed that Karl was yawning. Not once, not twice, but six, now seven times. Patrick's lips tightened and he almost forgot what he was saying to Captain Lachlann, so incensed was he with his slave's behavior. Watching Karl, one would almost think, thought Patrick angrily, that what Patrick had to say about his old home in Ireland and his friends and family before he was captured was not worth listening to.

Patrick's pale blue gaze skittered to Thomas Lachlann. Ah, that man seemed to find what he had to say fascinating enough. Very well, 'twas obvious that Karl was playing some kind of irritating game. Well, 'twould not work. Patrick's lips thinned. He would see to it that Karl was punished, later, in the privacy of their tent. Later. A thrill ran up and down his spine at the thought of how he would punish Karl and he forgot what he was saying.

Patrick stopped talking and glared at Karl. Karl, catching his gaze, stopped yawning and reddened.

"I am ready to sing," said Yngveld cheerfully.

Karl slumped in relief as Patrick glanced at Yngveld. Karl found that the closer they got to Ireland, the angrier his "master" became. He did not know what had possessed him to tease Patrick like that while he was talking. Some imp of misfortune, he guessed. Contrary to what Patrick obviously thought, Karl had actually listened to what Patrick was telling Lachlann. And it sounded to Karl as if Patrick had a huge, and rather strange family awaiting him in Ireland. Karl wondered wearily whether he would fit in.

Yngveld looked pale, Thomas thought. He wondered for a moment how she would take to Ireland. 'Twas different from Greenland. Better, in his opinion, but he had not grown up on Greenland soil. Mayhap her heart would long for the snow and ice and high meadows and rocky fjords of her home. His jaw clenched. 'Twas doubtful that Ivar would do much to help her. He would be busy leading military forays in and around the city, looking for Brian Boru, the Irish king who had sworn to take back Dubh Linn. And when Ivar was not pursuing Boru around the hills, he would probably be pursuing Jasmine around the tent. Ah, well, 'twas no affair of Thomas's. His orders were to bring back Yngveld Sveinsdatter— untouched, he reminded himself. And that was what he was doing, by Thor!

"Oh!"

Thomas looked down at the stick of firewood that had snapped loudly in his hands. He was more overwrought about this undertaking than he had realized. He smiled casually at Yngveld as he tossed the pieces onto the sandbox. "I did not mean to startle you. My apologies."

Yngveld nodded, wondering at her guest's sudden inattention. Then, dismissing it with a hesitant smile, she began to sing.

The evening sky behind her was painted in blues and purples. Leaning against the rail, unaware of the lovely picture she presented with her blond hair catching the breeze and her lovely face upturned, Yngveld sang a song of love, crooning at first, then lyrical with soaring notes.

Thomas could not take his eyes off her. Her singing this eve, rather than awing him as it had earlier in the day, touched his heart with a longing he could not name. He wanted to stride over and enfold her in his arms and clasp her to his breast. The words of the song were beautiful and powerful, and he felt shivers go through him at the high, pure notes she sang. Her voice added another dimension of beauty to her that made her irresistible to him. He clenched his fists at the thought of Ivar having her. Then he looked down at his hands and slowly unclenched them. She was Ivar's. He must not forget that. At that moment the beauty of the song escaped him, and he could only think of loss. He watched her broodingly until the song ended, and she glanced at him, obviously expecting some reaction.

Thomas swallowed and nodded. "Very lovely, my lady. Like you."

Yngveld smiled sweetly, and then launched into a happier, lilting song.

She is trying to lift the sorrow from me, thought Thomas, and he marveled at her sensitive perception of his mood. He knew the tune, 'twas one that his mother and other women had sung, though the words of the verses were different from those he had learned. The chorus, however, was the same, and before he realized what he was doing, he had joined her at the railing and was singing the song with her. Yngveld's eyes widened when he did so, but she lost not a beat and together they sang. At last, at the end of the song, his low notes echoed her high ones, and the song fell back to earth.

"You sing like a Valkyrie!" burst out Neill into the silence left after the song.

Yngveld swung startled eyes upon him and saw that the whole ship's company had been watching her sing with Thomas. She flushed.

Thomas bowed. "Why, thank you."

"Not you. Yngveld!" sputtered Neill amidst the laughter.

Thomas grinned. "Aye," he said, running his eyes over her fair form. "She does indeed." He went back and sat down with Patrick and Karl.

Yngveld watched him musingly. They had sounded well together, he and she. It had surprised her that he could sing so well. Somehow it did not fit the ruthless image that she had of him.

She shrugged her small shoulders and launched into another song, this one a ballad about a man who went off a-viking to raid and seek his fortune, only to return and find that his one true love had wed another. Yngveld sang the woman's part, and Thomas joined in on the man's.

Back and forth they sang the tender words, as the man tried to persuade her to leave her husband. Yngveld suddenly wished that she had not chosen that particular song. One could read more meaning into it, into their particular situation, than she had ever intended. She flushed in mortification at one graphic verse that Thomas sang, but she kept on doggedly until the end of the song. When she sang the last note, he swooped her up in his arms and held her up triumphantly as the men laughed and roared their approval.

He let her slide down him, watching her flushed face, and before he could stop himself, he bent and kissed her full on the lips. Caught up in the kiss, Yngveld put her arms around his neck and held his head in place, the better to kiss him back. Several heartbeats later, he lifted his head slowly, looking down into her darkened eyes. With trembling fingers she touched her lips where moments before his had been. 'Twas a kiss of forbidden passion, and they both knew it.

A polite cough caused Yngveld and Thomas to turn. Yngveld stared, with widened, horrified eyes, and Thomas with narrowed, glittering ones, at the ship's company that watched them both in silence.

Chapter Twenty-six

Thomas swept Yngveld behind him as if for protection from the hostile eyes. She peeked over his shoulder.

Neill cleared his throat. "You are supposed to be delivering her to Ivar. She is Ivar's betrothed."

Behind Neill the men grumbled and spoke amongst themselves. Thomas knew that while some of the men bore him a personal loyalty, most of them were bound in honor to Ivar. He cursed himself silently for letting the kiss happen. He should have foreseen the anger of the men were they to perceive even a hint that their military commander's betrothed was being compromised.

"Ivar will not like it." Torgils spoke up in his gravelly voice.

Thomas Lachlann, jaw clenched, watched them out of flinty green eyes. "It will not happen again."

Some of the men stirred, turning away to resume their seats at the oars. Most stayed, waiting.

"Ivar will kill you, mon, for touching her." Thomas could hear the anger in Neill's voice. Was his anger directed at Thomas for besmirching Ivar's intended, or at Thomas's foolishness in endangering himself? Neill could be most protective upon occasion and 'twas obvious that the men did not approve of Thomas's action.

Thomas took a step toward the crowd of men, his fists clenching and unclenching.

"And he *will* find out about it." Torgils' growling voice held a warning.

"Aye, he will," replied Thomas coolly. "For I shall tell him."

A collective sigh went up from the men. Murmurings were heard. Some of the men nodded. Others began to walk back to their seats, muttering as they went.

" 'Tis understandable . . ."

"She is a lovely woman, 'tis easy for a man to lose his head . . . once . . ."

"Has been a long voyage . . ."

"Ivar will understand. . . ."

"But he will no' like it."

Neill and Torgils stepped back, relief plain on both their faces. With a particularly piercing stare at Thomas, Neill turned and marched to his place at the tiller.

Torgils watched Neill go, and his white hair blew a little in the cool breeze. "You are asking for trouble," he said in his low voice to Thomas. "The men do not like it that—"

Thomas turned to him and met his concerned blue eyes without flinching. "Enough, Torgils! I said 'twill not happen again. And it will not." Privately, Thomas wondered if he could keep his word. He, who had never had his honor questioned, was being questioned now by Torgils, one of his own friends.

Torgils lifted a blond brow and said nothing. 'Twas clear to Thomas what Torgils thought.

He sighed. "Out with it, mon."

Torgils grinned slyly. "Just thought I would mention that I would back *you* in any fight against Ivar." Then he walked away.

Thomas watched him go. Would it come to that? Should it come to that, a fight between Ivar and him over this woman standing at his side?

Yngveld stood looking out over the water. She had heard every word spoken since the terrible moment she had turned to see the men watching her and Thomas. And now she swung to face Thomas, her blue eyes roaming his face. He looked tired, she thought. "What is the matter?"

Thomas gave a small grin. "The men do not like me kissing you."

Yngveld's chin went up. " 'Tis none of their business."

" 'Tis. You are Ivar's. They fight for Ivar. I

fight for Ivar. I am bound to defend the honor of my commander, not besmirch it."

Yngveld studied him thoughtfully. "Thomas," she said slowly. "There is something that you must know."

Thomas lifted a brow.

"I will not marry Ivar."

"You do not know him."

"Correct. And I do not want to know him. I certainly do not want to marry him."

Thomas said nothing. Part of him wanted to applaud her decision. Another part wanted to shake the rebellion out of her. "Ivar will not let you go." She might as well know what Ivar was like. "He will set a guard—two, three if he must—to watch you every hour of the day or night. They will follow you everywhere, watch whatever you do—even to piss."

Yngveld flushed at the image he conjured up. She stuck her chin out farther and her blue eyes flashed. "I will not marry him. I do not have to. I have money now."

"The dowry?"

"The gold," she corrected.

Thomas sighed. He had been afraid of that. Who knew what a woman with money would do? And Yngveld was wealthy. Thomas's old cynicism about rich women reared its head. His voice hardened. "Your money will not protect you. Ivar will marry you. What Ivar wants, Ivar gets."

Yngveld shook her head slowly. "*Nej*, Thomas Lachlann. I do not believe you. Were those not the very words that you once used to describe yourself? Who are we talking about here—you or Ivar?" She answered her own question. "Methinks we speak of you."

Thomas's hard eyes assessed her. She made a lovely opponent, he thought. He would rather she made a lovely mistress. But that line of thinking led too quickly to kisses, and kisses were proving dangerous with Yngveld. He wondered what Ivar would do when he learned that Lachlann had dared take the liberty of a kiss with her. Then he mentally shrugged his shoulders. 'Twas possible Ivar would do nothing. Ivar, himself, was not a sterling figure of propriety with women. But then, he was a man and men could have other women. . . .

"You are correct, Yngveld Sveinsdatter," Thomas acknowledged smoothly, none of his frustration showing upon his hard face. "We are speaking of me, for if I wanted you, I would take you." And he turned upon his heel and marched away.

Yngveld gasped, and her hands flew to her hot cheeks. How dare he? First he kissed her, then he insulted her. What did he want? 'Twas obvious that he did not want *her. Damn him,* she raged, whirling and running to the stern of the ship. She gripped the cold, curved wood of the back stem until her fingers looked like claws. How dared he think he could kiss her, stir her emotions, then turn upon his heel! Why, he was all but saying that he did not want her, that he would as soon throw her to Ivar. How dared he!

In her rage, she stared at the white churning wake of the ship as it sailed across the choppy gray waves. She would make Thomas rue those words. *Ja*. She would make him take them back, every last one of them!

Only later did she stop to ask herself why she was so angry, why his indifference should hurt so. 'Twas Ivar she should be concerned about, not Thomas Lachlann. But cool reason did not stand at Yngveld's elbow on that beautiful evening that had started out so well and ended so badly. Nor was cool reason likely to intrude for some time.

Chapter Twenty-seven

Yngveld was determined to run away. To stay on shipboard, under Thomas Lachlann's command, was to court a kind of slavery. After his kiss last night, his contemptuous words . . . Her hands clenched into fists just thinking about how angry she was with him. *Nej*, she could not stay around him. Every time he walked past her or took his shift at the tiller, her anger flared anew.

And she absolutely refused to passively wait for him to hand her over to Ivar Wolfson in marriage.

She must flee before 'twas too late. She *must* escape. She would flee the ship—and Thomas Lachlann.

But she must also have somewhere to go.

Norway, she thought. Norway would be the best place. She still had some family there. Well, one kinsman, 'twas all. 'Twas not much, but what else could she do? She refused to stay and be told whom to marry and where to go. *Nej*, she would choose her life for herself, not let others dictate to her!

But how to flee? And when?

Yngveld sat in her little tent making plans. Everything she owned was packed. She sat upon the blankets, fingering the gray one absently and wondering if she should take it with her when she fled. The nights were cold.

She stared past her little doorway to the green, rolling coast of Ireland. They had been sailing parallel to the coast since early morning.

Yngveld's first sight of the green isle had caused her heart to leap. Freedom! She had overheard Thomas telling the men that they would anchor for the night and that the men would camp ashore for the first time.

She wondered uneasily if she should make her escape attempt this night. Yngveld's mouth tightened in determination. She would escape, no matter what.

'Twas only that she must decide when. She had no inkling as to how many more nights ashore they would spend before reaching Dubh Linn. Should she take a chance and flee into the less populated Irish countryside and trust that she would not cross the path of any brigands or ruffians? She was no fool and knew that as a woman traveling alone she would present a ripe opportunity for unscrupulous men to rob, rape, or murder her.

Or should she wait until she reached crowded Dubh Linn and make her escape from there? The danger of waiting until Dubh Linn was that Ivar Wolfson would no doubt send his soldiers to hunt her down.

She pondered this and sighed. Were she to escape into the Irish hinterlands this night, then Thomas Lachlann would surely hunt her down. Either way, she would be a fugitive.

She tapped her long fingers on her knee thoughtfully as she considered her choices. Lachlann would be ruthless in his pursuit. She realized that. Not because he wanted her—*nej*, because of his commitment to deliver her to Ivar. And while she did not know Wolfson, she guessed that he had not been made military commander of Dubh Linn because of a gentle, retiring nature. She sighed. She must assume he would also be determined to find her. Mayhap more so, because she was his intended bride.

The Irish countryside or Dubh Linn? Back and forth she went, pondering her choices.

And, there was another problem—who would help her once she had eluded her pursuers? How would she find a ship to sail to Norway? Yngveld knew she could not be assured of finding sanctuary anywhere in Ireland. Would the people of the country be more willing to help a fleeing woman? She did not know the land or the people. She knew that there were men fighting in different parts of the land. That there were some towns where the Vikings ruled, and some where the Irish retained their hold. But she knew not a single soul on Irish soil. *Oh, what shall I do?* she agonized.

Her fingers stopped their nervous tapping as she pondered the seriousness of her situation. Then she smiled ruefully. It seemed she was always fleeing unwanted bridegrooms. First Bjarni Bearhunter and now Ivar Wolfson.

She shook her head and sighed. Why could she not choose her own husband? She would choose someone like . . . she closed her eyes tightly against the sudden image of Thomas Lachlann welling up in her mind's eye.

Thomas Lachlann was handsome; he was brave. He cared about his men. He had been kind to her. He had helped her get payment for her land. He kissed very well. She touched her lips gently at the memory. Then she started. How could she? she demanded of herself. How could she think that Lachlann would be the man she wanted for her husband? He had dragged her away from Greenland. Given her no choice in the matter. Told her she was going to marry Wolfson. And then, after giving her a kiss that had nearly undone her, he had casually announced that if he had wanted her, he would take her—even as he walked away!

She shook her head once more, her lips tight in disgust. *Nej,* Thomas Lachlann was not for her. She banished traitorous thoughts of him into the furthest mists of her mind.

Escape, that was what she must think upon.

And, she decided, if she was to escape, it would be best to escape from Dubh Linn. Immediately upon leaving the ship. At least there she could disappear into the crush of people.

Her heart fluttered in anticipation and fear. Her mouth was dry, and she had to swallow many times. For the fourteenth time, she packed and unpacked, then packed again her little bundle of belongings, carefully placing the precious sack of gold in the center of the soft, gray wool blanket. She touched the leather sack with one finger and smiled a tiny, satisfied smile. Her dowry. She shook her head. *Nej*, 'twas no longer her dowry. Now 'twas her freedom money, for with it she would buy a new life for herself.

A new life, she mused. *Ja*, it sounded good. She studied the green coastline that she could see from her little doorway as she pondered. Now was the time to think. Now was the time to decide what she wanted for herself and what she did not want.

She grimaced. She did not want Ivar Wolfson. She knew that. Yet, she did want a husband. She wanted someone to share her life with, someone who would love her, give her children, someone she could talk with on long winter evenings, someone she could laugh with, sing with . . .

Abruptly Thomas Lachlann's face rose before her mind again. *He* had sung with her. Last night. And his voice and hers had blended well. Beautifully, if she were to be truthful.

She shook her head. She must not think about him. She must think about what she wanted for her life. She wanted to go to Norway, *ja*, that was it. Yngveld gritted her teeth. She would go to Norway and find a husband and Thomas Lachlann would have nothing to do with it.

She closed her eyes and leaned back against the tent. After a while the tension left her. Her thoughts roamed lazily. She wanted children, someday. In her mind's eye she could see two beautiful girls, blonde, blue eyed—and a boy with black curls and laughing green eyes.

She sat up quickly. How did *he* get there, in her daydream? She slumped back down, willing her treacherous mind to forget, once and for all, about Thomas Lachlann.

Drowsily content, she imagined what her life was to be. She wanted a happy life. She wanted a good place to live, a farm with good, rich soil. She wanted land that was not stony and thin. She would grow her crops of barley, corn. . . . She would have a little herb garden. . . . And mayhap she would have a pair of goats. *Ja*, she would like a goat—one like Flowerface, a sweet gray-and-black goat that would listen to her sing.

She opened her eyes suddenly. She would not need to go away with her goat because she would never, ever have to flee her home again. Her father was dead, and with him, the strange madness that had forced her away from him, away from her home and far up into the hills. Never, ever again would she flee her home.

Frowning, she told herself that she would have a home where there was laughter and love—and no madness. That was what she wanted, she decided. A home with love, where she could sew and visit with her friends and sing with her husband and love their children. And madness would not be part of it. When she found her home, nothing and no one would ever again drive her from it. Of that, she was certain.

Chapter Twenty-eight

The Northern Irish Coast

Yngveld watched Neill lift a protesting sheep over the side of the ship. He staggered as he carried the struggling beast, and when he set her down upon the stony shale beach, she darted off as though her tail were afire. Torgils, carrying a large cheese, stopped to watch and laughed as Neill raced after the bleating ewe.

The spot where Thomas Lachlann had chosen to moor the ship was in a calm harbor at an isolated part of the northern Irish coast. Yngveld could see scattered clumps of trees, some large rocks, and green, rolling hills off in the distance. A forest of thick trees grew right to the water's edge on the other side of a small stream which ran to the sea. Yngveld relished the thought of drinking fresh water once more. The barrelled water tended to get tasteless quickly.

She gritted her teeth as Thomas lifted her over the rail, and her cheeks flushed. His touch was firm. She might as well be a sheep herself or—or a round of cheese for all the interest he showed. Yet she could not help glancing down at that handsome face. When she caught his gaze, so close to her own, she could see those green eyes brighten and a little thrill ran through her.

She quickly smothered it. It would not do to flatter herself that Thomas Lachlann found her worthy of his attention. Nor to let the great oaf know that even his impersonal touch while he lifted her off the ship could cause her heart to beat faster.

She looked away, murmuring a tiny thank you, and then she too, raced off across the green grass, much as the troubled ewe had done. Yngveld hoped that the similiarity ended there, for the sheep, once Neill caught her, was destined to be the main course at dinner.

The long grass felt slick under her bare feet as she ran. Her leg muscles stretched and felt good after so many days aboard ship. She finally stopped, panting, atop a little hillock. She swung around to observe the men back at the ship. Some were on the beach, some on the rolling grass, and some setting up campfires. She could see Thomas bending down to start a blaze, his back to her.

Suddenly a powerful thought struck her. Mayhap she should flee from Thomas Lachlann this very night! Mayhap, if she were to wait until Dubh Linn, she would not get as fortunate a chance to escape. She halted, staring thoughtfully at the men, as she turned the idea over in her mind. No one seemed to notice that she was not close to the ship. Were she to turn and run now, why, she might get a league away before their suspicions were roused.

"Ah, there you are, Yngveld." Neill, the runaway sheep in his arms, appeared over the round of the next little hillock. "I caught her!" he explained unnecessarily. "I love the taste of roasted mutton."

Yngveld's heart, pumping madly at the thought of freedom, almost came to a screeching stop with Neill's appearance. For a moment she felt sick and lost. Then, her terrible, lovely idea grew and her world righted. She could escape, she *would* escape—this very night! As the impulse grew into an idea, and the idea took shape and hardened, she suddenly smiled, lips trembling, in Neill's direction. Her mind raced as her feet had done only minutes before. "And does Thomas Lachlann, too, enjoy mutton?" she asked.

"Aye. Loves it."

"Good." She joined Neill in the walk back to the campfire. She could smile with him so easily, she thought, and still make her plans. Her mind on the pleasant prospect of immediate escape, she rambled and nodded and let Neill talk.

When she reached Thomas, she took a breath. Time to put the first part of her hastily constructed plan into action.

"Would—would you care to have me cook your dinner?" she stammered.

Thomas finished placing a large piece of driftwood upon the fire. He dusted off his hands and eyed her consideringly. "Aye," he nodded. "I should like that. Very much."

Yngveld smiled politely. She would need extra meat to take with her when she fled. What better way than to cook it and secrete it away when no one was looking? She smiled in satisfaction, unaware of Thomas's hot gaze.

Thomas wondered what the Fair Valkyrie of the North was up to now. How unusual that she should offer to cook for him. But she aroused his curiosity—and more, he admitted wryly—and so he had consented to try another of her meals.

The men clustered around several campfires, scattered over a wide area. Yngveld noticed that none of them had chosen to camp close to the stream. On the other side of the stream was the forest. She must remind herself not to glance at it too often and inadvertently give away her plan to flee.

With Thomas at his fire were Neill and Torgils. They were soon joined by Karl and Patrick.

Conversation was relaxed among the men. Yngveld, slicing at the still steaming, bloody meat, did not say a word because she was too nervous wondering if her plan to flee this night would work. A thousand times she said *'nej,'* a thousand and one she said *'ja.'*

When the flames were burning low and the embers glowed, she carefully placed the meat on the hot coals. The sizzling fat of the mutton dripped and a tantalizing aroma filled the air. Her mouth watered. She must be sure to set aside at least enough meat for herself for three days. It might take her that long to get help in finding a ship bound for Norway.

She looked toward the forest thoughtfully and bit her lip. She did feel uneasy about her gold. Mayhap she could sneak back aboard Thomas's vessel when he was not looking and bring it with her. If only she had thought to pick up her precious leather sack while she was aboard. But she had grown so flustered when Thomas had casually lifted her over the rail that all thought of anything else had fled her mind. Then again, how could she have known that such a fine opportunity to escape would present itself?

Around most of the campfires it appeared that the meat was done and men were falling silent as they ate. Yngveld narrowed her eyes at the mutton and flipped a slab over with a stick. The meat looked half-raw to her—obviously it needed more time to roast. Enough time, she gauged critically, for walking to the stream and back. Her tired feet could use a walk in the cool stream and her lips were dry.

She brushed a strand of hair out of her eyes

as she slowly wandered over to the stream. Her movements were slow and methodical. She did not want to alarm anyone who might be watching her. Let Thomas get accustomed to her frequent forays to the stream. Then, when he was not looking, she could run.

The water did indeed feel cool on her feet. She closed her eyes in bliss as the water swirled around her ankles. She opened her eyes and spied a broad leaf. Picking it, she carefully shaped it into a cup and dipped it in the water. Water dribbled down her chin as she drank. Ah, but that was refreshing! She dipped it again, turning idly to observe if she were being watched.

Ja. She was. Thomas Lachlann was staring at her, though he appeared comfortable enough sitting on a boulder near the fire. Still, she did not like it that his eyes had followed her. She lingered a little longer, carefully studying the forest in front of her. Then, with a sigh, she trudged back to the campfire. 'Twas twilight now, on an Irish summer evening. She hoped it would get darker.

Several pairs of eyes looked up as she approached the fire. A burnt smell filled the air. She ran the last few steps and fell to her knees by the fire. "Oh, *nej*," she moaned.

"Oh, *ja*," came the chorus from Thomas, Torgils, Neill, Karl, and Patrick.

The meat was burned. Again. She looked at it—a shrivelled, dry black mess.

Her eyes sought Thomas. She wanted to tell

him she had not done it apurpose this time, but something in his green gaze—a sparkle, mayhap—stopped her. "Why did you not take the meat off the coals?" she demanded, her eyes searching each man in turn. Grins and shrugs met her irritated question, though she thought Karl looked a little guilty.

She stood, hands on hips, foot tapping. "Thomas, this is all your fault!"

"My fault?" He looked taken aback.

"*Ja*. You. You stood there and let it burn!" she wailed.

He grinned. "Not I. I was gathering wood. And I did hear *you* offer to cook *my* dinner. Not the other way round."

"Humph," she muttered. How was she ever going to escape if they *noticed* her? And burning their dinner certainly had the effect of making them notice her. She made a face as she took a stick and gingerly removed what was left of the charred meat from the coals. "Anyone hungry?" she asked brightly, trying desperately to salvage the situation.

Groans greeted her. Thomas's green eyes twinkled and she wanted to smack him with the seared mess.

"I think I can find something else," said Patrick. "Come on, Karl." The two wandered off to another fire.

Torgils and Neill politely excused themselves. Yngveld grimaced as they walked over to the sheep's carcass. Neill sliced off a joint of meat. She noticed that they did not return, preferring to cook their meat at another campfire.

She swung back to Thomas. "Well?" she demanded.

He grinned. "I will eat it if you will."

She frowned at the black mess. "*Nej,*" she said slowly. "I find I am not hungry."

"That so?"

Something in his voice caused her to glance at him. He was watching her steadily. "Tell me, Yngveld," he asked casually, "did you do much cooking at home?"

She shook her head. "Dimples always did it."

"Dimples?"

"Our—our thrallwoman." It had always looked easy when Dimples cooked. The farmhouse would be full of delightful aromas as she baked. It had all looked so simple, then, thought Yngveld. Cooking did not appear simple now.

"Of course." Thomas' lips tightened. The woman was rich. She had never had to work. How had he forgotten?

He bowed, cold and distant now. "I find that I am still hungry, after all. Excuse me." And then he, too, left. Yngveld stood there, red-faced, watching as he sliced off a chunk of meat from the carcass. She should be glad that he had walked away. That Torgils and the others had found their own supper. But somehow, all she felt was lonely.

She gave herself a shake. She had spoken truly. Food was not on her mind. Her gold, however, was.

She glanced at the ship. Looking around,

apparently unconcerned, she saw that all the men were busily occupied. She started walking toward where the ship was drawn up in the shallow water. She expected at any moment to hear a cry to halt. But no one cried out. She kept walking. She reached the ship. She had made it. She swung herself up over the railing and listened. Still no outcry. Good.

She scrambled over to the tent and stared at the blanket-wrapped bundle of clothes and possessions she had packed earlier. 'Twas too bulky. 'Twould arouse suspicion.

She reached in and pulled out the sack of gold. She would take it with her. The rest she must leave behind. After all, Thomas would certainly get suspicious were she to drag all her belongings off the ship and past his campfire.

The sack was heavy, she thought. Hastily, she lifted the skirt of her tunic and belted the sack around her waist. She dropped the skirt and patted her stomach where the sack bulged ever so slightly. The bulk of the tunic hid most of it, she thought critically, though mayhap she did look a little pregnant. She shrugged her shoulders. There was no help for it. If she were to escape tonight, then the sack was all she could take. She must not arouse suspicions.

She grabbed another long piece of thin leather to use as a belt outside her tunic. She hastily dumped out all her precious possessions, her mother's amber breast pin, her own silver one. Eyes narrowed, she regarded her favorite silver armlets. These she placed on her upper arms.

She stood and put on her embroidered pantalets. She tied the colorful ribbons to the belt that held her sack of gold. One of the men might get suspicious were she to suddenly appear wearing them in her hair as she marched toward the forest.

She saw the tiny vial of floral scent. She looked at it longingly. Now that her chance to escape had come, she found she did not want to leave any of her precious possessions behind.

Quickly, before she could change her mind, she doused herself with the scent, patting drops of it into her hair, behind her ears, on her arms, everywhere that she could think to put it. Mmmm, she smelled beautiful. The smell was a little overpowering, but it still smelled wonderful.

She glanced around the little tent once more, tempted to take the gray blanket. But she decided that Thomas Lachlann would surely notice something odd were she to walk past him wearing the blanket. *Nej*, she would have to be content with what she had managed to secrete under her tunic.

She clambered over the rail, put her feet in the cold sea and waded to shore. She spied Thomas talking with some of his men at a fire none too distant. Striking out in the other direction, she ambled across to the fire where she had managed to char yet another meal. She looked down at the meat. Should she cook some more and hope that she did not burn it, or should she salvage what she could from the charred mess and take it with her on her flight?

No one was paying any attention to her. She bent down and picked up the knife she had used earlier to slice the meat. She should take the knife with her. 'Twould be a weapon. She carefully sliced off the most charred parts and found that some of the meat looked edible. She tasted it and made a face. 'Twas not as good as Dimples used to make, but it would suffice for her meat supply, she decided. She stuffed it into her belt, next to the knife. Fortunately, the campfire where she stood was in the shadows, closest to the stream, and she thought no one had noticed her.

Carefully rising, she glanced around. Everyone was talking. No one paid her any attention. Good. She started for the stream. First one step. Then another. Step by step, she walked slowly to the stream.

Chapter Twenty-nine

She had done it! She was free! Yngveld walked swiftly through the thick oak forest, pushing at low-hanging branches. The spongy mosses she walked upon softened her footfalls and she was able to make good progress. She swivelled her head once and could still see the little orange flares where the Irishmen had their campfires, but no one had noticed her leave. There had been no outcry raised. She was free!

The light was dimmer in the forest, almost dark, but it would confound any pursuers. She had been careful and cautious and had lingered near the stream until the men had grown used to her being there. Then—she smiled in satisfaction at the memory—she had quietly vanished.

The euphoria of her success at eluding her captors did not fade even after she had gone some distance. She had scratches on her hands and two on her left cheek from brambles, but her spirits were high. Thomas Lachlann was not as smart as he thought, she decided in glee. She had escaped him, had escaped marriage to Ivar. She was her own woman. At last!

Every little while she would stop and listen to see if she could hear sounds of pursuit, but nothing reached her ears. She wondered at the stillness, and at times she looked around the silent forest with a slight foreboding. It was quiet. It was dark. It was unknown.

Then, with an effort, she would remind herself that she was free. She was on her way to find help, and then she would sail to Norway. Such things weighed heavily against the paltry inconvenience of a silent, dark forest.

She had just finished heartily congratulating herself on her brilliant escape when the sound of a snapping twig came to her ear. She halted, frozen, afraid to turn in the direction of the sound, afraid not to. Slowly, trying to still her wildly beating heart, she swung to face the sound.

Nothing. No one. She almost slumped to the thick mossy floor of the forest in relief. For a moment, she had thought . . .

She heard a grunt to her left. She swung her head in that direction, eyes wide in fright, straining to see whatever she could in the dimness. She could see nothing. As quietly as she could, she stepped behind the trunk of a large oak, peering through the branches.

There 'twas again. Another grunt. Now she could see a dim shape, low to the ground. She slowly released her breath. Why, 'twas nothing but a pig! She could see him rooting around in a clump of brush. Snuffling sounds came to her distinctly. The boar was rather large and of a dark brown color with long yellow tusks, but she recognized him for what he was. Naught but a pig.

In Greenland she had known a neighboring family, the Gustavsons, who had raised pigs. Many times Yngveld had stood near the pig enclosure and watched as the animals grunted and rooted through the dirt. They ate whatever roots they could find and were messy animals. But they were not dangerous. Heaving a silent sigh of relief, she pushed on, careful not to disturb the foraging creature.

She was some distance from the boar when she heard him run off through the forest, crashing through branches as he ran. As he was headed in a different direction from her own, she merely shrugged and smiled to herself. Imagine being frightened of a pig!

She could still hear the pig occasionally, and she thought that her ears were playing tricks upon her. Sometimes she heard a snap of branches from the direction the wild pig had run in, other times she thought the sound came closer than that—from behind her. But whenever she swung her head to look, she saw nothing. She shrugged and moved on.

She stopped for a moment and put her arm to her nose and inhaled deeply. Ahh, how the perfumed scent lingered. She still smelled lovely. Laughing ruefully to herself, she skipped along, ducking her head now and then to miss a low-hanging branch. She sang happily in her newfound freedom.

Suddenly the sound of the boar was much closer, right behind her, and she whirled around. 'Twas no boar. 'Twas Thomas, running straight for her.

"*Nej!*" she cried and ran.

"*Ja!*" he said. In five swift steps he was upon her and grabbing the back of her tunic.

"*Nej!*" she cried, beating at the strong hands. He chortled softly and pulled her back to him, step by step. Yngveld's arms were still outstretched and she had not given up all hope of running away.

But slowly, inexorably, he drew her back.

The neck of her tunic cut into her throat, she could feel the back of her garment pulled tight and wondered if it would give. Then, remembering that Dimples had woven the garment, she knew that nothing would cause the sturdy cloth to tear. With a choking cry, Yngveld stopped pulling and swung around, eyes flashing, to face him.

Only to be held firmly by the shoulders and kissed soundly on the lips. "*Ja,*" Thomas breathed.

She wiped her lips and glared up at him.

He held her glance mockingly. "And where in

Thor's name did you think you were going?"

She studied him before answering. He did not look angry. He seemed more amused than anything. She stamped her foot and felt her cheeks grow hot. She would not be an amusement to this man. She would not!

"I was running away! That should be obvious!"

"Aye. 'Tis. Just where were you running to?" He waved a hand around the small glen they found themselves in. "Do you know anyone in this land? Did you have a destination in mind or were you just running blindly?" His sardonic manner told her he thought the latter.

She stuck out her chin, hands on hips. "I was making plans. . . ."

"As you ran?" he finished. He sniffed the air with flared nostrils. " 'Twas no' difficult to find you, Yngveld. I had but to follow your scent." More amusement in his voice.

She did not answer. She felt foolish.

"Know you that there are wild pigs in the forest?"

Her chin came up. "I saw one. I am not so blind as you think!"

"They are dangerous."

"Hmmph," she snorted. "Do not try to fool me. Why, the Gustavsons, back in Greenland, kept pigs. Tame, grunting things the animals were! Dirty, too. But not dangerous!" Her eyes flashed at his nerve in trying to scare her.

Thomas drew himself up to his full height and glared at her menacingly. "Listen to me!"

He wanted to shake her, but he took his hands from her shoulders. A man his size could hurt a woman, and he was careful about his strength. "That was a boar! An old one. They can be mean and vicious. And he could have charged you! Why, he could have killed you, woman!"

"Like the shark, I suppose," she demanded archly. "Well, the shark did not get me and neither did the boar!"

Thomas wanted to strangle her. "There are wolves in these forests!" he roared.

"Not any more," she replied saucily. "Your bellowing has scared them all away!"

Thomas ground his teeth in frustration. "You are not safe in these woods, woman. Get that through your head."

"I am not safe with you, you mean!"

'Twas clear to Thomas that Yngveld believed herself to be in no danger. He sighed, wondering what he could say or do that would impress upon the woman the seriousness of running off into unknown woods. He would try one more time.

He pulled her to him, then lifted her off the ground so that her feet swung in the air. Holding her up until they were eyeball to eyeball, he gritted, "Do not try to escape into the forest again! Not only are there wolves and wild boars, there are all kinds of brigands! There are Irish mercenaries, Norse mercenaries, bands of thieves, the occasional nasty farmer, lonely monks—"

"Sounds like Greenland," she said pertly.

He put her down. Carefully. His face red, he bellowed, "I am serious, woman!"

She shook his hands off her. "I can take care of myself."

"Like you did with Bjarni Bearhunter?" Sarcasm laced his voice.

"Bjarni Bearhunter," she said snidely, "was better left behind. Which is what I did. I left him behind."

Thomas gnashed his teeth. "You ran from Bjarni and got into worse trouble! You ended up with that foul captain, what's-his-name!"

"Olafson?" she answered sweetly. She waved a hand in dismissal. "He was not so bad."

"Not so bad! Do you know what he planned to do to you?" sputtered Thomas.

"*Nej*," she said airily. "Nor do I care to."

Thomas stood there, livid.

Yngveld, hands on hips, leaned into his face. "The only problem I have run into since I started my adventure is *you*!"

"Me?" said Thomas, taken aback. "Why, I have helped you, I have saved you—"

"For Ivar!" Her voice quivered with bitterness. "You are the most dangerous man I know."

Thomas looked at her blankly. "How—? Me?"

"You mutinied on my ship and took it back from me!"

" 'Twas mine!"

" 'Twas *mine*!" she shrieked.

"Well I paid you for it. Eventually. With Bearhunter's help."

"*Ja*. The gold. I—I thank you for that." She

squirmed in irritation. "How can I yell at you when I am thanking you!"

"You will find a way," he muttered.

"And furthermore," continued Yngveld, warming to her subject, "just now, who attacked me? Was it a wild boar? *Nej!* Was it a wolf? *Nej!* A band of thieves? Oh *nej*! 'Twas you!" She smirked triumphantly. "*You* are the one who is dangerous!"

Thomas stiffened. She looked so smug. "I am merely doing my duty—"

"Your duty as Ivar sees it! Your duty as *I* see it is to—"

"I do not take orders from a woman!"

"I meant what you should do with me. In the predicament you are in."

"I am in no predicament! 'Tis *you* in the predicament!"

"How very correct you are!" she agreed scornfully. "*My* predicament then. My predicament is being held captive by *you*. And I was attempting to resolve that predicament when you so rudely captured me once more!"

Thomas's eyes rolled heavenward for a moment in a futile bid for patience. He lost the bid. Seizing her by the arm, he propelled her back the way they had come. "The only advice I have for you, woman—"

"I do not need your advice!"

"Nevertheless, you will get it. And profit from it," he gritted. "Do not, I repeat, do not attempt to escape from me for the rest of the voyage. 'Twill not work!"

"You cannot scare me," she responded in a trembling voice.

"Ah, but I can," he said silkily. He stopped and glared at her, his eyes drawn by her quivering lips. He leaned down and pressed her mouth with his lips—hard. As the kiss lengthened, his lips softened. Yngveld moaned, reaching up to put her arms around his neck. He pulled her closer to him, and the two of them were caught up in their passion. Finally, with a deep sigh, Thomas released her, his green eyes curiously softened, her blue ones dazed.

She reeled back from his embrace and one hand flew to her mouth in dismay.

"See that you do not escape again," Thomas murmured. "Or there will be more kisses like that!"

There, that should keep the wench in tow, he decided. He liked the look of her half-closed eyelids when he'd finished kissing her. With a satisfied quirk of his sensuous lips, Thomas dragged her back through the forest toward the glowing fires.

Yngveld let him, she felt so dazed. What had Thomas promised? More kisses like that one, should she escape? And that was a *threat*? With a secret little smile to herself, she wondered how pleased with himself he would be if he knew that she was even now entertaining that very thought. And, when Thomas caught her again, if she could not have her freedom, mayhap his kisses would prove consoling!

Chapter Thirty

Who was she trying to fool? Yngveld demanded of herself. Thomas Lachlann's kisses were all well and good, but they were not worth staying captive for!

She sat huddled in front of her tent, frowning at the green Irish coast that flowed past her vision. The euphoria of his kisses had worn off at last. For a short time she had been under Lachlann's spell, but no more. No more! Kisses could not make up for loss of freedom.

And so she sat and plotted through the day. She had overheard Neill tell Torgils that 'twas only one more night before they arrived at Dubh Linn. Very well, that meant she had only one more chance for escape. She must escape this very night. Again. Only this time, she would be successful!

In late afternoon the ship sailed into a small cove. There was a rude hut built near the beach, and Yngveld was downhearted to see that small sign of human life. 'Twould make her escape attempt more difficult. Her lips tightened as she saw a man and two women emerge from the hut. One of the women started to plod across the beach to the water. She waved heartily at the ship in greeting.

Well, there was no help for it. Yngveld would escape despite these strangers. And mayhap she could even make their presence work for her.

"Thomas?" Yngveld approached him with what she hoped was a suitably meek smile.

Thomas looked up from where he was conferring with Neill. The sight of a humble pleading look upon the proud lips of Yngveld Sveinsdatter intrigued him. What did she want now? Showing no sign of his suspicions, he nodded pleasantly.

Yngveld took heart from his cool nod and pointed at one of the women. "It has been so long since I have seen another woman, talked to one. Do you mind if I visit—?" She could not go on. The humble words choked in her throat. She glared at the deck, knowing that if she met Thomas's eyes, he would read her intent to escape clearly written therein.

Thomas's narrowed glance took in Yngveld's mock humble look, then the woman to whom she had pointed. He smiled. 'Twas Fiona. Fiona was a good girl. Honest as the day was long. Belle and Martin, her parents, were good folk as well. Aye, Yngveld could do worse than make friends with them. He paused, considering. A quick glance at Yngveld out of the corner of his eye told him that she was holding her breath. Evidently his answer meant much to her. 'Twas probably hard on a woman to sail with a ship full of men. No doubt she did long for someone of her own sex to speak with. And Lord knew she would get little feminine companionship once she arrived in Dubh Linn. Once Jasmine got a look at her, Yngveld would be taunted and teased and Jasmine would play nasty little tricks on her. He had seen it happen before to Ivar's new conquests.

Thomas rubbed his chin thoughtfully. He supposed there was no harm in letting her visit with Fiona. And if she did try to flee again—here he shot another glance at Yngveld, but she was meekly studying the ship's deck—why, she would get a little surprise. They were near Swords, his home village, and he knew everyone in these parts. That he was not welcome should he run into Aelfred was of little account now that he had a ship full of fighting men.

"Very well, you may go and visit."

Yngveld was not fooled by the polite words. He was suspicious, she thought. She almost gave up her plan to escape then and there—but *nej*, she would dearly love to tear that asinine smirk off his face. And the only way she knew to do that was, by Thor, to escape!

So, committed irrevocably to her escape plan, she bowed in what she hoped was a suitably humble manner and fled to her tent to take a few last things with her. She had the presence of mind to not wear her armbands when she emerged from the tent. There were no ribbons fluttering from her hair to give away her plans. Her sack of gold was, of course, tied about her waist, but *he* did not know that. She was wearing her one precious set of embroidered pantalets, and her mother's breast pin and her own favorite pin were tacked under her hem where no one could see them. She was ready.

With a sweet smile, she waved to Thomas and the others and let Neill escort her off the ship. They waded through the cold water, and Yngveld shook the water off her feet once she reached the shale beach. "Do not be trying to escape," warned Neill.

Was she so transparent as all that? "Why, Neill, how could you say such a thing?"

Neill frowned. " 'Tis no secret that you ran last night. I must warn you, do not try it here. This land is Thomas's—"

"I am aware that Ireland is his country, Neill!" she snapped. Then, in a softer voice, she added, "I assure you that I will not be running blithely off into the forest." *Nej*. This time, it will be over one of those green hills. But she bit her tongue and felt a slight twinge of guilt at lying to Neill. He had been kind to her, and she hated that her last words to him would be a lie. She placed her hand on his arm as he was turning away. "Neill, I—"

"Aye?" Curiosity was in his glance.

If she thanked him for all his help, his suspicions would be raised. So she smiled sadly and said, "Thank you for walking me to the beach."

He looked at her warily, and she wished she had not given in to her guilt. But then the look vanished, and he glanced at the young woman crossing the beach to them. "I must help Thomas," he answered gruffly and strode back to the ship.

With a sigh, Yngveld watched him go. Then she turned to face the approaching woman. She pasted a bright smile to her lips and cursed that she must be as deceitful as Einar ever was in order to escape. Still, what must be done . . .

The young woman, Fiona, proved to be as guileless as a friendly puppy, and Yngveld felt doubly guilty for falsely confiding that she longed to go for a walk to stretch her legs. She almost hated to make the woman party to her escape, but she suspected that Thomas would not hurt the woman, once he learned she was duped. *Nej*, his wrath would be reserved for her, Yngveld, but by then she would be far away.

Gradually Yngveld led the unsuspecting woman into a discussion of the area and the local people. "Any large farms in these parts?" she inquired. If she could learn where the local leaders lived, she could ask them to help her find a ship to sail to Norway.

Fiona answered carefully. "There is one family that owns most of the land. . . ." she broke off and glanced from the ship to her visitor.

"And?" prodded Yngveld eagerly.

"Ummmm." Fiona was proving a reluctant informant. "They are not well-liked." Neither was Einar, remembered Yngveld. Yet he had been the most influential man in the Godthab District of Greenland. Mayhap 'twas the same here. The merchant or farmer who managed to become wealthy was not always dear to his neighbors. Well, she had managed Einar. She could manage this family, whoever they were.

"Where do they live?" Yngveld asked brightly. She and Fiona were now walking across the shale beach toward the green, rolling hills. Yngveld made sure that their pace was slow, stately even, so that any watching green eyes would not narrow in suspicion. She wanted to glance at the ship to see if Thomas was indeed watching, but with a great effort, she refrained.

Fiona waited until they topped the crest of a low hill to answer Yngveld's question. She pointed in the direction of the setting sun. "That is their mansion," she said solemnly.

Yngveld could see a large dark shape that cast a great shadow. The building appeared to be made of stone, in the manner of a monastery. Small huts or outbuildings half-circled it. "Mansion? It seems very luxurious. . . ." Yngveld murmured.

"Aye, 'tis." Fiona glanced at Yngveld. "Where did you say you came from?"

"Greenland. But there are no houses like that one in Greenland." Yngveld was properly awed. The house was the largest she had ever seen. "Is the family strong? Can they protect their lands?" She had to know if they would put up a fight if Thomas came looking for her. No point in seeking help from them if they had no capability to help her.

Fiona frowned at Yngveld's eagerness. "They can fight, aye. They fight too much."

Yngveld glanced at Fiona at that enigmatic statement. Well, there was no help for it. She was looking at her new sanctuary. Her toes wriggled restlessly in the green grass.

"I—I need privacy," Yngveld murmured suddenly, and her face burned. She glanced around, pretending to search for a bush or tree or rock that she could squat behind. Fiona guessed the obvious, and obligingly took a few steps back toward the small hut she shared with her parents.

"No need to wait," Yngveld called, waving a hand casually as she headed for a large cluster of boulders that stood between her and the great mansion.

Fiona, duped once more, smiled and waved back. "You are invited to sup with us," she called. "Methinks 'twill be a pleasant change from sea fare."

Yngveld could but nod, miserably guilty now at using the kindly Fiona. She could only hope that Thomas would go easy on the girl once he learned of Yngveld's escape. Yngveld bent suddenly and fiddled with the hem of her gown. "Wait!" she cried. Grasping her favorite brooch in her hand, she ran over to Fiona. "Here," she said breathlessly, thrusting the finely made object into her surprised new friend's hand. "Take this."

"But—" Fiona looked at her a little oddly. She glanced down at the piece and, seeing the fine workmanship, her eyes widened. "Are—are you sure?" At Yngveld's nod, she clasped the precious brooch to her chest and exclaimed, "My thanks, Yngveld. Oh, 'tis truly beautiful!"

With a tiny smile, Fiona fixed the lovely piece of jewelry to her own tunic. Yngveld smiled back, some of the guilt at her deception lessened. "It looks lovely on you," she assured Fiona. And it did.

She watched as Fiona skipped happily back to the shore and started across the shale beach. With a frown, Yngveld swung for one last, irresistible glance at the ship. Several of the men were gathered around two men who splashed in the water. Yngveld narrowed her eyes. 'Twas Karl and Patrick. Fighting. In the water. Now Karl ducked Patrick, then Patrick got up and heaved Karl into the cold waves. A huge splash drenched the cheering, boisterous onlookers.

With a groan, Yngveld turned from the scene. That her last glance of Karl and Patrick should be of them trying to drown each other seemed too sad. Yet her own opportunity for escape would never get better.

Now. This was her chance, while everyone's attention was on the fighting men! With a tiny skip, she picked up the front of her tunic and started into a slow lope toward the dark, forbidding mansion in the distance.

* * *

Patrick was furious, raging, foaming, furious. What he really wanted to do was to kill Karl. The man made a poor slave, Patrick thought in contempt, watching Karl flailing under the waves. Everything Patrick told his new slave to do, Karl did. But it was *how* he did it: slowly, feet dragging, with many sad looks over his shoulder at Patrick, until Patrick wanted to gnash his teeth and scream his frustration. What the hell did Karl think slavery was about? Karl should know! He'd kept Patrick a slave for fourteen years, fourteen long, lost years that Patrick would never get back.

Karl surged out of the water, a murderous look ravaging his face. Patrick was ready for him. He gripped Karl's tunic just under the chin and hauled him up. "I'll kill you," he spat in Karl's face, then gave a great heave and Karl sank beneath the waves once more. The older man was having a hard time of it in the physical contest, and his wet clothes weighted him down. Patrick watched, a contemptuous look on his face, as Karl tried to stand, then fell back into the water. Good! Patrick thought. Let him drown!

Loud cheering from the watching soldiers finally cut through Patrick's preoccupation with Karl. Swinging around, Patrick realized that the grinning faces and cries were urging him on. The soldiers, too, were avid to see Karl drown. It added excitement to their day.

Suddenly Patrick looked at Karl, actually

looked at the coughing, sputtering, bedraggled man who swayed on his feet as he gasped for breath. *I could kill him*, Patrick thought in sudden wonder. *This man whom I have loved for fourteen years, I could kill him now.* And then Patrick realized with a cold, clear clarity that the only end that he and Karl could ever come to would be death. If they kept on as they had, locked in mortal combat, each one struggling for power, each one struggling to be in control of the other, then that struggle could end only with one, or both, of their deaths. There was no other way out.

Now sickened at the cries urging him on, Patrick turned away for a moment. He had already lost fourteen years to this man. Did he want to lose another moment tied in a sick, destructive bondage of hate with him? The thought revolted Patrick and he suddenly saw himself as the grinning onlookers must. It was merely a fight to them. It mattered not if a master killed a slave. There were always more. Except that this was Karl. Loved, hated Karl.

At that moment, Karl, steadier on his feet now, and breathing heavily, staggered through the thigh-high water to Patrick. He grabbed out at Patrick's neck, his hands curved into claws. A look of pure hate contorted Karl's face.

Calmly, Patrick put out both hands to stop Karl's clumsy onslaught. In that moment, Patrick knew what he must do. To save his own soul . . . he must do it.

"You are free," he said. His voice carried on

the clear air. "You are free. I no longer call you my slave."

Karl's face twisted in disbelief. Groans and hisses from the men around him told Patrick that they did not approve of this compassionate gesture. But Patrick knew their approval mattered little. What mattered was that he stop this duel to the death, this terrible dance of hate and despair. To do so, he must set Karl, and himself, free.

"All men here may witness it: I hereby set you free, Karl Ketilson. No man may call you slave."

Patrick gazed into Karl's startled blue eyes and for a heartbeat Patrick's face softened. Then, abruptly, before he could change his mind, he turned and strode out of the water and up to the beach. He left behind a bewildered, bedraggled former slave staring openmouthed and uncomprehending after him.

Chapter Thirty-one

"Well, well, and what do we have here?" smirked Aelfred as Yngveld stood uncertainly in the great doorway of the mansion.

"Naught but a peasant wench," snorted Helmut, looking up blearily from his horn of ale where they sat at table. Suddenly, he dropped the drinking horn into his bowl of meat. He ignored the gravy that splashed on his tunic as he half-rose to his feet. He peered at the woman standing in the doorway. "But what a wench! I have not seen the likes of her about," he murmured, getting fully to his feet and waddling to the door.

"I saw her first," cried Aelfred petulantly.

Helmut ignored him as he strode to the door,

sucking in his gut as he approached the woman.

Helmut attempted a bow, but it was so swift that Yngveld missed it. She did not, however, miss the dirty, heavy hand that clamped around her wrist and dragged her forward into the gloom.

"I—" she began.

"No need to speak, wench," said Helmut hoarsely, dragging her toward the table. He was headed for a back room. "I want her all to myself," he barked at Aelfred, who had risen and now followed them as a dog follows a suspicious scent. "She's mine!"

"We can share," whined Aelfred.

Helmut drew his sword, one hand still grasping the now struggling Yngveld. "Stop it," he snarled at her. To Aelfred he ground out, "You can have her later. When I am done with her."

"But Helmut," protested Aelfred. "You know we always share the new wenches."

"Not any more. This one is mine." His little blue eyes watched in satisfaction as he saw the very moment that Aelfred decided to back down. "Good," Helmut grunted, and slid his sword back into the scabbard. "Come with me, wench."

"Where—where are we going?" cried Yngveld, bewildered. "Is there no one here I can speak with? The—the lord, or mayhap the lady?"

Helmut jerked a careless thumb at Aelfred as he propelled her before him. "That's the lord," he snorted. "And the lady is blind."

"Well, let me speak with someone." Yngveld pulled at the heavy hand squeezing her wrist. "Let me go, you wretch!"

"None o' that now! You be kind to Helmut. And mayhap Helmut will be kind to you. If you are good."

Yngveld uneasily watched the smirk on his coarse mouth. His face red from his exertions, his nose squashed from too many fights, his body heavy from too many years of eating and drinking and raping peasant wenches, Helmut was a ghastly sight.

What is he doing? thought Yngveld in panic. "Where—where are you taking me?" she cried.

"To my chamber," he said.

"*Nej!*" she cried. She threw all her effort into pulling at the madman's hand. Succeeding in releasing herself, she darted for the door. She almost made it past the table, but Aelfred reached out and grabbed her long hair as she ran past. The terrible yank on her hair burned her scalp and halted Yngveld in mid-step. She whirled on the blond, thin Aelfred. "Let go of my hair," she growled savagely and pulled the flaxen mass from his hand.

Aelfred smiled, and she saw that several of his teeth were lined with rot at the gums. "I believe she likes me," he said to Helmut, who was panting up to them, "better than you."

"Nah. She is just teasing me," said Helmut, as his grasp closed once more over Yngveld's sorely used wrist. "She likes *me*!"

They began to argue over her as they stood there.

Yngveld tried desperately to shake the madman's hand loose. "Let me *go*!" She cast her eyes about the large room looking for aid, any kind of aid. "Help!" she squeaked.

A score of men sat at the table watching her as though this was a usual occurrence. Which it no doubt was, thought Yngveld. Two of them got to their feet and tottered over, looking to be in their cups. At last, she thought. Some help. They too looked big and heavy, but at least they had responded to her cry for help.

"Helmut," said the first. His long blond beard was spattered with dried meat. A stench of old sweat rose from him, and Yngveld recoiled visibly, then wished she had not. He was, after all, trying to help her.

" 'Tis time," said the bearded one, "that we have *our* turn first. You always get the prettiest wenches."

Yngveld's mouth gaped open. She recovered herself quickly. "You are no help!" she yelled at them.

They ignored her, preferring to put their suit to Helmut. The second one had drawn his sword. He was dark-haired and shorter, and looked cleaner than his bearded companion. He, however, had mean little pig eyes. "Oh, my God," she squealed, "I must get out of here!"

The short, dark one grabbed her other hand and yanked on it, hard, trying to get Helmut to loosen his grip. Yngveld thought they would tear her in two. When he saw that Helmut would not let go, the short man raised his sword, obviously intent on bashing Helmut to subdue him. That Yngveld would get hurt in the fray seemed of little concern to him.

In terror, she screamed at the top of her lungs.

"Shut up," growled Helmut, and he raised his beefy paw to backhand her.

But before he could follow through with the blow, the huge front door crashed open.

Chapter Thirty-two

"Thomas!" screamed Yngveld at the huge black shape that blocked the doorway.

With a bloodcurdling roar, Thomas Lachlann hurled himself forward. Behind him, yelling like the ferocious warriors they were, rushed Neill, Torgils, and the whole of Thomas's crew.

Never in her life had she been so glad to see anyone, thought Yngveld. Never!

Helmut let go her wrist and spun her aside as he whirled to face the swarming invasion.

Yngveld sagged against the wall in relief.

Her dark-haired attacker roared as he ran, sword out, straight at the charging Vikings. Thomas grabbed up a bench and slammed it into him, and the man collapsed on the floor, oblivious to the invaders trampling over him.

Yngveld watched the milling men in dismay. Cries and grunts and yells bounced off the stone walls of the big hall. Men were everywhere, fighting, twisting, leaping, slashing with broad dull swords that bounced off little round shields, wrenching heads back with muscular arms, attacking each other with axes, swords, and even pieces of wood. In terror, Yngveld watched as Karl and Patrick, too, entered the fray. She blinked. For a moment, she thought she saw Karl laughing gleefully as he stabbed with a sword at a fat defender. Then her attention flew to where Thomas and the madman battled.

"This one's mine!" bellowed Thomas above the terrible din. Then he whacked at Helmut with his sword and laughed as the bulky one jumped. "Come on, come on," coaxed Thomas harshly. "Fight!"

The battle fever was upon him, and Thomas felt invincible and glorious. In a lightning quick glance, he had seen that Yngveld was safe against the wall. And now he had his chance to kill the man who had laughed at him so many years before when he had driven Thomas from his own land.

Helmut, shaking his head like a great shaggy beast, rushed at his foe. But his days of wenching and high living and little exercise save for the beatings of peasants told against Helmut. It took only three well-placed blows before Helmut sank to the floor, gasping like a dying fish. From then on his body constantly tripped up his drunken comrades as they fought desperately against the clear-eyed, hard-visaged invaders.

The battle was over in minutes. Drunk and dying men lay scattered across the hard stone floor. The cheery fire burning in the fireplace at the end of the room cast a warm glow on the grisly scene. Heartrending groans filled the smoky air and echoed through the building.

Thomas, a slash wound to his leg, limped over to Yngveld.

"Thomas! You are hurt!" She fell at his feet and examined the injured limb.

He winced. " 'Tis nothing."

"Oh, Thomas," she moaned.

"Get up, Yngveld."

"*Nej*. Thomas, I cannot. You are wounded. I must help you!"

He closed his eyes briefly. "You can help me more if you are not touching the wound."

"Oh, *ja*, of course." Belatedly she realized that her compassionate touches were of little use. The wound was bleeding. She ran to grab up some cloths off the table and raced back to Thomas. She patted the wound with them, then eyed the cut cautiously. It had stopped bleeding and was not deep. Still . . . "It does not look too bad," she said doubtfully.

He eyed her. "Aye."

She helped him to sit down upon a bench. He leaned back against the wall and closed his eyes once more, his face tired.

"Is it so very bad, Thomas?" she asked in a small voice.

His green eyes shot open at that. " 'Tis nothing, I tell you."

She nodded, understanding that he had no doubt been taught not to let the pain show.

"Thomas, never was I so glad to see you as the moment you burst in that door."

"Aye."

"Truly, Thomas. They—they were going to hurt me." She closed her eyes tightly at the memory. Her hands trembled now at the delayed reaction. "I—I was verily glad to see you."

"Aye."

"You saved me, Thomas! You saved my life."

"Aye."

She waited, but he added nothing to his cryptic assent. "Thomas?"

He opened his eyes.

"Thank you," she said softly.

He closed his eyes once more and sighed. No need to remind Yngveld that he had saved her for Ivar.

"What will we do with this 'un?"

Thomas's eyes jerked open and he beheld his half-brother, Aelfred, standing before him, tightly gripped by Neill and Torgils on either side. His weariness fled, and Thomas got up from the bench to face his half-brother.

Aelfred looked wrathful, his slightly bulging blue eyes furious as they centered on Thomas's pale face. "So, 'tis you! Come back, like you said!"

"Aye," answered Thomas wryly. "Though 'twas not quite as I had planned." His glance shot to Yngveld, then back to Aelfred.

She thought she saw a twinkle in that green gaze, but then thought she had been mistaken.

"Get out," snarled Aelfred. He glared around the room where most of his men lay dead. "You have done what you came for. You have killed my men. Killed Helmut, my good friend—"

"He was no friend," objected Thomas.

"What do you know about it?" snarled Aelfred. "Helmut helped me! He told me what to do. How to keep the land. Why, he even picked my men." Aelfred struggled to free a hand. Neither Neill nor Torgils relaxed their grip. Teeth clenched, Aelfred gritted, "And now you have killed them all. Get out, I say!"

"No," said Thomas and his voice rang with quiet authority. "This is my home now. You are the one who must leave." At a nod from Thomas, Neill and Torgils released Aelfred.

Aelfred glared at Thomas, blue eyeballs bulging, mouth gaping. He leaped at the table and snatched up a sword. Fire in his eyes, he swung at Thomas. "I will kill you!" He lifted the sword above Thomas's head.

Thomas ducked and stepped aside. Still he did not reach for his own sword. He did, however, grab up a round shield to defend himself with. Aelfred's blade bounced off the rim.

Aelfred hacked furiously at him for several minutes and in that time, Thomas went through three shields, throwing the broken one to the side and snatching up another before his half-brother could bestow another blow.

Aelfred was panting now. "I will never give the manor over to you. Never!" he gasped.

"Think you not? What choice do you have? Your men are dead. You have no one to defend you."

Aelfred's lips were a thin white line of fury. His eyes bulged from his head. "I will see you dead!"

"Get a grip on yourself," barked Thomas. His half-brother straightened reflexively. "There will be no more talk of killing, of dying, of death. By Thor, have you not had enough?" Thomas looked around the room, loathing on his face. "How many good men died to protect you?" Contempt was on his face. "Get out, Aelfred, whilst I can still stay my hand." He reached for the hilt of *Thor's Bite*.

Aelfred backed up a step, as though he suddenly realized the tenuous position he was in. "Where—where will I go?" he whined.

Thomas looked exasperated. "I care not. But leave my lands. And do not come back!"

Aelfred turned on his heel and ran for the great door. He was just stepping across the threshold when a high voice intruded. "Aelfred? Where are you, Aelfred?"

Entering the large hall from a small side room came an old woman, thin and very straight. She walked unseeing across the red-splashed carpet of dying men. Thomas saw that her once-blond hair was now white; her blue eyes, once so bright, were now covered with an opaque film. A young serving maid led her; even so, she stumbled as she came forward.

"Greetings, Lady Ingrid," said Thomas evenly. He did not bow.

"Who?" she quavered. "Who is it?"

Thomas saw that Aelfred barely paused as he fled through the door and out into the yard. Torgils followed him. "'Tis I, Thomas Lachlann."

"Lachlann? Is it you then?" She held out her hands in the manner of the blind. "Closer, girl," she ordered the maid imperiously, in her old manner.

She had not changed, thought Thomas. But her circumstances had. He suffered the woman to come within several paces. "You are in my manor now, Lady Ingrid." His voice was firm. "And on my lands."

"So!" she snarled. "You have returned. And now you are sending away my son, and Harald's son, the rightful lord of the land."

"I am also Harald's son, madame, lest you forget."

He saw her face whiten, and her lips looked bloodless. "Your son could not hold the land, madame. Therefore, it is now mine." Though he had oft dreamed of it, Thomas realized now that he had never actually thought to speak those words. That Lord Harald's vast lands and huge manor should now be his felt fitting and right. He was of this land, and his mother's family had been of this land for centuries. Now it had been returned to him.

"Would you turn a blind woman out into the forest?" she asked, her voice suddenly piteous. A crafty look flitted across her face and was gone.

Thomas's grim mouth relaxed. He was a man now. This dragon could not order him around, could not grind him into the dust as she had when he was a small boy. "Nothing has been said about turning you out. However, you are free to leave the manor and seek other lodgings." The serving maid at her side looked nervous.

"Where would I go?" came the quavering voice, and this time Thomas thought the fear was real.

"That is for you to decide, Lady Ingrid. But I will not have you in my home."

Her head, so proud on the thin stalk of her neck, shook as though palsied. She turned away and started for the door. The serving maid ran after her.

"You may take any belongings you wish," added Thomas. Lady Ingrid halted where she stood but did not turn to face him. "You may continue to reside on the lands—in a small house mayhap. You may have your maid and shall not suffer for want of food or wood or water."

Lady Ingrid resumed her stiff walk to the door, the little maid guiding her by the arm. Thomas watched her go, grudgingly admiring the old woman's unbending pride. When the door quietly closed behind her, he felt that a part of his past—a sad, troubling part—had also closed.

"You are too soft," growled Torgils. "You treat her far better than she deserves."

Thomas shrugged. "She is old and blind. And pitiful. I choose not to punish her for her past cruelty to me." He looked curiously at Torgils. "Why did you pursue Aelfred? He is already a beaten man."

Torgils grinned. "Aye. But I wanted to make certain that he did not return. Ever."

Thomas lifted a questioning brow.

"I told him what you should have told him," said Torgils.

"And what was that?"

"That if he ever returned, I would cut out his heart."

Thomas looked at his friend lazily. "He has none."

Whilst walking among the wounded, Thomas was surprised to see Neill approach, one arm around his father, Caedmon. "Caedmon!" exclaimed Thomas. "You are injured."

"'Tis nothing, a mere scratch," panted the old man.

Thomas set out a bench and helped the old man to sit. He peered at the bleeding wound on Caedmon's arm. "I see now where your son gets his bravery."

Caedmon's wrinkled face relaxed at the compliment. Thomas was still peering at the wound.

"Best you get some herbs on that," he advised. "See what old Bess can do. If she is still alive?" Much had changed in ten years, he reminded himself. And old Bess, the herb woman, had always been old, even when Thomas was a boy. Mayhap she now lay in her grave.

Caedmon smiled. "Aye, Bess is still about. Hardy, that one." He gave a little chuckle, then winced and moved his injured arm closer to his body. "Bess is no doubt visiting your old mother."

"How is she?" asked Thomas.

"Your old mum? Why, the same as ever. No better, no worse."

"Your wound pains you."

Caedmon shrugged off Thomas's concern. "You took your time coming back to us."

Thomas heard the reproach in the old man's voice. "Aye," he agreed.

"Glad I am," muttered Caedmon, "that you wiped out that nest o' vipers. Aelfred and his henchman, Helmut, made life very difficult for the folk. Very difficult." He peered at Thomas. "But then, you must have known that. Connall carried messages many times to tell you how it was with us."

"Aye. Until now I did not have the men to help you. And still would not have, had not Yngveld Sveinsdatter escaped from me. Again."

Thomas sighed and glanced around the smoky room to see how Yngveld had fared in the fighting. He went still. "Where is Yngveld?" he asked, anger darkening his visage.

Torgils and Neill glanced about the room and then they both shrugged. A swift, thorough search of the hall and environs failed to reveal her whereabouts.

"Where in Thor's name has that woman gone now?" roared Thomas.

Chapter Thirty-three

Under a spreading oak tree, Yngveld awoke to singing birds and a growling stomach. Her ribs hurt from where her sack of gold had pressed into her as she slept. She sat up and glanced around, remembering now that she had escaped from Thomas Lachlann and his men the night before. She remembered, too, how handsome Thomas had looked as he had hurtled through the manor's doorway with his men to rescue her.

She sighed. Mayhap she had been a fool to flee him this time. But she could not go to Dubh Linn and be married off to Ivar. She *could not*. Especially not when the mere sight of Thomas Lachlann made her heart beat faster, and a mere word from him made her pale cheeks flush.

For Dubh Linn was where he meant to take her. She knew him well enough now to know that nothing would sway him from his cause—and from Ivar.

She got to her feet, yawned, and stretched, then fumbled at her waist for a dried chunk of pork that she had scooped up off the manor's cluttered table the night before. She wished now that she had picked something more appetizing.

The dried piece of meat looked hard, but 'twould have to do. She bit off a piece and chewed. 'Twas stringy and tasted like shoe leather, but resolutely she continued chewing as she walked. When her jaws ached, she put the meat away.

She started singing to herself, happy to be walking in the green forest. In the midst of the chaos after the fighting last night, no one had noticed her leave. Once outside the manor, she had realized that she could not return across the smooth green hills to the beach where Thomas had moored his ship. Glancing frantically about, she had spied the forest, at some distance behind the manor. As though she had wings upon her feet, she had run to the welcoming dark shelter of the trees.

Yngveld stopped singing when a meadow presented itself to her eyes. The clear morning light shone on the dew of the crescent-shaped meadow and made the grass look light green. Yngveld could easily pick it out from the darker green and black splashes of bog. The meadow would be the best place to walk, she thought judiciously. She glanced around once more and then, serenaded by the trills of birds, she started forward.

The morning was truly lovely in this new land, she thought, swinging her arms as she skipped along. A small creek ran at one end of the meadow, and she knelt to taste the water. She had taken several mouthfuls of the wonderfully fresh water when all of a sudden she noticed that the birds had stopped chirping. Startled, she lifted her head and glanced around. Only meadow and oak forest met her eyes. Rising slowly to her feet, she swung her head about, nostrils flaring, trying to determine if there was danger.

There was. Leaning against a tree and now watching her was Thomas Lachlann.

With a gasp, Yngveld was on her feet and running away from the creek. Her bare feet flew over the wet grass and she prayed that she would not slip.

She had a good start on him, she told herself as her feet pumped swiftly. But now a pounding tread behind her told her that she was quickly losing her advantage. A jolt of fear lent her a burst of speed. Mayhap she should jettison the gold, she thought, casting a panic-stricken look over one shoulder. 'Twas slowing her down. But she could not bring herself to cast her treasure aside.

On she ran. It seemed almost as if Thomas Lachlann was content to keep a distance between them. He did not seem to be making an effort to catch up to her. Taking hope, she lengthened her stride. Her breaths were now coming in short pants. Her lungs ached, but her leg muscles felt strong. She knew that she could run a long distance before they gave out.

Ahead of her stretched more open meadow and vast, rolling green hills. Clumps of alder and oak dotted the landscape and she saw many bogs scattered across the small, dish-shaped green plain in front of her. She must avoid them. Thomas would surely catch her were she to stumble into one of those swampy peat bogs.

Yngveld glanced back over her shoulder. Still he came on, looking barely winded. His sinewy leg muscles moved effortlessly as he ran across the smooth terrain. She saw that his sword flapped at his side.

She glanced behind him. No one else had joined the chase. He had come alone. Was he so confident he would catch her? She put on a new burst of speed, desperate to outrun him. She would not go to Ivar. She would *not*.

Suddenly she could hear Thomas Lachlann drawing closer, much closer. Still she ran, her blond hair streaming loose behind her. She would not give up, she would run until he cut her down with his sword, if it came to that!

Then with a terrible lunge, Thomas was upon her. He bowled her over and she went rolling across the grass. Immediately she tried to scramble to her feet, but he threw himself over her and she sank back against the ground. He lay upon her, hot green eyes looking down into shimmering blue ones.

Yngveld wanted to cry in disappointment and despair. So close! She had been so close to freedom. Bitterness rose in her mouth, and she tightened her lips, willing herself not to cry and add further to her humiliation.

Thomas watched her small breasts rising and falling under the bulky tunic. His narrowed fierce gaze moved back to her face and he saw the fear thereon.

And she should be afraid, he thought. When he had first discovered that she was missing, *he* had been the one to feel fear—for her safety. There were hungry wolves in the Irish forests, and ill-tempered, unpredictable wild boars. As she already knew. His blood still hot from the fight against Aelfred, Thomas had delayed finding her, knowing that he might betray his own honor and Ivar's were he to come upon her while fresh from battle. It was only later, as he was following her trail through the forest, that he had stopped to think that he had followed her for his own purposes, not Ivar's—for Thomas had realized that he did not want to lose her.

In fear for Yngveld, he had increased his pace until he had discovered her asleep under a large oak. Seeing how deeply she slept, satisfied that she would sleep several hours, he had taken his own rest nearby. Unfortunately, he had slept deeply himself and had not heard her rise.

Something had awakened him, and he had hurried after her, only to discover her kneeling at the stream.

Now, as he looked down into those wide, frightened blue eyes, he smiled, a fierce, angry smile. "Did you enjoy your run?"

Goaded, Yngveld hissed, "Get off me!"

Thomas's eyes, hot, lustful, stroked her face. He did not have to get off her yet. He could play with her a little.

Yngveld's eyes fluttered shut, as though she could not face his lust.

"I do not think so," he purred. "I like it just where I am."

Yngveld's eyes flew open. "Get off me, you lout!"

He reached out and his long fingers grabbed a handful of hair at the back of her head. He lifted her face to his, her mouth mere inches from his own. "Do not try to escape me again!"

"I will!" she cried. "I will try again and again until I am free—of you and of Ivar!"

His green eyes raked her, her words bringing pain to him. Through clenched teeth he gritted, "You cannot escape me. I will run you to the ends of the earth!"

His voice was harsh and unyielding, and Yngveld shivered a little. "Let me up!" she demanded, for she felt a new fear now. Something hard was pressing against her hip, and 'twas not her gold coins. "Let me up!"

But Thomas, confident that he was still in control of himself, was too stubborn to listen to what *she* wanted. Instead, he dipped his head and ground his lips into hers.

Yngveld pushed frantically at his shoulders and tried to tear her mouth away.

Thomas followed her with his own and clutched her head closer. When he finally released her, they were both panting heavily. Mayhap 'twas not such a good idea to kiss her, he thought dazedly.

Yngveld touched her throbbing lips, her eyes wide and frightened. "Why—why did you do that?"

His conscience asking him the same thing, Thomas lowered his head once more and kissed her into silence.

Reproaching himself, Thomas slowly let the kiss end, then raised his head and looked down at her. He loosed his tight grip on her hair and slowly lowered her head to the grass. Her hair was pale as it fanned out around her head against the green.

In a fit of despair and defiance, Thomas pulled her to him and laid his head against her breasts. His grip tightened. He did not want to let her go. He did not want to take her to Ivar. He wanted to keep her for himself. The thought shook him, and he gripped her all the tighter to keep from trembling.

Yngveld slowly, tentatively, touched a dark curl of his head. She felt the possessiveness of his hold and wondered at it.

Where he gripped her, Thomas could suddenly feel something hard and coinlike. "What is this?" He reared back suspiciously, not enough to lift himself off the length of her body, but enough that he could place a warm, firm hand on her belly. "Why, Yngveld Sveinsdatter, I do believe you took your gold with you."

"*Ja*, I did. I meant to escape!"

"Then you are a bigger fool than I thought. Do you know what could have happened to you, a woman traveling alone with a fortune in gold?" His gaze darkened as he fought to restrain his anger. The woman would have been easy prey for any man. "You stumbled upon my family's manor. You know that, do you not?"

She looked at him and shook her head slowly. "*Nej*," she said. "I went to them, asking for help—"

"Asking my half-brother, Aelfred, for help, or his henchman, Helmut. . . ." he shook his head. "I would sooner ask a wolf to help a rabbit."

She glared at him. "Is that who they were? Your family?" She sniffed, obviously not impressed with his bloodlines.

Thomas grinned. "One of them. The one with the blue eyes is my half-brother. The other is dead." Thomas rolled over onto his stomach, putting a little distance between himself and Yngveld. Some of his anger subsided. His eyes wandered over her, and he felt his groin stir.

Yngveld's cheeks flushed. "How was I supposed to know?" she cried.

He shrugged. "One of the risks you take when you run." He chewed a piece of grass meditatively. "Why are you always running, Yngveld?"

She looked at him, bewilderment on her face. "I—? Running—?"

"Aye. When I first met you, you were running. You have escaped me twice."

"Thrice," she corrected him. "Once the first night in Ireland, once to your family's home, and once to this forest." She looked disgruntled as she said it. The reminder that he had caught her irritated her, and her eyes glittered with unshed tears at the unfairness of it. That Thomas had caught her was the biggest blow to her pride and her hopes.

"Twice, thrice." He shrugged again. " 'Tis of little matter. What interests me is, why do you run? Why do you not stay and face your fear?"

"Would it do any good?" she demanded of him. "Would it have done any good to say to Bjarni Bearhunter, '*Nej*, I will not marry you. Leave.' Think you he would have listened?"

Thomas looked at her, his green eyes thoughtful.

Yngveld answered her own question. "*Nej*, Thomas Lachlann. Bjarni Bearhunter would have not listened. He would have taken what he wanted, my land and me, and I would have had no say. That is why I ran from him."

"And me?" he breathed. "Why have you run from me?"

" 'Tis obvious," she snapped. "You would take me to Dubh Linn and your precious Ivar. And as I have told you before, I do not want to marry Ivar!"

"What *do* you want, Yngveld?" The green eyes were not mocking, but serious.

She leaned forward and locked her blue gaze on his. "I want to be free," she snarled. "I want to be free to choose my own fate!"

Thomas continued to watch her, a thoughtful expression on his face. "And what would you choose, fair Valkyrie of the North?" he breathed. He looked alert, as though every muscle and drop of blood in his body was concentrated on her.

It gave her a heady feeling, and Yngveld relished his attention to the utmost. "What would I choose?" she muttered. "I would choose . . ." Her voice died out. She had been about to say that she would choose to be with him, to marry him, to have his children, to live in his fair green land with him. She bit her tongue in time. How foolish! He would laugh if he knew that she longed for him. He certainly did not long for her! She would have noticed. "I—I will not tell you," she said instead.

A little light went out in those beautiful green eyes. What was there about this woman? Thomas wondered. Now *he* was the one running from his own fears. He wanted to keep her with him, not take her to Ivar. But he did not say the words. Fear held him back, fear that she would laugh at him, dismiss his suit or—his eyes dropped to her waist—accuse him of wanting her for her money. No, he could not bear that rejection and so he kept silent.

He sighed. "I am bound to take you to Dubh

Linn and Ivar. You know that, Yngveld."

"*Ja*," she said bitterly. "I know it. You have never, ever let me forget it, even knowing as you do that I want nothing to do with the man!"

'Twas of no use to argue with her. That he was bound by actions he had helped to set in motion was as bitter to him as it was to her. When he had first consented to go to Greenland, he had given his word to bring her to Ivar. How little he had known then. About himself. About loving a woman. About freedom and honor. He sighed heavily. He was committed to bringing her to Ivar and bring her to Ivar he would. Safely. At least he could do that. 'Twas a small thing, but it was something. "I will keep you safe," he promised her aloud.

She glared at him, her blue gaze locked with his. Then her eyes softened. "I—I know you will. You have proved that often enough."

He chuckled. "Aye, I have." They both went still, staring into each other's eyes. "Yngveld," he breathed. All reason fled. Nothing mattered but Yngveld, beautiful Yngveld. Thomas's blood pounded thickly through his veins as he reached for her.

"Thomas," she murmured and came into his arms.

Thomas clasped her to him and slowly lowered his mouth to hers. He took his time in an exploratory, tentative kiss.

Yngveld was quite unprepared for the gentleness of it. Then his tongue demanded entrance to the soft inner part of her mouth. "Oh, *nej*," she moaned.

"Oh, *ja*." Thomas moved his lips over hers, at the same time pressing his hard frame against her. The gold sack under her tunic dug against his ribs. He brought a hand up to push it away, but somehow his hand made it past the gold to the gentle mound of her breast. He cupped her /gently.

She struggled to sit up. "*Nej*, you must not."

"Ah, but I must."

He kissed her again. Yngveld took a breath, desperate to stop his devastating assault on her senses. But before she could gasp out a word, he was kissing her once more, his lips moving languorously over her mouth. Slowly, slowly, he lowered her back down upon the soft grass.

Yngveld whimpered softly. *I should not be doing this*, she thought. Then all thoughts were driven from her mind as he continued his relentless kisses. His mouth became hot and devouring, and Yngveld's world centered on where he would kiss her next.

Her clothing was a frustrating barrier, and Thomas was not about to put up with it. Carefully he slid his hand up her leg to her thigh. When she did nothing to stop him, he gently lifted the offending tunic. He had it bunched up to her waist and his hands were doing wonderful things to her lower torso, when Yngveld suddenly raised her hands to stop him. Swiftly she untied the sack of gold and cast it to the grass where it clanked dully. She turned back to him.

"Let me," whispered Thomas over her murmured protests as he quickly helped divest her of the bulky tunic. He held his breath as he stared at her naked beauty. His heart, already pounding fiercely, beat faster. Lord, she was lovely. Her graceful form, her legs, her breasts . . . He leaned forward and kissed the delicate pink tips.

Yngveld looked down at the dark head pressed against her bosom, and her breathing quickened. She could feel the warmth of him, the scratchiness of his cheek as he pressed against the soft skin.

Then his head came away and he was stripping off his own garments and tossing his sword aside. It lay, silver against the green grass, sparkling in the morning sun. Thomas turned back to her with muscular arms open. She went into them.

"Ah, Yngveld," he murmured. "I have wanted to do this for so long."

She smiled and rubbed her cheek against his crisp chest hair. "I have wanted it too," she admitted softly.

He drew back at that. "Truly?"

"Truly." She glanced away shyly. "I thought surely you knew. I could not keep my eyes from you."

He was kissing her again, her cheeks, her lips, her throat. . . . "Oh, I saw you gaze at me. But I thought 'twas fear."

"Not fear—excitement," she gasped, startled at what he was now doing with his tongue. He laved the tender skin behind her ear and warm shivers darted down her spine. Her head lolled back and she sighed happily.

"Yngveld?"

"Mmmmm?"

"Thank you for lying atop me."

She knew immediately that he was referring to the time he had been dragged through the freezing waters of the sea.

"I would have died."

"*Ja,*" she acknowledged softly. "You would have."

He could not help himself. He had to ask. This time she would tell him the truth. "Why, Yngveld, why did you do it?"

It was her turn to pull away and look at him. Her wide blue eyes locked with his. "Because I wanted you to live. From the first moment I saw you, I thought you were so beautiful. . . ."

He closed his eyes, and a look, as of pain, crossed his darkly handsome face.

She saw it. " 'Tis true, Thomas," she said gently. "I admired you. Your way with your men. Your standing up to Einar. I did not want you to die. . . ."

He opened his eyes, and they were a clear green, the pain gone from his face. "I believe you," he said at last. "I believe you. Now. When you are naked and have nothing to hide from me."

She smiled, and her hand brushed his savage jaw line. "I am glad I did it."

He heard the satisfaction, almost smugness in her voice, and his lips twisted. He bent to kiss her again.

Yngveld felt the warmth of him, his stroking hands, his lips, and she sighed and gave herself up to the sensations he elicited. When he nudged at the very entrance to her, she parted her legs and he gently slid into her.

It took all of Thomas's considerable will to keep from plunging wildly into the woman who lay beneath him, the woman he wanted with all his soul. He did not want to hurt her, though he knew he would. "Yngveld," he murmured, voice strained. "'Twill hurt for a short time."

She opened her eyes to stare up into his green ones. "I am ready," she said. He plunged then and she gave a cry, her arching back lifting from the ground. He held her to him, murmuring soft, endearing words until she gradually relaxed once more. He began to move slowly, carefully, the tempo increasing until he stiffened suddenly. A triumphant, hoarse cry issued from his lips. Then he wilted over her, panting heavily.

After a time, he lifted himself off her a little and stared down at her. She watched him with calm eyes. He grinned and kissed her forehead. "'Tis not over yet," he said.

"'Tis enough, Thomas."

He chuckled. "You think so?"

She smiled, a tiny relaxed smile, and then stretched and yawned.

Thomas watched her through suddenly narrowed eyes. "You think we are done so soon, Yngveld Sveinsdatter?"

She nodded and smiled. "I have pleased you, have I not?" Her blue eyes watched him in placid amusement. "What say you, Thomas? Was it good for you?" Mild feminine satisfaction laced her voice.

"Aye," he said through clenched teeth. "It was good." He kissed the tip of her nose. "And now *I* will please *you*." And he bent to kiss her once more, his mouth taking hers firmly. She arched and stretched, thoroughly relaxed under him, and he smiled to himself. She had utterly no idea what love-making was about. But she would soon find out, by Thor!

Yngveld enjoyed his kisses. They were pleasant and relaxing. She liked the way he held her, the warmth of his strong frame, his strong arms. She snuggled into his embrace and breathed deeply of his scent. She liked everything about him, she decided.

Now he was kissing her neck, his breath whispering across the sensitive skin. She felt the return of the shivers she had felt earlier and giggled. Thomas, hearing her, rolled his eyes and buried his face in her mussed, blond hair. He was still a moment.

"Thomas?"

"Aye."

"Are we done?"

His body quivered with what suspiciously seemed like laughter. "*Nej*," came his hoarse response. "We are not done."

"Oh. I thought mayhap—"

"Shhh . . ." and his lips silenced her with more kisses. This time Yngveld started to notice that her heart was pounding faster and her breathing, *ja*, 'twas definitely becoming more labored. "Thomas?"

"Aye?"

"I feel funny. . . ."

"Good," he grunted.

"Good?"

And then there was only the sound of her distinctly labored pants as Thomas slowly slid down the length of her, kissing as he went. He stopped to give attention to her breasts, and each one hungered for his touch. Yngveld's head tossed back and forth on the grass and she moaned something that suspiciously sounded like, "More."

Thomas arched over her and then pressed himself against the very center of her. She parted her legs willingly, but he did not avail himself of the opportunity to enter, and she soon forgot to wonder why as he moved down to her stomach, his lips seeking and finding every tender spot. Ripples of desire started in her lower abdomen and moved through her. She gasped at the shivery feeling. His hands ran over her buttocks, squeezing and playing, and it seemed to her that she could not get enough of his touch. "Oh, Thomas!"

"Where, fair Valkyrie? Tell me where to touch you."

"Here," and she guided his hand to where she had a terrible ache. He rubbed her gently and she lifted herself to meet him. "Oh, *ja*!"

Thomas kissed his way lower and Yngveld suddenly grabbed the thick curling locks of his head. She tried to pull him up. "*Nej*, do not—! I never—!"

"Ah, but I must," he murmured, his fingers seeking and finding the delicate, sensitive flesh. Then Yngveld's whole body lifted and she stopped breathing. A huge spasm of delight ripped through her as Thomas's wonderful hands caressed her.

"Oh, my God!" She quivered and trembled, and saw blinding flashes of light, and then a terrible sweetness seeped through her. With a great sigh, she lay still. Possibly she had died.

Some time later, she opened her eyes and moved her head. Where had Thomas gone? Ah, there he was.

He had rolled off her and was watching her with a distinctly masculine grin of satisfaction as he chewed lazily upon a blade of grass. "Was it good, Yngveld?"

Those beautiful green eyes were laughing at her! She chuckled weakly, and then a small shudder shook her frame. She held out her arms to him. "Again."

And he obliged.

Chapter Thirty-four

"Thomas?"

"Aye."

Yngveld sat looking at Thomas. She had finished dressing, the sack of gold carefully tied around her waist once more. Thomas was belting his sword onto his left hip.

Yngveld marveled at what they had shared. Never in her life had she dreamed that such sensations, such feelings, could be possible between a man and a woman.

"What will Ivar Wolfson say?"

Thomas's fingers froze. Then he resumed his task. "He will say nothing, fair Valkyrie."

She watched him, waiting.

" 'Tis what he will do."

She got a flash of his white, even teeth. When

Thomas would say no more, she prodded, "And what will he do?"

"Why, fair Valkyrie of the North, he will try to kill me."

Yngveld gasped.

Thomas glanced at her. "That thought bothers you?"

"*Ja!* Of course! Oh, Thomas"—she was wringing her hands—"what are we to do?" Without waiting for him to speak, she hurried on. "We could flee. We could run away—"

Thomas held up a hand. "Yngveld," he said softly.

"We could flee to Norway. No one will find us there. I have a kinsman. . . ." She could not let Thomas be killed. Not now, when they had just discovered each other. She would throw herself on the mercy of her Norwegian kinsman. *Anything*. "Your men . . . Thomas, will they help us?"

Thomas looked down into her blue gaze, and his heart almost stopped beating at the passionate look he saw there. She cared for him, he knew it.

"Thomas," she said, crossing the short distance between them. She took his hands in hers and pulled him to her. "We must not let Ivar—"

"Yngveld," he said again. "Listen to me."

"*Ja*, Thomas," she said obediently. Thomas would know what to do. Thomas would have a plan for them to get away, safe from Ivar.

"Yngveld." he took her hand and started in

the direction of the oak forest.

They were heading back to the manor.

There was a new warmth in his voice, a kindness that she had not heard before. 'Twas love, she knew. She loved him. And he loved her. Oh, how fortunate they were to have discovered each other and their love before they reached Dubh Linn. Now they could be together and safe, and Ivar—why, Ivar would be as nothing to them! She smiled up at him and then burst into a joyous love song. She gave her heart in song to him. She sang of her love and her feelings, the words twisting and turning around them until he too, was caught up and joined her in the song.

Never had Yngveld felt so happy. She was with the man she loved. They would marry, have children together, grow old together. She looked into his green gaze and laughed with the sheer happiness of being with him.

Thomas felt a lump in his throat as he looked down into the blue eyes of the beautiful woman at his side. He would give anything, anything he possessed now or ever would possess to be able to make her his—in his own eyes, in the world's eyes. His heart felt a heaviness, a dread, that was unmatched by anything he had ever felt in his life. Oh, why had he found Yngveld, only to lose her?

He must give her to Ivar. Viking honor, his sense of being a man, everything he had ever learned about being an honorable human being screamed at him that he must set aside his own desires and feelings. It was his duty to bring Yngveld to his commander. There was no other honorable choice.

Ivar would treat her kindly. Ivar would find her easy to love—God knew Thomas did. When Thomas told Ivar that he had raped Yngveld, thereby taking any and all blame upon himself, Ivar would console Yngveld and take her to wife. In the event he did not, Ivar would provide for her. Ivar, too, was an honorable man. Thomas glanced away and swallowed, unwilling to destroy the happiness that was so evident upon Yngveld's lovely face. He tried once more. "Yngveld."

Something of his sorrow came through in his voice and she halted. "Thomas? What is wrong?"

He brushed a wisp of pale hair from her forehead. "We cannot—I cannot—" Lord, this was difficult! "We cannot run away together." There, he had said it.

"Thomas?" Shock was upon her face. "You do not want me?"

"I want you," he bit out savagely. "I want you, Yngveld. But I cannot have you. You belong to Ivar."

"*Nej*, I do not." Her chin went out, and he recognized that stubborn look of hers. "I belong to no one but myself."

He smiled, grimly. "That is certainly true."

"And I give myself to *you*. Not to him!"

He stroked her hair and pulled her gently against him. She looked up at him, blue eyes full of unshed tears. " 'Tis you I love, Thomas!" she said fiercely.

"Yngveld!" The cry tore from his throat and he lowered his mouth to hers. They kissed, long and slow, and it was all Thomas could do to keep from sinking to the forest floor and taking her again. *I love her,* he thought, heart pounding from his emotions. *Lord, I love her so much!* He stood there, eyes squeezed tightly together, cursing the fate that had decreed he should find her only to lose her. *Why?* he cried in fierce, silent agony. *Why?* He could not, would not, break his loyalty to Ivar.

Something about Thomas's terrible stillness seeped through to Yngveld. She lifted her head. "Thomas?"

He looked down at her, already feeling himself withdraw. Already seeing Ivar's cold, impassive face. Hearing him ask about his bride. His bride! In his agony, Thomas turned away.

Yngveld put a shaking hand to her lips. Something was wrong, horribly wrong. Her hand dropped. Thomas did not love her! That was it! *He* did not love her! The enormity of it, the terrible loss, the grief, hit her and she wanted to die. She wanted to lie down there on the soft forest floor and never get up. "Oh, Thomas," she moaned, one traitorous hand still reaching for him despite her newfound knowledge.

Thomas did not see her, caught up in his own agony.

Yngveld let her hand drop. "I—I see." She saw, *ja*. Only too well. He did not love her. Did not want her. "You"—she could barely whisper the words—"you will give me to Ivar." It was not a question. And she knew the damning answer before it left his lips.

"Aye." He could not look at her. To look into those precious blue eyes would be to tear himself apart. He stared at an oak tree, studied its gnarled trunk and rough bark. "Aye." It was a groan.

Yngveld let out her breath. A long, deep, suffering breath. The forest was still. No birds, no rustle of leaves in the wind. She knew they would soon reach the manor and the others. "I—" What could she say? *I understand?* But she did not. *I love you?* He did not want to hear that again, certainly. So she muttered only, "Very well."

She lifted her chin and he caught the movement—that proud, stubborn chin. His eyes played over her face, her beautiful, beloved face. "Yngveld, I—"

She lifted her hand to cut off his words. A tremulous twist wrenched her lips in a parody of a smile. "I will not tell him," she said. She wanted to assure him that, despite his betrayal of her heart, she would not tell Ivar, she would not be the one to place his life in jeopardy.

Thomas admired her more in that moment than in the whole time he had known her. That she felt terribly hurt, he could read plainly on her unguarded face. Yet she did not want to hurt him back, to have Ivar kill him. That, that was an honorable woman. Ivar little knew the value of the woman he was getting, thought Thomas bitterly. He would soon leave her for Jasmine, or one of his other favorites, and Yngveld, beautiful Yngveld, would be left alone and neglected and betrayed. He closed his eyes at the terrible thought. *Nay,* he cried in silent agony. *Ivar would not do so—it is your own fears talking thus.*

He reached for her hand. There was nothing else to be said. "Come."

She did not take his hand, and he shrugged, letting her fall into step behind him. They walked like that through the rest of the forest, he in front, she behind, head down, stopping now and then to look at a leaf but actually to wipe at her eyes when she thought he was not watching.

Thomas ran several possible scenes over in his mind. Him confronting Ivar. Them fighting. Thomas winning. Ivar winning. If Thomas won, he could take Yngveld away with him, offered a little voice. If Ivar won, he would kill Yngveld, knowing that she had come to Thomas willingly.

As he and Yngveld stepped up to the manor, he could feel his men's eyes upon him—some in speculation, some in boredom, some merely curious. He ignored them all and headed directly into the huge house, Yngveld tagging along behind him.

Yngveld did her best to keep her face impassive, afraid the men could read what had happened. She did not want them to suspect. Thomas could be killed if it was known they had made love. *And what about you*, demanded an inner voice. *Think of yourself. What will happen to you?* She bit her lip as she pondered that question.

She had time to ponder it as Thomas spoke with Neill, spoke with Torgils, spoke with an old wrinkled man with a wounded arm. But Yngveld paid no attention to what was going on around her. Her thoughts and feelings were all of her own pain.

Sometime later, she saw Karl and Patrick waving good-bye to her as they stood in front of the manor. She waved numbly, heard Thomas tell Neill that he would return in a fortnight, heard Thomas say something to Neill about guarding the lands. And then they were leaving, Thomas prodding her to walk across the green hills. Somber Torgils marched at her side, and she was grateful for his silence as she stumbled along in a daze. They reached the shale beach, crossed it.

She followed Thomas to the ship, and he boosted her over the rail, giving a hand to steady her. She felt his touch briefly, then snatched her hand away and marched toward the safety of her tent. She refused to meet the curious eyes of the men who clambered aboard around her. When she reached her tent, she sank to her knees in its protecting dark depths to cry.

Chapter Thirty-five

Dubh Linn

Yngveld watched in wide-eyed wonder as *Raven's Daughter* sailed into Dubh Linn harbor, where fresh water from the wide mouth of a river flowed and mingled with the salt. Long docks jutted out into the river, and a sickle-shaped rock wall kept the harbor waters smooth and still. She could see more anchored ships than she could ever count. Even more ships were drawn up onto the muddy beach near the riverbank.

And everywhere Yngveld looked there were houses. They covered the low hillsides, neat, tidy rows of single-room homes made of wooden posts and wattle. All had thatched roofs. A low fog hovered over the town and was fed by the smoke curling from the roof openings in the homes. The distinctive wood smoke smell entered Yngveld's nostrils and she would ever after associate that smell with Dubh Linn. Low wattle and the occasional stone fence separated each dwelling from its neighbor. The narrow streets gave an orderly look to the town.

Yngveld turned to see Torgils not far from her side. She was not surprised, nor did she give more than a pleasant nod to the man. He, or some other crew member, and sometimes even Thomas Lachlann himself, had been at her side ever since her unsuccessful escape attempt at Swords village. Yngveld had put up with her guards patiently, though how Thomas thought she could escape whilst aboard ship still puzzled her.

The activity on the beaches and on the streets caught Yngveld's attention once more and Torgils was forgotten for the nonce. Yngveld craned her neck and stared. Never in her life had she seen such a large gathering of people. Why, 'twas the biggest village she had ever seen.

As the ship drew nearer to shore, Yngveld leaned over the rail the better to watch. Her glance centered on an open space where many people walked and talked. Some of them were looking at wares displayed in stalls, others contented themselves chatting with friends. The women wore brightly colored dresses and tunics, and decorated themselves in heavy jewelry. She saw one woman wearing several gold chains, gold earrings, gold armbands, and a huge breast pin. Yngveld feared the woman was about to topple over from all her jewelry. Another, a pert young woman with brown braids, wore red and yellow ribbons fluttering from her hair. Her dress was a beautiful purple. Yngveld gawked in awe.

"Would you like to walk through the market, Yngveld?"

Yngveld froze at the sound of that deep-timbred voice. She wrenched her eyes away from the market, past Torgils who was wandering away to another part of the ship, and she faced Thomas. Though his green eyes glittered, a mild smile was fixed upon his lips. She wondered how he could look so, so relaxed, so distant—as if nothing had ever passed between them. Belatedly, she chastised herself for her muteness, but she truly felt tongue-tied. Whatever could she say to this man who had kissed her, rescued her, insulted her, then protected her and made love to her? And now he was about to coldly hand her over, a virtual prisoner, to his military commander? She must have nodded her head, for she saw that he was turning away as if in acceptance of her acquiescence.

From somewhere deep inside herself, she found the courage to call him back. He came, a question shadowed in those beautiful green eyes. "Thomas . . ." she took a deep breath. She fumbled with the sack of gold that now hung at her waist. She held it up and it swayed back and forth and made little clinking sounds.

"What is it?" He turned, his hard gaze devouring her.

"Think you that I can find a ship to sail to Norway upon?"

He frowned.

"I—I want to see my kinsman." 'Twas a lie. She did not want to see her kinsman. She wanted to stay with Thomas, marry him, and raise those children she had dreamed of, the two girls and the boy with the black curls. But Thomas had made it clear to her that he did not consider her a part of his life, that he was very willing to hand her over to Ivar despite what they had shared. She choked back a shudder.

He took a step toward her. "This sounds too familiar, Yngveld. Was this not the way we met?" he offered at last. "You were trying to purchase passage to Norway, as I recall."

"*Ja*," she said defiantly, "I was."

He surveyed her with cool green eyes. "And now you again want to go to Norway." Thor's blood! His heart pounded violently, and some part of him wanted to ask her to stay with him, to tell her that he loved her, that he wanted her for his wife. But the call of duty was too strong. He *must* deliver her to Ivar. He looked at the shoreline, squinting irritably. Why was she doing this? She knew he had no choice! Why was she making it so difficult? She knew he could not, would not help her escape to Norway!

"I have kin," Yngveld said proudly. She was

holding on to the last shreds of her tattered pride. Thomas did not want her, she knew, but mayhap he would help her evade Ivar. Mayhap the lovemaking they had shared had given Thomas cause to doubt the need to give her to Ivar. . . .

"By Thor!" swore Thomas savagely. "Do not ask it of me! I cannot give you leave to take ship to Norway. I must take you to Ivar!"

"Thomas"—her voice took on a terrible note of desperation—"you have accused me of running. Well, I am not running now. I am facing you, with the truth." She clutched at his tunic front now, all pride gone. "If you care for me, have any feeling at all for me, *please* do not deliver me up to Ivar!" Her blue eyes locked on his, willing him to understand her desperation, her fear—her need for him.

She had dared to say it because she thought he cared for her a little—*nej*, she must be truthful, she thought he cared a great deal for her. He had kissed her, he had protected her, he had made love to her.

Thomas jerked as though she had struck him, and his eyes went dark, whether with passion or with anger, she could not tell. He reached out to touch her chin gently, raising her face to his.

Her gaze swept past the strong tanned column of his throat and up to meet his eyes.

He swallowed and took both her hands in his. He prised her tight grip off his tunic. "I cannot do otherwise, Yngveld Sveinsdatter. No matter how much I may wish otherwise, you belong to

Ivar Wolfson." A shudder seemed to go through him at those words and he took a step back, his hands dropping to his side. His eyes were veiled, and she could read nothing in them, no sorrow, no regret, nothing. She saw him suddenly as his men and as Ivar Wolfson must see him—cold, hard-bitten, menacing.

"Thomas?" Of their own volition, her hands reached out to him. She could not let it end thus between them.

Thomas stayed where he was as though rooted to that particular piece of the ship, but his heart cried out to her, *Yngveld, my love, my love—*

"Thomas?"

'Twas better if she thought she meant nothing to him, decided Thomas in a flash. He needed to give her the courage to go forward to meet Ivar, not to persist in looking to him for hope. And there was a way he could yet protect her against Ivar's ruthlessness.

Reluctantly, Thomas drove the words from his throat. "You are an attractive woman, Yngveld Sveinsdatter. Do not put so much on a few kisses. A man can kiss—make love even"—he forced himself to look at her as he said the cruel words—"and not give his heart."

Yngveld jerked as though she had been struck. "And was it that way with you, Thomas Lachlann?" she asked sadly, her own heart shriveling inside her. "Did you make love to me and not give your heart? Did you not care for me? I thought—"

He grinned. "Why, Yngveld Sveinsdatter. You were but an amusing diversion on a long voyage, a way to pass the time. Surely you knew that."

He could not go on, could not face the stricken look in those beautiful blue eyes. *Lies, lies*, his heart told him. *But what can I do?* he raged back silently. *She is already claimed. I can do nothing!*

Yngveld turned away, humiliated to the core. She had thought—but what matter what she had thought? She faced the pain. She had thought that Thomas cared for her, had hoped that he loved her. More fool, she. Thomas did not care for her, had only found her an amusing diversion. She bit on her fist to keep from crying out as she turned away.

"Get your things," he said quietly. "I will walk you through the market. Then we will go to Ivar."

"*Nej*," she said, and she did not know her own voice. "Not you. It is best if—if Torgils escorts me to Ivar. I—I cannot go if you—you are—" Another word and she would have broken down and cried.

Thomas must have sensed it, for he said only, "Very well. I will see that Torgils escorts you." And then he was gone, striding away and leaving her with a broken heart.

Chapter Thirty-six

Even with the numbness of her wounded heart, Yngveld found herself occasionally glancing about as Torgils, with a gentle touch upon her elbow, guided her through the Viking city of Dubh Linn. An armed escort of crewmen from the ship accompanied them. She had seen Thomas leave the ship ahead of her, and her traitorous eyes had followed him until he was swallowed up in the crowd.

She stared in wonder as a beautiful woman, her skin completely black, her hair in tight curls, hurried past. Yngveld stared after her until, prodded by Torgils, she had to run to join the rest of her escort.

They walked down narrow streets of wattle and daub huts wherein individual families dwelt. Each hut had a single hole in the roof to let out the smoke. A wide, flowing river meandered to the north of the town, and Torgils informed her in his gravelly voice that it was the River Liffey. In the distance, she could see a large stone structure—a church, she was informed, named St. Patrick's.

"And Dubh Linn is an important center for slave trading," remarked Torgils. He slanted a glance at Yngveld to see if she was listening. Satisfied that she was, he continued, "Slaves are gathered together here. Most of them are taken in raids locally or from England. Sometimes slaves are even caught in raids on the Barbary coast of Africa." Seeing her puzzled look, he waved a hand. "From far, far away to the south and east. It takes many days to sail there."

She nodded.

Torgils continued. "From here in Dubh Linn the slaves are shipped north to Scandinavia. Occasionally they are shipped to Arab Spain, or even North Africa."

Yngveld nodded again, struggling to make sense of his words. People moving to many places, she thought. That must account for the many different types of faces she passed on the streets. The red and blond hair of the long, narrow-headed Norse men and women, and their pale or ruddy complexions she was familiar with. Even the smaller-boned, dark haired Irish—she had seen their like before, in Greenland. But the dusky ones, and the black ones, these she had never seen before. Never had she dreamed that people could look so different! And she liked it. She liked it that people came in all shapes and sizes and colors. She stopped to gawk once more, this time at a short blond dwarf scurrying by. Torgils had to tug at her arm to get her to move along.

" 'Tis also the home of many tradesmen," Torgils continued his tour doggedly.

"What?" she murmured absently, barely ducking out of the way as a man led a string of ponies past her. Yngveld narrowly missed getting her foot stomped upon by an unshod hoof.

They were in the market now, and the sights and sounds and smells held Yngveld spellbound. Everywhere she looked were booths and tradesmen and women with colorful wares. Red and yellow and purple ribbons fluttered gaily from the sides and roofs of the booths.

Beautiful satins and red, purple, blue, and pink embroidered sheets were draped over the sides of one booth. An embroidered quilt blew gently in the breeze. Yngveld gazed at the lovely yellow and green dragon that curled around its border and sighed. Never in her life had she seen such fine work.

"Over there is a goldsmith," pointed Torgils helpfully. "And there, next to him, a silversmith. That man makes the loveliest brooches in the whole city. Why, he can make a brooch look like a silver rose you just plucked from its stem, dewdrops and all." Torgils nodded at a small muscular man studiously bent over his craft. The man's plump wife called a greeting to a passerby. Then she spotted Yngveld. "Come, come, sweetnose," she called. Yngveld wanted to shrink into Torgils' side. "*Nej, nej*, I mean no harm. Merely gaze upon the fine work my man does. I know you will want to buy!"

Yngveld clutched her little sack of gold tighter and shook her head. The woman shrugged good-naturedly and called out to someone else.

They passed a woman who sat nursing a baby. Spread around her on a yellow blanket were many carved stone bowls. "Why, these bowls are much like the ones we use at home," she exclaimed.

"Aye," nodded Torgils. "Traders from Iceland and Greenland occasionally bring their wares. Thomas will get a good price for the goods he took from Einar."

At the mention of Thomas's name, some of the glow left Yngveld's face. Unbelievably, she had forgotten about him. She peered through the crowd ahead and was rewarded with a glimpse of his dark, curl-covered head as he bent to speak with a merchant at a booth. "No doubt he makes arrangements for the sale of our goods this very moment," observed Torgils in a satisfied voice as he followed her glance. Then he saw the flush on Yngveld's face and cleared his throat abruptly.

"Here, Yngveld Sveinsdatter, this ribbon would look pretty on you." Trying to distract her, he held up first a wide turquoise satin ribbon, then a narrow blue one. "Why, the blue brings out the color of your eyes—"

"'Tis no good, Torgils," she said solemnly. "He has ruined my life. There is nothing you can do to change that. Except let me go." Why was she even suggesting such a thing? she wondered. Torgils would never release her, either. He was too much Thomas's man.

"Hmmmph," muttered Torgils noncommittally. He continued his guide role, loitering in the market, pointing out interesting shops here and there, talking about the town, but much of the fascination of his tour had died for Yngveld. Not only was she being abandoned by Thomas Lachlann, that seducer and betrayer of women, but she was being given to Ivar Wolfson, a man who had ordered her plucked from Greenland and dragged to his very lair. Soon she would meet him.

"Is it not hot this day?" she asked Torgils.

He saw the sheen on her forehead. "Not overly hot."

She fanned herself with her hand. Her palm, too, was slick with sweat. "Must be me, then," she muttered nervously.

"Aye," agreed Torgils, wondering what Yngveld Sveinsdatter would do upon meeting Ivar Wolfson. He suspected that his friend Thomas had some regrets about the situation. However, 'twas none of Torgils' business.

"There." He pointed. "There is the military encampment, our destination."

They had passed through the market and were now walking along narrow streets of wattle homes once more, though still paralleling the wide River Liffey. As the houses became fewer and they approached the wooden walls of the military enclosure, Yngveld found that her footsteps correspondingly slowed.

And then they were there—at the gates of the military encampment. Yngveld took a deep breath, squared her shoulders, and went forward to meet the wolf in his lair.

Chapter Thirty-seven

Thomas faced Ivar across the military tent.

"So. You have returned," observed Ivar. His eyes were in shadow from where Thomas stood, and he could not read what his commander was thinking. Not that Ivar Wolfson ever showed much on his face, Thomas thought ruefully.

Ivar came forward into the light from the door. "And my bride?" he asked harshly. "Is she here?"

Thomas nodded. He watched relief creep across Ivar's lined face and he wondered at it. Thomas took a step farther into the tent. "She is here. Safe."

Ivar nodded. "Very good," he said, and Thomas could hear the excitement in Ivar's voice. Ivar brushed by him, obviously anxious to greet his new bride. He stepped out of the tent and looked about in bewilderment.

Thomas was behind him. "She is not here yet, Ivar. She wanted to see the market." It was not exactly true. Thomas had been the one to decide that touring the market would give Yngveld time to adjust to her meeting with Ivar. "Torgils and the men are escorting her. I took the opportunity to come directly here to inform you of our arrival." Thomas heard the formal words, knew that he was keeping Ivar at more of a distance than had been his wont in the past. But he had wanted to speak with Ivar—alone—to tell him what his own conscience and loyalty demanded that he say.

"Is she pretty?" asked Ivar softly.

"Beautiful."

"Ah, very good, very good." Ivar looked at him, head tilted on an angle. "Any problems?" His voice held mild curiosity; that was all that Thomas could detect.

Thomas shrugged. "We were shipwrecked upon our arrival in Greenland. Taken into slavery. But we managed to recapture the ship and sail it back."

His cursory summation left out many details, but Ivar looked satisfied. "And my bride? Was she hurt? Injured?"

Thomas shook his head. "*Nej*. She is—"

"Here she comes now!" Ivar exclaimed. Thomas swung to watch the approaching troop of men. The small, lone woman in their midst looked impossibly delicate, ethereally beautiful to Thomas's eyes. Ivar grunted in satisfaction.

"Ivar, there is something I must tell you."

Ivar dragged his eyes away from his bride. "Aye," he said impatiently. "What is it?"

"She is no longer a maiden."

Ivar's face flushed, and the skin went tight over his low cheekbones. "What are you telling me?" His voice was cold.

"She is no longer virgin."

"Why did you not protect her?" cried Ivar. "That was your duty! That was why you were assigned to guard her!" His face was florid now. He began pacing back and forth in front of his tent.

With dread, Thomas continued, "I did not protect her, because it was I who—" For the first time in his life, Thomas did not have the words to communicate with his commander.

Rage flashed in Ivar's eyes. "It was you!" he said, his voice low and vicious. "It was you that—that—" He sputtered in his fury.

Thomas nodded, coolly. "Aye."

Ivar's lips drew back and he snarled, "You have ruined everything! Everything!"

Taken aback, Thomas could only stare at Ivar. Ivar's words made little sense to Thomas. What in Thor's name did Ivar mean by 'everything?' Did he mean that he would not go forward with the marriage? Thomas heart beat a little faster, and he wondered if he had told Ivar not only for honorable reasons, but because he had hoped that Ivar would cast Yngveld aside. Once Ivar no longer wanted her, then Thomas could—

"Dirk! Ingolf! Seize him!" Around the corner of the tent came Ivar's two bodyguards. Thomas should have known they would not be far away. Neither questioned Ivar's command to seize his third bodyguard, one of their own. The two made straight for Thomas. Thomas did not fight them. He had anticipated this moment, dreaded it, but had been unable to foresee any other possible outcome. He had betrayed Ivar's trust. To lie about it would be to compound that betrayal. "Tie him."

Ingolf went about his task of tying Thomas's hands behind his back with particular zeal. Once, Thomas thought he caught a hint of inquiry in Dirk the Dane's blue eyes, but then it was gone.

Ingolf gave a quick jerk of the knot and almost lifted Thomas off his feet. "That should hold," he drawled insolently. Thomas kept his face impassive. Ingolf had never liked him, and now he did not trouble to hide his animosity.

"Put him in the prisoner's hut," growled Ivar.

He kicked at Thomas. Thomas turned aside in the nick of time, and Ivar's foot barely missed his groin. Thomas gazed into Ivar's hate-contorted face and knew that Ivar was furious—might, in fact, kill him.

Dirk gave a push and Thomas lurched in the direction of the tiny, dark, dirty hut that was used to house recalcitrant captives. As he turned away, Thomas spoke the one lie that he must needs tell Ivar. It was the only way he could save Yngveld Sveinsdatter from Ivar's wrath. " 'Twas rape." His cold green eyes met Ivar's furious blue ones, and Thomas thought the man would explode with his anger. " 'Twas rape," he repeated, wanting no mistake. Ivar must know that Yngveld was innocent.

Ivar looked away from his prisoner to where his bride approached—his fair, soiled bride. "Ingolf," he snarled, "when you have locked him up, report back to me!"

Ingolf, a smirk upon his thin lips, nodded and gave Thomas a brutal shove. The two bodyguards marched him away just as Yngveld and her escort approached.

Yngveld watched the two large men lead Thomas away. He completely ignored her, she saw, and sadness swept through her. She wondered if he was going to be imprisoned somewhere. She guessed that Thomas himself had told Ivar what had happened and she wondered at his stubbornness and foolishness. She sighed and straightened, preparing herself to deal with Ivar Wolfson.

Ivar was staring at her, no welcoming smile upon his face. Ah, well, thought Yngveld. What had she expected? To be told that your bride preferred another must come as a cruel blow to a man of Ivar's importance.

Just then, a black whirlwind raced around the side of the tent. The whirlwind was a screaming woman with nails as sharp as talons, who launched herself at Yngveld.

Yngveld stepped back, putting up her hands barely in time to protect her face. The infuriated woman, still screaming at her in an unintelligible language, clawed and groped at Yngveld's face and the terrible scratches meant for her countenance scored her arms instead. When her attacker found that she could not gouge out Yngveld's eyes, she tried to throttle her. Yngveld fell to the ground, knocked down by her opponent's weight. Yngveld struggled frantically to get the woman to release the deadly grip upon her throat.

Yngveld felt herself fading in and out of blackness. She fought desperately against the grip at her throat, but could not dislodge it. Yngveld was about to succumb to darkness a third time when suddenly her throat was released. She coughed and choked, holding her throat against the terrible pain.

Torgils had wrenched the screaming woman off her. Yngveld lay dazed, eyes half-closed, heart pounding, as Ivar half-carried, half-dragged her attacker back behind the tent. He was gone some minutes, leaving Yngveld time to recover under the solicitous attentions of Torgils, who helped her to her feet and inspected the scratches on her throat and arms. He shook his head in silent disgust.

Ivar Wolfson soon reappeared, an amused look upon his face. He shrugged amiably at the men, his good humor insulting and bewildering to Yngveld.

Ivar glanced at her briefly, then stepped aside and bowed. He swept one arm toward his tent in what Yngveld understood to be a bid for her to enter.

"Welcome to Dubh Linn, Yngveld Sveinsdatter."

Chapter Thirty-eight

Thomas sat in the dark, arms numb from the wrist up. Sitting in the little hut for some time, he had had plenty of leisure to ponder the seriousness of his position. That it was serious he had no doubt. Yet he could not have let Ivar learn of what had happened with Yngveld from anyone but himself. Had one of his returned men, guessing at what had taken place, informed Ivar, then Yngveld would have been in danger. Thomas knew that 'twas his loyalty and his honesty that kept a place for him in the Viking world. The confessed rape of Ivar's betrothed had sealed Thomas's doom with Ivar. There would be no forgiveness, no overlooking it. He had hoped—

The door to the little hut opened, and a crack

of light entered, along with a shadowy figure that Thomas recognized as Ingolf.

"So. 'Tis you."

"Aye," answered Ingolf placidly enough. He approached, carrying a small lamp that cast its glow in the tiny, dirty room. Ingolf grinned and said conversationally, "Ivar sent me to kill you."

Thomas stared at his assassin. Ingolf's sword was in his hand, the grin tight upon his thin lips. " 'Tis what I would expect of you, Ingolf," sneered Thomas. "You would think it sport to cut down a tied, unarmed man."

Ingolf frowned and set the lamp down on the floor. "Ivar did not say how to do it, he merely said to kill you."

"What does Ivar plan to do with the girl?"

"Sveinsdatter?" Ingolf shrugged and licked his lips. "Did not say." Then, to irritate Thomas, he added, "Said he would give her to me."

Thomas knew it was a lie, a lazy one at that. He let it pass.

Thor's blood, how was he going to get Ingolf to untie him and make it a fair fight? Thomas's hopes sank. Ingolf had never been one to be particular that his fights were fair. Thomas remembered one time at the end of a battle, when the battlefield had been littered with groaning and dying men, Irish and Norse. Ingolf had plunked himself down beside a groaning, dying Irishman. Taking out his knife, Ingolf had lazily sharpened the blade. Thomas had watched the strange scene because he was too exhausted to move. After Ingolf carefully tested the blade on one finger to ensure that it was sharp, Thomas had watched in amazement as Ingolf suddenly buried his blade to the hilt in the dying man's chest. Turning away in disgust, Thomas had heard Ingolf chortling happily as he plucked up the man's jewelry and weapons.

The memory of the brutal incident did not hearten Thomas now. He knew that Ingolf would not hesitate to decapitate him whilst his hands were tied behind his back. His best chance was to keep Ingolf talking, Thomas decided, until he could think what to do. Ingolf unwittingly helped him in that direction. "But I do know what Ivar plans to do with you," taunted Ingolf.

"After you kill me?"

"Aye. Ivar has plans for you." Ingolf snickered to himself.

Thomas turned away, yawned, and pretended boredom.

"Ivar plans to hang you in Odinn's grove."

Thomas's head whirled back to his tormenter. "You lie!"

Ingolf grinned. "*Nej.* No lie, Lachlann." He played with the shaft of his sword, hefting it lightly in a nervous little pattern. "Ivar Wolfson has become quite the Odinn worshipper in the time since you were sent to Greenland."

Thomas said nothing, but his green eyes glared.

Ingolf moved closer. "Ivar needs bodies, Lachlann. Nine of them, to be exact. Nine male bodies to hang in Odinn's grove. Along with the nine dead horses and the nine dead dogs, of course." He paused. "Mayhap Ivar will need to kill some of your men to make the nine." He grinned slyly. "I will suggest it to him. He could kill Torgils. *Ja*, I think Ivar will like my suggestion."

Thomas's guts churned, but his green eyes grew cold. "Ivar does not sacrifice men to Odinn! He never has, not in all the years I have known him!"

"Ivar's changed, Lachlann." Ingolf smirked. "Now he does. He has become a most enthusiastic follower of Odinn."

Something in Ingolf's voice told Thomas where this was heading. "You," sneered Thomas, "*you* are the one who turned him to Odinn. As a berserker, you were already under Odinn's favor."

"I?" Ingolf grinned. "*Nej, nej*, not I. I merely showed him how effective a sacrifice can be upon the eve of battle." Ingolf held up his weapon and ran a calloused finger along the blade carefully. "Animals, of course, are pleasing to Odinn." He brought the sword down onto his palm with a *splat*! "But strangled humans are so much better."

"Strangled? Then you will be doing Odinn out of a victim if you decapitate me, Ingolf."

Ingolf grinned reassuringly. "No decapitation, Lachlann. Just a few fatal stabs to the body. We can wrap a rope around your neck later."

"All planned."

Ingolf took a step nearer, a stealthy look upon his face. Clearly he had grown bored with the conversation and was about to carry out Ivar's plan.

Both Thomas and Ingolf were so caught up in their confrontation that the door crashing against the wall made them both jump. With a muttered oath, Torgils leaped into the room, and with two furious hacks of his sword, Ingolf's head was separated from his shoulders. It went rolling across the floor—a look of utter surprise still on the face before the severed muscles went slack. Blood spurted from the stump of the neck and spattered the front of Thomas's tunic.

Thomas stared at the head, then at Torgils. Neither said anything for a moment; Torgils was panting, Thomas trying not to heave up his last meal. Then Torgils walked over and, with a knife, sliced through the rope binding Thomas's hands.

The pain in his hands as the blood rushed back into them made Thomas wince. Torgils knelt beside Ingolf's body and wiped his bloody blade on the back of Ingolf's embroidered vest.

At last, Thomas gritted, "My thanks. He planned to kill me."

"Aye, I heard him. I hid outside Ivar's tent and overheard him tell Ingolf to finish you off."

Thomas stood up, his face grim. "We'd better leave."

Torgils snatched up Ingolf's sword and tucked it into his waistband. He now carried two swords.

"Did you know that Ivar planned to hang my body in Odinn's grove?"

Torgils nodded. "And I heard Ingolf's kind suggestion about my joining you." His white teeth flashed in the dark hut; he was clearly amused. Then his smile vanished. "There is more." The seriousness of Torgils' tone alerted Thomas. "Ivar plans to hang Yngveld Sveinsdatter tomorrow."

Thomas went cold at the words. "Yngveld? But—"

"Ivar does not want her. I will tell you the rest later. For now, we must hurry!"

"Where *is* Yngveld?" demanded Thomas, running alongside his friend.

"With the Angel of Death!"

Chapter Thirty-nine

Yngveld giggled as she watched the old woman rise from a place in the corner and slowly swung her head around. Where was whatever-was-his-name—Ivar? Where was Ivar? Ivar should be here to laugh with her at the old woman. *Ja*, she looked funny with that strange, gap-toothed smile. Funny, but kind. Yngveld could tell that. The old woman's dark rags fluttered around her as she forced yet another cup of the strange-tasting brew into Yngveld's mouth. 'Twas cold and sweet and tasted so delicious. . . .

Yngveld swirled the contents around in her mouth, then another laugh seized her and she sprayed it out at the little woman. Yngveld laughed anew at the astonishment on the old wrinkled face. The old woman clucked and dabbed at her rags with another rag. Then she dabbed at Yngveld's chest.

Yngveld glanced down. Red dribbles stained her embroidered tunic. Shrugging happily, she chuckled as the old one wiped the dirty rag across her tunic and then tossed the rag in a corner. Yngveld put her hand to her head, trying to focus her wandering gaze, trying to keep her head from nodding. Now what was the old woman up to? And what had she said her name was? Oh *ja*, 'twas Angel. How very odd.

Ah, this was interesting. Angel was twisting a cord around in her hands, knotting it and talking to it in a sing-song voice. Yngveld giggled. How very amusing of—what-was-his-name?—Ivar, that was it—of Ivar to provide such fine entertainment for Yngveld's enjoyment. She must remember to thank him.

Yngveld put her hands over her ears to keep out the guttural keening of the old one. Who had ever told Angel she could sing? Shaking one amused finger at the old crone, Yngveld burst forth into song. Now this, *this* was singing! She finished the song and glanced, head nodding, at Angel to see if she had appreciated Yngveld's lovely music.

Nej. She was staring as another form crept into the tent. Yngveld blinked. Whoever it was was dressed from head to toe in black—only eyes peeped out—and the form looked vaguely familiar. Yngveld tried to peer at her in concentration but soon gave up the effort. Mayhap she should sleep. *Nej*, she was only a little tired. She opened her eyes.

The other woman—*ja*, 'twas a woman, she had taken off her heavily veiled cloak—slowly approached Yngveld.

"Is she ready?" she heard the younger woman ask the old crone, but the words sounded strange, as if there were an echo in Ivar's tent. Mayhap she was in a cave—a deep, dark, black cave. Yngveld giggled.

The younger woman seized Yngveld's chin and jerked her face around. Yngveld pushed at the woman's hand. But nothing happened. How odd. Her hands were not obeying her. She lifted her nodding head to peer at the woman. Deep black eyes with long thick eyelashes glared back at her. Yngveld smiled. She burst forth into song once more.

The woman let go her chin in disgust. "What is this croaking she is doing? Methinks that she is ready. What think you?"

Yngveld wanted to sleep. She wanted to ignore the two women. The old one was now poking and prodding at her neck. Get away! Yngveld reached up a hand to slap away the old one's probing fingers. That is, she thought she reached up, but her hands were lying quietly in her lap. At first bewildered, then lethargic and uncaring, Yngveld yawned.

"Not quite yet," decided the old woman judiciously. She smiled at Yngveld, that sweet, kind smile.

Yngveld held up her arms. They would not move. "Mother?"

The old crone tossed her head back, and her chortling laugh careened off the pillows and the thick rugs at the side of the tent. "Soon," she soothed. "Soon, you will see your mother."

Yngveld sank further into the turquoise and pink pillows. She was so tired. . . .

"I just want to see her hanged," said the young woman with the black eyes as she stared at the beautiful blond woman lying half-asleep on the cushions.

Yngveld could hear their words, but it was too much effort to open her eyes. She would listen, she decided, listen to their funny talk, and she would laugh.

"I told Ivar she would be trouble, naught but trouble. I told him he had no need of a wife. He has me!"

"No need for you to fear now, dear Jasmine," said the old one. "I will take care of it all. She will be no threat to you."

Jasmine's eyes narrowed thoughtfully. "When you are acting as the Angel of Death, even I must treat you with respect." Her voice held a tinge of awe.

The old crone crept to her and took the fine brown hands in her own and patted them. Lifting the hands to her cheek the old one closed her eyes. "'Twill go well, dear Jasmine, fear not. Soon, soon she will be hanging in Odinn's grove and Ivar will be yours once more."

Jasmine turned away. "If only you could

bestow the gift of life as successfully as you bestow the gift of death." Bitterness crept into Jasmine's voice. "I would bear Ivar's child." Her shoulders slumped.

"The potions take time," soothed the old woman as only moments before she had soothed the blond woman.

Jasmine's heavy-lidded doe eyes dropped, and for a moment a tear glistened on her cheek.

The old woman wiped it away in consternation. "The child will come," she assured her, "in his own time."

Jasmine nodded.

"But," croaked the old woman, "I must warn you. When your child comes, you must beware of Ivar. Take great care that he does not try to sacrifice your son, too."

Jasmine nodded. "That is what he is doing with *her*." Jasmine's lip curled as she regarded the sleeping woman. "She is a fool. She walked right into Ivar's plan."

"She did not know," said the old woman. "The hate that Ivar carries for her family runs deep."

"He does not hate me. There is no reason for him to kill my child."

"Ivar can be a desperate man," observed the old woman. "At times, he will give anything, *anything* at all to succeed in battle." She glanced at the half-asleep woman. "When the usefulness of her sacrifice has worn off, he will look for another sacrifice. Do not be in his path when he comes looking."

Jasmine shrugged, not convinced. "I have known him a long time. He will not hurt me." She glanced again at the sleeping woman, then at the Angel of Death. "Will—will you garrote her here? Now?"

The old woman smiled. "Would you like that?" she teased.

Jasmine shuddered. "No. I do not want to watch you choke her. Do it in the other tent!" she added imperiously.

The old woman tautened the knotted cord between her hands. "Very well."

"Will they hurt her?"

"So much curiosity," the old woman clucked. "What does it matter?"

"I wondered, that is all."

The old woman sighed and lowered the cord. She stared at her young charge for a moment. "*Nej,*" she said at last. "They will not hurt her. They will go into her one at a time. When one is done, the next will take his place. . . ." She held up her hands, palms open. "The woman will not even know what it is that they do to her. The potion I gave her is very strong."

"Ah," said Jasmine, thoughtfully. "So many men. I wonder what it is like to feel so many men between one's legs. . . ."

The old woman shrugged. " 'Tis part of the ritual. 'Tis our way of sending her on to the next world."

"Pity that she will not be awake to feel it," snickered Jasmine. "I wonder if Thomas

Lachlann will be one of the men who goes into her."

The old woman laughed. "Why should he be? He is sitting in the prison hut, waiting to die. Ivar is going to hang him in Odinn's Grove also."

Jasmine nodded. "I always did like Thomas. He will make a fine sacrifice."

"You have learned our ways well," said the old woman. "Your people, the Moors, do not make sacrifice to Odinn."

Jasmine sighed. "Not to Odinn. But they do make sacrifice. They do it carefully, when no one is looking. A knife in the stomach of a sultan. Poison in the food of some princeling."

" 'Tis not the same." The old woman shook her head. "We do it for Odinn! *Nej*, 'tis not the same at all."

Jasmine merely regarded her impassively with those black eyes. She glanced down at the sleeping woman. "I like it when your ways and mine work together."

The old woman smiled. "Take her legs. Help me carry her to the other tent."

"Can we get no help?" complained Jasmine. "I do not want to have to lug her. She looks heavy."

" 'Tis not far," coaxed the old woman. "And when we have done, I will tell you a story—a story of Odinn and his eight-legged horse, Sleipnir. And"—she lowered her voice to a whisper—"I will give you a most pleasant sleeping potion."

Jasmine smiled. "Very well."

The two women staggered as they carried the unconcious Yngveld from the tent.

Soon she was settled in a smaller, bare tent. Two thick carpets on the ground were the only furnishings. "Now we need not soil Ivar's tent," observed Jasmine. "So messy."

"Death is," agreed the Angel.

Chapter Forty

The wooden-walled, circular military encampment was quiet. The men had bedded down for the night in the long barracks and only two sentries were posted at the main gate, the only entrance into and out of the camp.

Two silent shadows crept up to where a small tent was set apart from the others. Ribbons decorated the tent and fluttered in the night breeze.

"Where's Ivar?" Thomas whispered.

"In his tent. With Jasmine."

"And the old woman?"

"Asleep."

"Where is Sleipnir?" Sleipnir was Ivar's prize dun stallion and named after Odinn's mythical eight-legged horse.

"Bridled and ready. Tied near the main gate in that small copse of trees," answered Torgils. "When I found him in the barracks stable, there was a wreath of flowers draped around his neck."

"Oho. Sounds like Sleipnir was bound for Odinn's Grove tomorrow evening too. No doubt he was to carry me to the underworld."

Torgils chuckled low. "Is there anyone that Ivar was not planning to hang? 'Twas to be you, I, Yngveld, Sleipnir . . . quite a crowd."

"Hush," cautioned Thomas. "We do not want to wake anyone."

"Except Yngveld."

Thomas frowned. He hoped he *could* wake Yngveld. "Listen. I will take Yngveld with me upon Sleipnir. You leave the camp separately. Torgils, look at me. That is better. Now, heed my words. You must escape tonight! Do not stay behind. Ivar will be in a killing mood once he discovers his precious sacrifice is gone. I do not want you to be here when that happens. Take Connall and any of the men you are certain are loyal to me. Sigurd, Rolf, Harald, and Eric are loyal to me." These were the four men Thomas had rescued in the cold waters of Greenland when first they had been shipwrecked there. "Take them and any others that wish to join us and meet me at Swords village, at the manor."

Torgils nodded.

"Go!" whispered Thomas urgently. Within the space of a few heartbeats he was alone.

He entered the tent. A small lamp burned at

one corner of the thick pile rug that Yngveld lay upon. Her hair cascaded around her. Lord, she was lovely, Thomas thought. His heart wrenched within him to see her so helpless. "Yngveld. Wake up!"

He shook her gently. "Yngveld. Fair Valkyrie of the North," he pleaded. "Awaken!"

No response.

He bent and kissed her. Her breaths were slow and shallow. "Yngveld." He shook her again. She did not even stir. He placed his hand over her heart and felt the slow, steady thump. Relief crept through him. Realizing that he had little time, he lifted her in his arms, her head dangling over one arm, her feet over the other. She was completely slack and relaxed. Whatever the Angel of Death had given her had certainly put her into a deep sleep. He wondered suddenly if she would ever awaken from it. The thought sent a stab of fear through him. She had to awaken. She had to!

Thomas willed himself to be calm. Once they were away from here, she would wake up. He had to believe that. His face was set and grim.

With quick, sure steps, he left the tent and walked the perimeter of the camp. He stopped once to lay down his burden and reconnoiter. No one was alerted. Everything was quiet. He picked her up and went swiftly to where Sleipnir was tied to a tree.

When Thomas placed Yngveld face-down across the horse's back, Sleipnir snorted and pranced sideways. Thomas cautioned the horse and patted him, whispering reassuringly to the nervous animal. When Sleipnir calmed, Thomas mounted. Then he lifted Yngveld into his arms, his grip secure on her frame. He urged Sleipnir forward. Soon they were racing along the dirt trail that ringed the encampment.

Thomas guided the galloping beast toward the main gate. The two sentries glanced up at the sound of rapidly beating hoofs, but neither appeared alarmed yet. When they saw Sleipnir approach, one of them pushed open his half of the wooden gate, thinking that 'twas Ivar, the military commander. Suddenly he realized his mistake, and he reached to pull the gate closed.

Thomas had only enough time to yell at him to get out of the way before Sleipnir raced full tilt at the gate. The sentry swung at Thomas with the flat of his sword as Thomas whirled by. Thomas ducked his head, still clutching Yngveld, then threw his weight over Sleipnir's shoulders to urge him on. Sleipnir hurtled through the gates, his hooves lashing dangerously. Thomas heard a guard cry out in pain and fear. Then they were through and on the other side of the gate, racing for freedom. Stretched out at a full gallop, Sleipnir swiftly put distance between Thomas and any pursuers.

From far behind him, Thomas heard the sentries yell the camp awake.

Chapter Forty-one

Thomas's grip on Yngveld tightened and he wrapped the reins around his other hand to better control the high-strung stallion. He urged Sleipnir on. Thomas could hear men behind him—those who pursued on foot shouted in frustration; those who followed on horseback cracked and broke branches as they floundered through the forest after him.

He kicked the stallion's sides. They must go faster! 'Twas a well-known fact that Sleipnir was the fleetest horse in the barracks stables, and Thomas could feel the bunched power of the beast as the stallion responded to his urging and lengthened his stride. They flew through the woods, crisscrossed obscure trails, and galloped through brooks until Thomas was certain that pursuit would be impossible.

Heading south from Dubh Linn, Thomas hoped to throw any pursuers off his path and his intended direction. Even should Ivar pick up his trail, he would not guess Thomas's true destination.

Or so Thomas hoped. For Swords village and his manor lay about a day's travel to the north. Thomas planned to go south for a time, then circle around Dubh Linn to the west, ford the River Liffey in the shallows, and strike out to the north for Swords village. 'Twould take two extra days, if the valiant stallion did not falter, but the time could not be helped. Thomas hoped that Ivar would never discover where his quarry had fled to.

Sleipnir's sides were lathered before Thomas finally pulled him to a walk. Yngveld moaned and stirred in Thomas's arms. He glanced at her worriedly, but then his eyes softened and he traced her face lovingly. She had been so still and silent since their flight, and now he felt suddenly heartened by the tiny sound she had made. His fear that she would never awaken from the drugged sleep lessened a little.

He peered through the thick forest, trying to determine where he was. Some of the return journey to Swords would be through forest, some of it across open land. He would avoid the villages and even the lonely monasteries, Thomas decided. He wanted to leave no one for Ivar's men to question in their search.

He wondered if Wolfson would guess that

Swords was his destination. Thomas grimaced. Ivar had never indicated an interest in Thomas's origins and Thomas had never told him much. That lack of interest boded well now. But if Torgils or Connall or any of the other men were captured, Thomas knew that Ivar would force them to divulge anything they knew about Thomas's destination. Thomas could only hope that the others, too, had escaped in the excitement.

A fierce light appeared in his eyes. Should Ivar discover his whereabouts, then he, Thomas, would fight Ivar wherever and whenever the time came. 'Twas worth it for Yngveld, for his land!

Once he and Yngveld arrived at the manor, they would be safe. He glanced down at the unconscious woman in his arms. The memory of her desperately pleading face as she begged him not to give her to Ivar appeared in his mind. He sighed heavily. At the time, it had seemed like the manly, honorable thing to do, though he was prepared to admit it could not have seemed so honorable to Yngveld. He had felt torn then, and he felt torn now.

He was torn between his honor as a man and his love for Yngveld. To Ivar had gone his word, his honor, his loyalty—the very commitment that made him an honorable man. And up until now, that commitment had come first. But now, with the sickening knowledge of what Ivar had planned for Yngveld roiling in his mind, Thomas knew he had been misguided in his loyalties. He knew he was now justified in ending his commitment to Ivar. Thomas would not stand by and see Yngveld threatened with bodily harm.

That Ivar had promised his bride as a sacrifice to Odinn was still difficult to believe. The man had to be insane. Or obsessed. Thomas shook his head, marveling that Ivar had changed so much.

But was it true that Ivar had changed? Or had Thomas never truly known the man? Thomas shrugged; the answer was not clear, but the thought that Ivar had deceived him did not sit well with Thomas. He had thought himself to be a better judge of character than that.

Thomas smiled grimly, feeling as if he had awakened somehow from a dream. If nothing else, he had learned to give his loyalty with more discretion. He would still give it, 'twas part of his world and the warrior path he trod, but no longer would he assume that a strong sword arm or military might warranted unwavering loyalty. *Nej*. He would give loyalty, but to those who were worthy of it, who gave loyalty to him in return, and who were honest with him.

Yngveld stirred briefly in his arms. His lips tightened grimly. He would keep her safe. Never again would he give away her love.

Thomas's thoughts kept him morose company as the stallion carried him and Yngveld along. Finally, he halted the stallion in the middle of a small creek as he looked about. Thomas deemed that they had traveled far enough south. He pulled on the rein, and the big dun's head willingly turned west.

Thomas's hand gripped the rein hard as he remembered his boast to himself years earlier. He had vowed that he would return and take over the manor house, the lands, and the men of his father. He had succeeded in that promise, but he must still elude Ivar and his men to achieve it fully.

He halted Sleipnir once more and listened to the forest sounds. All seemed quiet. He urged the horse forward.

Fortunately, Thomas had made a fair bargain with the merchant he had spoken with in Dubh Linn. For a share of the Greenland goods, the man was willing to sell the furs, furniture, and other rarities that had filled the ship. The merchant's eyes had lighted with interest when Thomas had mentioned the narwhal tusks. Aye, Thomas should get a fair price, a very fair price indeed.

He would use his newfound wealth to restore and improve the manor, making some changes for defense, too. He would look to improve the lands. The fields had been overfarmed, and the livestock had become skinny and diseased in the ten years that Aelfred had run Swords and the manor. Thomas knew that he would need to replenish the stock and get new seed for the farmers. Mayhap they would clear some of the forest, open new fields. Aye, 'twould be much work ahead, but Thomas relished the thought of building up the land. *His* land.

He glanced at the sun. 'Twas now low in the sky. His stomach growled. He had traveled since early morning with only two stops for water, and he had not eaten.

Yngveld was still asleep. What had the Angel of Death given her? Then he calmed. The Angel had no doubt drugged Yngveld heavily in expectation that Odinn's ceremonies would last for some time. Thomas knew that the dancing and feasting and speeches that preceded Odinn's sacrificial ceremonies usually took up most of the day. Night was when the victims were garroted and then hung. Thomas clenched his jaw. Aye, the Angel of Death would have wanted Yngveld pliable and willing for the ceremonies and for what came later. Thomas felt a surge of relief that he had been able to rescue Yngveld from Ivar.

Yngveld moaned and Thomas halted the stallion. He glanced around the small forested glade. A clear-running stream ran near the trail. 'Twas as good a place as any to camp, he reflected. He swung down from Sleipnir's back, carefully balancing Yngveld in his arms. He placed her on a bed of moss and touched her forehead. 'Twas cool to his touch—no fever. Good.

With brisk, efficient movements, he gathered sticks for a small fire, but he did not light it for fear of driving away any game.

He left the stallion and Yngveld for a short time while he scouted the area for food. He returned with a large hare he had managed to kill with a rock. *Thor's Bite*, though a finely crafted weapon for fighting against men, was of little use when it came to hunting game. Thomas had also dug up some tasty roots he had recognized. They would add variety to the meal.

To Thomas's great relief, Yngveld was awake and sitting up when he approached the camp. He flung aside the hare and the roots and strode over to her. "Yngveld."

"Thomas!"

They looked at each other awkwardly for a few moments. "How did you—?" they both began.

Yngveld giggled. Her head nodded, and she looked around. "Where is Angel?" she asked languidly.

Thomas sighed. "I assume you mean the Angel of Death. She is back at the military camp. In Dubh Linn."

Yngveld nodded, but he could not tell if she understood. Then she cocked her head. "What are you doing in the forest, Thomas?" She glanced around and frowned. "Where are we?"

Thomas squatted down beside her and took both her hands in his. "Yngveld, Ivar was going to hang you. I took you with me and fled."

She frowned, uncomprehending, and pulled her hands from his. "I seem to remember something . . ." She shook her head. " 'Tis gone." She looked at him with frightened eyes.

He read her fear. " 'Tis the potion that the Angel gave you, Yngveld. It makes you sleepy and befuddles your thoughts. 'Twill wear off."

He tried to keep his voice calm, but truly he did not know if she would get better. He had a peculiar dread of people whose minds had been hurt. His mother, for one . . . What would he do if Yngveld's mind was never fully restored? Pain shot through him at the thought, and he found himself speaking very gently to her as he skinned and gutted the hare.

Yngveld insisted that she do the cooking. Thomas, eyes narrowed, thought that she was not recovered enough, but he saw that she was gradually becoming her own self. As his fear for her lessened, he was willing to indulge her. "Very well," he said and made the fire.

The warm fragrant odor of the hare as it baked in the ashes tickled Yngveld's taste buds, and her mouth watered. Gradually, as she rested, her mind cleared, and she began to feel much better.

Thomas had gone to gather more wood, and when he returned night had fallen. As he dropped several thick oak limbs and scraps of alderwood beside the fire, Yngveld asked him, "Why did you rescue me, Thomas? I thought you were determined to give me to Ivar."

Thomas sat down and gazed at her from across the fire. She looked delicate in the red aura of the flames, and her blue eyes reflected the flickering light in a way that he could not tell what she was thinking. He sighed. "I sought to do the honorable thing, Yngveld."

"Well, 'twas not honorable to me," she snapped.

"*Nej*," he agreed. " 'Twas not."

"I do not like Ivar's worship of Odinn, either."

"*Nej*." Neither did Thomas.

"One Odinn worshipper in the family is enough. My father used to worship Odinn. Did you know that?"

"*Nej*."

"Well, he did." She frowned.

Thomas picked up a stick and restlessly stirred the coals.

Yngveld glanced at him. "You seem very quiet," she observed.

"Aye." Thomas visibly shook himself. " 'Tis that I do not know what to do."

"With me?" she asked archly. "Oh, do not trouble yourself on my account. I have plans."

Thomas groaned. He should have expected something like this. "What? What plans?"

Do you care? Yngveld wanted to ask, but she pressed her lips tightly together instead. She must remind herself that he thought her but an amusing diversion. Yet, if that was so, why had he rescued her? She looked at him uncertainly, trying to puzzle out his motives. At last she could hold back no longer. "Thomas?"

He grunted.

"Why did you rescue me? Did you think you owed it to me?"

"Aye," he answered. "I thought that as I was responsible for getting you into danger, I was also responsible for getting you out."

"Oh." She thought about that. "Very—uh, very commendable." She sighed. She could not tamp down the huge swell of disappointment that he had not told her that he loved her. She picked up a stick and poked at the red embers. She pushed the hare's carcass around a little.

"Where will you go?" asked Thomas after a while.

"Norway," she answered brightly. "I have a kinsman there."

Thomas grunted. 'Twas best that she had family to take care of her, he told himself, ignoring the part of him that wanted to cry out his disappointment. He had thrown away her love, tossed it away like something unwanted. He winced. But he did want her love. Very much.

He gazed across at her, wondering what the rest of his life would be like without her. Sad, he thought. Sad and lonely.

"I am remembering now, Thomas. It is starting to come back. Ivar was going to hang me, Thomas. He—he wanted to sacrifice me to Odinn!" She shivered and moved closer to stare at the flames.

Thomas noticed that she did not move closer to him. He nodded. Despair swirled with guilt inside him. His loyalty to Ivar had almost cost him the life of the woman he loved. Had he ever told her that he loved her? he mused, watching her. He thought not.

He did remember, however, telling her that she was an amusing diversion. He closed his eyes as he recalled the cruel words.

"Are you in pain?"

He opened his eyes. *Aye, Yngveld, I am. In more pain than you could ever know*. But he shook his head, denying his feelings.

She watched him closely.

He wondered if she still loved him, and for a moment hope flared.

Yngveld's eyes locked with his. "Thomas, I am furious with you for handing me over to Ivar! I begged you, *pleaded* with you not to do it! I would have gotten down on my knees to you if I had thought it would help!"

"Aye." He swallowed. *Would it help now if I got down on my knees to you, fair Valkyrie?*

"Yet you still handed me over! 'Twas not right, Thomas! Not right at all."

"I did what I thought I had to do, Yngveld."

Her eyes blazed. "And I did not like Ivar. I do not like his friends, the Angel and that—that Jasmine!" she sputtered. "Why you ever followed a man like that—!"

"Aye." Thomas shifted uncomfortably on the log. "Ivar was not always so—so obsessed," he said half-heartedly.

"Do not defend the man to me. He was going to kill me!"

"And me," he pointed out with a little more spirit.

"I fail to see why you had to tell him anything about us." She frowned.

He sighed. "The man trusted me to bring him his bride. After we—after I made love to you—well, I could not keep silent. He had a right to know."

"He did not!"

Thomas sat up straighter on the log. "He did. He had a right to know that he was getting a woman who was not a virgin."

" 'Twas none of his business." Her jaw was set mulishly.

"Yngveld," Thomas said patiently. "Ivar contracted with me to bring his bride from Greenland. And when I left Dubh Linn to fetch you, he warned me that he wanted a virgin. I was to keep you safe—from others, and myself."

"So? Those were his requirements, not mine."

"And I agreed to his requirements," said Thomas irritably. "But I did not live up to them," he muttered. "Worse, I knowingly broke them."

"That is what bothers you then, Thomas? That you broke your word to Ivar?"

He grunted.

She waited. When he did not continue, she prodded, "Viking men pride themselves on their word."

Thomas looked at her.

"My father," she explained.

"Aye." He sighed. Presently he said, " 'Tis not that I broke my word to Ivar that now bothers me, though I have suffered over that. No, 'tis that he intended to murder you. Had I known those were his plans, I would never have given you to him." He looked at her then, those green eyes solemn. "Do you believe me?"

Yngveld stopped breathing. How strange, she thought, that she had never considered that mayhap Thomas had known of Ivar's plans to kill her. She stared at Thomas across the flames. *Nej*, she thought, he had not known, and that realization went to the very depths of her being.

Her heart thudded in her chest, and she placed a hand over it, certain he could hear it across the fire. "*Ja*, Thomas," she answered softly, starting to breathe once more. "I believe you knew nothing of Ivar's plans."

Thomas's green eyes were locked on her blue ones. He heard the truth of her words in her voice.

"My father betrothed me to Ivar," she said, realizing that she wanted Thomas to know all that had happened. She looked away from the green intensity of his gaze and stared at the fire instead. "But Ivar did not want me." At Thomas's surprised glance, she added, "Ivar hated my father for killing his only brother. And for seducing that brother's wife. If I can believe Ivar—"

"What *did* Ivar tell you?" Mayhap Thomas could discover if Ivar had plotted betrayal from the very first.

"Ivar said that he sent for me because of the betrothal and because my family owed his a son." At Thomas's thoughtful look, she explained, "Ivar claimed that my father killed his brother. Therefore my family owed his a male. He also admitted that when he looked at me, he saw only my father and"—she winced—"he was repulsed. He could not take me to wife."

Thomas nodded slowly.

"Then Ivar said that because of losses he suffered in battle after you left for Greenland, he had decided to sacrifice to Odinn the most valuable possession he had." She paused, weighing Thomas's reaction. "And that was *me* as the mother of his yet-to-be-born son." Her eyes were dark in mystification. "He would sacrifice *me* and our son. Does that make sense to you, Thomas?"

"It does if you know Ivar." So Ivar had sent Thomas to Greenland in good faith. Thomas straightened, feeling that Ivar had not completely betrayed him. Ivar had changed his mind, aye, about what to do with Yngveld, but he had not coldly plotted to avenge himself on her. Some of Thomas's heated anger against Ivar lessened. "A man will do many things to succeed in battle, Yngveld. If he is not careful, killing becomes a way of life, a way to solve problems." He stared at her. "For such men, after a time it becomes the only way.

"Ivar had a desperate desire to win the battle for military supremacy over Dubh Linn. To win, he would do anything. I know this; I have seen that part of him."

Yngveld watched Thomas closely, weighing his words.

" 'Tis almost as if Ivar's desperation overruled his instinct to nurture the young, growing, good part of himself. Thus he chose to kill his son—and to kill you." Thomas stared sadly into the orange flames. "You might say that Ivar lost the battle waging in his own soul. He sacrificed to

Death that little kernel of Life that was starting to make itself known to him." Thomas shook his head. "'Twas a sad, awful decision, and I will warrant one that Ivar will live to regret deeply."

Thomas sighed, the mystery of Ivar's decision to kill Yngveld becoming clearer to him at last. Ivar's decisions and life were no longer a part of Thomas's, and he would strive to keep it that way.

He must return to Swords, Thomas thought with renewed determination. Return to Swords and take up a way of life that would nourish and cherish that kernel of Life in his own soul. He glanced at Yngveld, to see the effect of his words upon her. But she gave no answering glance, only stared thoughtfully into the fire, until Thomas too, went back to the hypnotic flames. They sat like that for a while.

"I had a dream," said Yngveld slowly. "In my dream, I was aboard ship with my father and a second ship came. You were aboard it. I"—she blushed painfully, glad that the red firelight hid her—"could feel your desire for me. I felt—desire for you. But behind you was Odinn, his mouth a great, yawning chasm. I was very much afraid. It was stormy. Then, in my dream, my father lifted me up and threw me down into the sea. After that, I woke up." Her eyes held his. "I think now that my dream was warning me that 'twas not you I needed to fear, but Odinn. And that my father started me on this journey, but he could not complete the full journey. So he threw me into the sea, like a sacrifice, but 'twas *I* who had to make the voyage, *I* who had to swim in the depths of the sea, into the depths of my soul, before I could know the direction my life would take."

Thomas nodded, unwilling to say anything. Yngveld must sort out her thoughts for herself, must find the meaning in her own dreams. Thomas could listen, but he could not undertake her journey for her. When she was silent for a time he said, "Yngveld, there is something else. . . ."

He looked away from her eyes first, and she shuddered at the pain she had glimpsed there.

"Yngveld," the words poured out of him urgently, willing her to believe him. "I did not find you an amusing diversion—"

She looked shocked.

He cursed for not making himself clearer. "I enjoyed our lovemaking, Yngveld," he assured her hurriedly.

"*Ja?*" she asked uncertainly.

"I did not make love to you as if it were some—as if you were some—" By Thor, why would the words not come out? He took a breath. "As if you were some passing entertainment." There. He looked at her, hoping for a glimpse of understanding in those blue eyes.

Yngveld stared at him. Whatever was the matter with Thomas? In the whole time she had known him, she had never seen him so unsure of himself. "Thomas," she asked at last, "are you trying to tell me that you cared about me when we made love?" She held her breath, waiting for his answer.

He nodded.

Slowly, wordlessly, as if she were still drugged, she stood up and walked around the fire to him. He watched her approach, step by step. When she finally stood in front of him, she reached up and put her arms around his neck. "I cared about you, too, Thomas," she whispered.

"Yngveld," he murmured, bending to press his forehead to hers. He inhaled her sweet scent. "Is it possible? Can you still have some feeling for me?"

"I think I might find a fragment or two," she purred.

With a whoop, he grabbed her hand and scooped her up into his arms. Jauntily, he carried her off to a patch of soft moss near a screen of trees that he had noticed earlier.

Heart pounding, Thomas set her down, smiling into those glorious blue eyes. With his body he could tell her of his love in ways his lips could never say. Gently he helped her off with her clothes, then slowly sank to his knees, pulling her down with him. He leaned over her and entered her, his eyes still locked on hers. The fused intimacy of their bodies rent his heart, and he had to close his eyes against the love he saw upon her face. Sorrow crept over him at the sudden memory of the danger he had placed her in, and he bent to kiss the pain away from her, his lips soft and gentle. Then with powerful thrusts he showed her his resolve to never let her out of his life. He clutched her when their mutual climax came, and the quiet of the glade was shattered by their cries. And afterward, the sweet kiss he bestowed upon her panting lips was to tell her of the hope that had been rekindled in his heart, the hope that he could have, and hold, her precious love.

Yngveld watched him make love to her and her heart filled with love at how gently he touched her. He made each caress an act of worship. "This is all I wanted," she whispered as they rocked together. "This is all I ever wanted, Thomas. Only you. . . ." And then she was lost in the maelstrom of sensation that took her body to heights she had never dreamed, to scale mountains she had not known existed. And when they were done, and had come back to earth, and she once again found herself lying under him, she gazed up lazily into those beautiful green eyes and smiled at him with every drop of love she had in her heart.

He bent his head to her then, pressing his lips to hers, and she wanted to melt and die from the beauty of it. She loved him, oh Lord, how she loved him!

Gradually they both came round, down out of the swirling clouds they'd but recently inhabited. Yngveld felt so satiated and replete with satisfaction that she could barely move. She leaned over Thomas and kissed him playfully on the cheek.

He grinned up at her. "I love you, Yngveld

Sveinsdatter," he said hoarsely.

"And I love you, Thomas Lachlann."

Later, they slowly got dressed. Thomas sorted through the words he wanted to use to tell her of his love, of what they would do together, of how their lives were now intertwined, of how he wanted her with him for always.

A smiling Yngveld held his hand as they sauntered back to the campfire. She sighed happily and held his hand to her face. She rubbed her cheek against his hand. "I am so fortunate to love you, Thomas."

He laughed. "Aye, that you are."

"I am serious," she scolded. "I am fortunate to find someone as wonderful as you to love."

"Yngveld, *I* am the fortunate one." His voice lowered. "I know you feel I did you wrong by insisting that you marry Ivar. But Yngveld, for me, I had to do that, I had to complete my task of delivering you to Ivar. I had given my *word*." His eyes met hers, his intensity willing her to understand. "Methinks you and I will never agree upon this, Yngveld, but I also think we can put it behind us, that we can each allow the other to hold values that differ from our own. Can you? Can you see your way to forgiving me? Or will this always be between us?"

"I do not know," she answered just as seriously. "I—I need some time, Thomas. Although," she added thoughtfully, "I did seem to forgive you when we were making love. . . ."

"You did, did you not?" His face lit up at the

memory. "You forgive very well, Yngveld."

She laughed, then sobered. "But that does not mean that I can let this go by so easily, Thomas. 'Twas a serious thing to do," she said, "to force me to marry him, I mean."

"Aye, 'twas."

She saw his big fists clench in the flickering light and wondered at his torment. But she had torments of her own. He had almost ruined her life. If he had not rescued her from Ivar . . . she shuddered at what would have surely been a painful, ignoble death. "I thank you for coming to my aid," she said primly. "That you rescued me goes a long way to making amends."

"Aye." He decided not to push her. If she forgave him, or if she did not, 'twas up to her. As for him, he did have the consolation that he had righted the wrong he had done her. He had saved her from Ivar. Mayhap she would come to see that.

They started walking back to their camp. "Yngveld." He halted and took both her hands in his. He could not let her go, could not let her walk out of his life, or sail off to Norway. Suddenly the words spilled out, "Yngveld, will you marry me? Will you come with me to Swords and share my life?"

Yngveld's eyes widened when she looked into those radiant green eyes. She would have promised him anything. Her throat worked with emotion. "*Ja*, Thomas," she murmured when she could speak. "I will marry you. With joy!"

He smiled then, and his arms closed around

her. "It is good, fair Valkyrie of the North." Yngveld settled into his arms, her eyes closed, her cheek against his broad chest. A peaceful knowledge settled into her heart that she had come home at last.

Their embrace seemed to last forever. At last, reluctantly, they broke apart. Then together they walked hand in hand the remaining distance to their camp.

They reached the fire.

"Yngveld?"

"Mmm?"

"The meat is burnt."

"Oh." She frowned, then glanced ruefully at him, her forehead wrinkled.

"Charred, Yngveld."

She looked at him; he was so serious.

"In fact," he took a stick and poked at the blackened mess, " 'tis quite, quite cremated."

She grinned.

He grinned and threw the stick aside. Reaching for her, he drew her into his arms and they both burst into laughter. They laughed until the forest rang with the happy sound.

Author's Note

In 999 A.D., one year after this story takes place, Brian Boru, the first absolute High King of Ireland, defeated the Danes of Dubh Linn and thoroughly sacked the city, burning wicker homes and taking citizens into slavery. A series of sackings and defeats further weakened the Viking hold until the Battle of Clontarf in 1014 A.D. when the Vikings, joining an Irish force, fought against Brian Boru and lost to his forces. Dubh Linn continued to grow as a trading center and gradually the two cultures merged.

References

Byrne, Dymphna 1988. "Viking Dublin Comes to Life" in *Cross Current*, September 1988.

Carter, Samuel III 1972. *Vikings Bold: Their Voyages & Adventures*. Thomas Y. Crowell Co., New York.

Coggins, Jack 1966. *The Horseman's Bible*. Doubleday & Co., Inc., Garden City, New York.

Ferguson, Sheila 1981. *Growing Up in Viking Times*. Batsford Academic and Educational Ltd., London.

Haliday, Charles 1969. *The Scandinavian Kingdom of Dublin*. Introduction by Breandan O Riordain. Irish University Press, Shannon, Ireland. First edition Dublin, 1881.

Jones, Gwyn 1984. *A History of the Vikings*. Oxford University Press, Great Britain.

LaFay, Howard 1970. "The Vikings" in *National Geographic Magazine*, Vol. 137, No. 4., pp. 492–541.

Pendlesonn, KRG 1980. *The Vikings*. Albany Books, London.

Ranelagh, John 1981. *Ireland, An Illustrated History*. Oxford University Press, New York.

Simpson, Jacqueline 1980. *The Viking World*. St. Martin's Press, New York.

Somerville-Large, Peter 1981. *Dublin*. Granada Publishing Ltd., London, England.

Stubbs, Helmer 1972. *Vikingships and Their Masters*. Postal Instant Press, San Diego, CA.